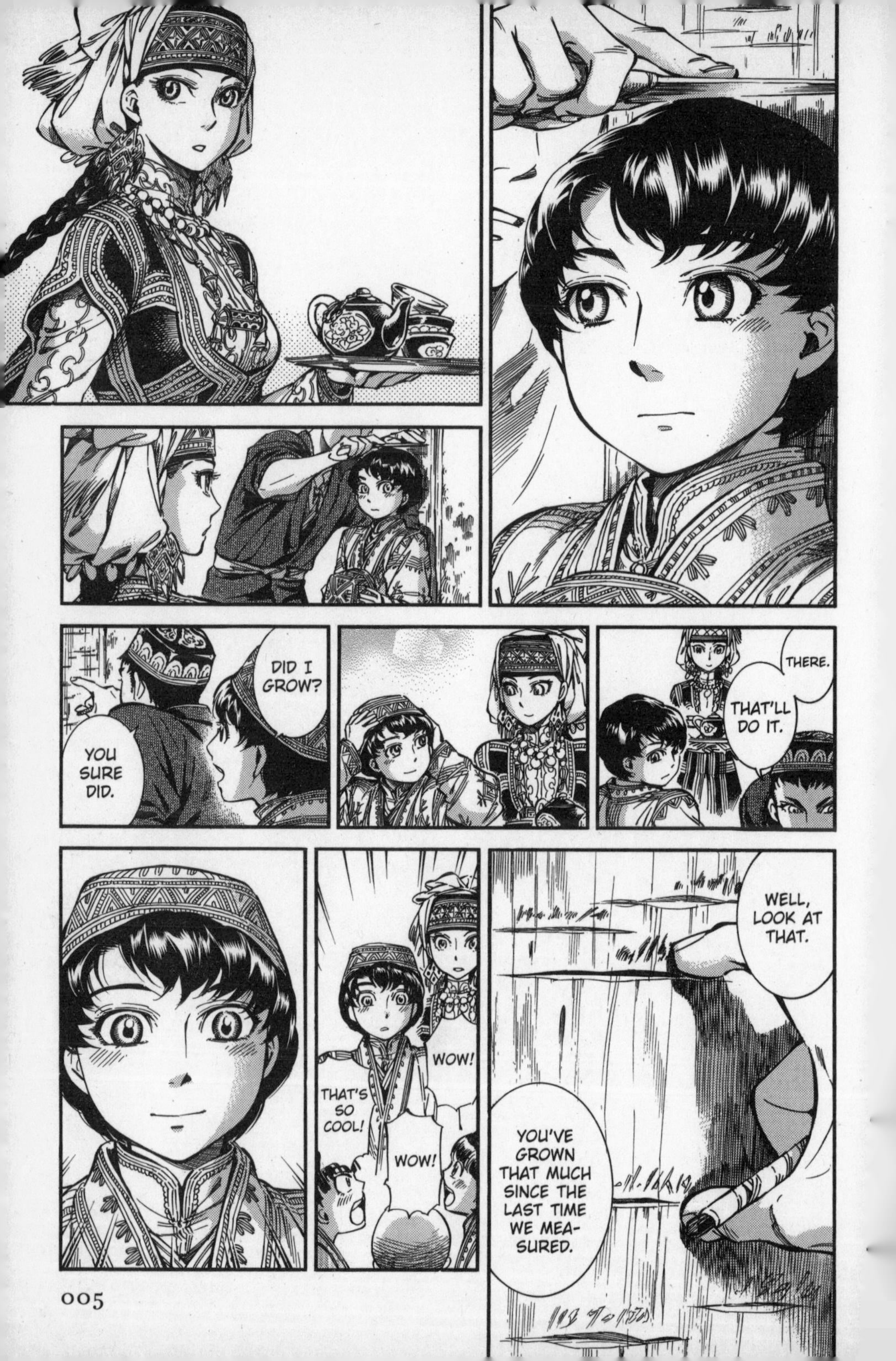
THERE.
THAT'LL DO IT.
DID I GROW?
YOU SURE DID.
WELL, LOOK AT THAT.
YOU'VE GROWN THAT MUCH SINCE THE LAST TIME WE MEA-SURED.
WOW!
THAT'S SO COOL!
WOW!

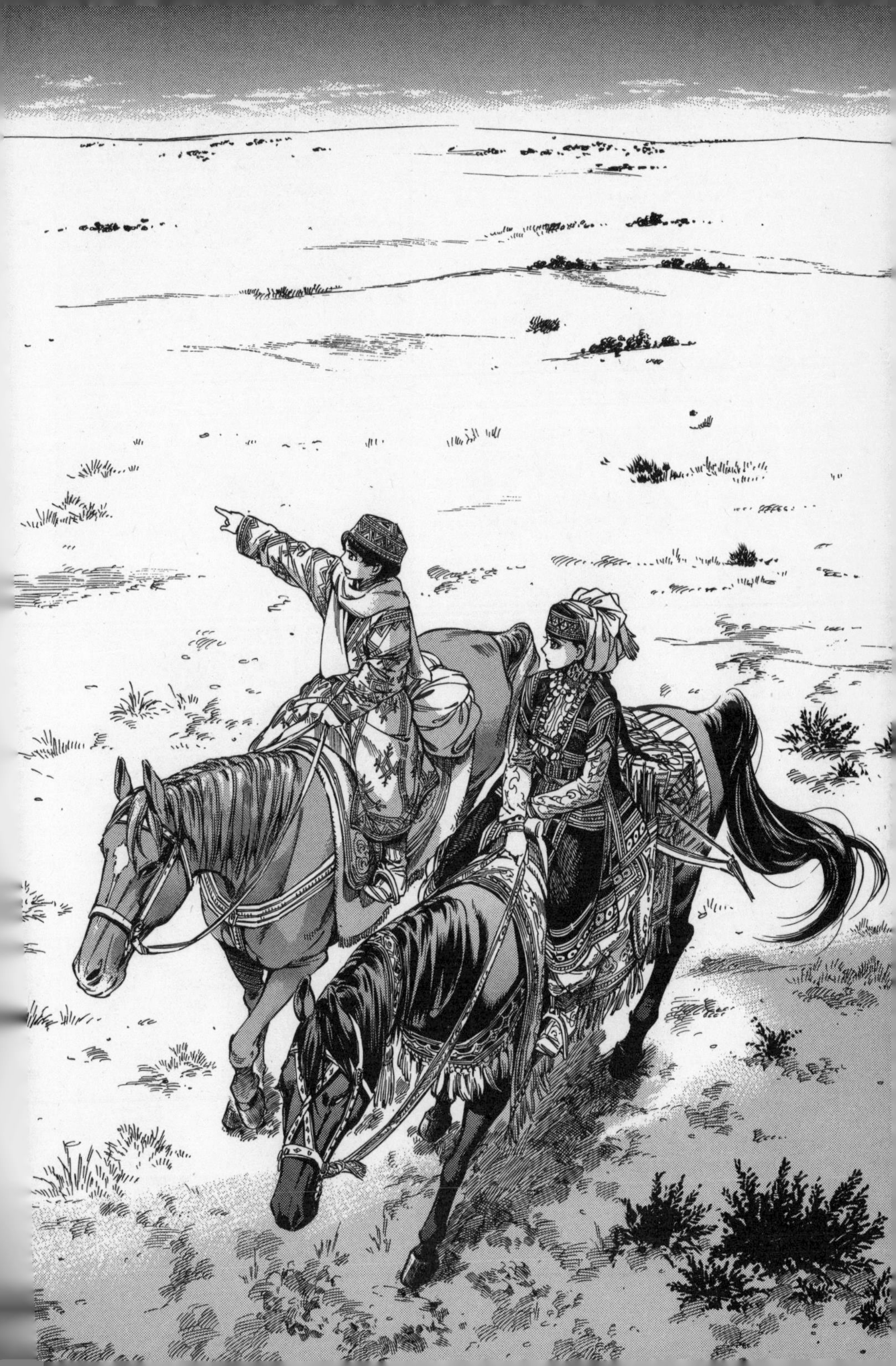

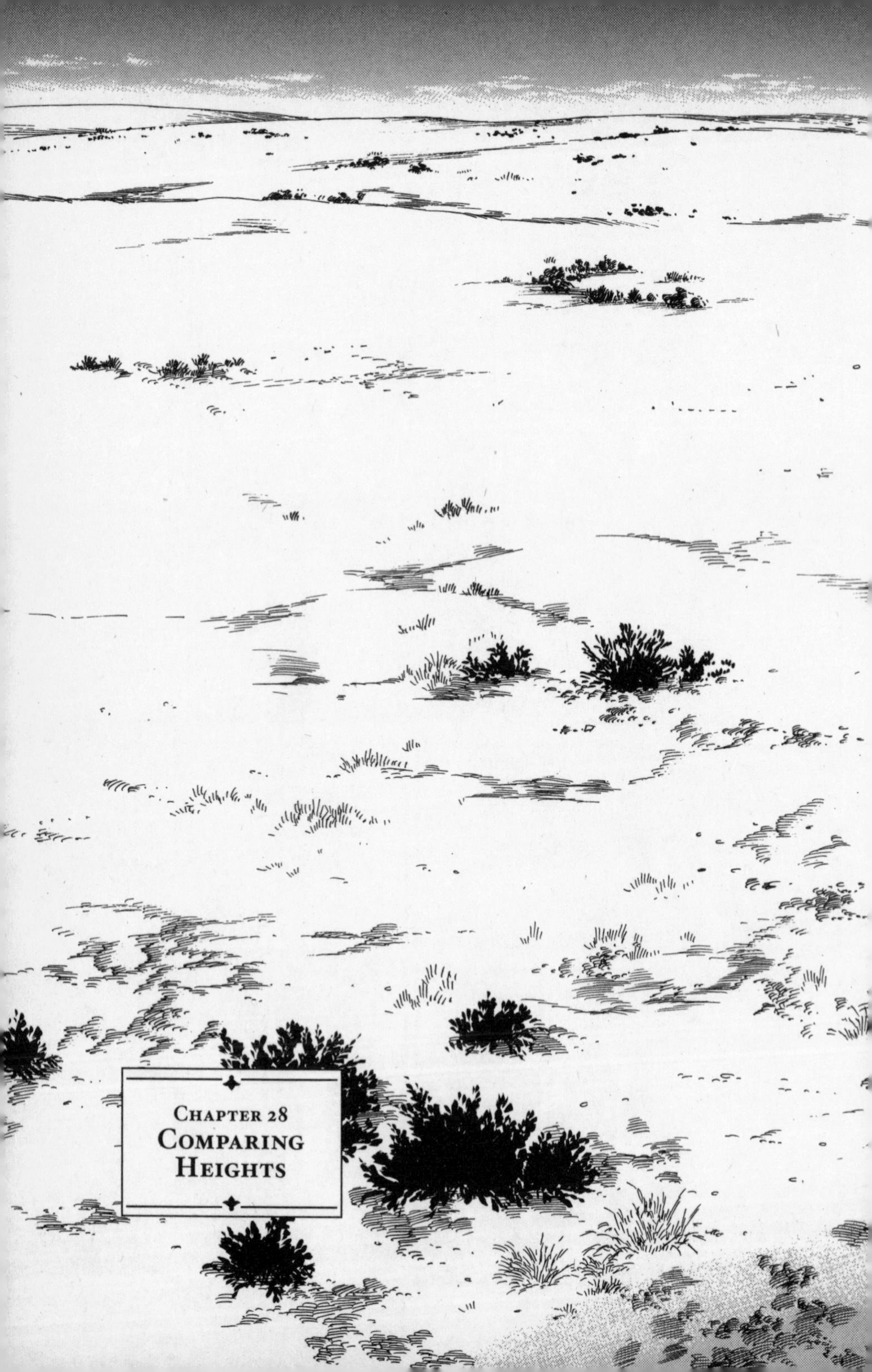

Chapter 28
Comparing Heights

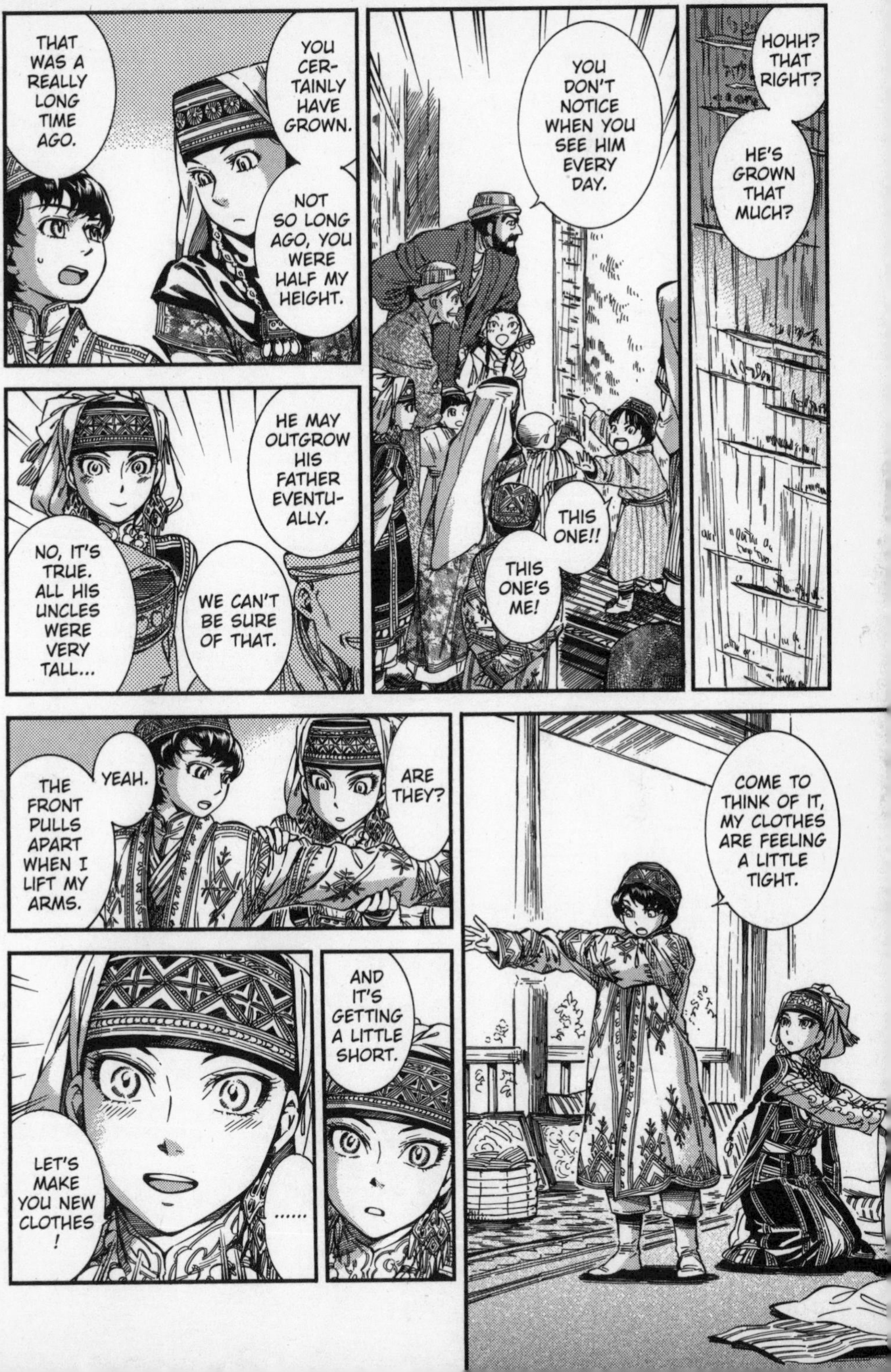
HOHH? THAT RIGHT?
HE'S GROWN THAT MUCH?
YOU DON'T NOTICE WHEN YOU SEE HIM EVERY DAY.
THIS ONE!!
THIS ONE'S ME!
YOU CERTAINLY HAVE GROWN.
NOT SO LONG AGO, YOU WERE HALF MY HEIGHT.
THAT WAS A REALLY LONG TIME AGO.
HE MAY OUTGROW HIS FATHER EVENTUALLY.
WE CAN'T BE SURE OF THAT.
NO, IT'S TRUE. ALL HIS UNCLES WERE VERY TALL...
COME TO THINK OF IT, MY CLOTHES ARE FEELING A LITTLE TIGHT.
ARE THEY?
YEAH.
THE FRONT PULLS APART WHEN I LIFT MY ARMS.
AND IT'S GETTING A LITTLE SHORT.
......
LET'S MAKE YOU NEW CLOTHES!

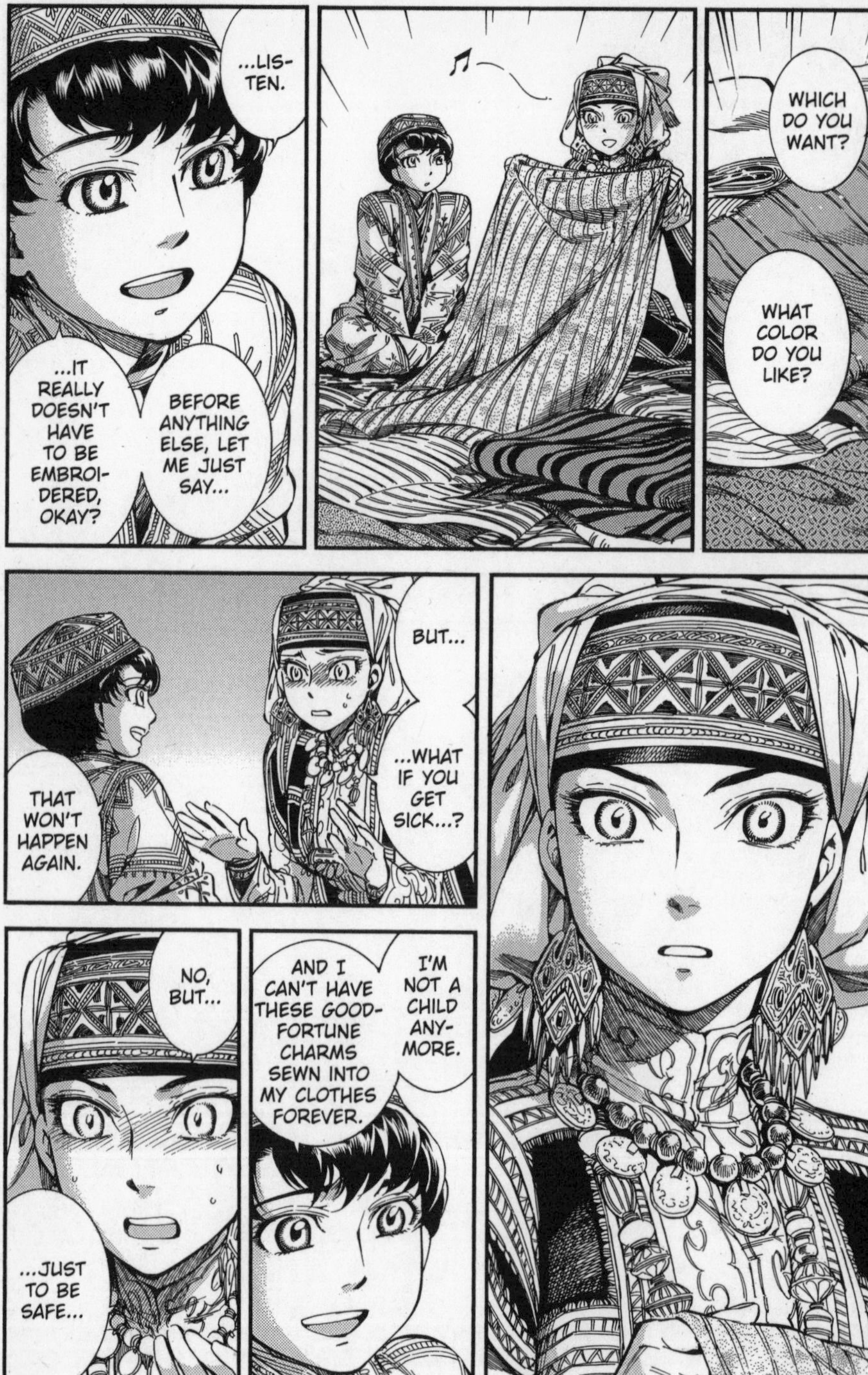
WHICH DO YOU WANT?
WHAT COLOR DO YOU LIKE?
...LIS-TEN.
BEFORE ANYTHING ELSE, LET ME JUST SAY...
...IT REALLY DOESN'T HAVE TO BE EMBROIDERED, OKAY?
BUT...
...WHAT IF YOU GET SICK...?
THAT WON'T HAPPEN AGAIN.
I'M NOT A CHILD ANYMORE.
AND I CAN'T HAVE THESE GOOD-FORTUNE CHARMS SEWN INTO MY CLOTHES FOREVER.
NO, BUT...
...JUST TO BE SAFE...

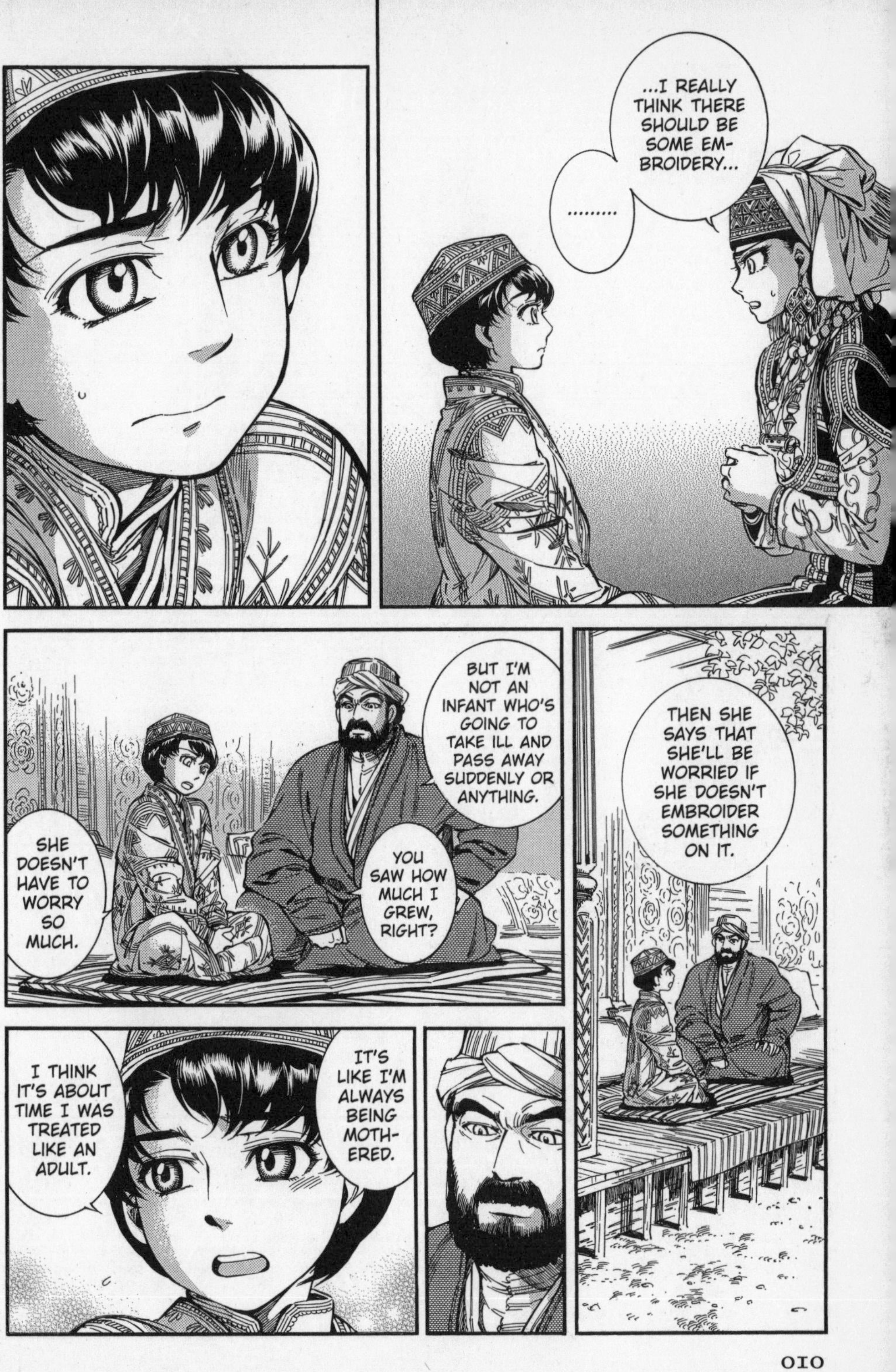

...I REALLY THINK THERE SHOULD BE SOME EM-BROIDERY...
....
THEN SHE SAYS THAT SHE'LL BE WORRIED IF SHE DOESN'T EMBROIDER SOMETHING ON IT.
BUT I'M NOT AN INFANT WHO'S GOING TO TAKE ILL AND PASS AWAY SUDDENLY OR ANYTHING.
YOU SAW HOW MUCH I GREW, RIGHT?
SHE DOESN'T HAVE TO WORRY SO MUCH.
IT'S LIKE I'M ALWAYS BEING MOTH-ERED.
I THINK IT'S ABOUT TIME I WAS TREATED LIKE AN ADULT.

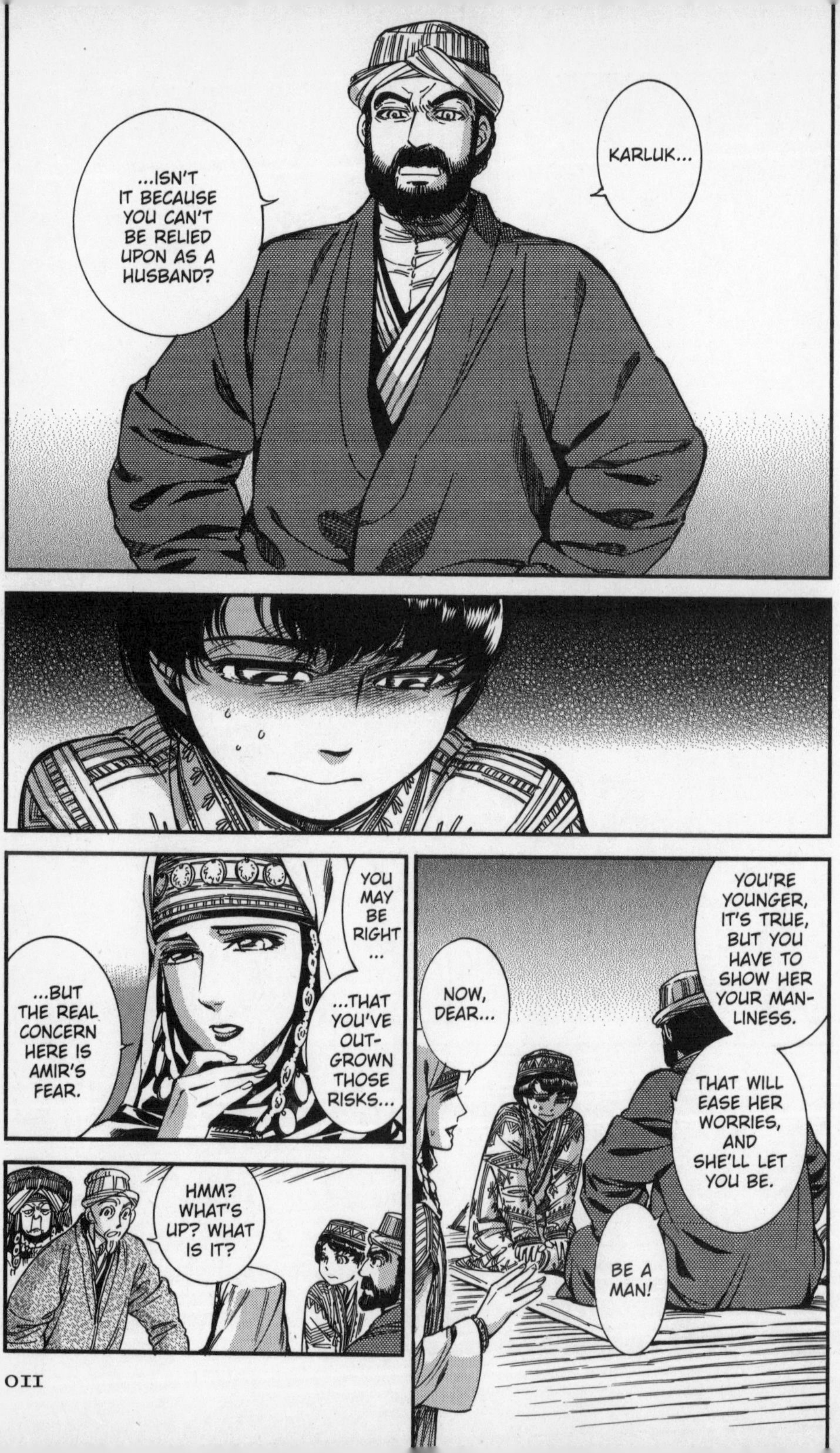
KARLUK...
...ISN'T IT BECAUSE YOU CAN'T BE RELIED UPON AS A HUSBAND?
YOU'RE YOUNGER, IT'S TRUE, BUT YOU HAVE TO SHOW HER YOUR MAN-LINESS.
NOW, DEAR...
THAT WILL EASE HER WORRIES, AND SHE'LL LET YOU BE.
BE A MAN!
YOU MAY BE RIGHT...
...THAT YOU'VE OUT-GROWN THOSE RISKS...
...BUT THE REAL CONCERN HERE IS AMIR'S FEAR.
HMM? WHAT'S UP? WHAT IS IT?

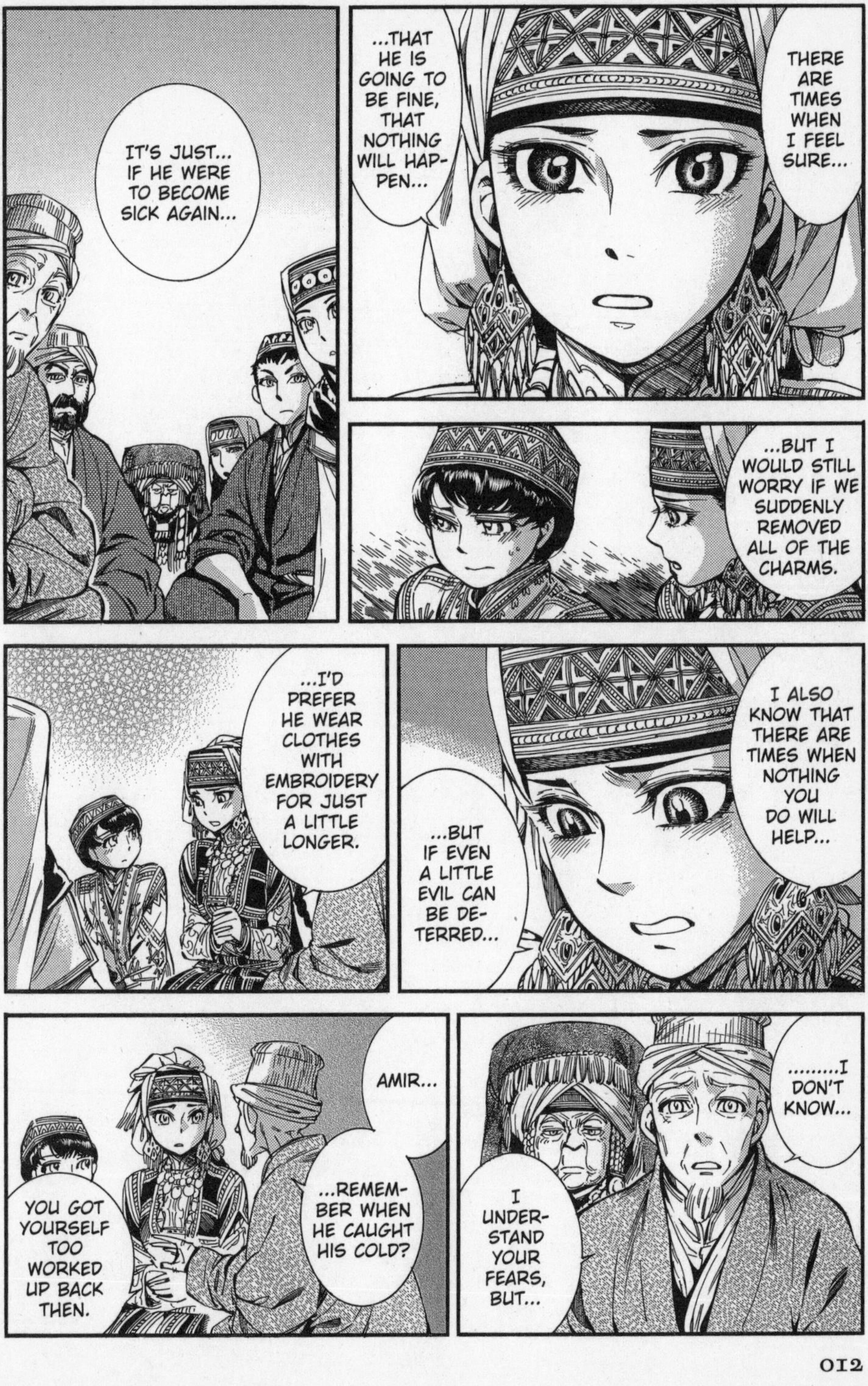
THERE ARE TIMES WHEN I FEEL SURE...
...THAT HE IS GOING TO BE FINE, THAT NOTHING WILL HAP-PEN...
...BUT I WOULD STILL WORRY IF WE SUDDENLY REMOVED ALL OF THE CHARMS.
IT'S JUST... IF HE WERE TO BECOME SICK AGAIN...
I ALSO KNOW THAT THERE ARE TIMES WHEN NOTHING YOU DO WILL HELP...
...BUT IF EVEN A LITTLE EVIL CAN BE DE-TERRED...
...I'D PREFER HE WEAR CLOTHES WITH EMBROIDERY FOR JUST A LITTLE LONGER.
........I DON'T KNOW...
I UNDER-STAND YOUR FEARS, BUT...
AMIR...
...REMEM-BER WHEN HE CAUGHT HIS COLD?
YOU GOT YOURSELF TOO WORKED UP BACK THEN.

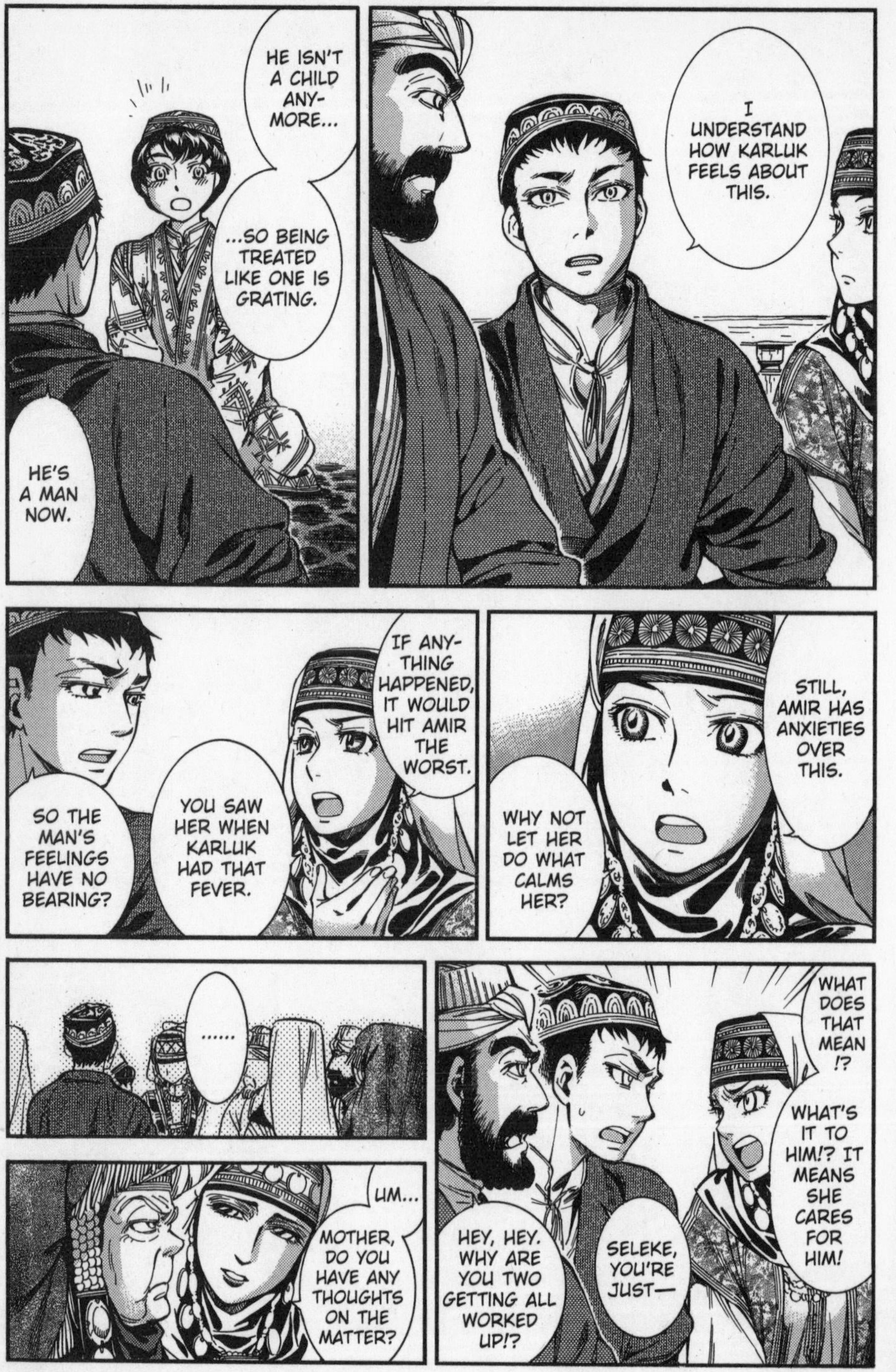
I UNDERSTAND HOW KARLUK FEELS ABOUT THIS.
HE ISN'T A CHILD ANY-MORE...
...SO BEING TREATED LIKE ONE IS GRATING.
HE'S A MAN NOW.
STILL, AMIR HAS ANXIETIES OVER THIS.
WHY NOT LET HER DO WHAT CALMS HER?
IF ANY-THING HAPPENED, IT WOULD HIT AMIR THE WORST.
YOU SAW HER WHEN KARLUK HAD THAT FEVER.
SO THE MAN'S FEELINGS HAVE NO BEARING?
WHAT DOES THAT MEAN!?
WHAT'S IT TO HIM!? IT MEANS SHE CARES FOR HIM!
SELEKE, YOU'RE JUST—
HEY, HEY. WHY ARE YOU TWO GETTING ALL WORKED UP!?
......
UM...
MOTHER, DO YOU HAVE ANY THOUGHTS ON THE MATTER?

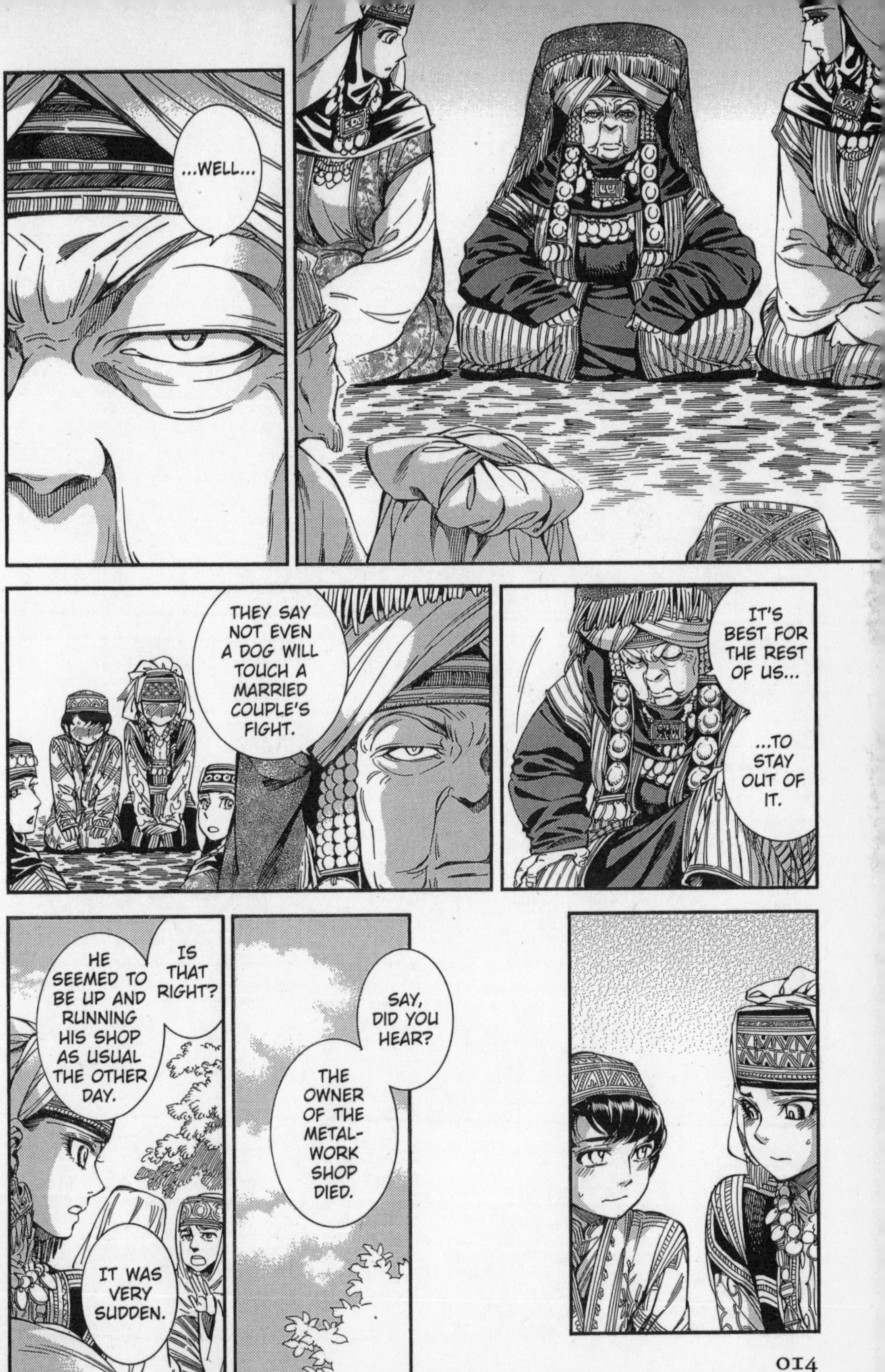
...WELL...
IT'S BEST FOR THE REST OF US...
...TO STAY OUT OF IT.
THEY SAY NOT EVEN A DOG WILL TOUCH A MARRIED COUPLE'S FIGHT.
SAY, DID YOU HEAR?
THE OWNER OF THE METAL-WORK SHOP DIED.
IS THAT RIGHT?
HE SEEMED TO BE UP AND RUNNING HIS SHOP AS USUAL THE OTHER DAY.
IT WAS VERY SUDDEN.

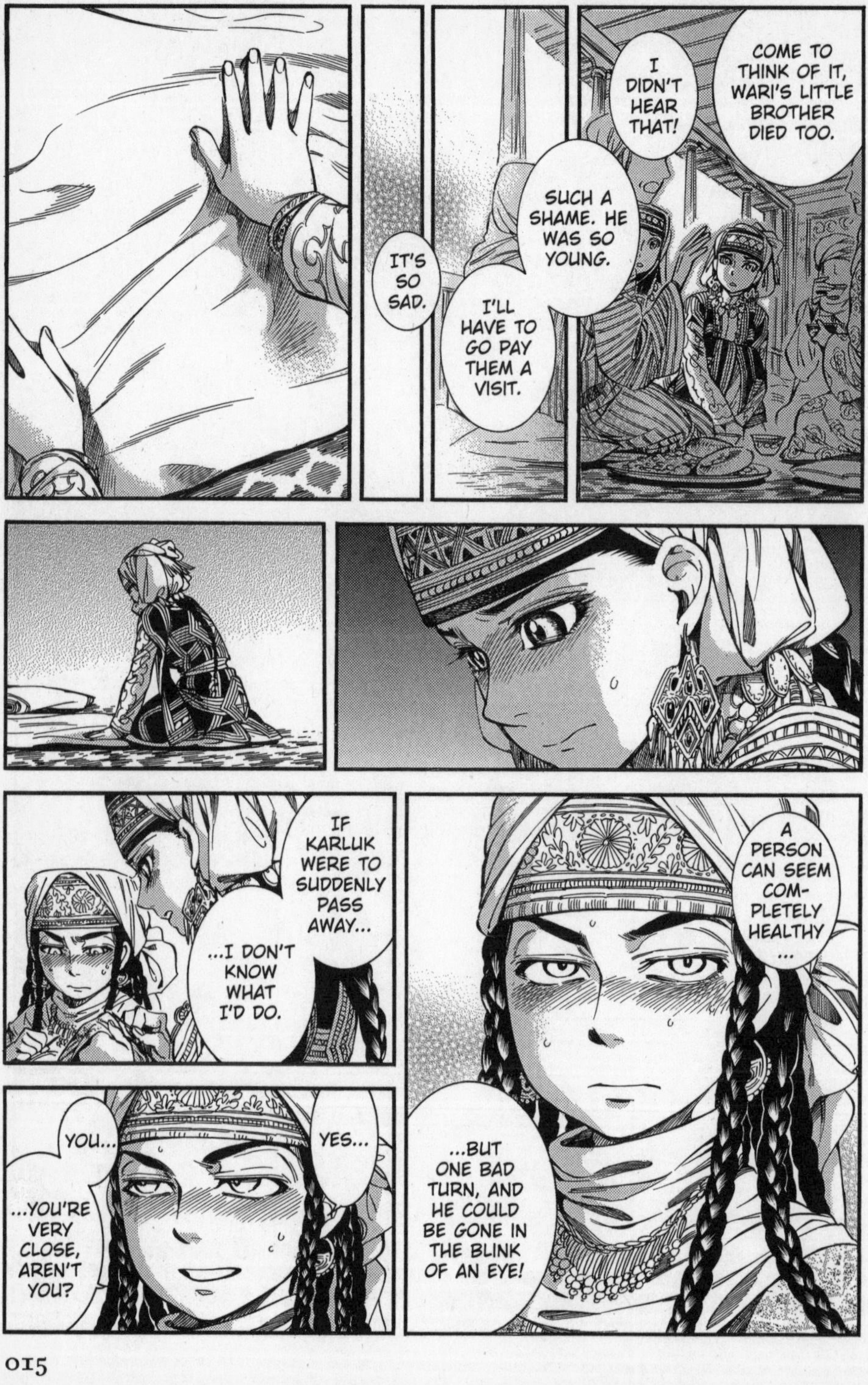
COME TO THINK OF IT, WARI'S LITTLE BROTHER DIED TOO.
I DIDN'T HEAR THAT!
SUCH A SHAME. HE WAS SO YOUNG.
I'LL HAVE TO GO PAY THEM A VISIT.
IT'S SO SAD.
A PERSON CAN SEEM COM-PLETELY HEALTHY ...
...BUT ONE BAD TURN, AND HE COULD BE GONE IN THE BLINK OF AN EYE!
IF KARLUK WERE TO SUDDENLY PASS AWAY...
...I DON'T KNOW WHAT I'D DO.
YES...
YOU...
...YOU'RE VERY CLOSE, AREN'T YOU?

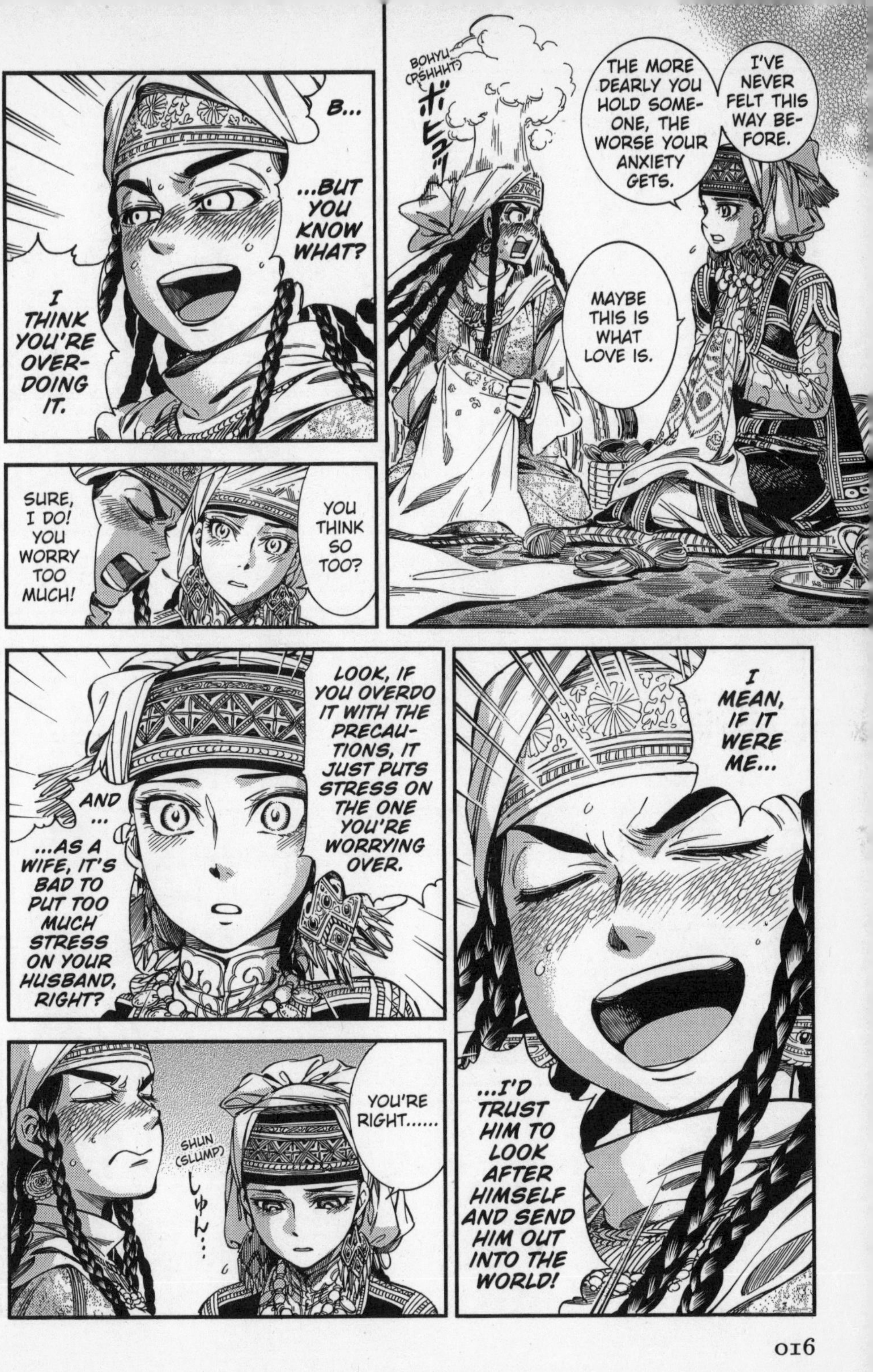
I'VE NEVER FELT THIS WAY BE-FORE.
THE MORE DEARLY YOU HOLD SOME-ONE, THE WORSE YOUR ANXIETY GETS.
BOHYU (PSHHHT)
ボヒュッ
MAYBE THIS IS WHAT LOVE IS.
B...
...BUT YOU KNOW WHAT?
I THINK YOU'RE OVER-DOING IT.
YOU THINK SO TOO?
SURE, I DO! YOU WORRY TOO MUCH!
I MEAN, IF IT WERE ME...
...I'D TRUST HIM TO LOOK AFTER HIMSELF AND SEND HIM OUT INTO THE WORLD!
LOOK, IF YOU OVERDO IT WITH THE PRECAU-TIONS, IT JUST PUTS STRESS ON THE ONE YOU'RE WORRYING OVER.
AND ...
...AS A WIFE, IT'S BAD TO PUT TOO MUCH STRESS ON YOUR HUSBAND, RIGHT?
YOU'RE RIGHT......
SHUN (SLUMP)
しゅん…

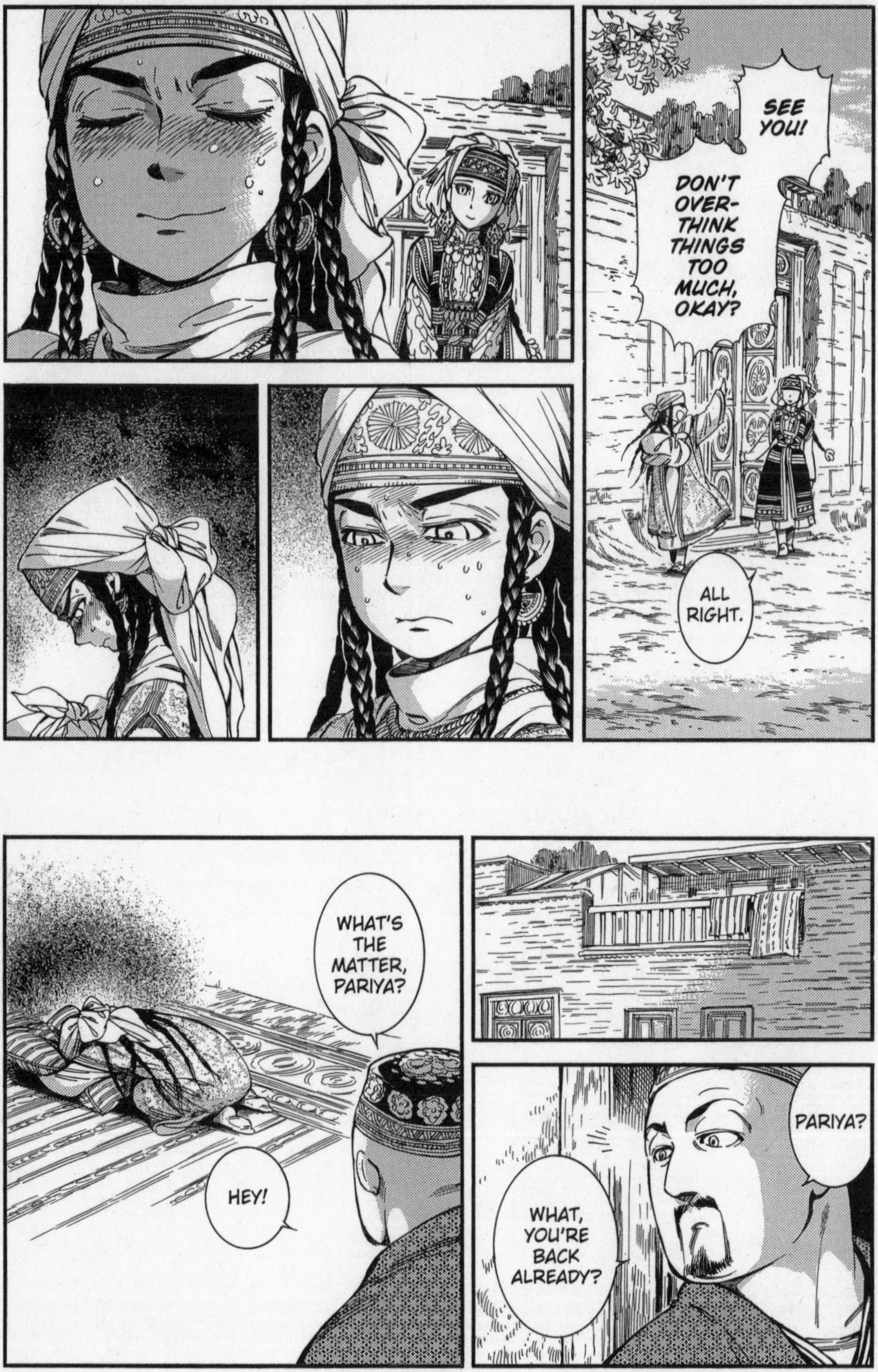
SEE YOU!
DON'T OVER-THINK THINGS TOO MUCH, OKAY?
ALL RIGHT.
PARIYA?
WHAT, YOU'RE BACK ALREADY?
WHAT'S THE MATTER, PARIYA?
HEY!

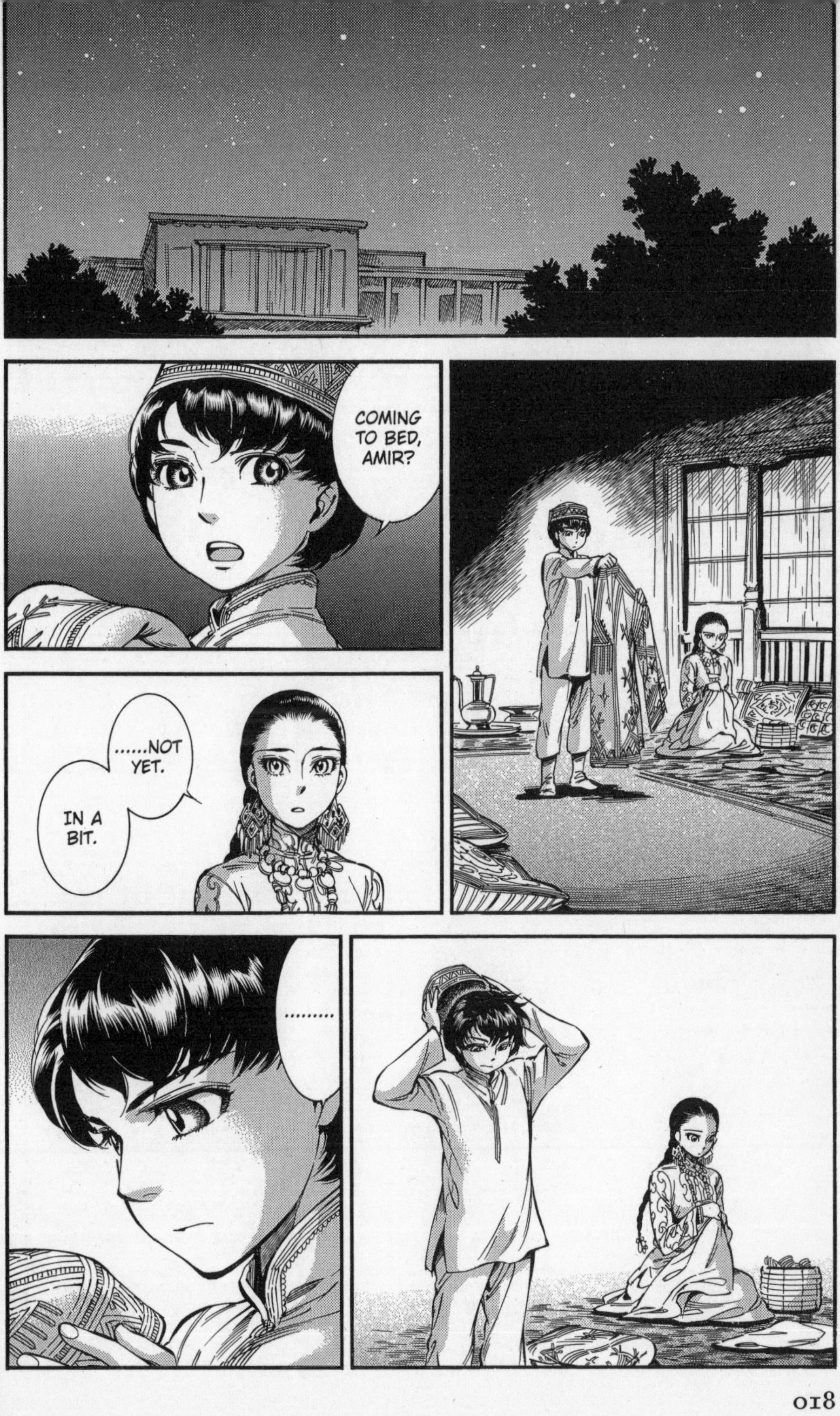
COMING TO BED, AMIR?
......NOT YET.
IN A BIT.
....

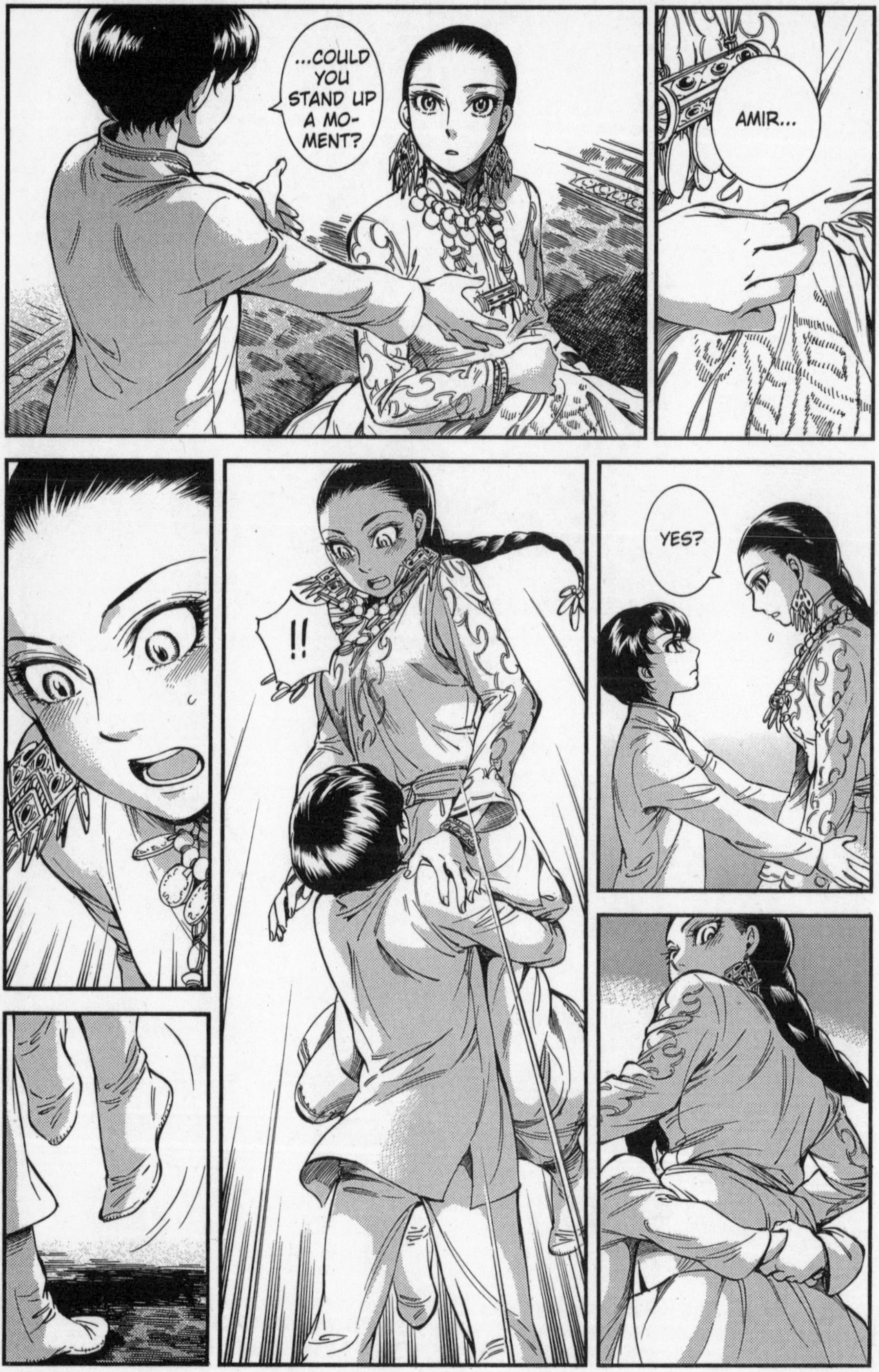
AMIR...
...COULD YOU STAND UP A MO-MENT?
YES?
!!

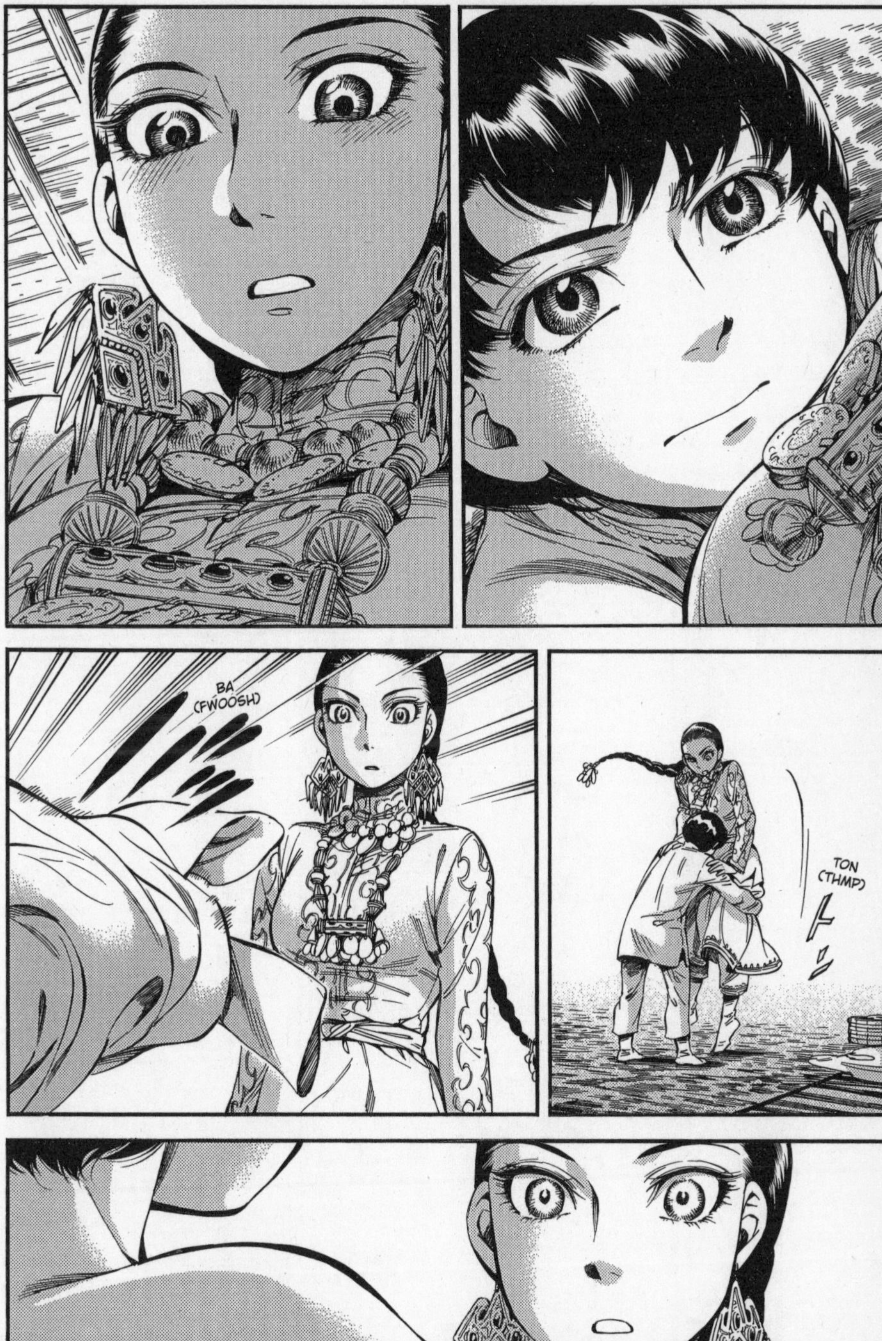
TON
(THMP)
BA
(FWOOSH)

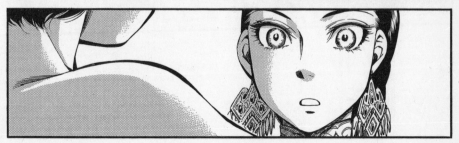

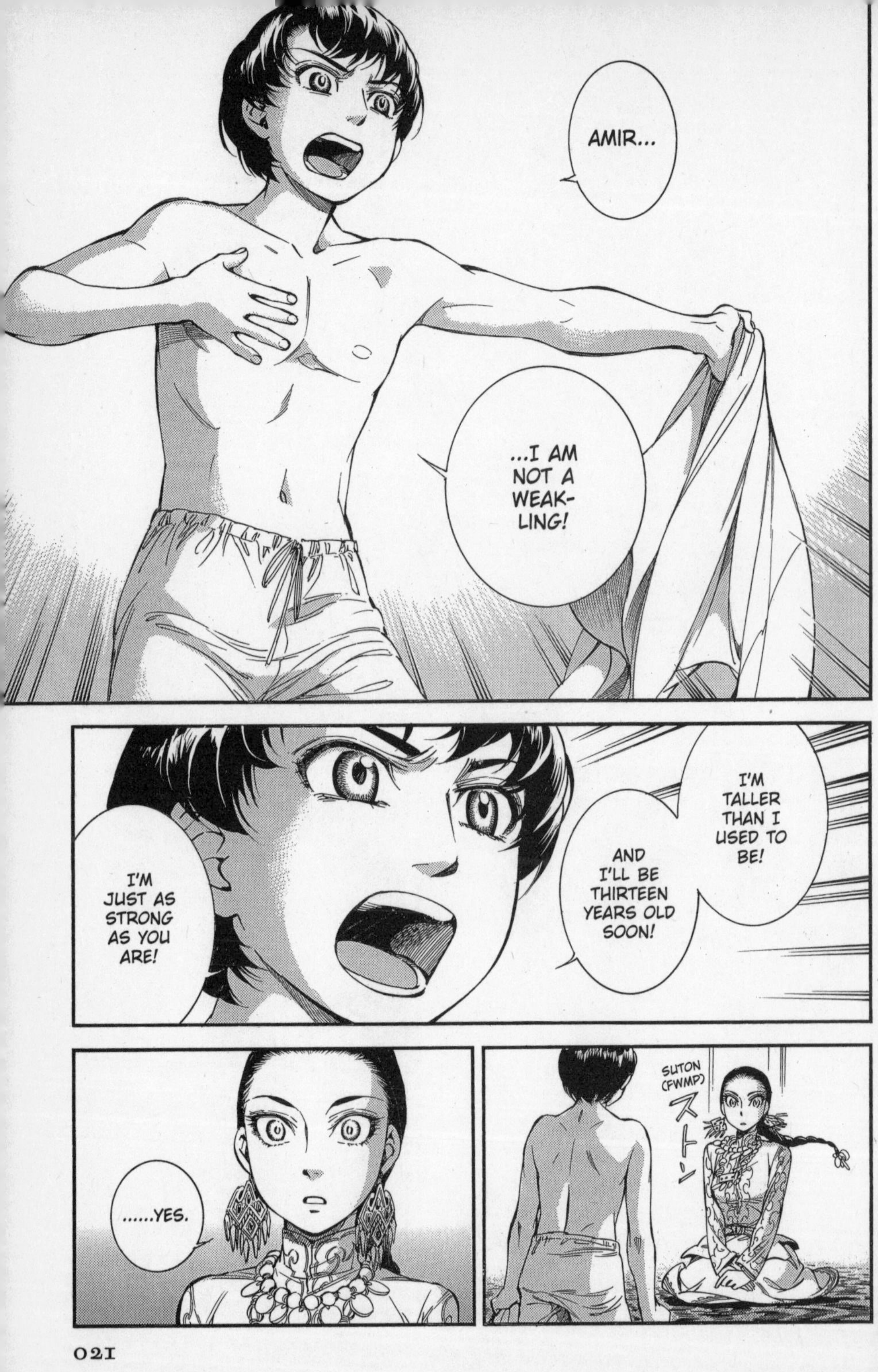
AMIR...
...I AM NOT A WEAK-LING!
I'M TALLER THAN I USED TO BE!
AND I'LL BE THIRTEEN YEARS OLD SOON!
I'M JUST AS STRONG AS YOU ARE!
SUTON (FWMP)
ストン
......YES.

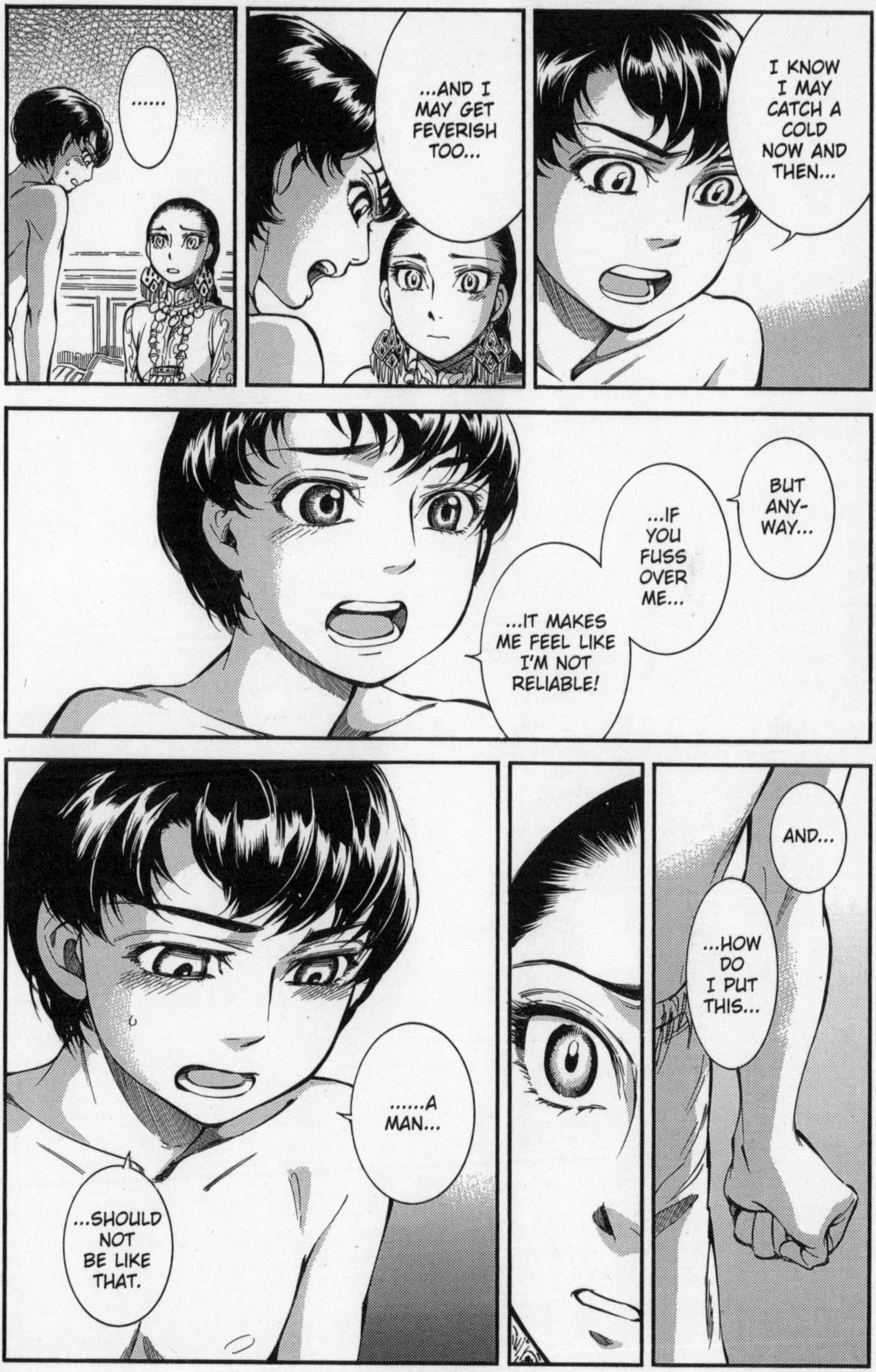
I KNOW I MAY CATCH A COLD NOW AND THEN...
...AND I MAY GET FEVERISH TOO...
......
BUT ANYWAY...
...IF YOU FUSS OVER ME...
...IT MAKES ME FEEL LIKE I'M NOT RELIABLE!
AND...
...HOW DO I PUT THIS...
......A MAN...
...SHOULD NOT BE LIKE THAT.

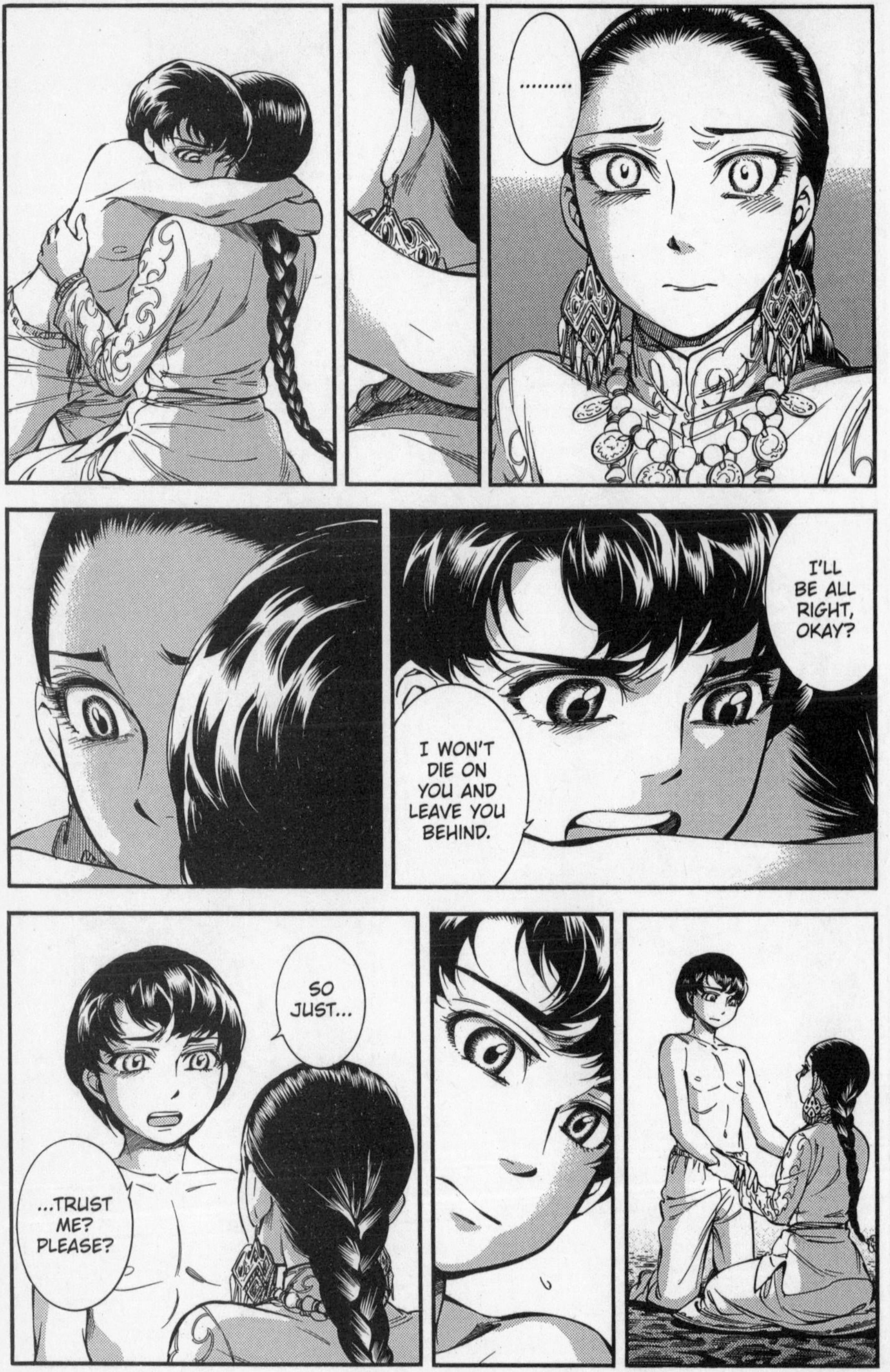
....
I'LL BE ALL RIGHT, OKAY?
I WON'T DIE ON YOU AND LEAVE YOU BEHIND.
SO JUST...
...TRUST ME? PLEASE?

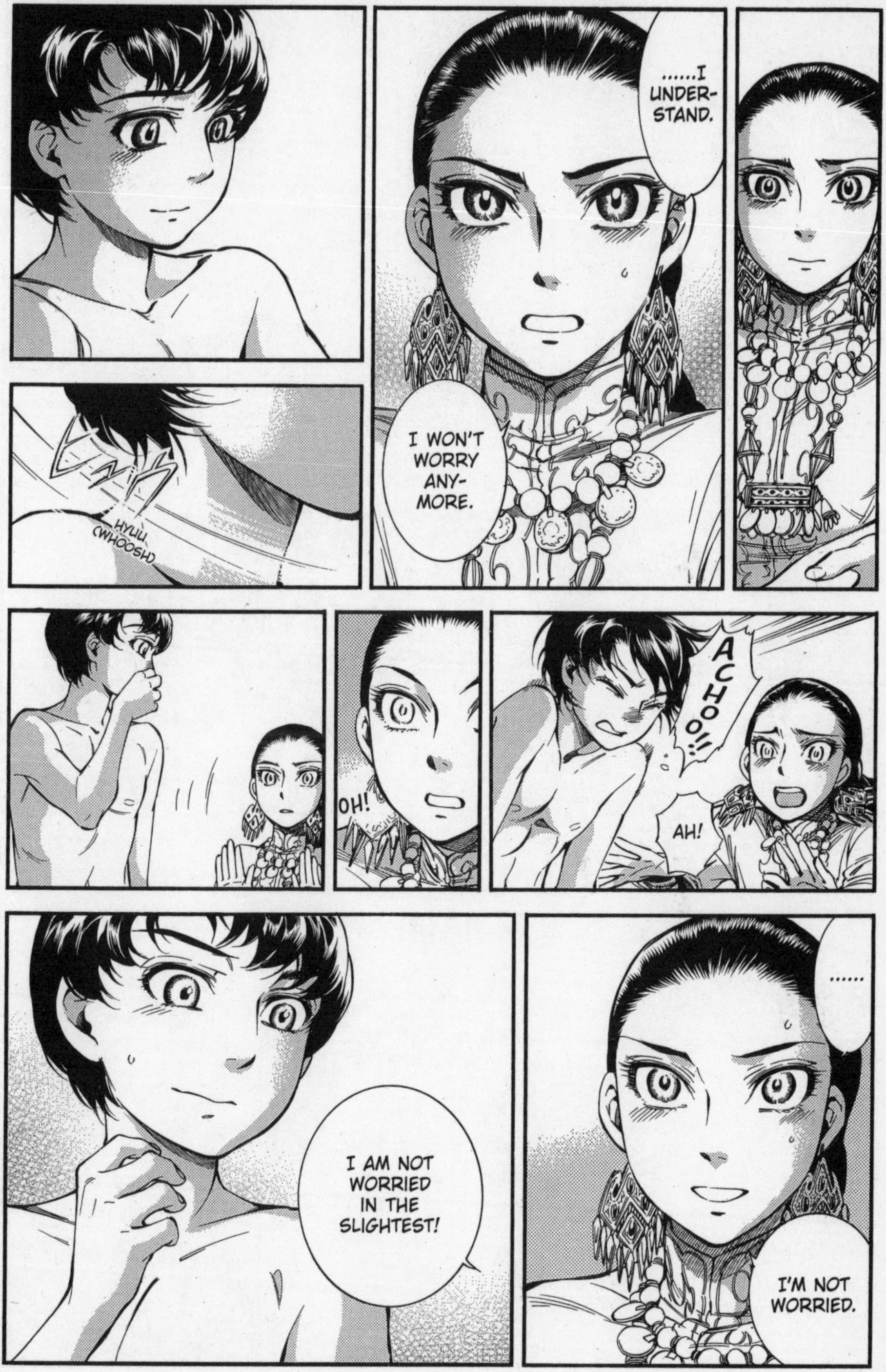
......I UNDER-STAND.
I WON'T WORRY ANY-MORE.
HYUU (WHOOSH)
ACHOO!!
AH!
OH!
......
I'M NOT WORRIED.
I AM NOT WORRIED IN THE SLIGHTEST!

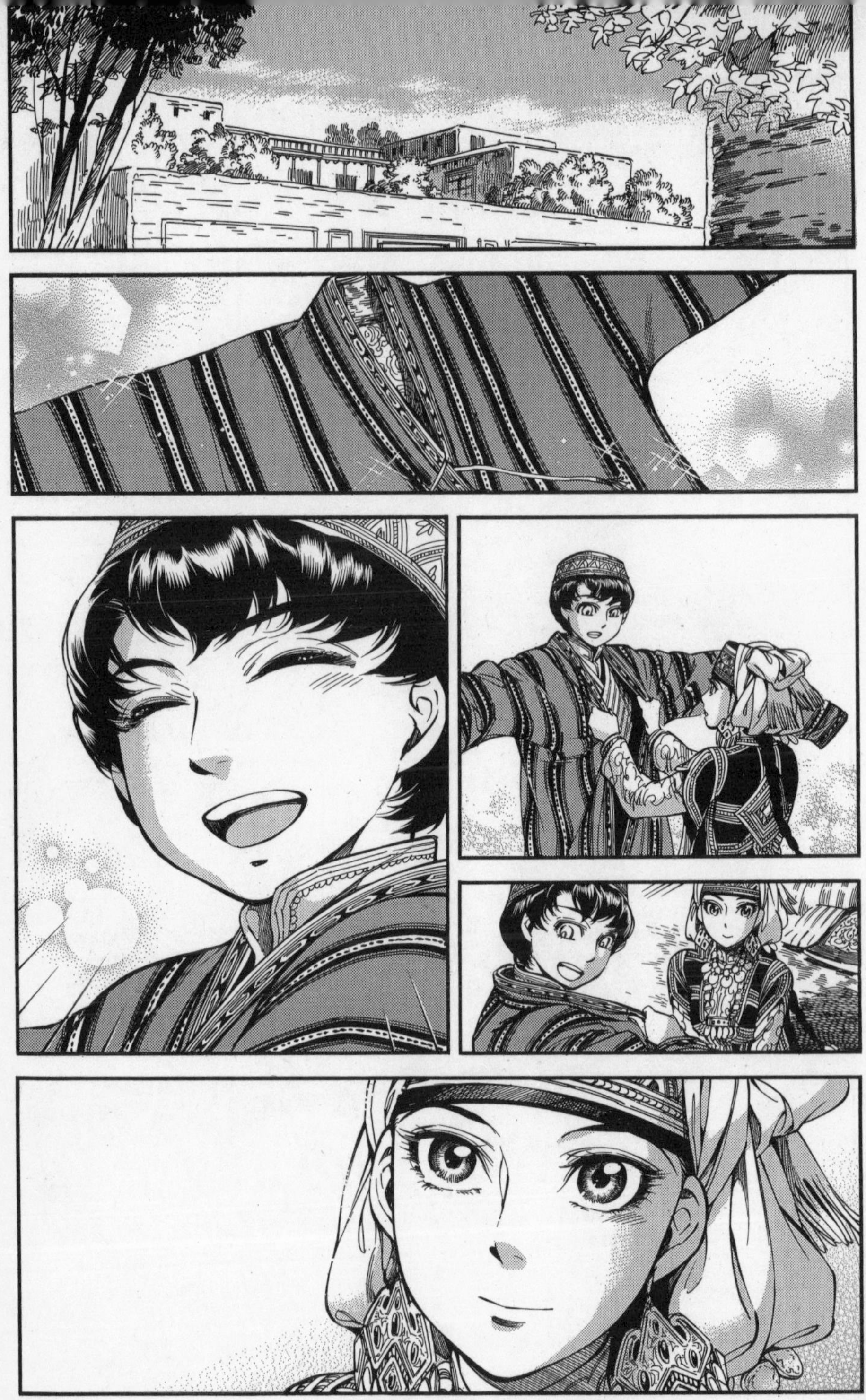

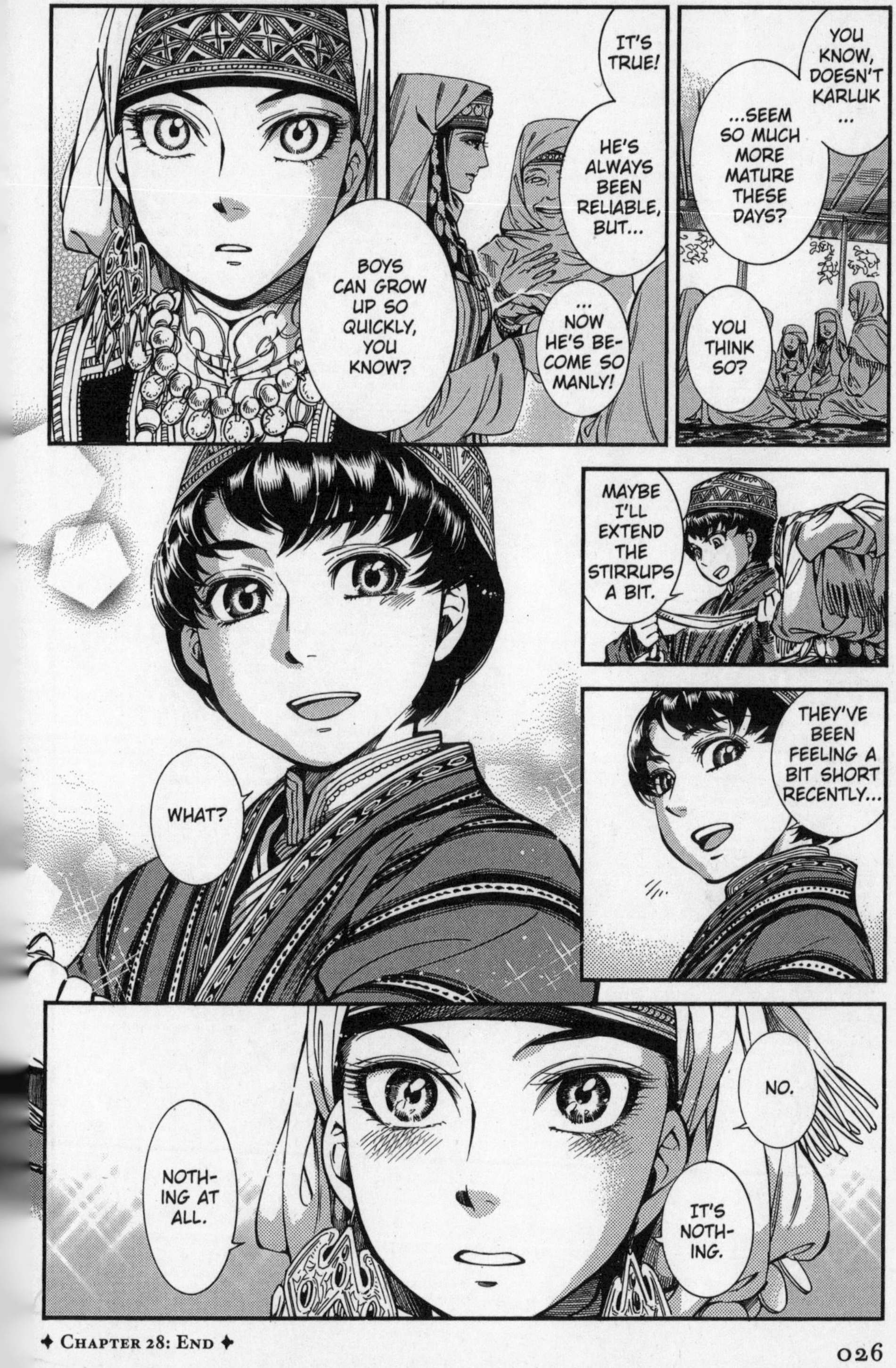
YOU KNOW, DOESN'T KARLUK ...
...SEEM SO MUCH MORE MATURE THESE DAYS?
YOU THINK SO?
IT'S TRUE!
HE'S ALWAYS BEEN RELIABLE, BUT...
... NOW HE'S BE-COME SO MANLY!
BOYS CAN GROW UP SO QUICKLY, YOU KNOW?
MAYBE I'LL EXTEND THE STIRRUPS A BIT.
THEY'VE BEEN FEELING A BIT SHORT RECENTLY...
WHAT?
NO.
IT'S NOTH-ING.
NOTH-ING AT ALL.

✦ CHAPTER 28: END ✦

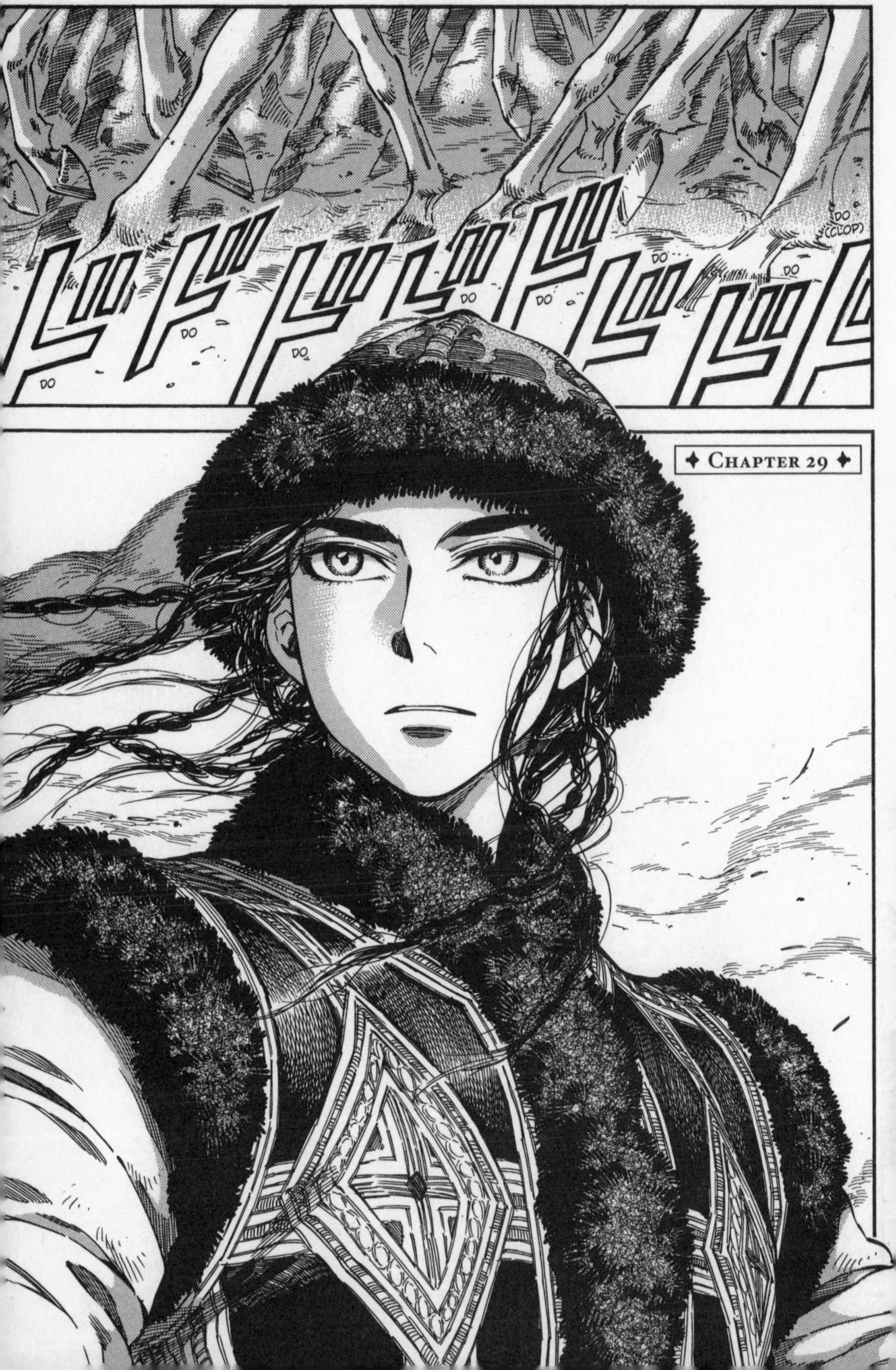
DO (CLOP)
DO
DO
DO
DO
DO
DO
DO
✦ CHAPTER 29 ✦

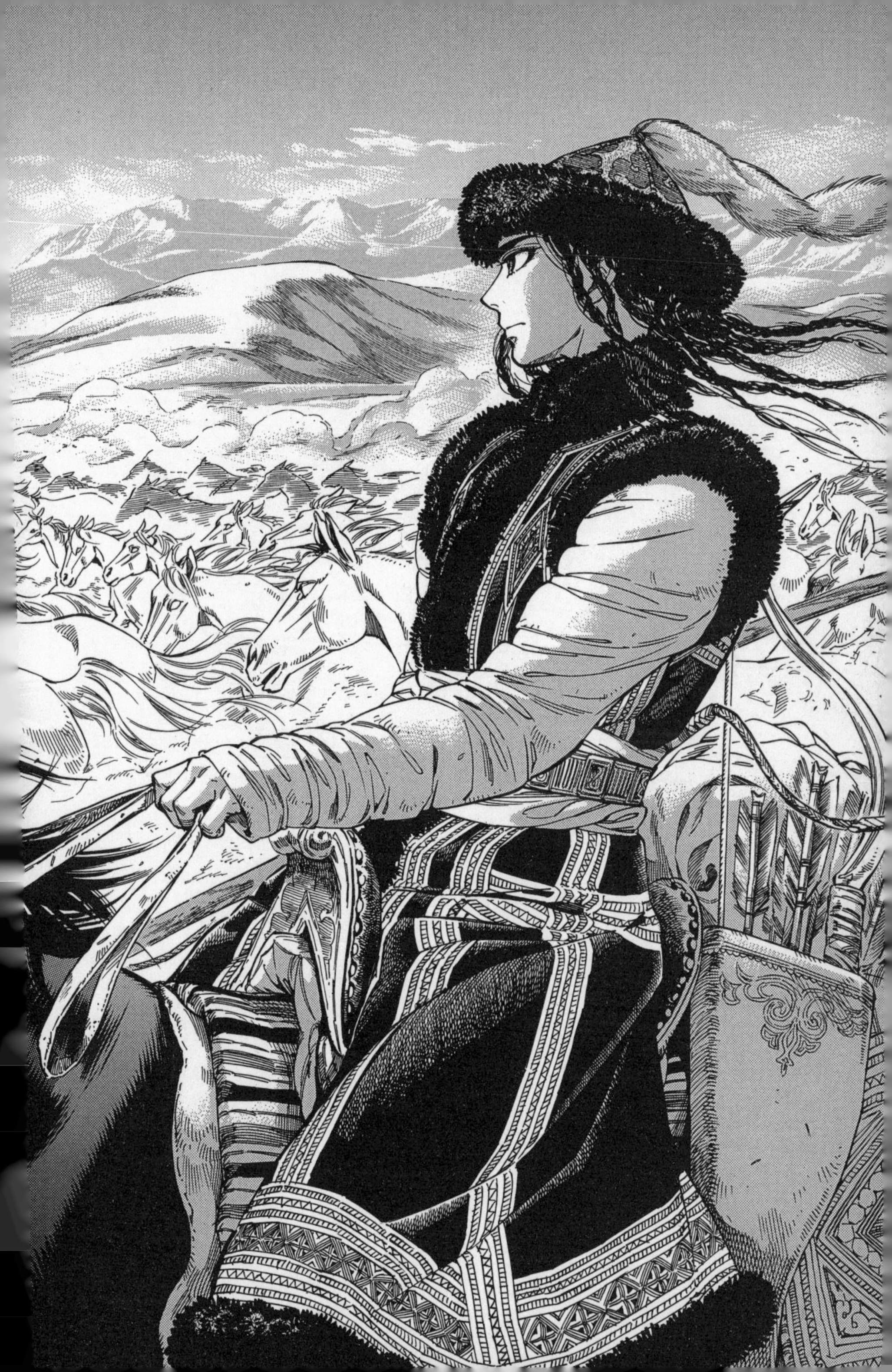

Chapter 29
Grazing Land

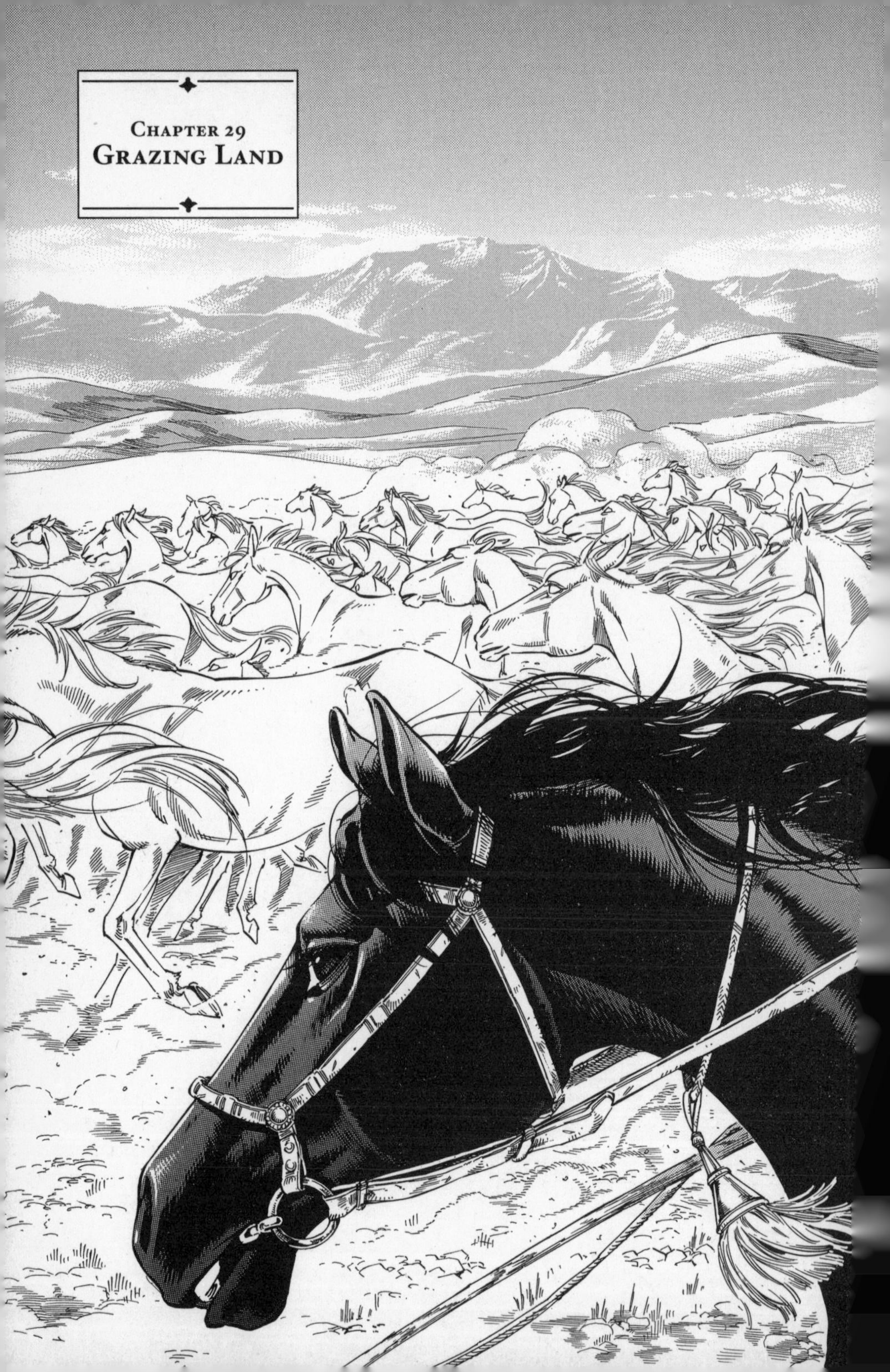

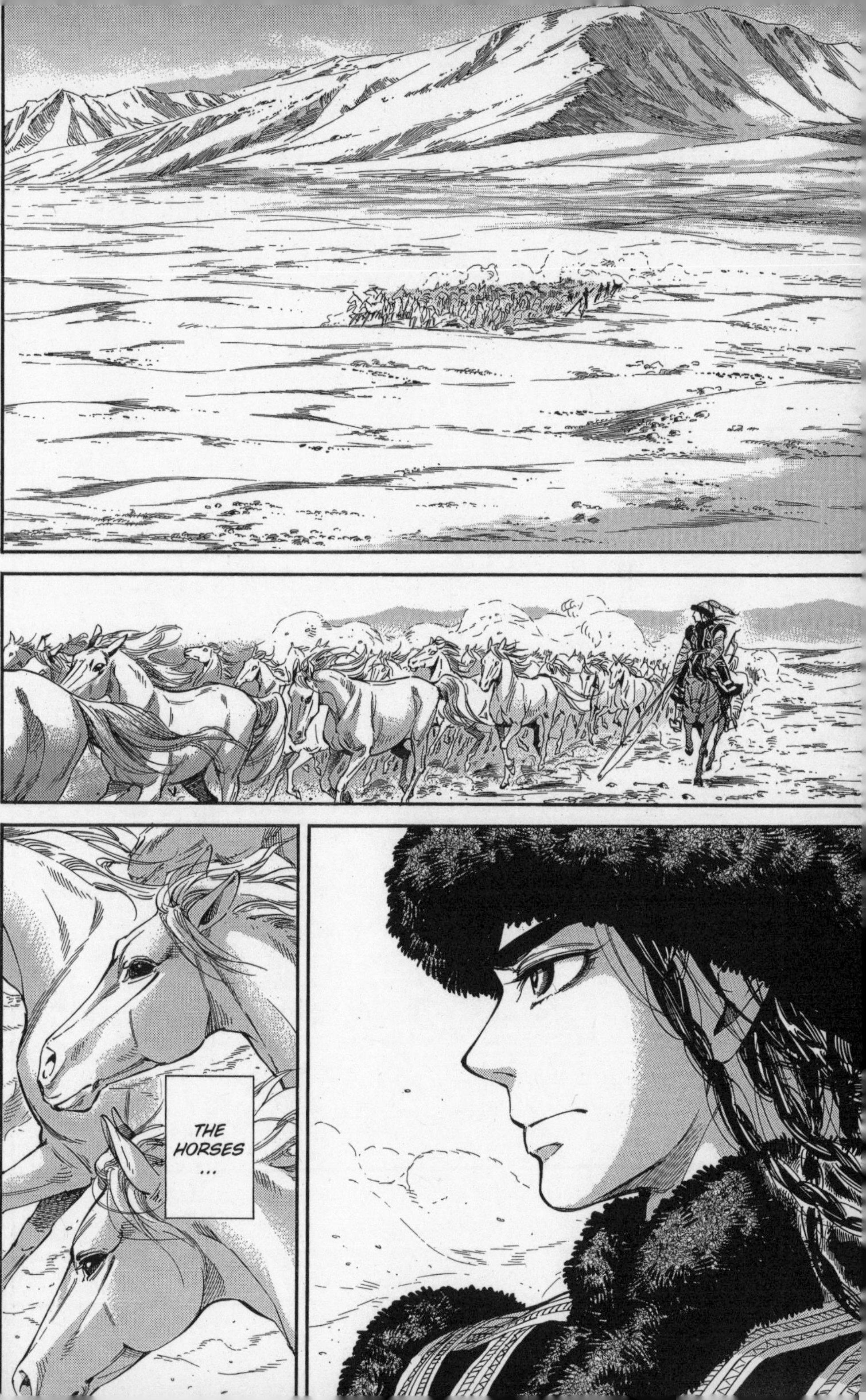
THE HORSES ...

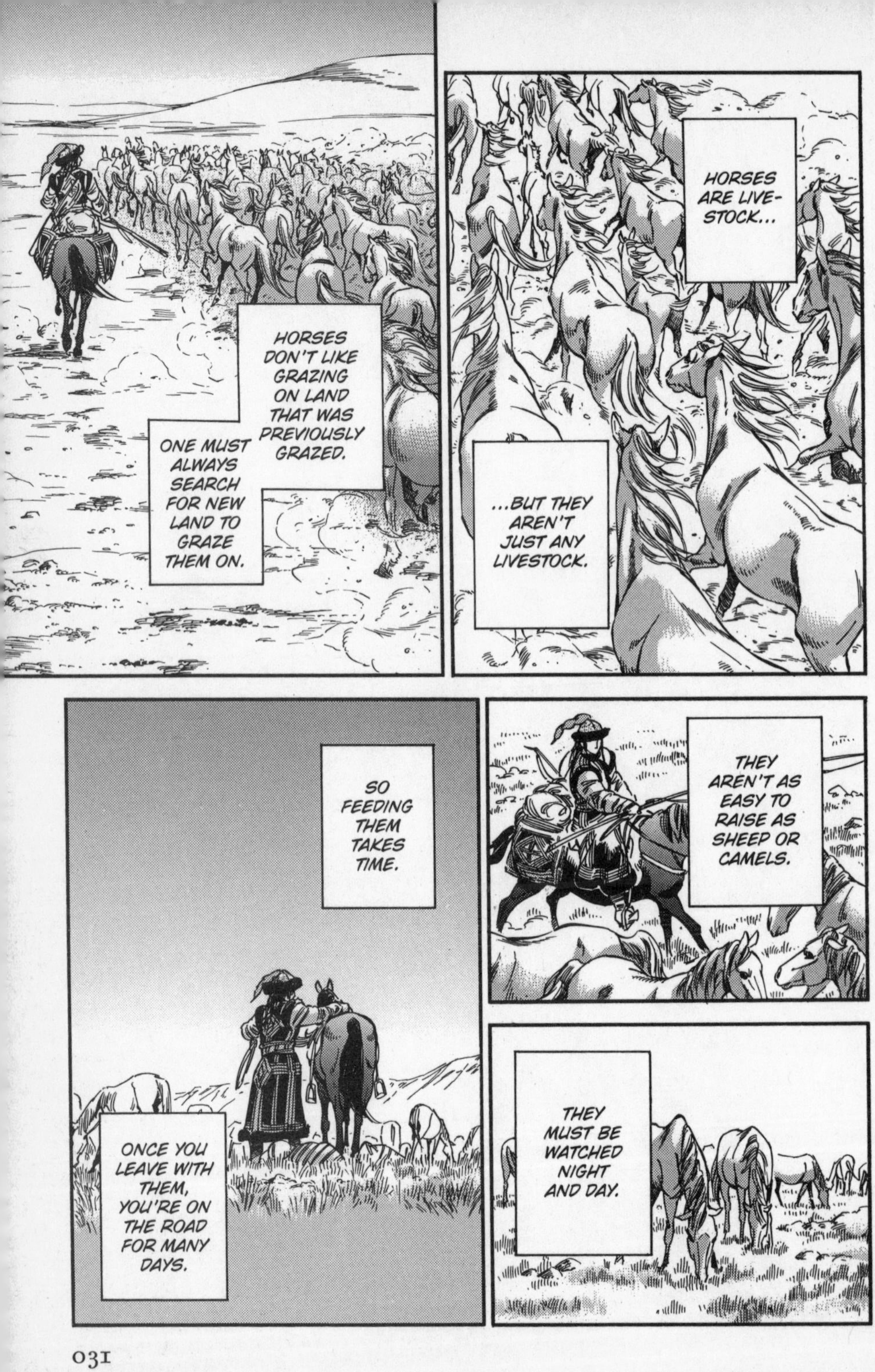
HORSES ARE LIVE-STOCK...
...BUT THEY AREN'T JUST ANY LIVESTOCK.
HORSES DON'T LIKE GRAZING ON LAND THAT WAS PREVIOUSLY GRAZED.
ONE MUST ALWAYS SEARCH FOR NEW LAND TO GRAZE THEM ON.
THEY AREN'T AS EASY TO RAISE AS SHEEP OR CAMELS.
THEY MUST BE WATCHED NIGHT AND DAY.
SO FEEDING THEM TAKES TIME.
ONCE YOU LEAVE WITH THEM, YOU'RE ON THE ROAD FOR MANY DAYS.

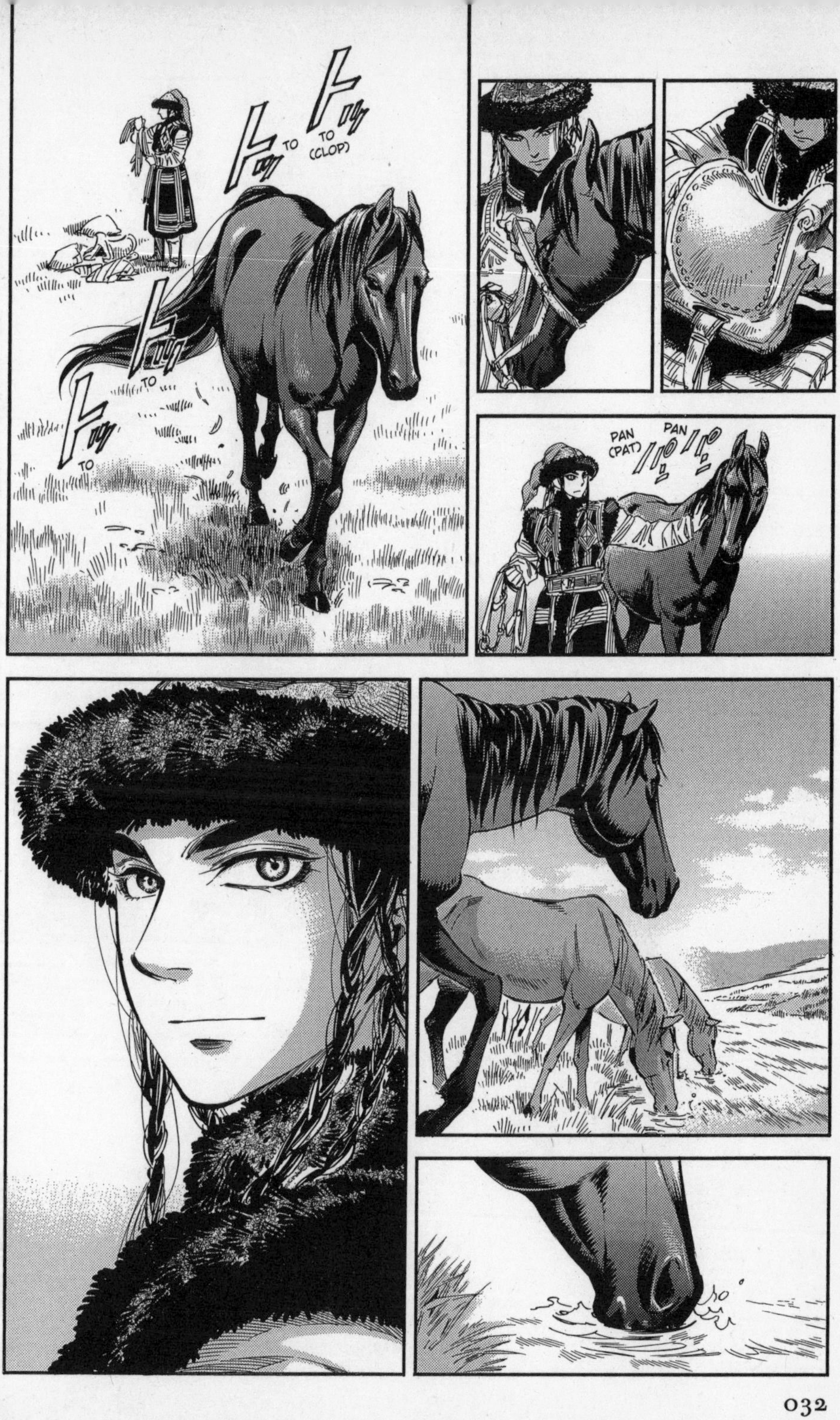

パン
PAN
パン
PAN
(PAT)
トッ
TO
(CLOP)
トッ
TO
トッ
TO
トッ
TO

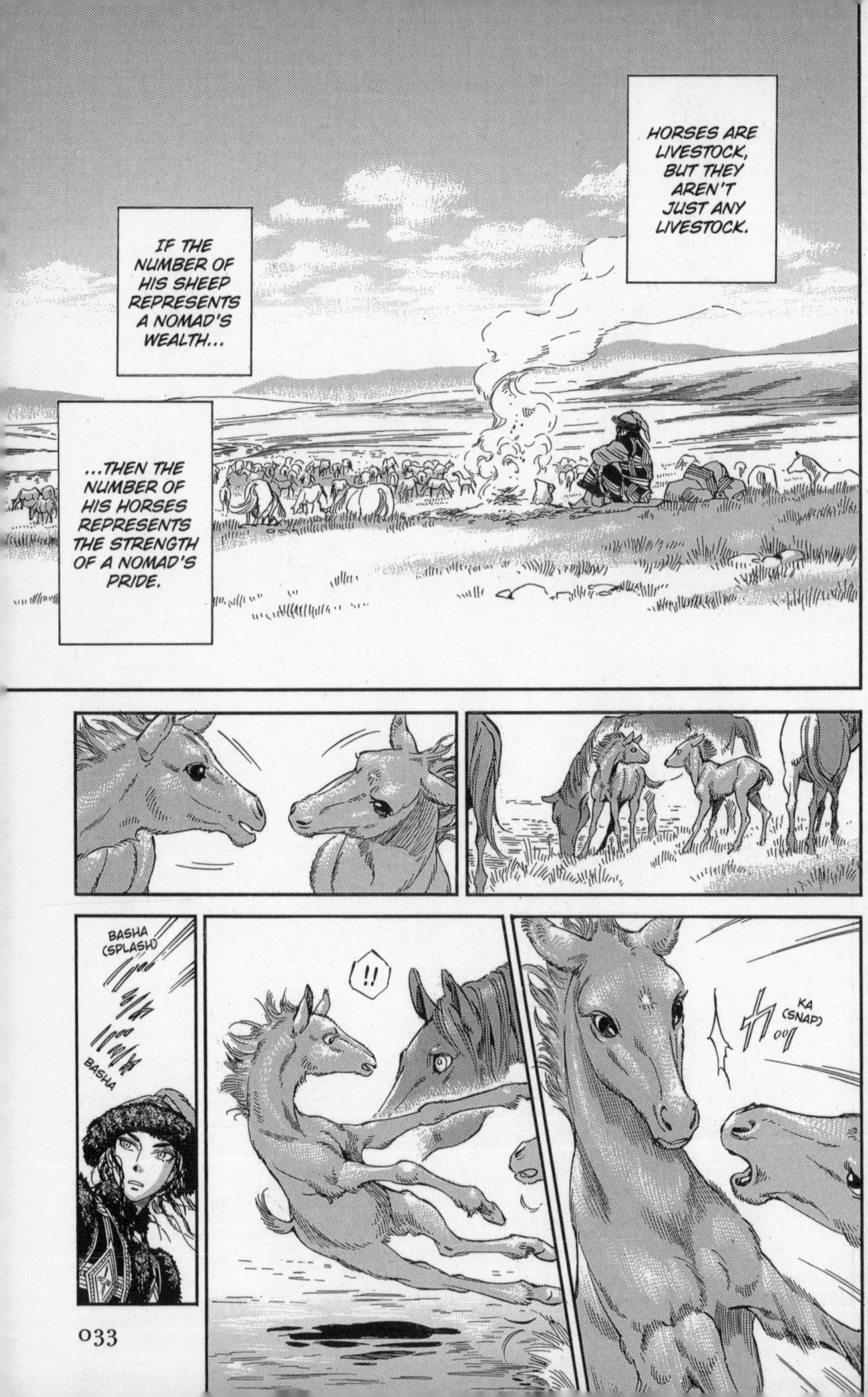
HORSES ARE LIVESTOCK, BUT THEY AREN'T JUST ANY LIVESTOCK.
IF THE NUMBER OF HIS SHEEP REPRESENTS A NOMAD'S WEALTH...
...THEN THE NUMBER OF HIS HORSES REPRESENTS THE STRENGTH OF A NOMAD'S PRIDE.
KA (SNAP)
!!
BASHA (SPLASH)
BASHA

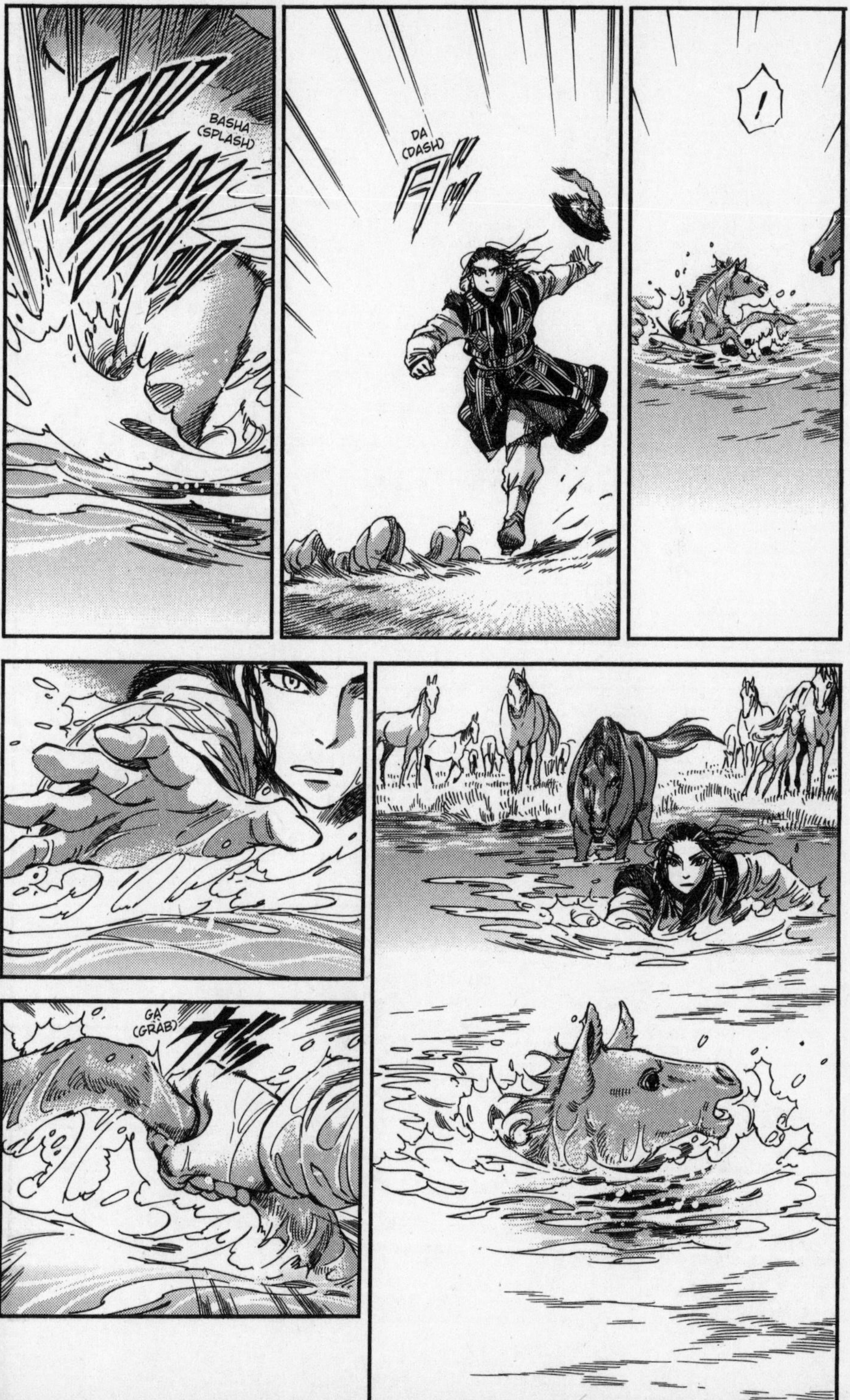
!
DA
(DASH)
BASHA
(SPLASH)
GA
(GRAB)

SFX: BURURURURU (SHAKE)

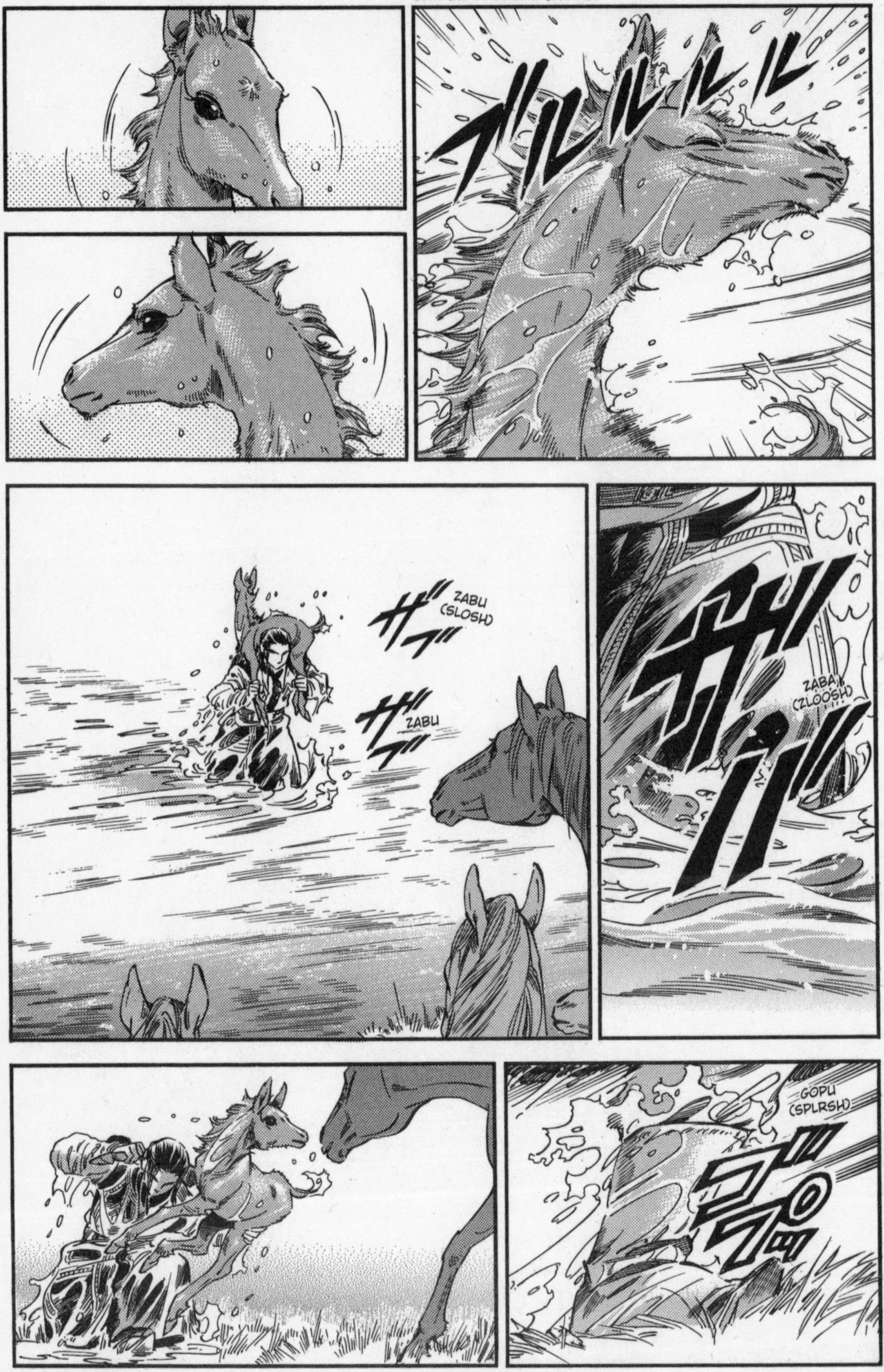

ZABA (ZLOOSH)
ZABU (SLOSH)
ZABU
GOPU (SPLRSH)

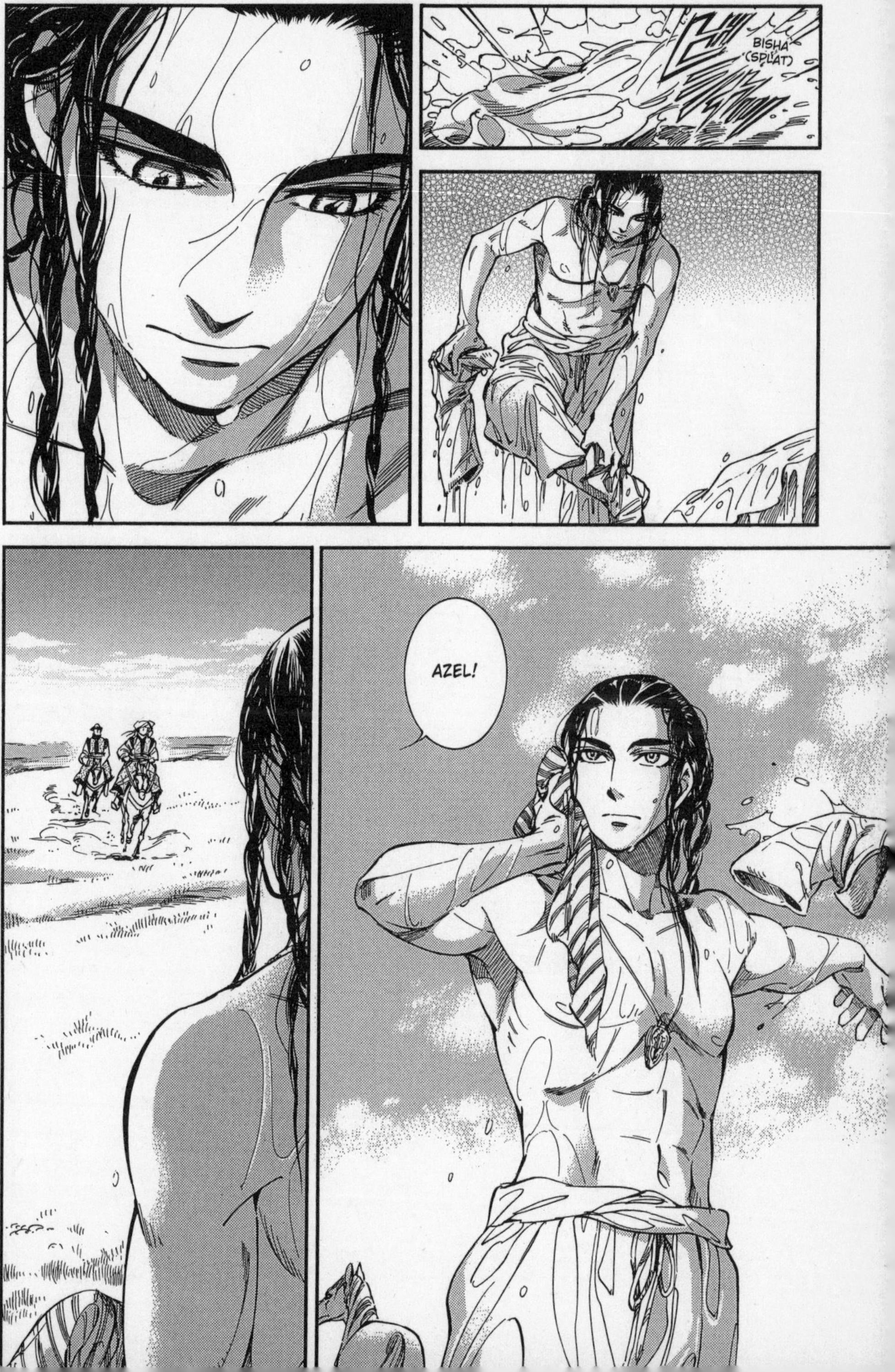
BISHA (SPLAT)
AZEL!

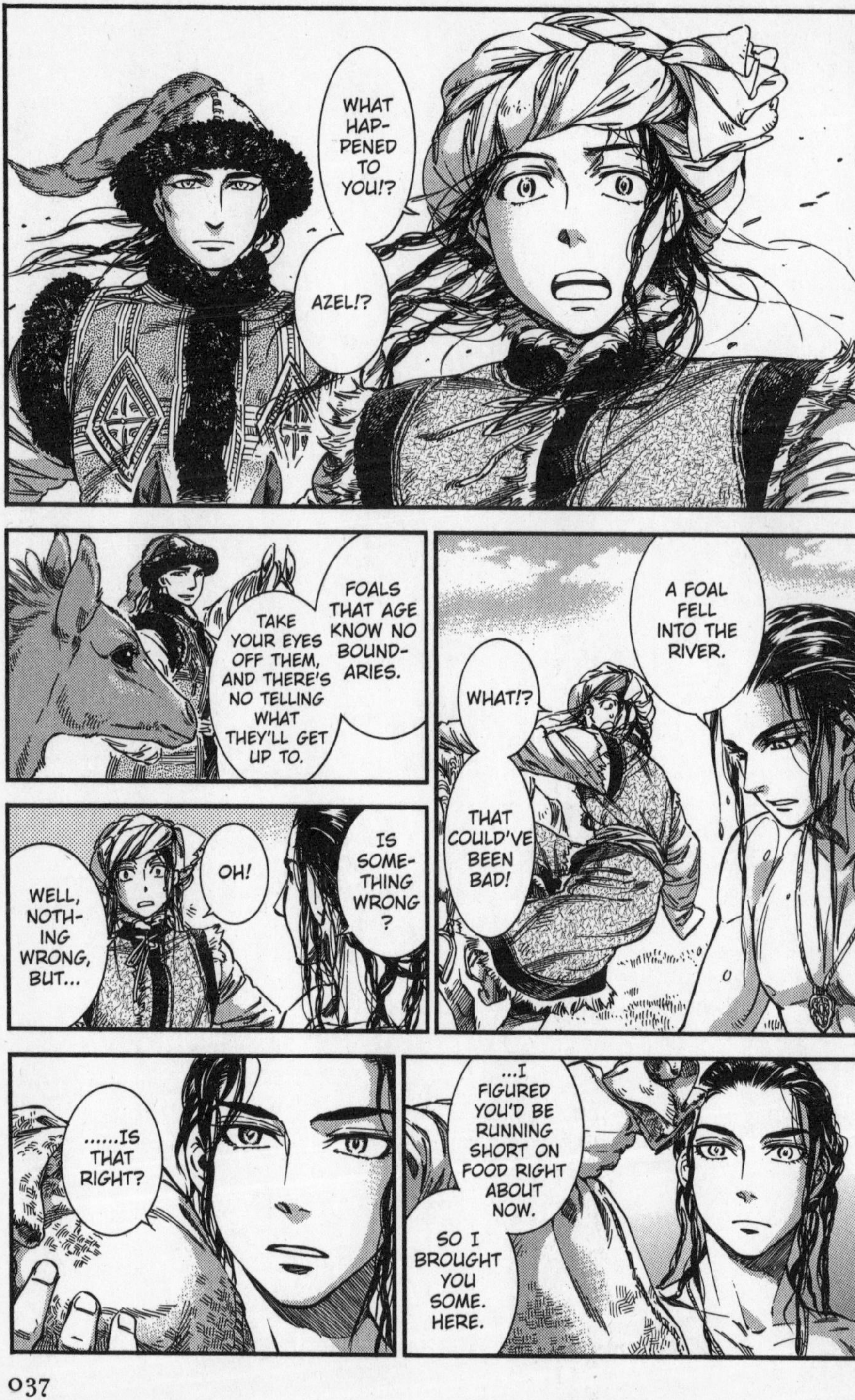
WHAT HAP-PENED TO YOU!?
AZEL!?
A FOAL FELL INTO THE RIVER.
WHAT!?
THAT COULD'VE BEEN BAD!
FOALS THAT AGE KNOW NO BOUND-ARIES.
TAKE YOUR EYES OFF THEM, AND THERE'S NO TELLING WHAT THEY'LL GET UP TO.
IS SOME-THING WRONG?
OH!
WELL, NOTH-ING WRONG, BUT...
...I FIGURED YOU'D BE RUNNING SHORT ON FOOD RIGHT ABOUT NOW.
SO I BROUGHT YOU SOME. HERE.
......IS THAT RIGHT?

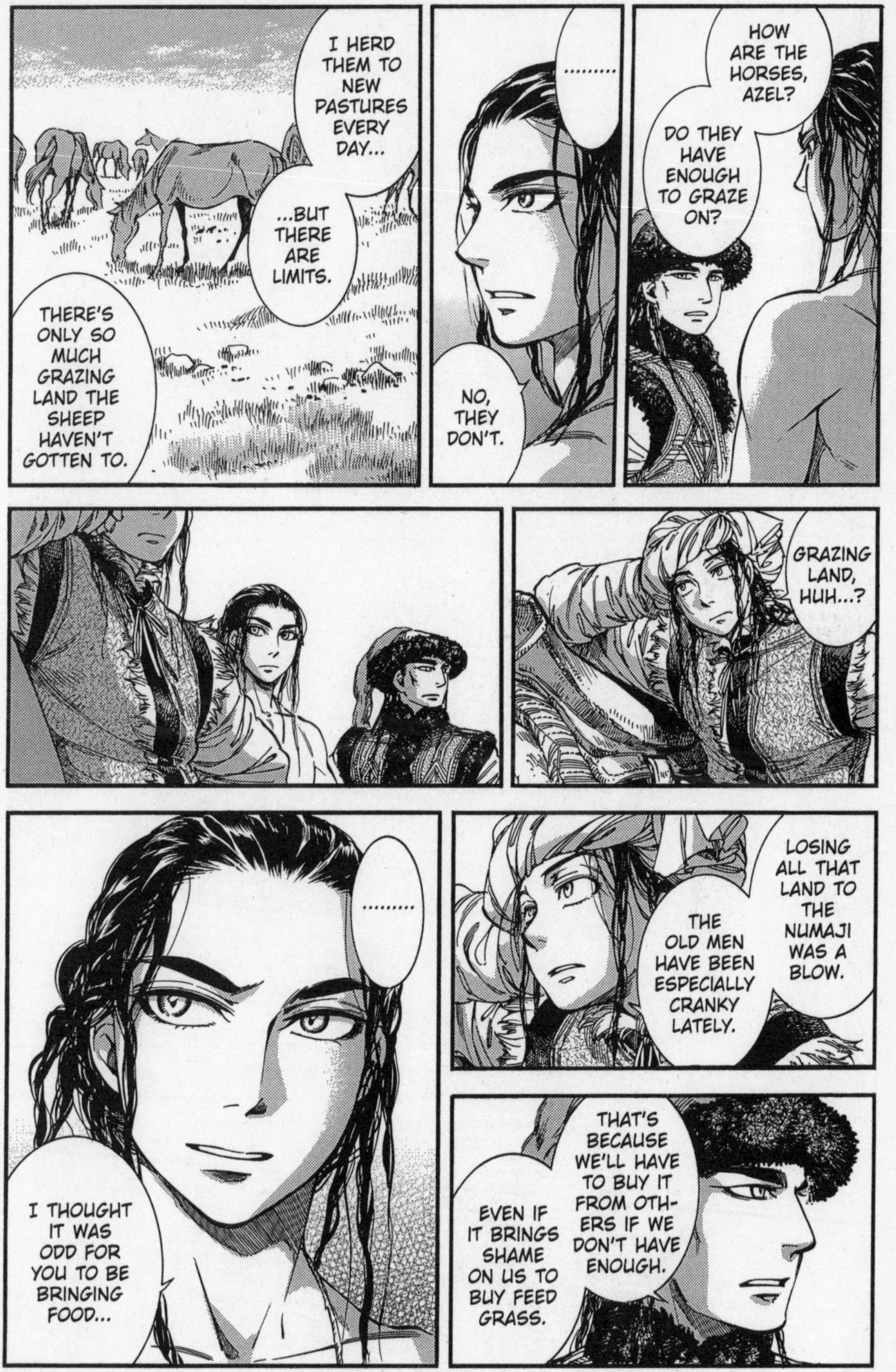
HOW ARE THE HORSES, AZEL?
DO THEY HAVE ENOUGH TO GRAZE ON?
....
NO, THEY DON'T.
I HERD THEM TO NEW PASTURES EVERY DAY...
...BUT THERE ARE LIMITS.
THERE'S ONLY SO MUCH GRAZING LAND THE SHEEP HAVEN'T GOTTEN TO.
GRAZING LAND, HUH...?
LOSING ALL THAT LAND TO THE NUMAJI WAS A BLOW.
THE OLD MEN HAVE BEEN ESPECIALLY CRANKY LATELY.
THAT'S BECAUSE WE'LL HAVE TO BUY IT FROM OTH-ERS IF WE DON'T HAVE ENOUGH.
EVEN IF IT BRINGS SHAME ON US TO BUY FEED GRASS.
....
I THOUGHT IT WAS ODD FOR YOU TO BE BRINGING FOOD...

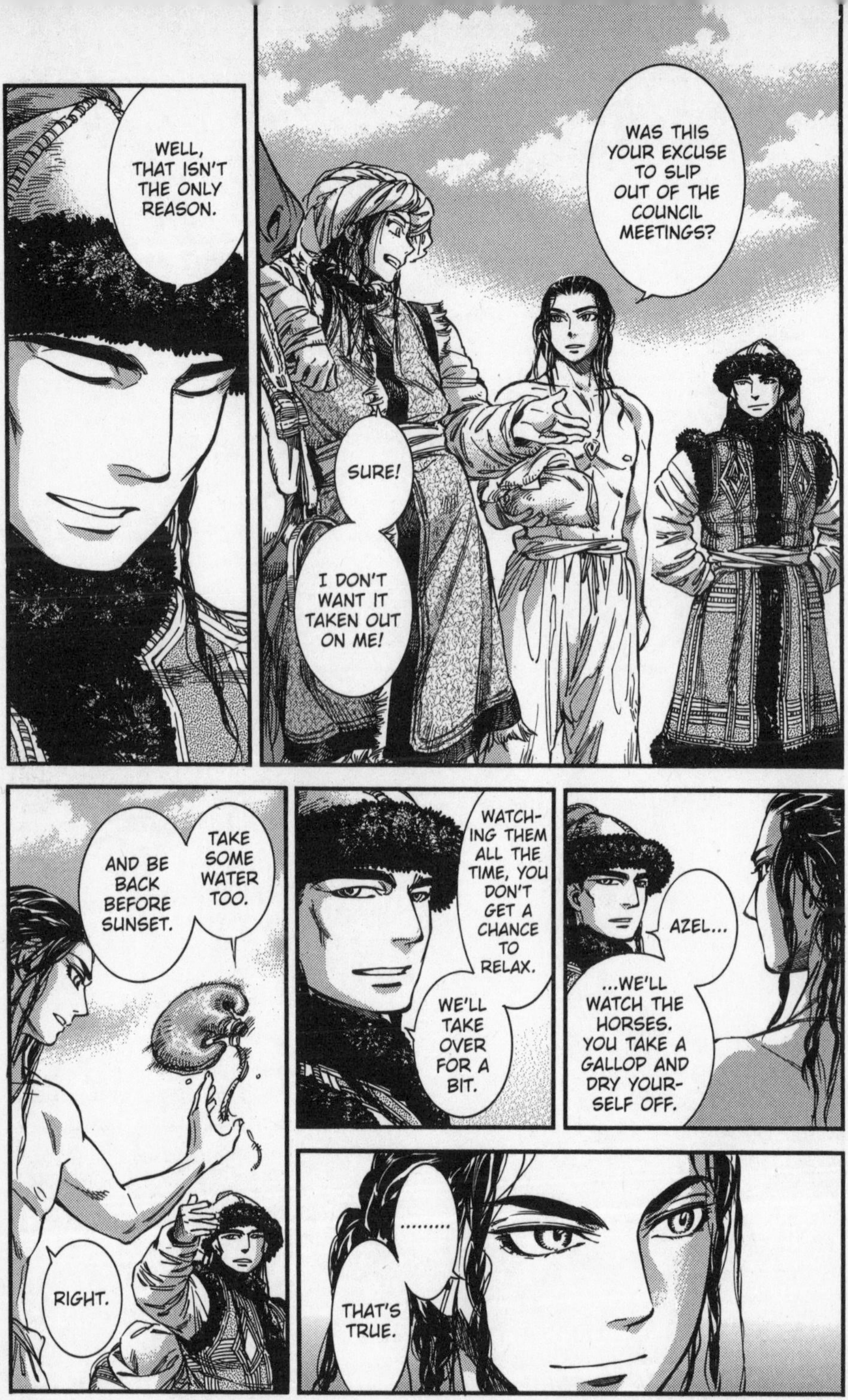
WAS THIS YOUR EXCUSE TO SLIP OUT OF THE COUNCIL MEETINGS?
SURE!
I DON'T WANT IT TAKEN OUT ON ME!
WELL, THAT ISN'T THE ONLY REASON.
AZEL...
...WE'LL WATCH THE HORSES. YOU TAKE A GALLOP AND DRY YOURSELF OFF.
WATCHING THEM ALL THE TIME, YOU DON'T GET A CHANCE TO RELAX.
WE'LL TAKE OVER FOR A BIT.
....
THAT'S TRUE.
TAKE SOME WATER TOO.
AND BE BACK BEFORE SUNSET.
RIGHT.

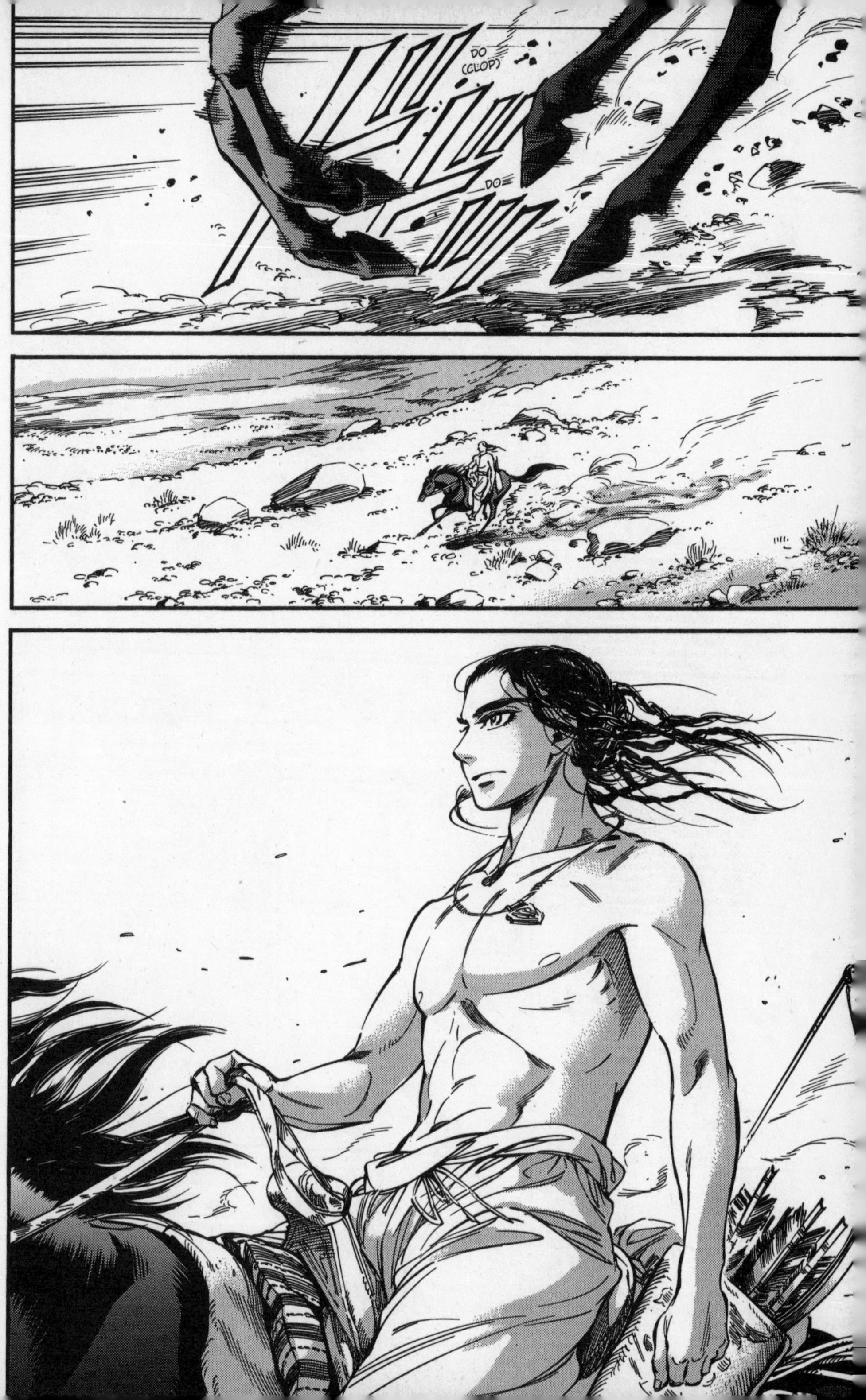
DO (CLOP)
DO

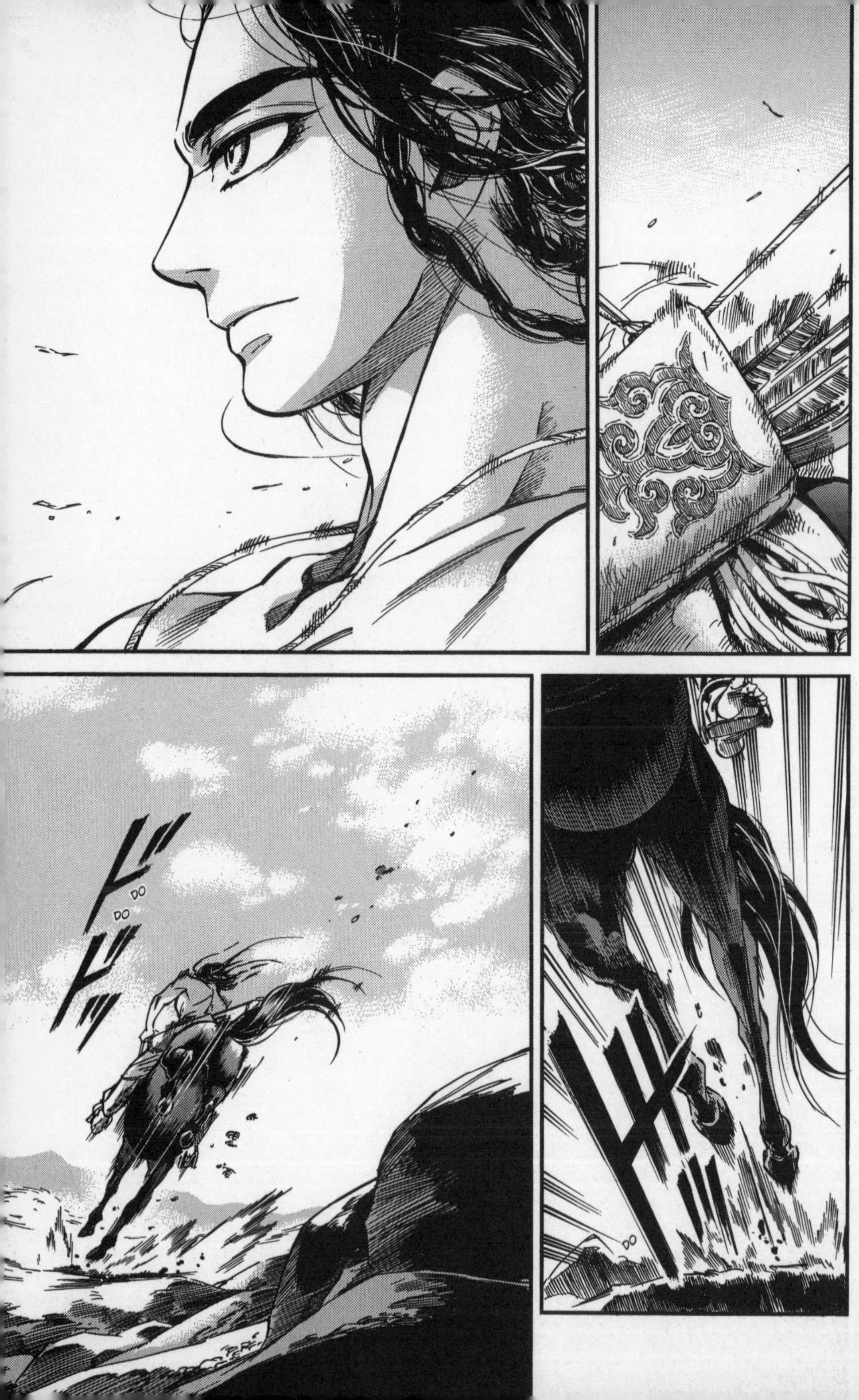
DO
DO
DO

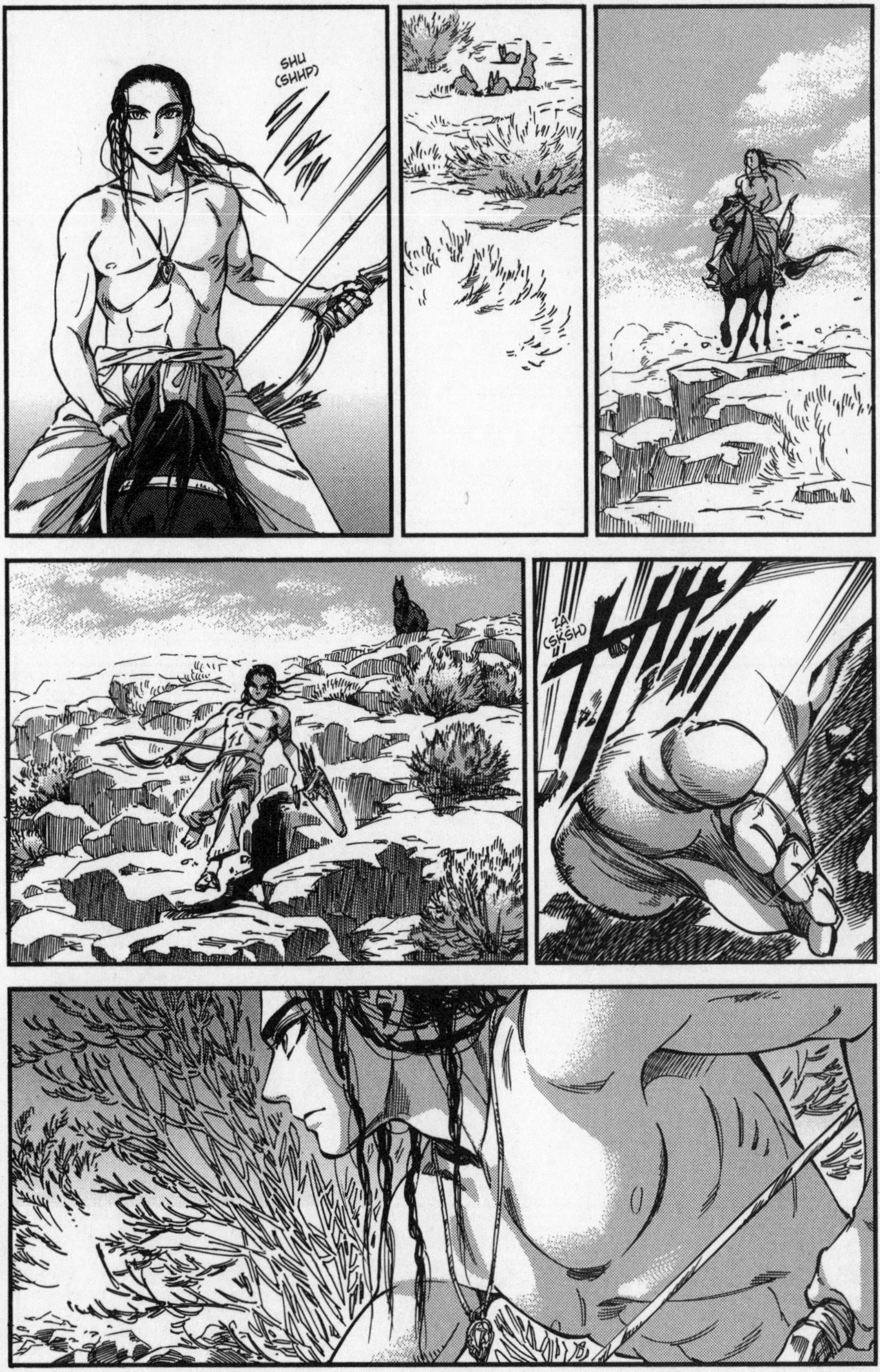
SHU
(SHHP)
ZA
(SKSH)

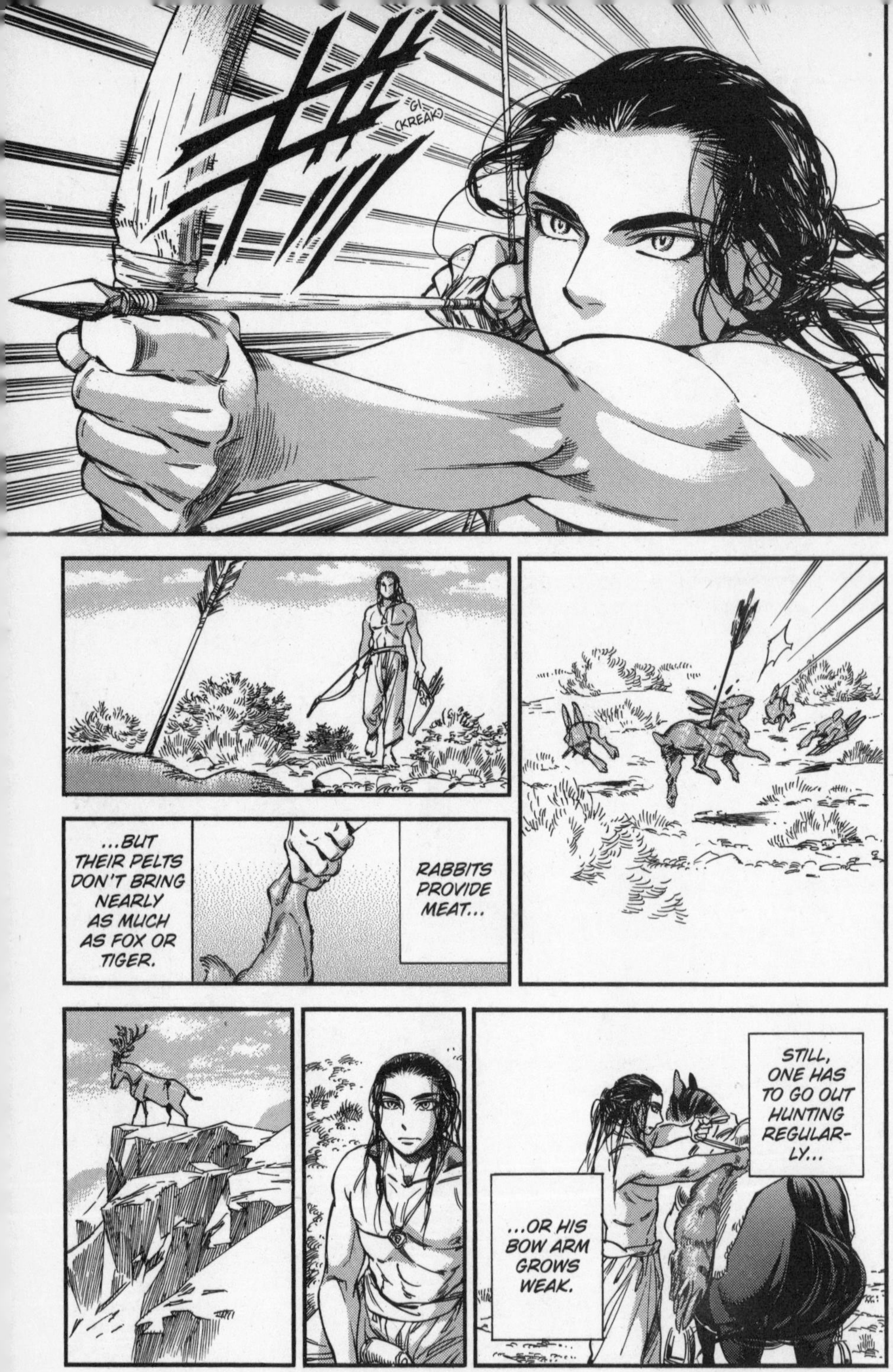
GI
(KREAK)
RABBITS PROVIDE MEAT...
...BUT THEIR PELTS DON'T BRING NEARLY AS MUCH AS FOX OR TIGER.
STILL, ONE HAS TO GO OUT HUNTING REGULAR-LY...
...OR HIS BOW ARM GROWS WEAK.

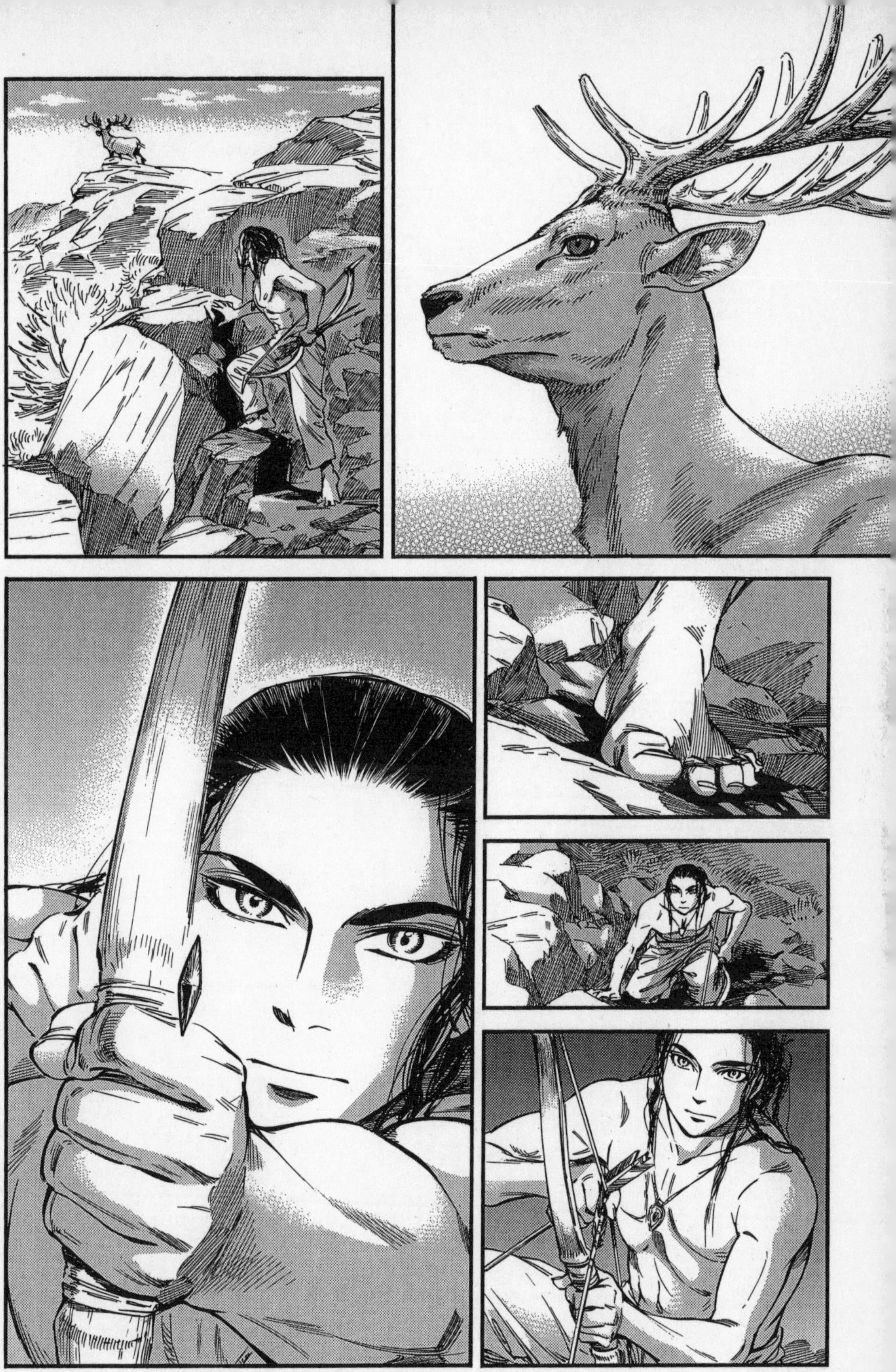

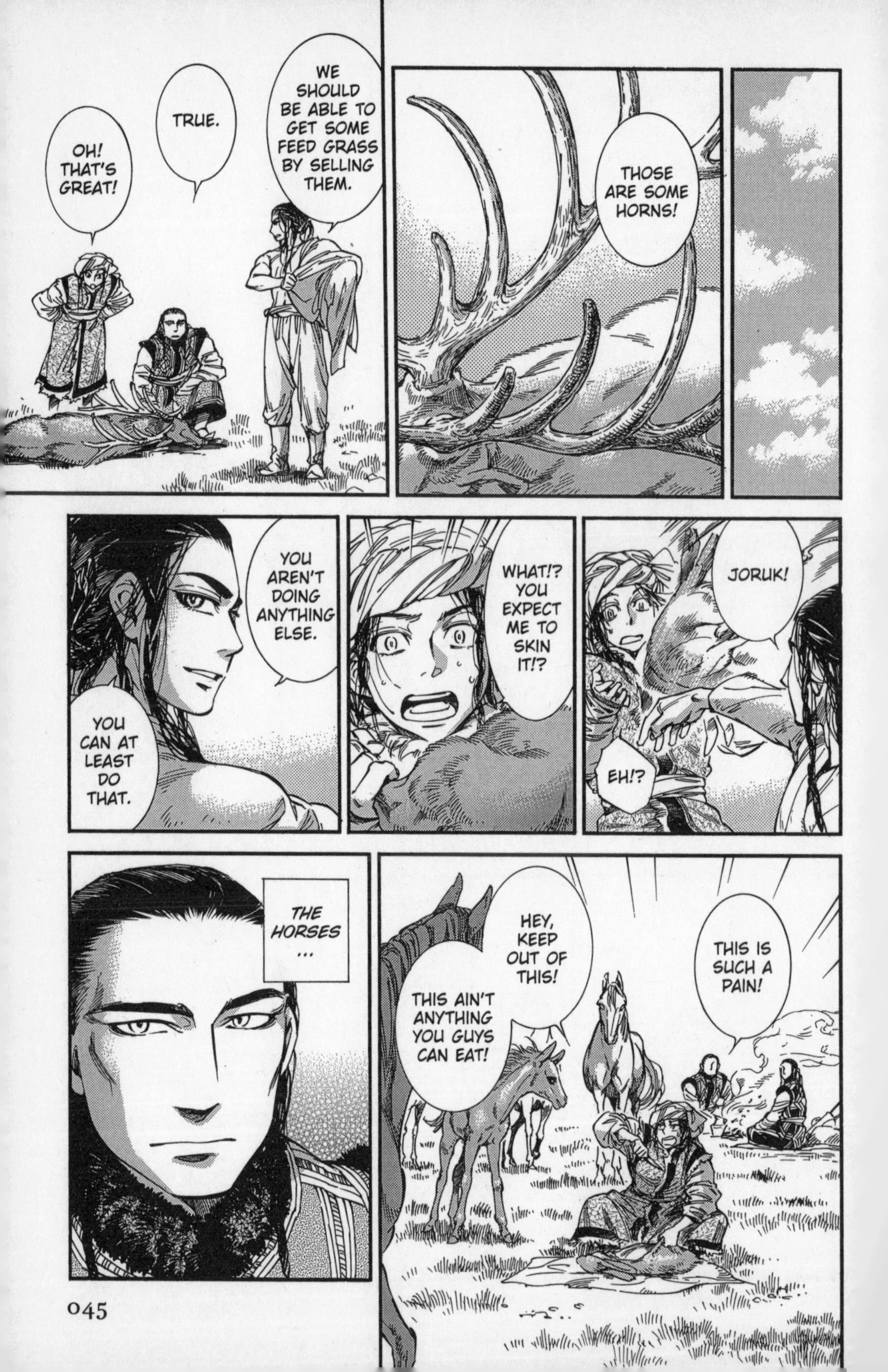
THOSE ARE SOME HORNS!
WE SHOULD BE ABLE TO GET SOME FEED GRASS BY SELLING THEM.
TRUE.
OH! THAT'S GREAT!
JORUK!
EH!?
WHAT!? YOU EXPECT ME TO SKIN IT!?
YOU AREN'T DOING ANYTHING ELSE.
YOU CAN AT LEAST DO THAT.
THIS IS SUCH A PAIN!
HEY, KEEP OUT OF THIS!
THIS AIN'T ANYTHING YOU GUYS CAN EAT!
THE HORSES...

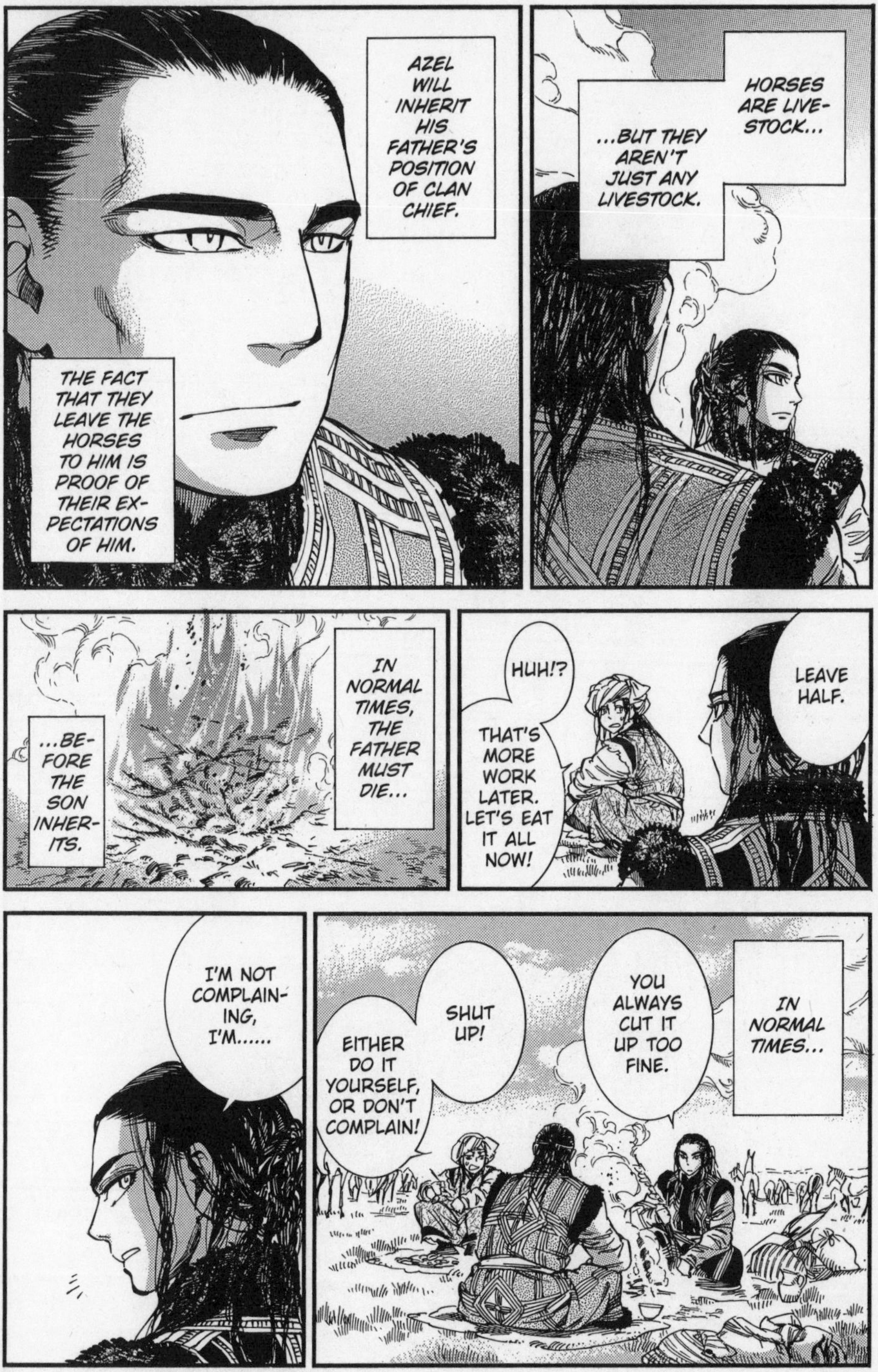
HORSES ARE LIVE-STOCK...
...BUT THEY AREN'T JUST ANY LIVESTOCK.
AZEL WILL INHERIT HIS FATHER'S POSITION OF CLAN CHIEF.
THE FACT THAT THEY LEAVE THE HORSES TO HIM IS PROOF OF THEIR EX-PECTATIONS OF HIM.
LEAVE HALF.
HUH!?
THAT'S MORE WORK LATER. LET'S EAT IT ALL NOW!
IN NORMAL TIMES, THE FATHER MUST DIE...
...BE-FORE THE SON INHER-ITS.
IN NORMAL TIMES...
YOU ALWAYS CUT IT UP TOO FINE.
SHUT UP!
EITHER DO IT YOURSELF, OR DON'T COMPLAIN!
I'M NOT COMPLAIN-ING, I'M......

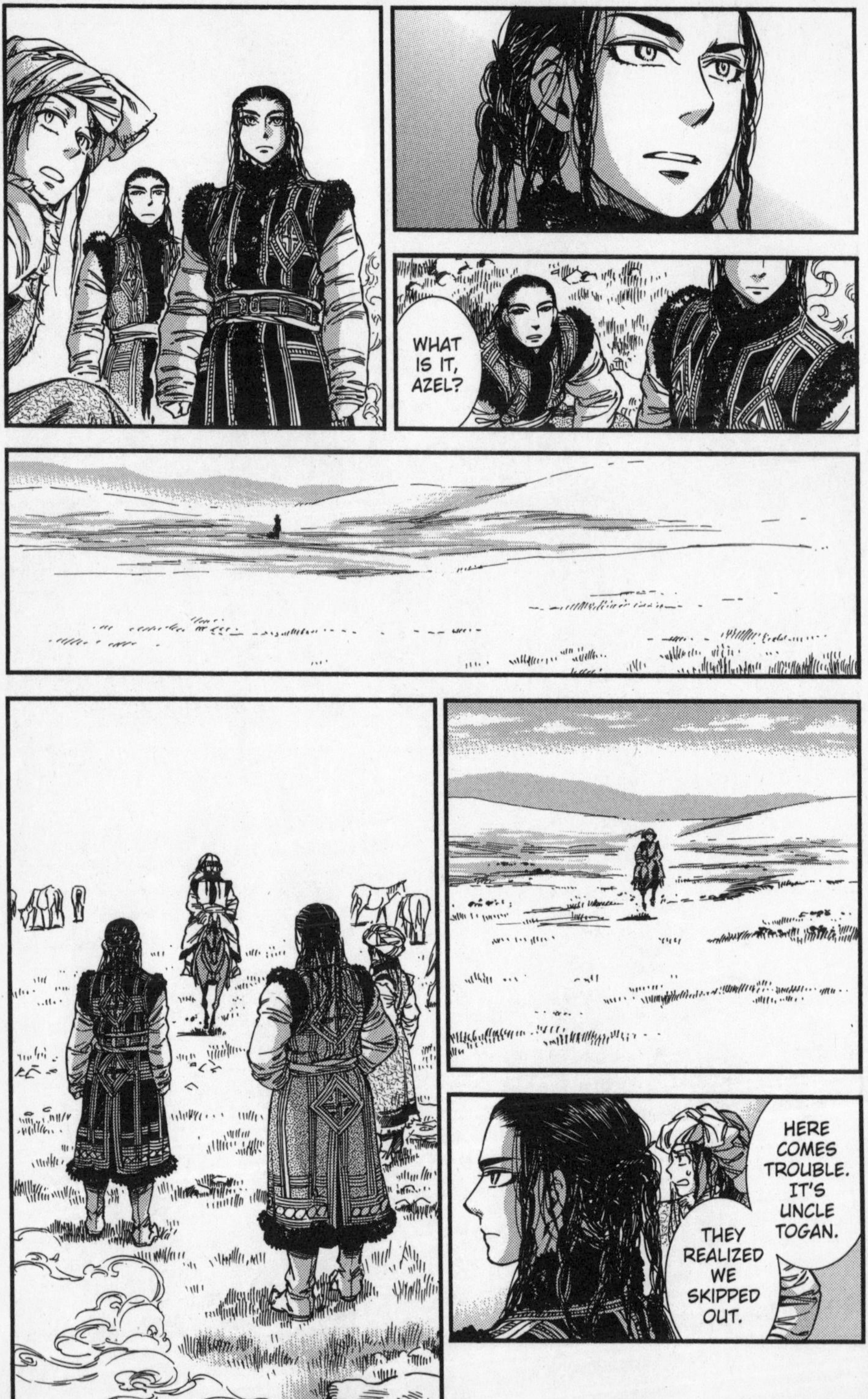
WHAT IS IT, AZEL?
HERE COMES TROUBLE. IT'S UNCLE TOGAN.
THEY REALIZED WE SKIPPED OUT.

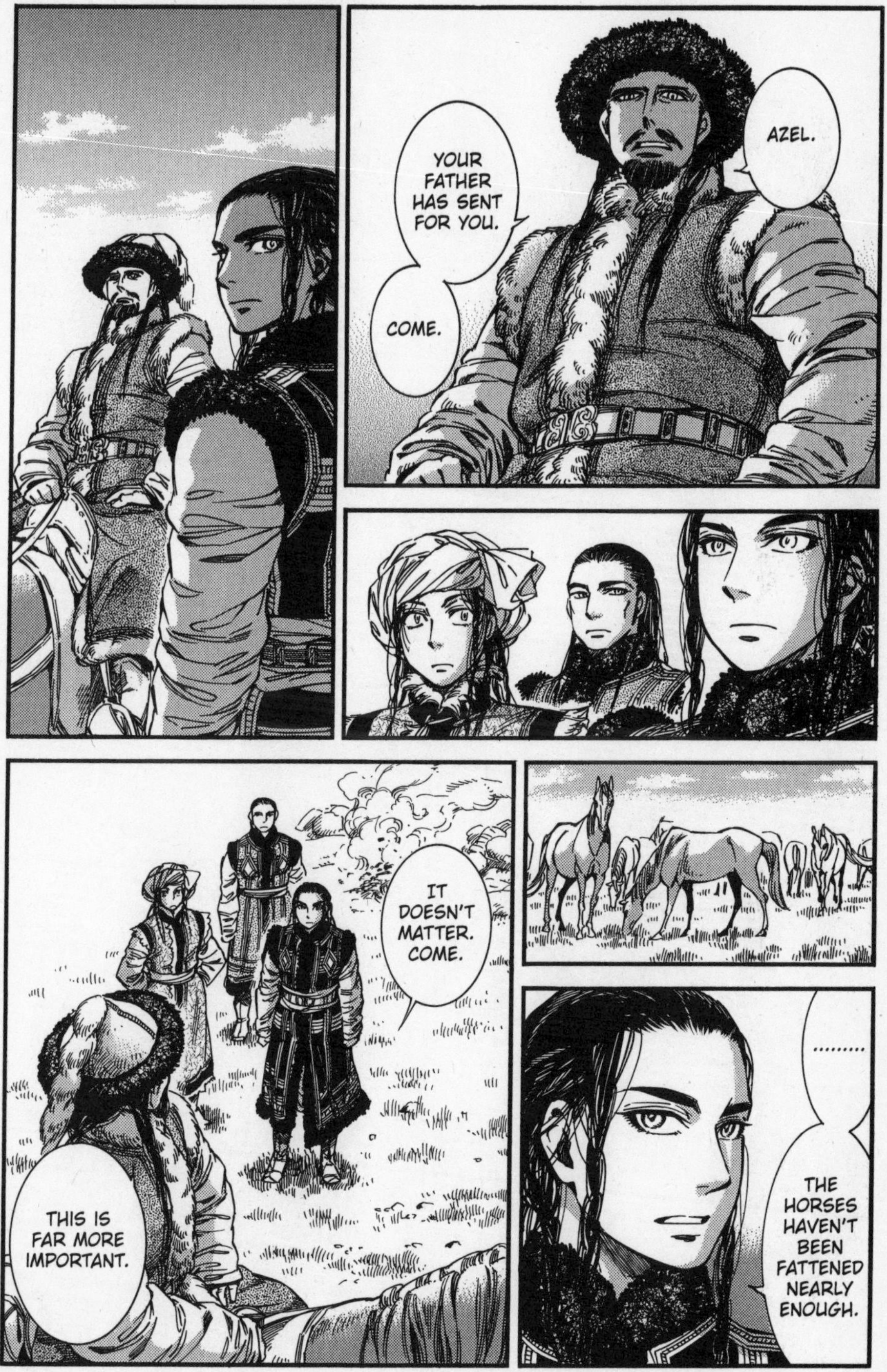
AZEL.
YOUR FATHER HAS SENT FOR YOU.
COME.
....
THE HORSES HAVEN'T BEEN FATTENED NEARLY ENOUGH.
IT DOESN'T MATTER. COME.
THIS IS FAR MORE IMPORTANT.

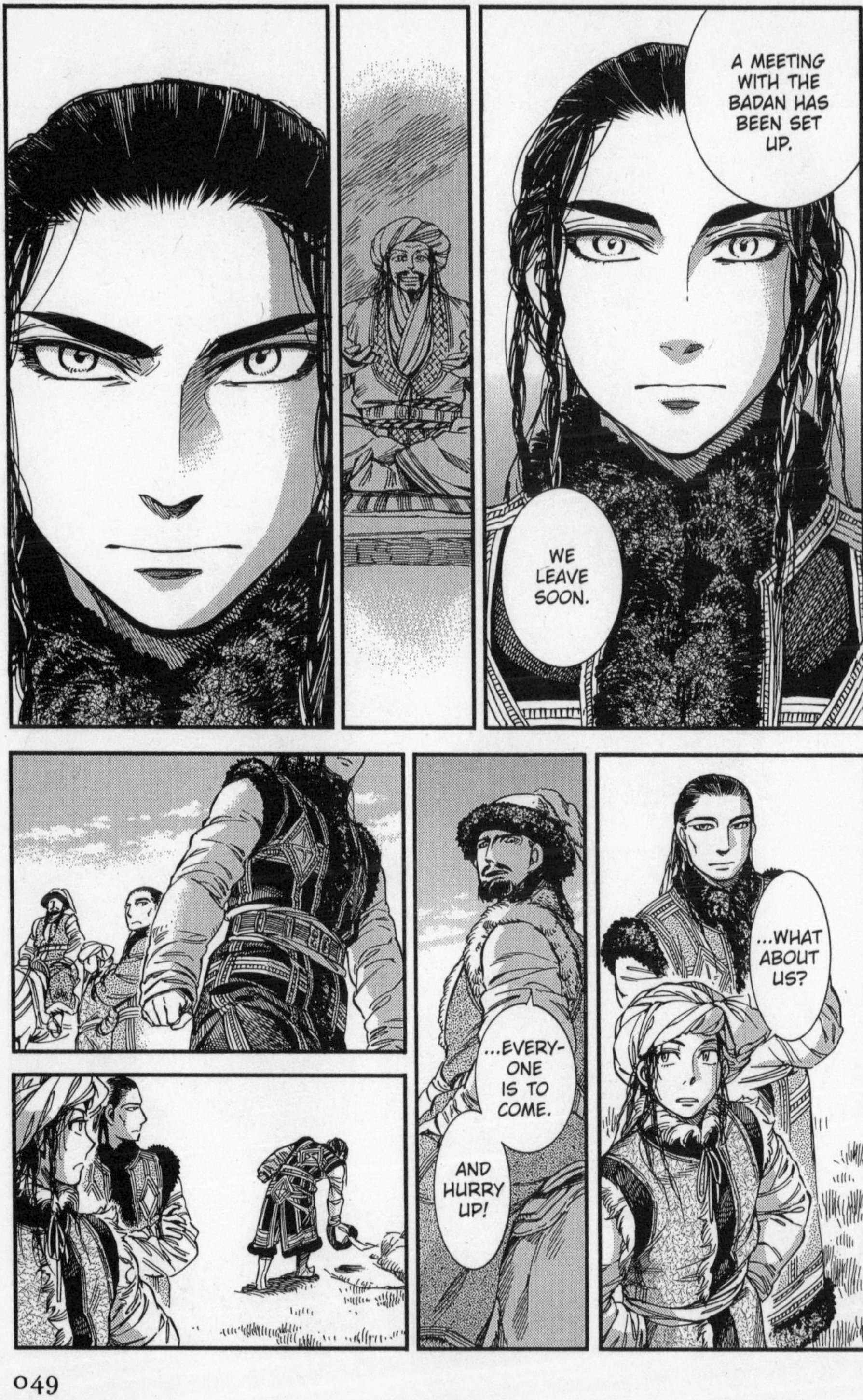
A MEETING WITH THE BADAN HAS BEEN SET UP.
WE LEAVE SOON.
...WHAT ABOUT US?
...EVERY-ONE IS TO COME.
AND HURRY UP!

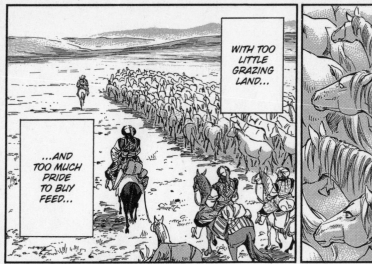

WITH TOO LITTLE GRAZING LAND...

...AND TOO MUCH PRIDE TO BUY FEED...

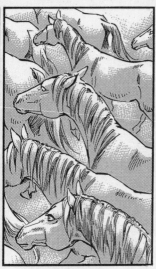

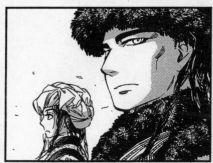

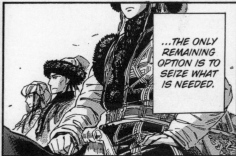

...THE ONLY REMAINING OPTION IS TO SEIZE WHAT IS NEEDED.

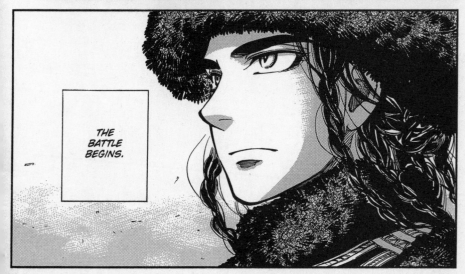

THE BATTLE BEGINS.

✦ CHAPTER 29: END ✦

Chapter 30
Meeting with the Badan

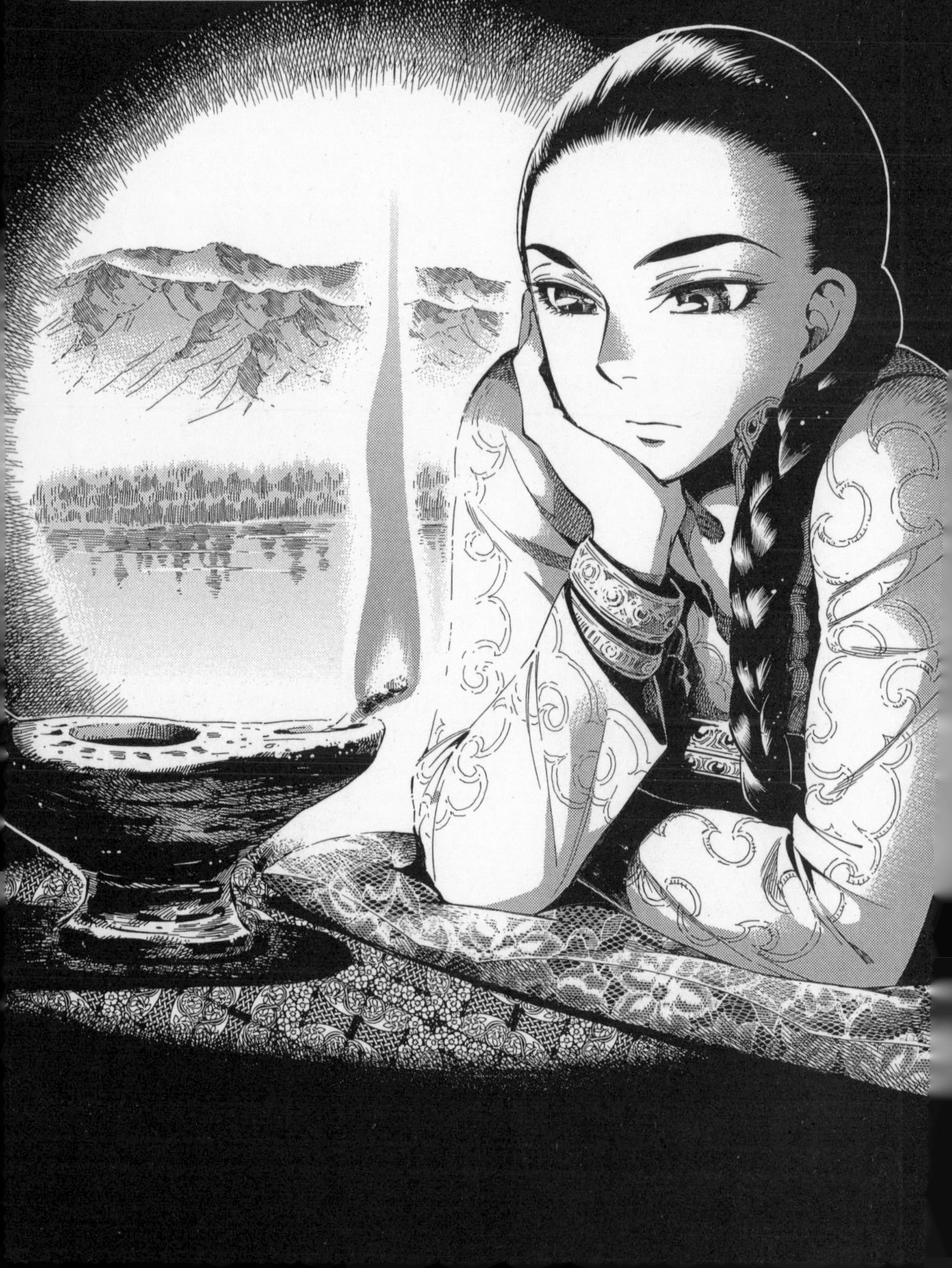

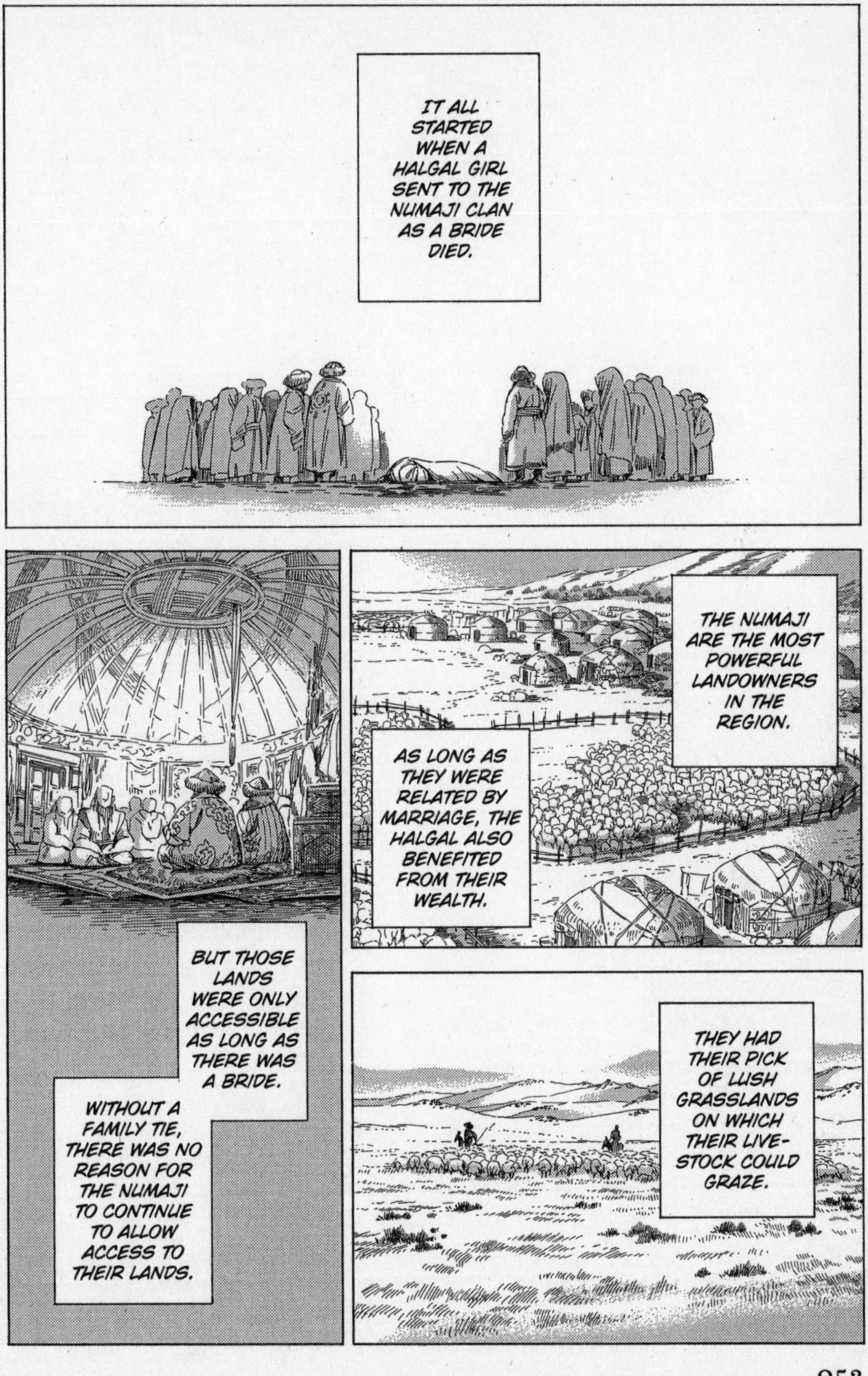
IT ALL STARTED WHEN A HALGAL GIRL SENT TO THE NUMAJI CLAN AS A BRIDE DIED.
THE NUMAJI ARE THE MOST POWERFUL LANDOWNERS IN THE REGION.
AS LONG AS THEY WERE RELATED BY MARRIAGE, THE HALGAL ALSO BENEFITED FROM THEIR WEALTH.
THEY HAD THEIR PICK OF LUSH GRASSLANDS ON WHICH THEIR LIVE-STOCK COULD GRAZE.
BUT THOSE LANDS WERE ONLY ACCESSIBLE AS LONG AS THERE WAS A BRIDE.
WITHOUT A FAMILY TIE, THERE WAS NO REASON FOR THE NUMAJI TO CONTINUE TO ALLOW ACCESS TO THEIR LANDS.

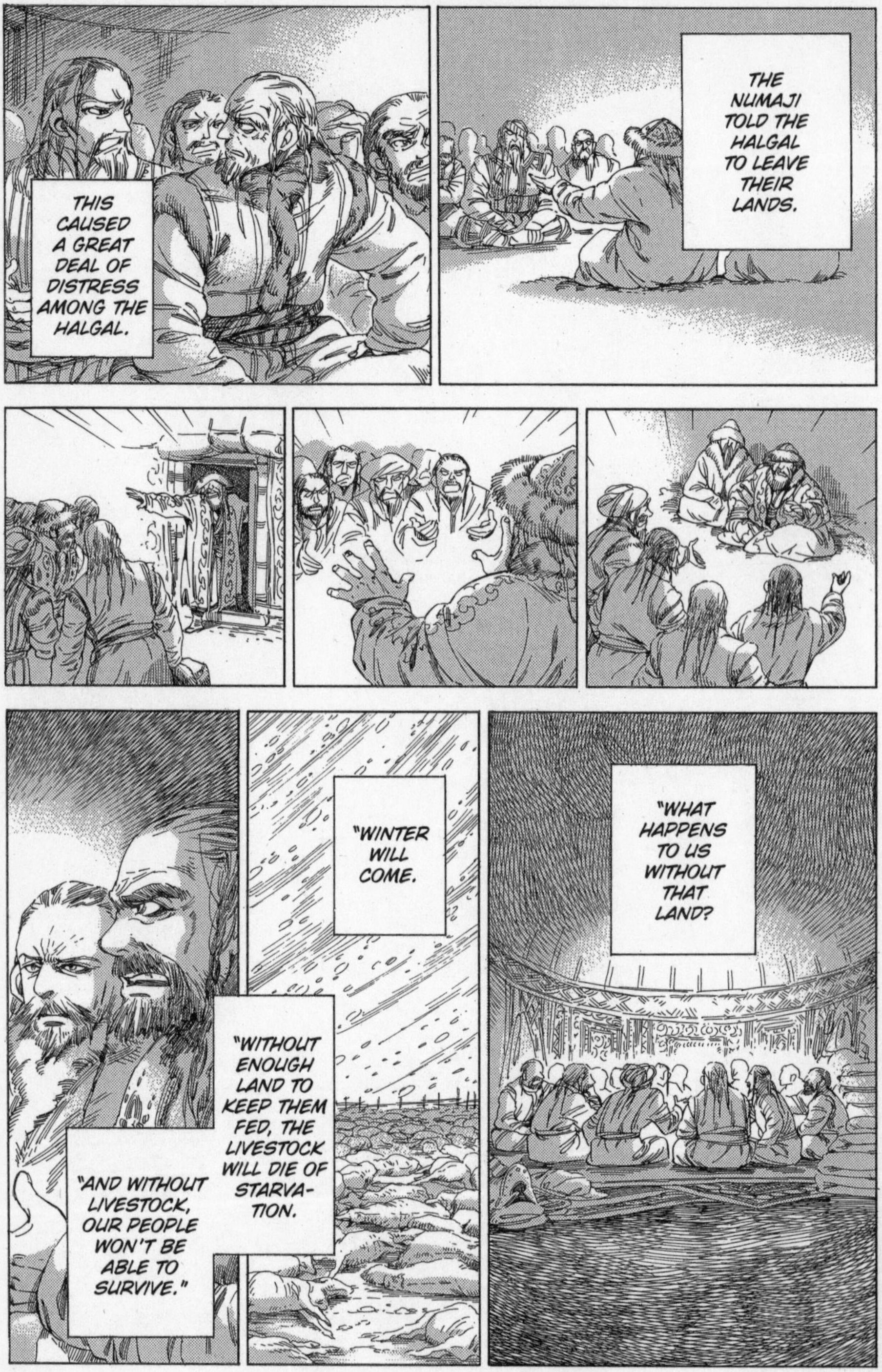
THE NUMAJI TOLD THE HALGAL TO LEAVE THEIR LANDS.
THIS CAUSED A GREAT DEAL OF DISTRESS AMONG THE HALGAL.
"WHAT HAPPENS TO US WITHOUT THAT LAND?
"WINTER WILL COME.
"WITHOUT ENOUGH LAND TO KEEP THEM FED, THE LIVESTOCK WILL DIE OF STARVA-TION.
"AND WITHOUT LIVESTOCK, OUR PEOPLE WON'T BE ABLE TO SURVIVE."

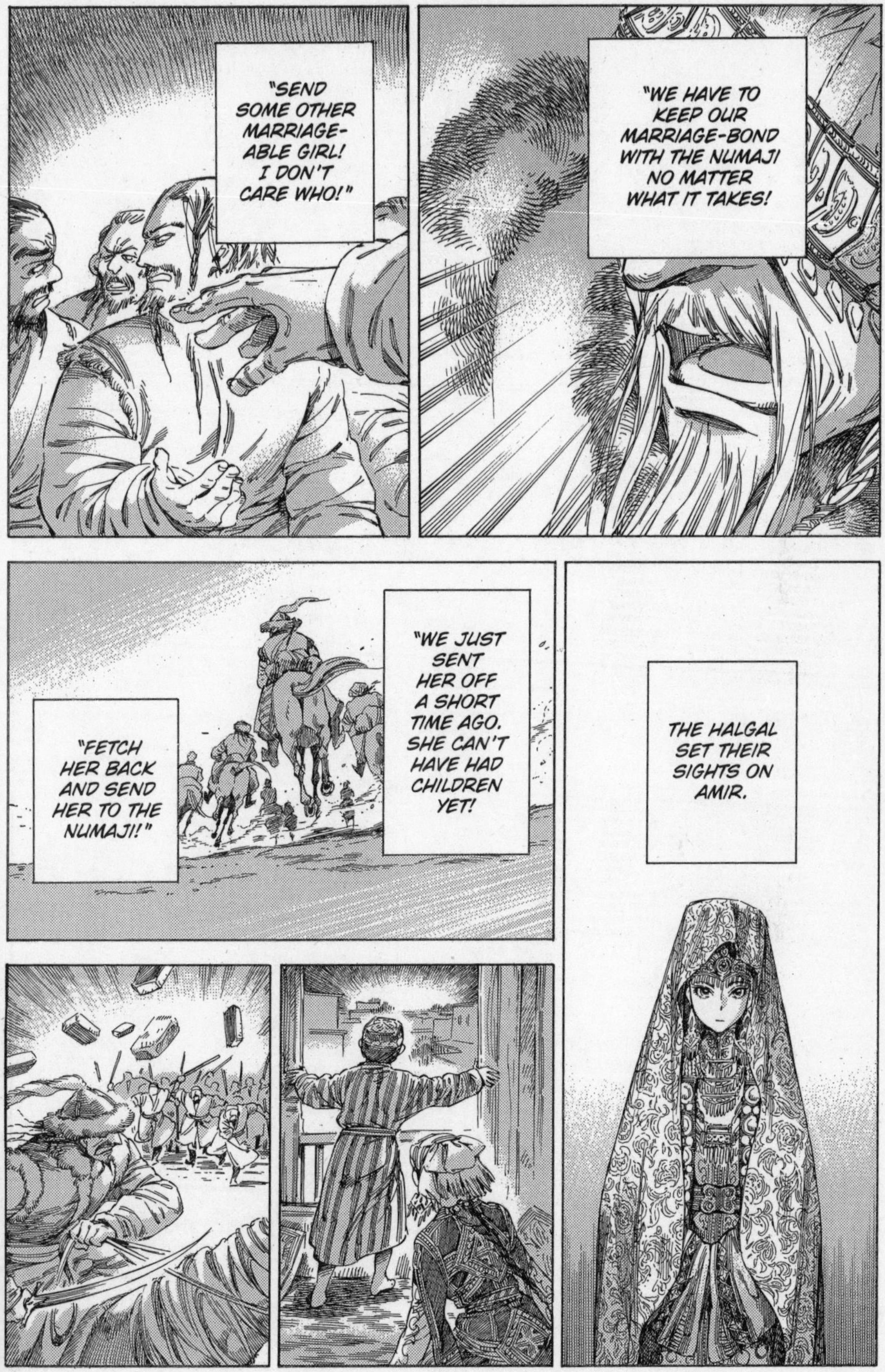
"WE HAVE TO KEEP OUR MARRIAGE-BOND WITH THE NUMAJI NO MATTER WHAT IT TAKES!
"SEND SOME OTHER MARRIAGE-ABLE GIRL! I DON'T CARE WHO!"
THE HALGAL SET THEIR SIGHTS ON AMIR.
"WE JUST SENT HER OFF A SHORT TIME AGO. SHE CAN'T HAVE HAD CHILDREN YET!
"FETCH HER BACK AND SEND HER TO THE NUMAJI!"

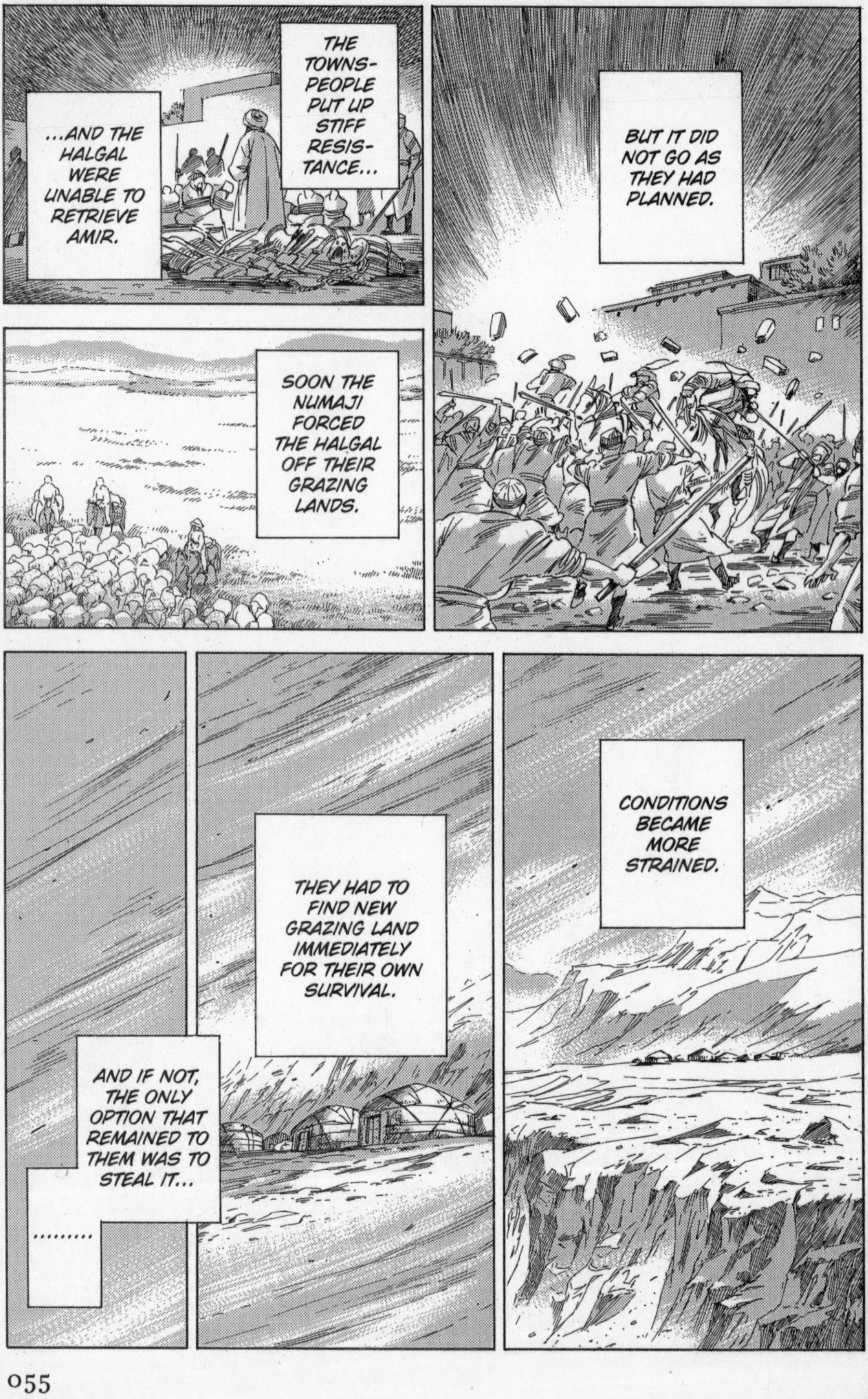
BUT IT DID NOT GO AS THEY HAD PLANNED.
THE TOWNS-PEOPLE PUT UP STIFF RESIS-TANCE...
...AND THE HALGAL WERE UNABLE TO RETRIEVE AMIR.
SOON THE NUMAJI FORCED THE HALGAL OFF THEIR GRAZING LANDS.
CONDITIONS BECAME MORE STRAINED.
THEY HAD TO FIND NEW GRAZING LAND IMMEDIATELY FOR THEIR OWN SURVIVAL.
AND IF NOT, THE ONLY OPTION THAT REMAINED TO THEM WAS TO STEAL IT...
....

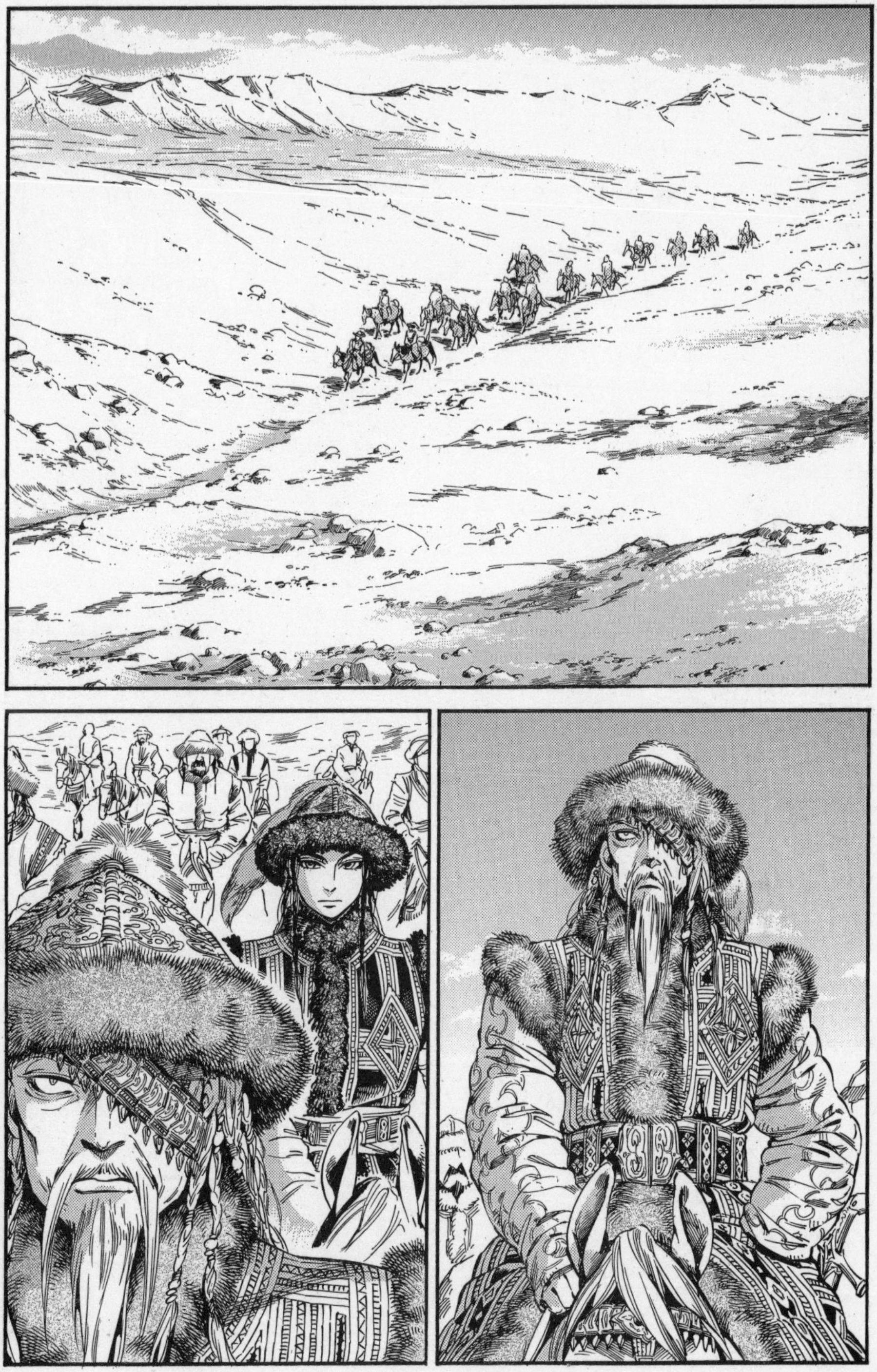

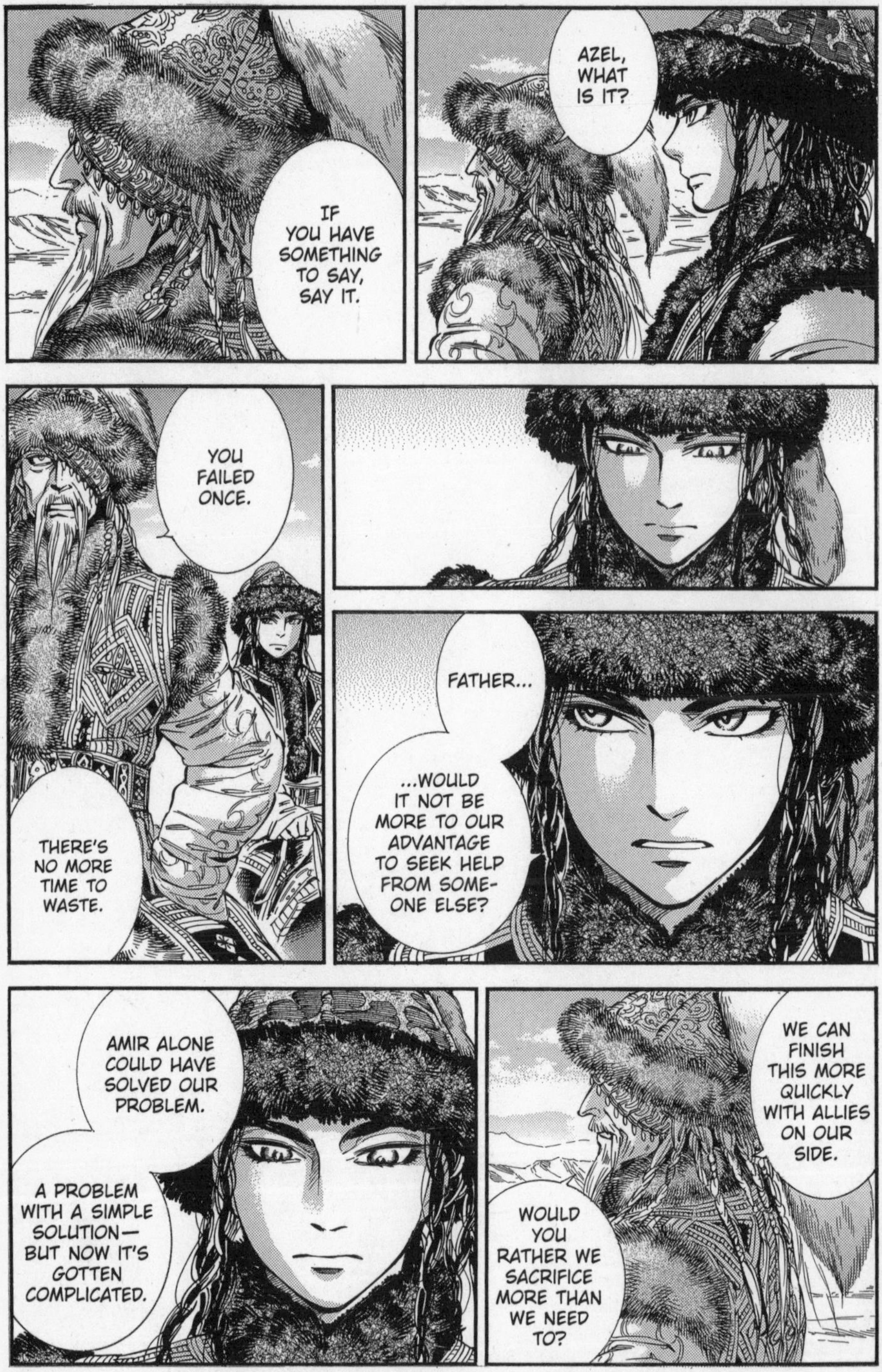
AZEL, WHAT IS IT?
IF YOU HAVE SOMETHING TO SAY, SAY IT.
FATHER...
...WOULD IT NOT BE MORE TO OUR ADVANTAGE TO SEEK HELP FROM SOME-ONE ELSE?
YOU FAILED ONCE.
THERE'S NO MORE TIME TO WASTE.
WE CAN FINISH THIS MORE QUICKLY WITH ALLIES ON OUR SIDE.
WOULD YOU RATHER WE SACRIFICE MORE THAN WE NEED TO?
AMIR ALONE COULD HAVE SOLVED OUR PROBLEM.
A PROBLEM WITH A SIMPLE SOLUTION—BUT NOW IT'S GOTTEN COMPLICATED.

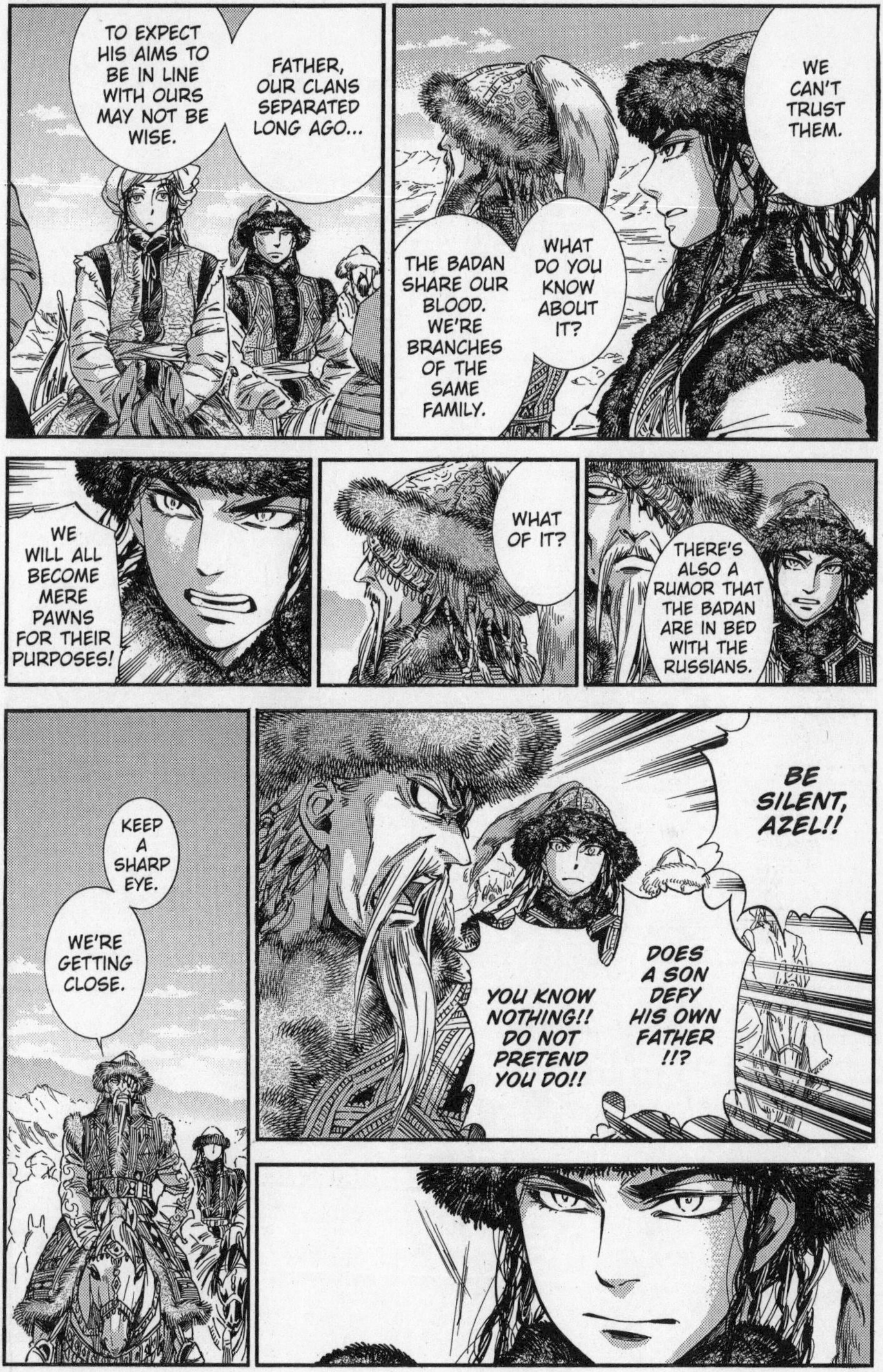
WE CAN'T TRUST THEM.
WHAT DO YOU KNOW ABOUT IT?
THE BADAN SHARE OUR BLOOD. WE'RE BRANCHES OF THE SAME FAMILY.
FATHER, OUR CLANS SEPARATED LONG AGO...
TO EXPECT HIS AIMS TO BE IN LINE WITH OURS MAY NOT BE WISE.
THERE'S ALSO A RUMOR THAT THE BADAN ARE IN BED WITH THE RUSSIANS.
WHAT OF IT?
WE WILL ALL BECOME MERE PAWNS FOR THEIR PURPOSES!
BE SILENT, AZEL!!
DOES A SON DEFY HIS OWN FATHER !!?
YOU KNOW NOTHING!! DO NOT PRETEND YOU DO!!
KEEP A SHARP EYE.
WE'RE GETTING CLOSE.

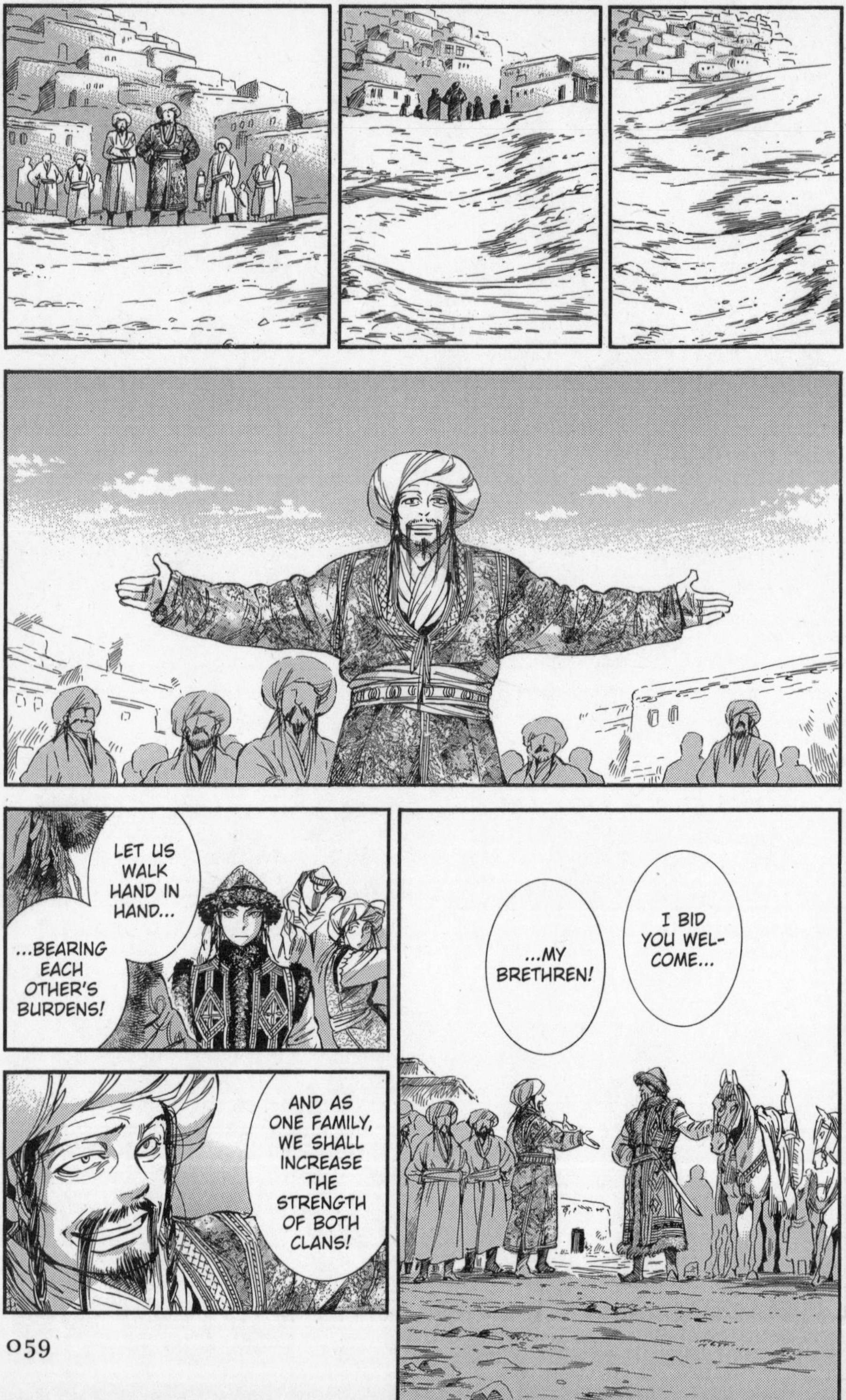
I BID YOU WEL-COME...
...MY BRETHREN!
LET US WALK HAND IN HAND...
...BEARING EACH OTHER'S BURDENS!
AND AS ONE FAMILY, WE SHALL INCREASE THE STRENGTH OF BOTH CLANS!

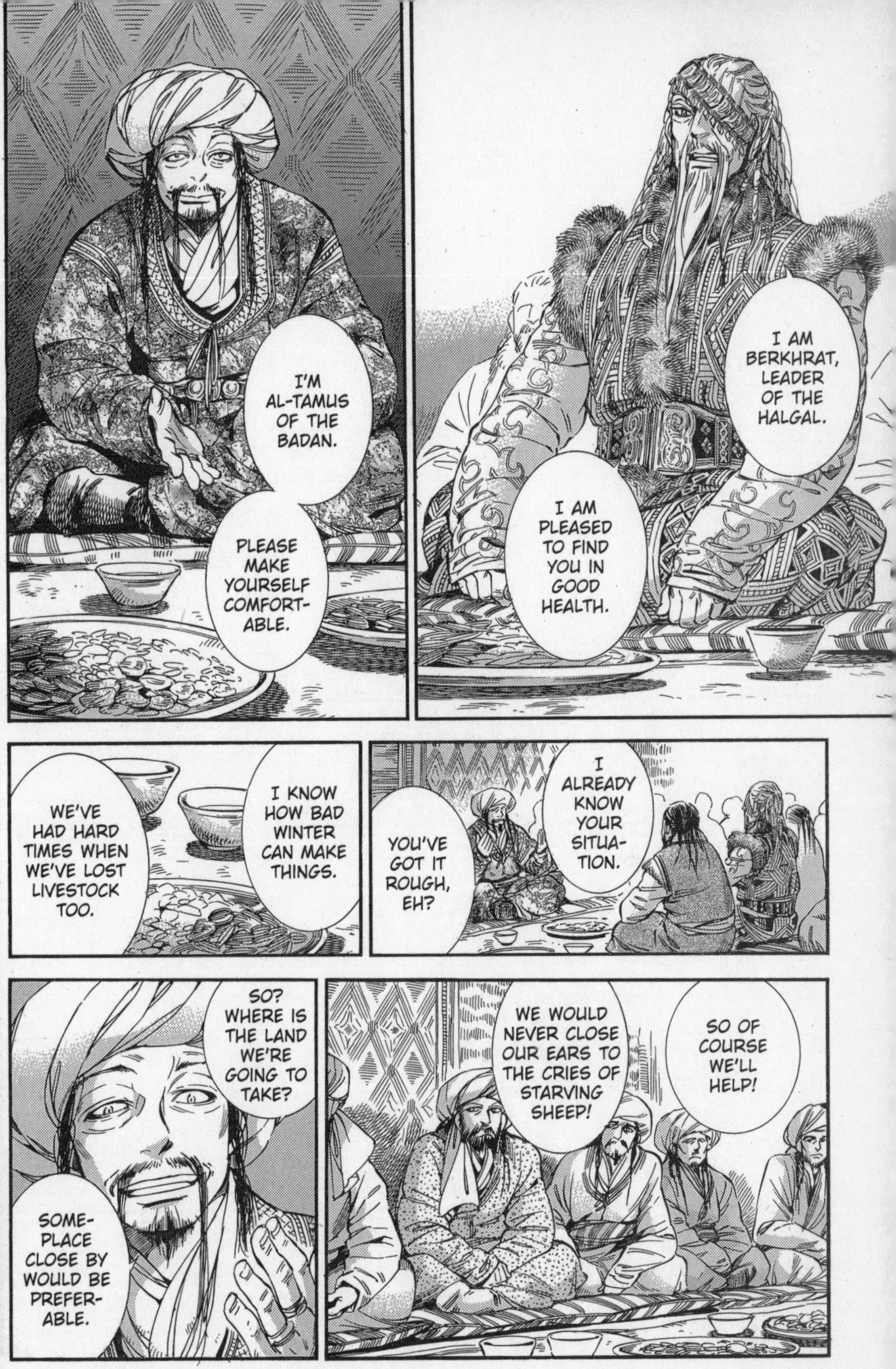
I AM BERKHRAT, LEADER OF THE HALGAL.
I AM PLEASED TO FIND YOU IN GOOD HEALTH.
I'M AL-TAMUS OF THE BADAN.
PLEASE MAKE YOURSELF COMFORTABLE.
I ALREADY KNOW YOUR SITUATION.
YOU'VE GOT IT ROUGH, EH?
I KNOW HOW BAD WINTER CAN MAKE THINGS.
WE'VE HAD HARD TIMES WHEN WE'VE LOST LIVESTOCK TOO.
SO OF COURSE WE'LL HELP!
WE WOULD NEVER CLOSE OUR EARS TO THE CRIES OF STARVING SHEEP!
SO? WHERE IS THE LAND WE'RE GOING TO TAKE?
SOMEPLACE CLOSE BY WOULD BE PREFERABLE.

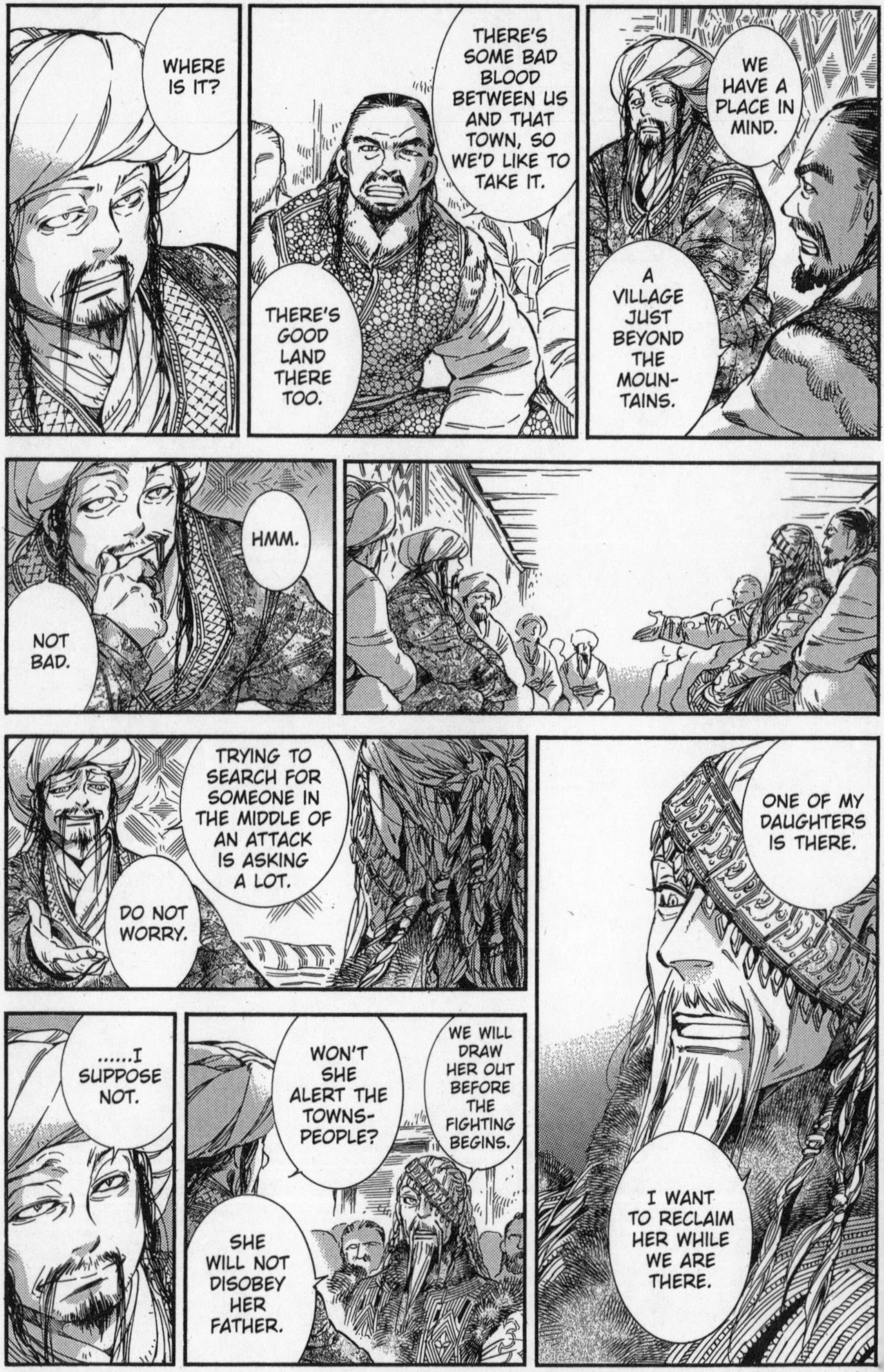
WE HAVE A PLACE IN MIND.
A VILLAGE JUST BEYOND THE MOUNTAINS.
THERE'S SOME BAD BLOOD BETWEEN US AND THAT TOWN, SO WE'D LIKE TO TAKE IT.
THERE'S GOOD LAND THERE TOO.
WHERE IS IT?
HMM.
NOT BAD.
ONE OF MY DAUGHTERS IS THERE.
I WANT TO RECLAIM HER WHILE WE ARE THERE.
TRYING TO SEARCH FOR SOMEONE IN THE MIDDLE OF AN ATTACK IS ASKING A LOT.
DO NOT WORRY.
WON'T SHE ALERT THE TOWNS-PEOPLE?
WE WILL DRAW HER OUT BEFORE THE FIGHTING BEGINS.
SHE WILL NOT DISOBEY HER FATHER.
......I SUPPOSE NOT.

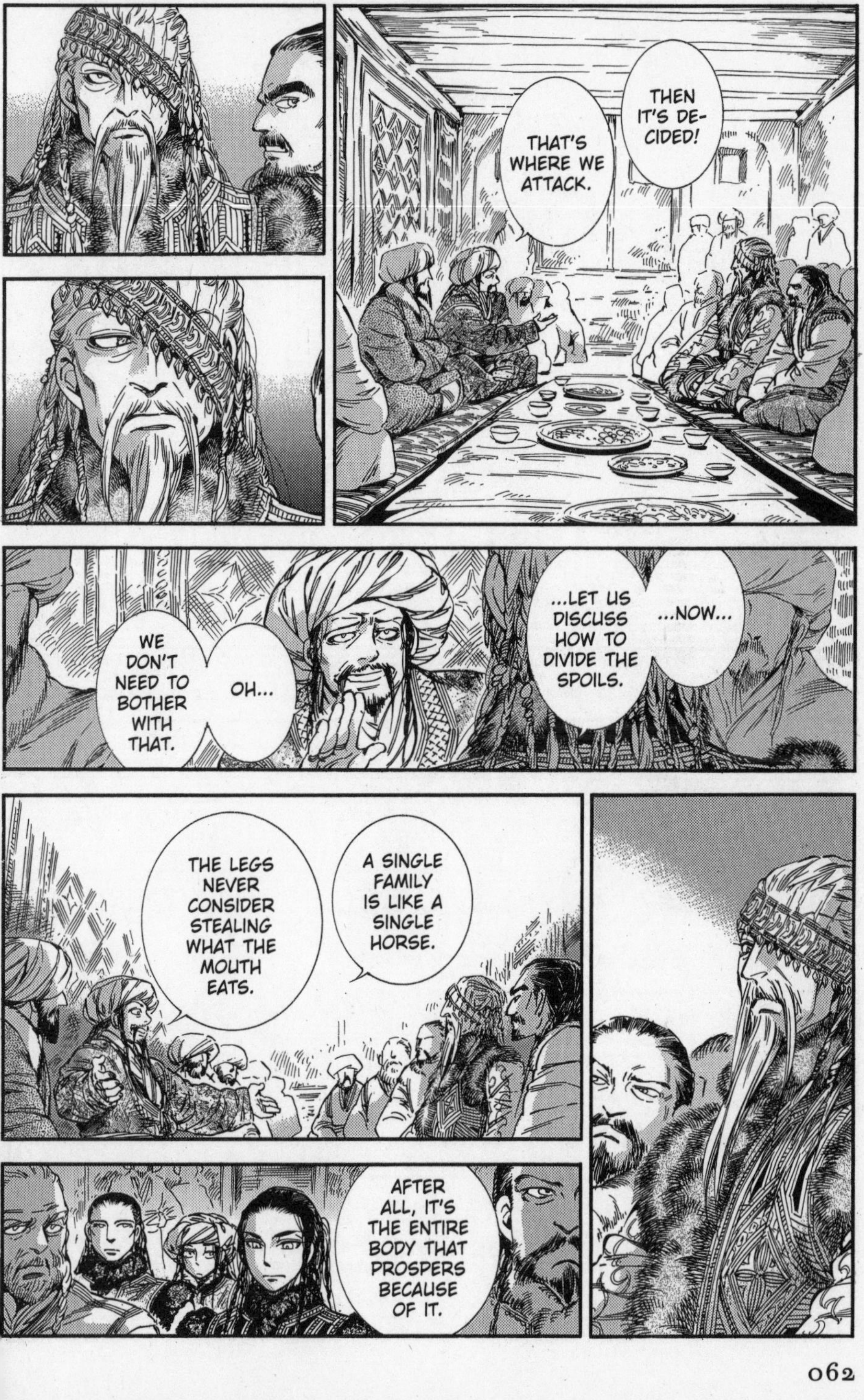
THEN IT'S DE-CIDED!
THAT'S WHERE WE ATTACK.
...NOW...
...LET US DISCUSS HOW TO DIVIDE THE SPOILS.
OH...
WE DON'T NEED TO BOTHER WITH THAT.
A SINGLE FAMILY IS LIKE A SINGLE HORSE.
THE LEGS NEVER CONSIDER STEALING WHAT THE MOUTH EATS.
AFTER ALL, IT'S THE ENTIRE BODY THAT PROSPERS BECAUSE OF IT.

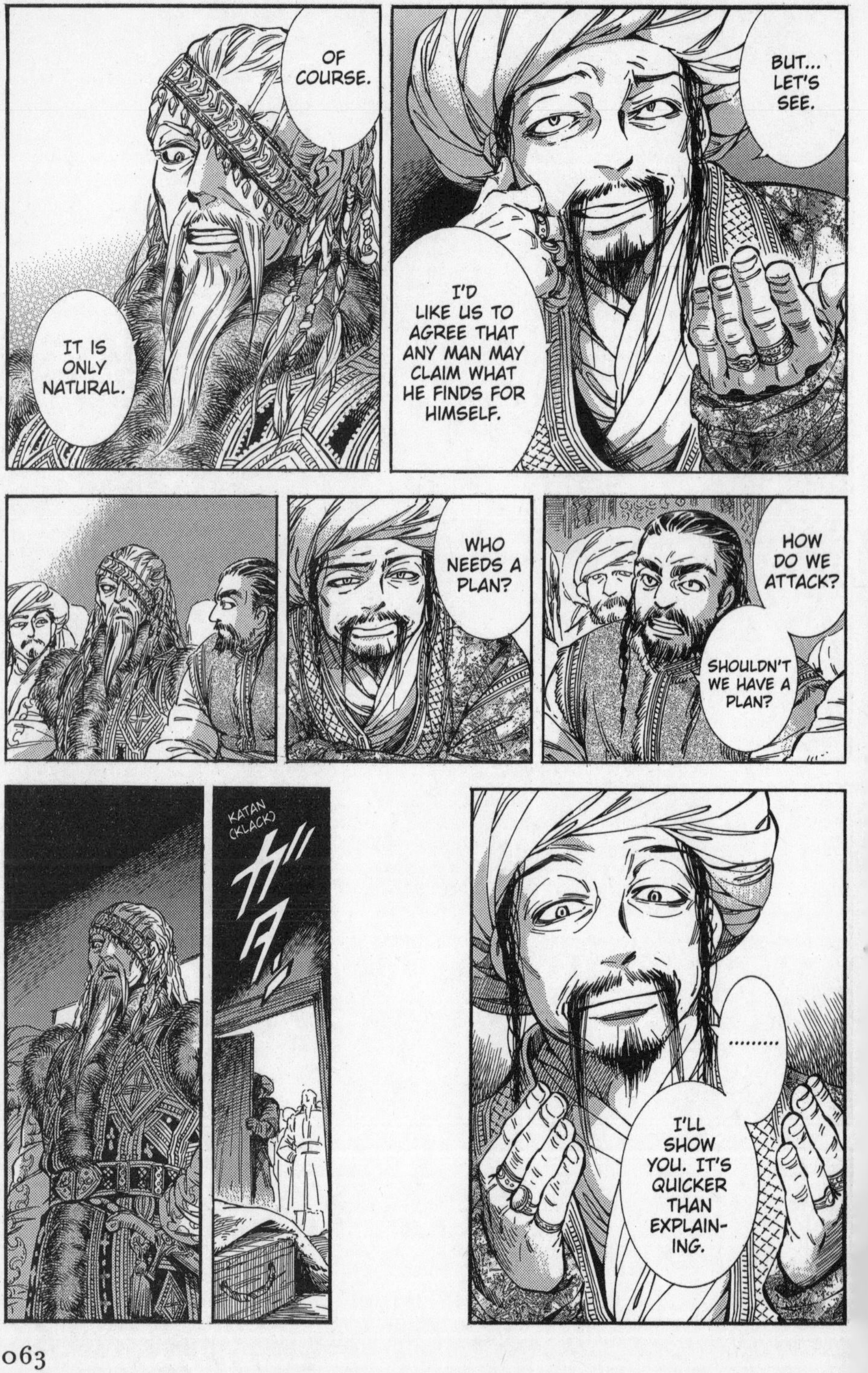
BUT... LET'S SEE.
I'D LIKE US TO AGREE THAT ANY MAN MAY CLAIM WHAT HE FINDS FOR HIMSELF.
OF COURSE.
IT IS ONLY NATURAL.
HOW DO WE ATTACK?
SHOULDN'T WE HAVE A PLAN?
WHO NEEDS A PLAN?
....
I'LL SHOW YOU. IT'S QUICKER THAN EXPLAIN-ING.
KATAN (KLACK)

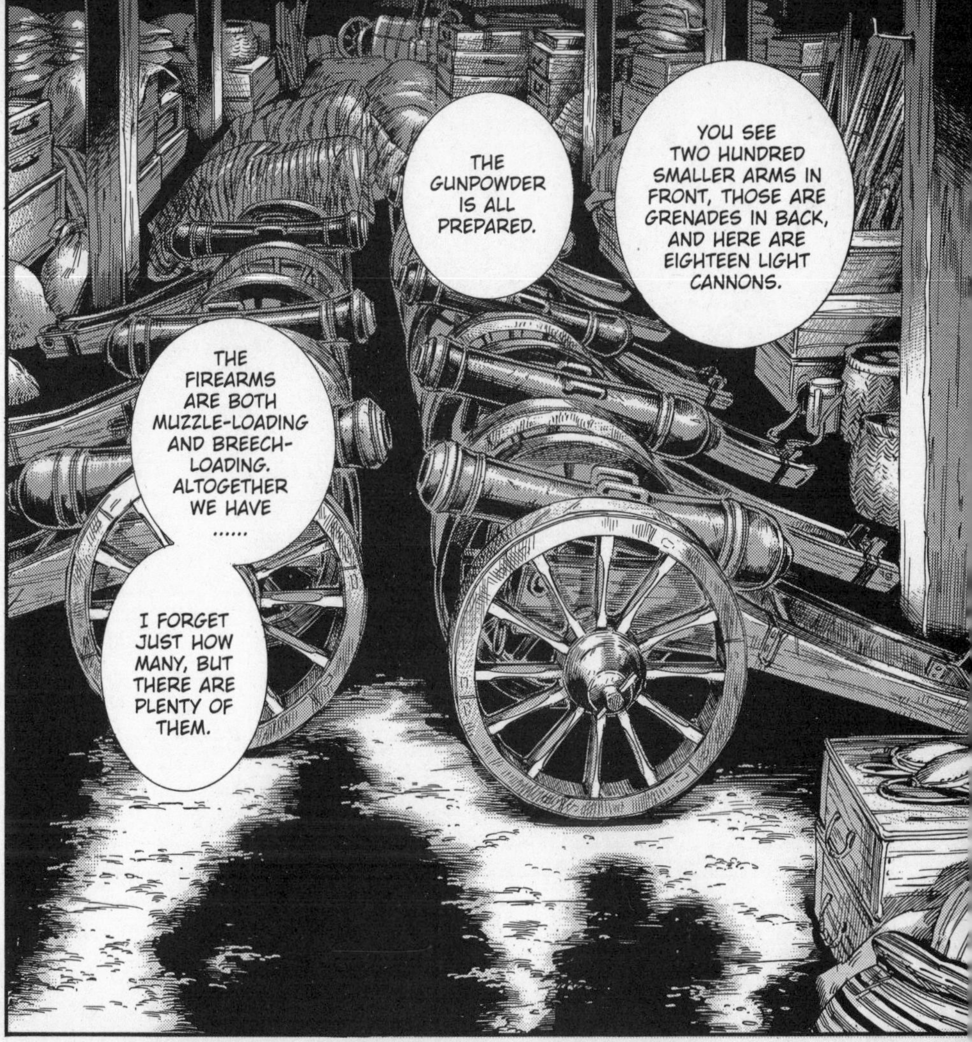
YOU SEE TWO HUNDRED SMALLER ARMS IN FRONT, THOSE ARE GRENADES IN BACK, AND HERE ARE EIGHTEEN LIGHT CANNONS.
THE GUNPOWDER IS ALL PREPARED.
THE FIREARMS ARE BOTH MUZZLE-LOADING AND BREECH-LOADING. ALTOGETHER WE HAVE ......
I FORGET JUST HOW MANY, BUT THERE ARE PLENTY OF THEM.

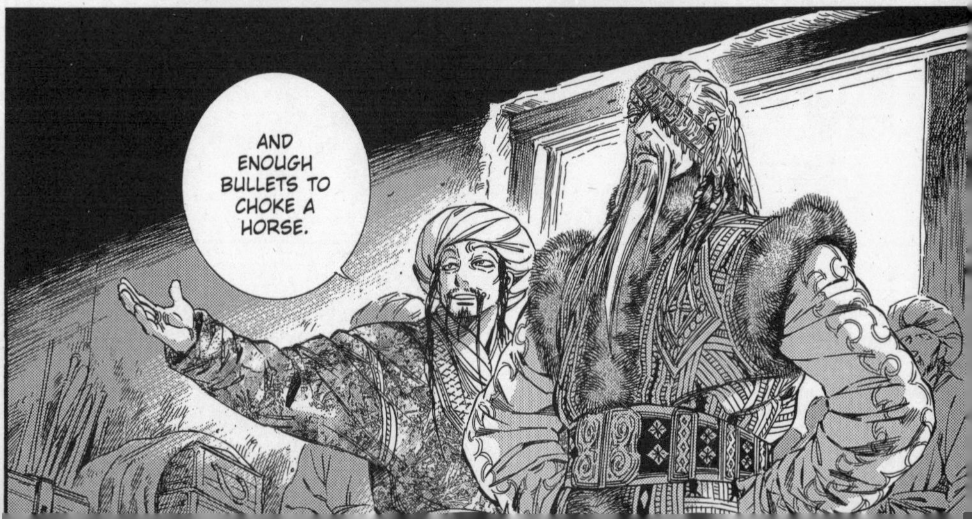
AND ENOUGH BULLETS TO CHOKE A HORSE.

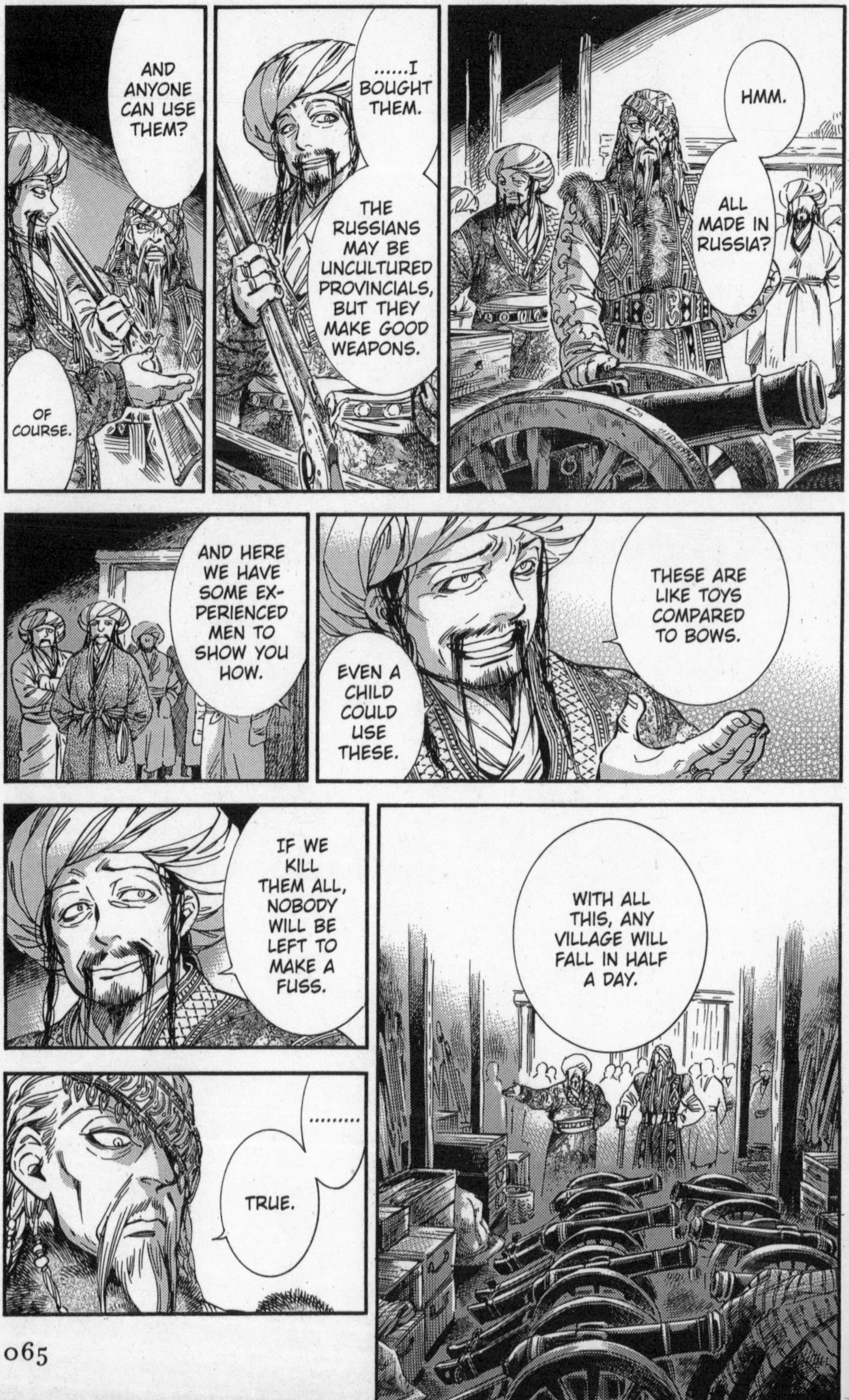
HMM.
ALL MADE IN RUSSIA?
......I BOUGHT THEM.
THE RUSSIANS MAY BE UNCULTURED PROVINCIALS, BUT THEY MAKE GOOD WEAPONS.
AND ANYONE CAN USE THEM?
OF COURSE.
THESE ARE LIKE TOYS COMPARED TO BOWS.
EVEN A CHILD COULD USE THESE.
AND HERE WE HAVE SOME EX-PERIENCED MEN TO SHOW YOU HOW.
WITH ALL THIS, ANY VILLAGE WILL FALL IN HALF A DAY.
IF WE KILL THEM ALL, NOBODY WILL BE LEFT TO MAKE A FUSS.
....
TRUE.

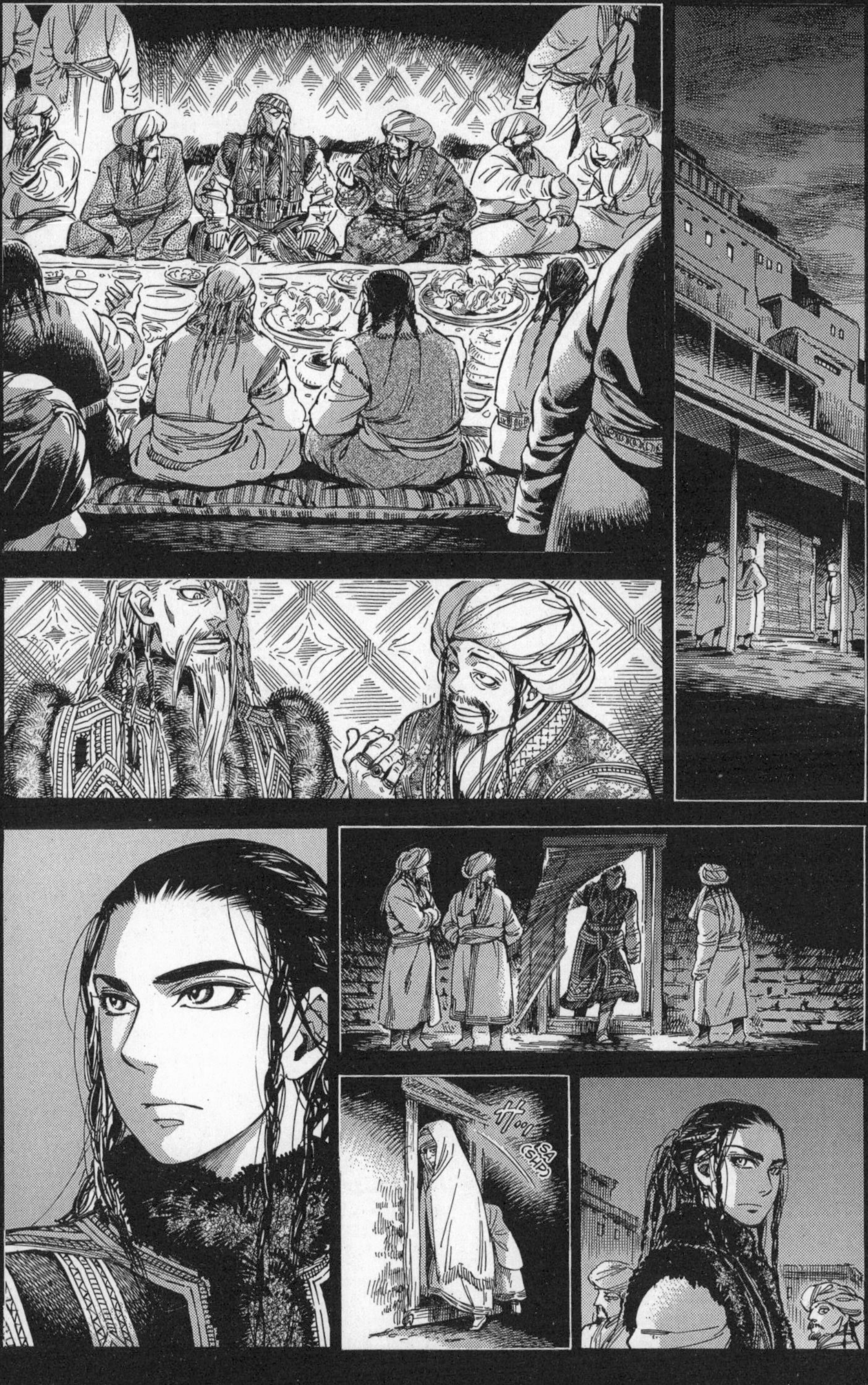
SA (SHP)

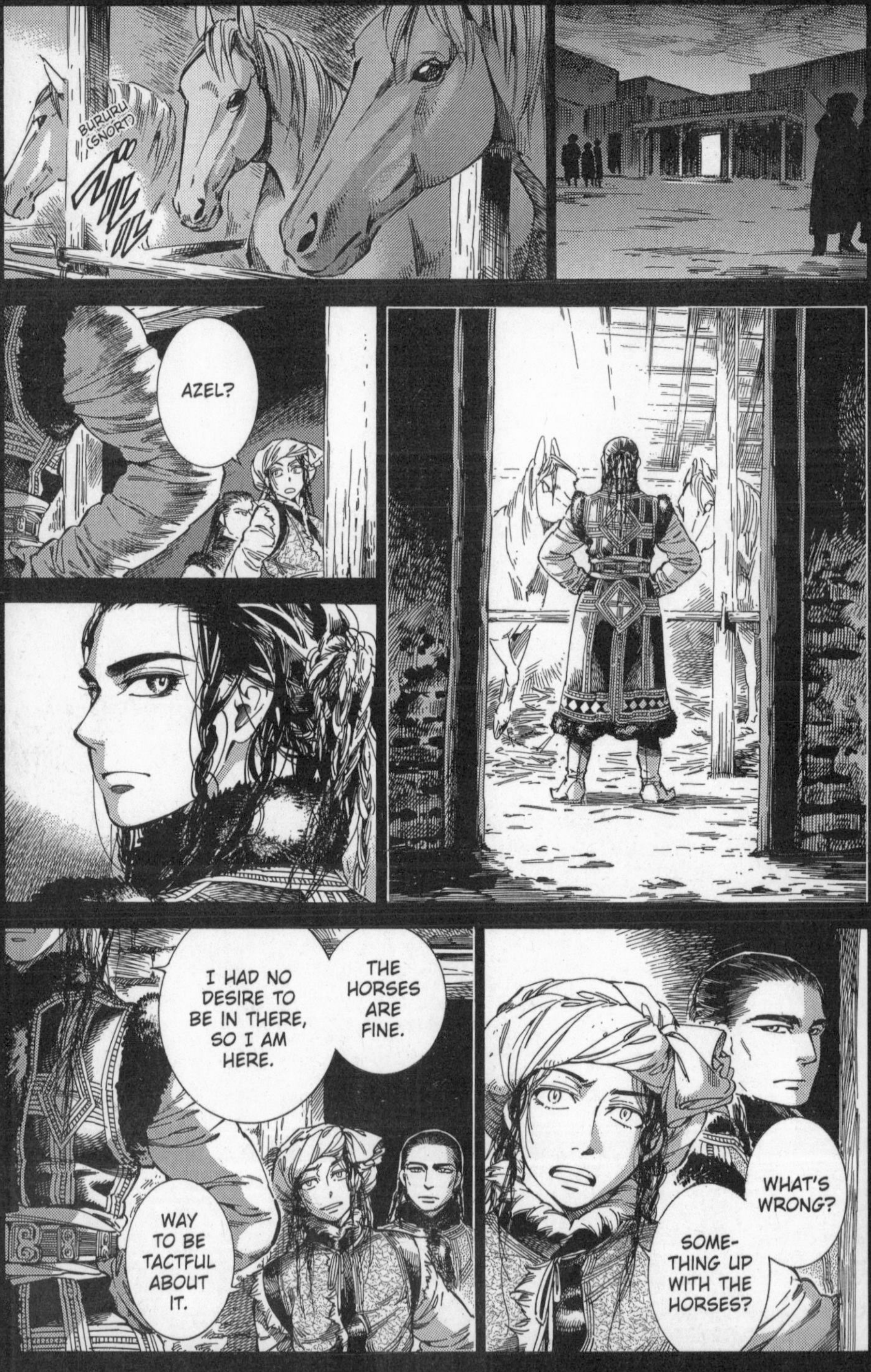
BURURU (SNORT)
AZEL?
WHAT'S WRONG?
SOME-THING UP WITH THE HORSES?
THE HORSES ARE FINE.
I HAD NO DESIRE TO BE IN THERE, SO I AM HERE.
WAY TO BE TACTFUL ABOUT IT.

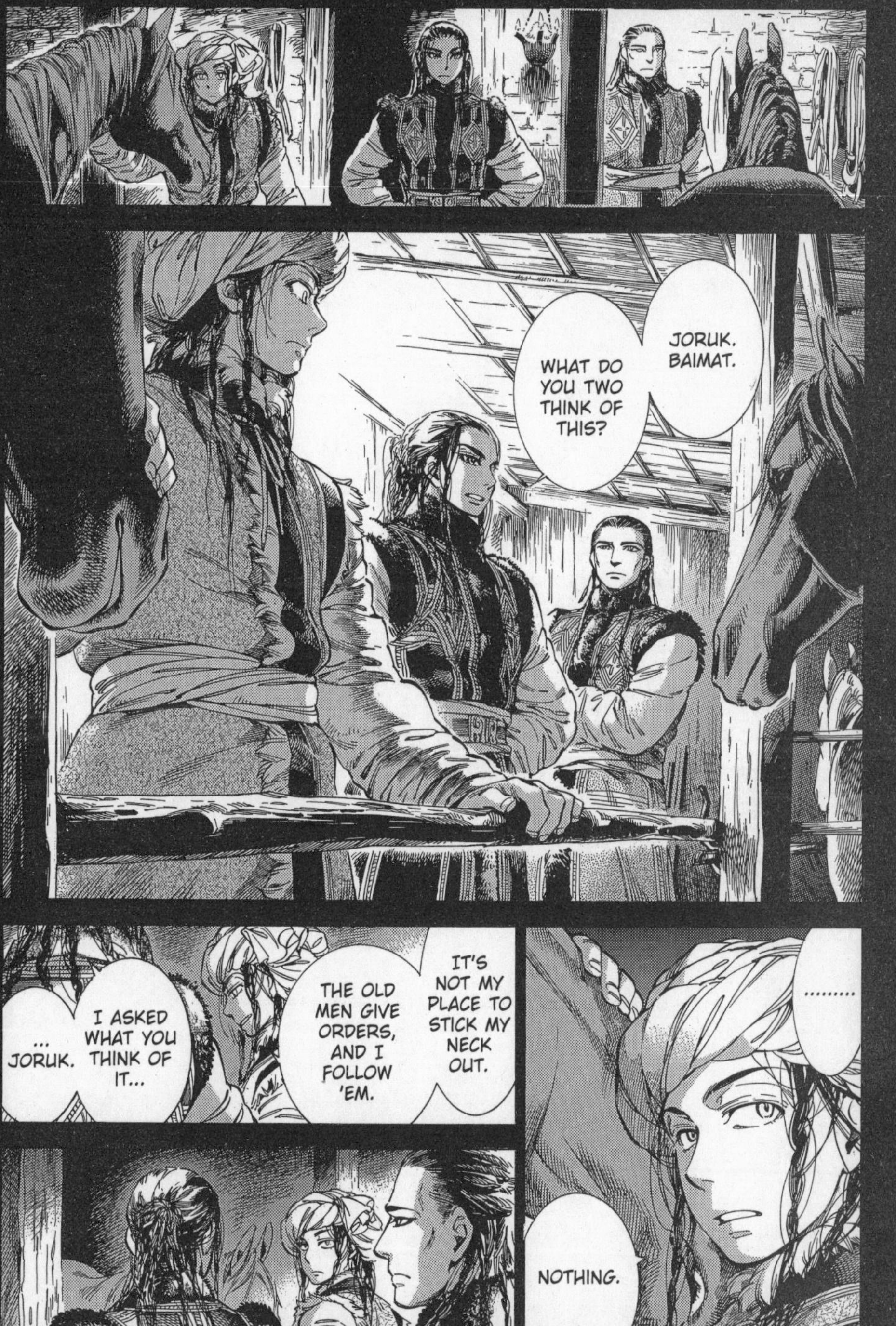
JORUK. BAIMAT.
WHAT DO YOU TWO THINK OF THIS?
....
NOTHING.
IT'S NOT MY PLACE TO STICK MY NECK OUT.
THE OLD MEN GIVE ORDERS, AND I FOLLOW 'EM.
I ASKED WHAT YOU THINK OF IT...
... JORUK.

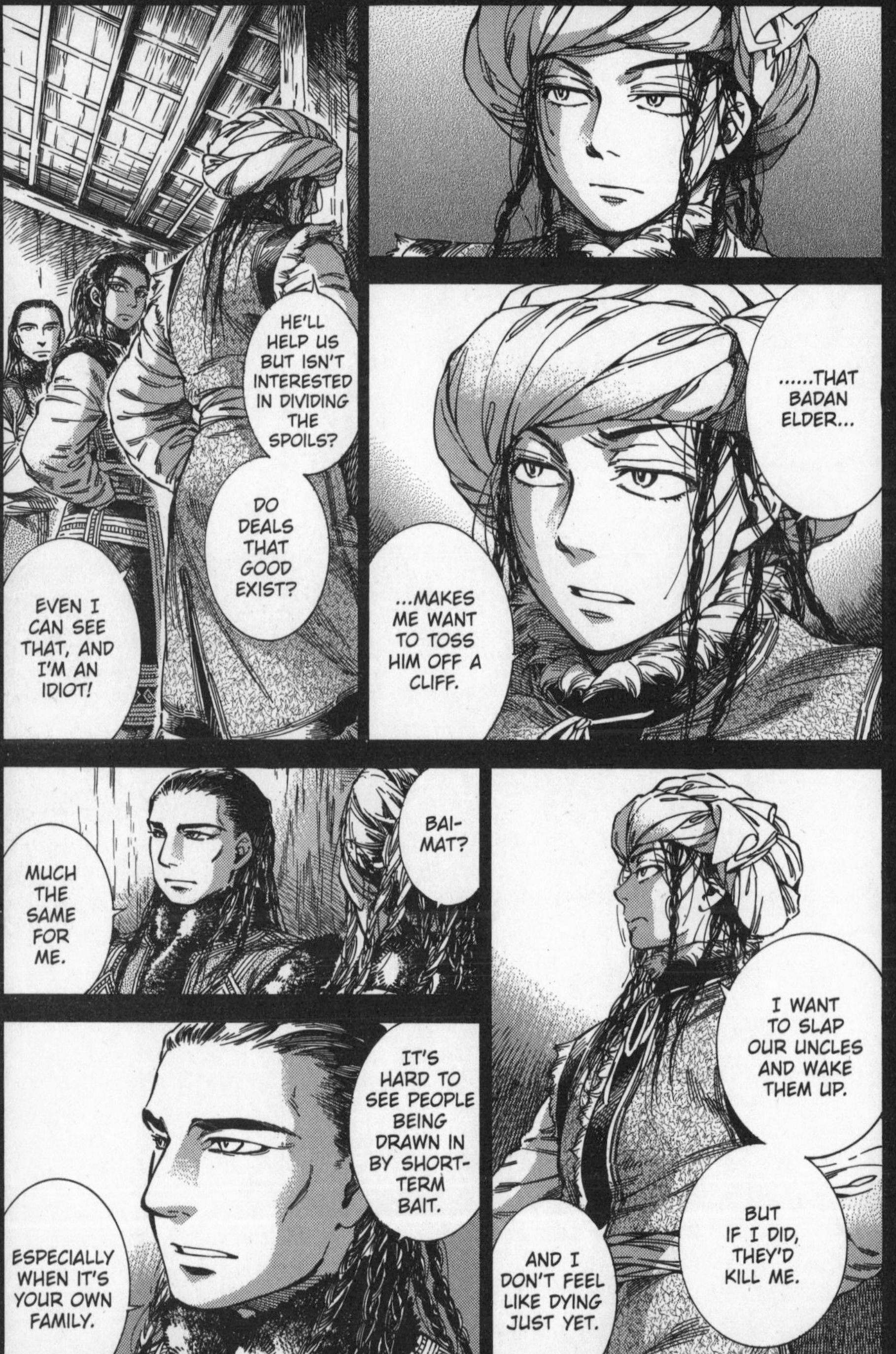
......THAT BADAN ELDER...
...MAKES ME WANT TO TOSS HIM OFF A CLIFF.
HE'LL HELP US BUT ISN'T INTERESTED IN DIVIDING THE SPOILS?
DO DEALS THAT GOOD EXIST?
EVEN I CAN SEE THAT, AND I'M AN IDIOT!
I WANT TO SLAP OUR UNCLES AND WAKE THEM UP.
BUT IF I DID, THEY'D KILL ME.
AND I DON'T FEEL LIKE DYING JUST YET.
BAI-MAT?
MUCH THE SAME FOR ME.
IT'S HARD TO SEE PEOPLE BEING DRAWN IN BY SHORT-TERM BAIT.
ESPECIALLY WHEN IT'S YOUR OWN FAMILY.

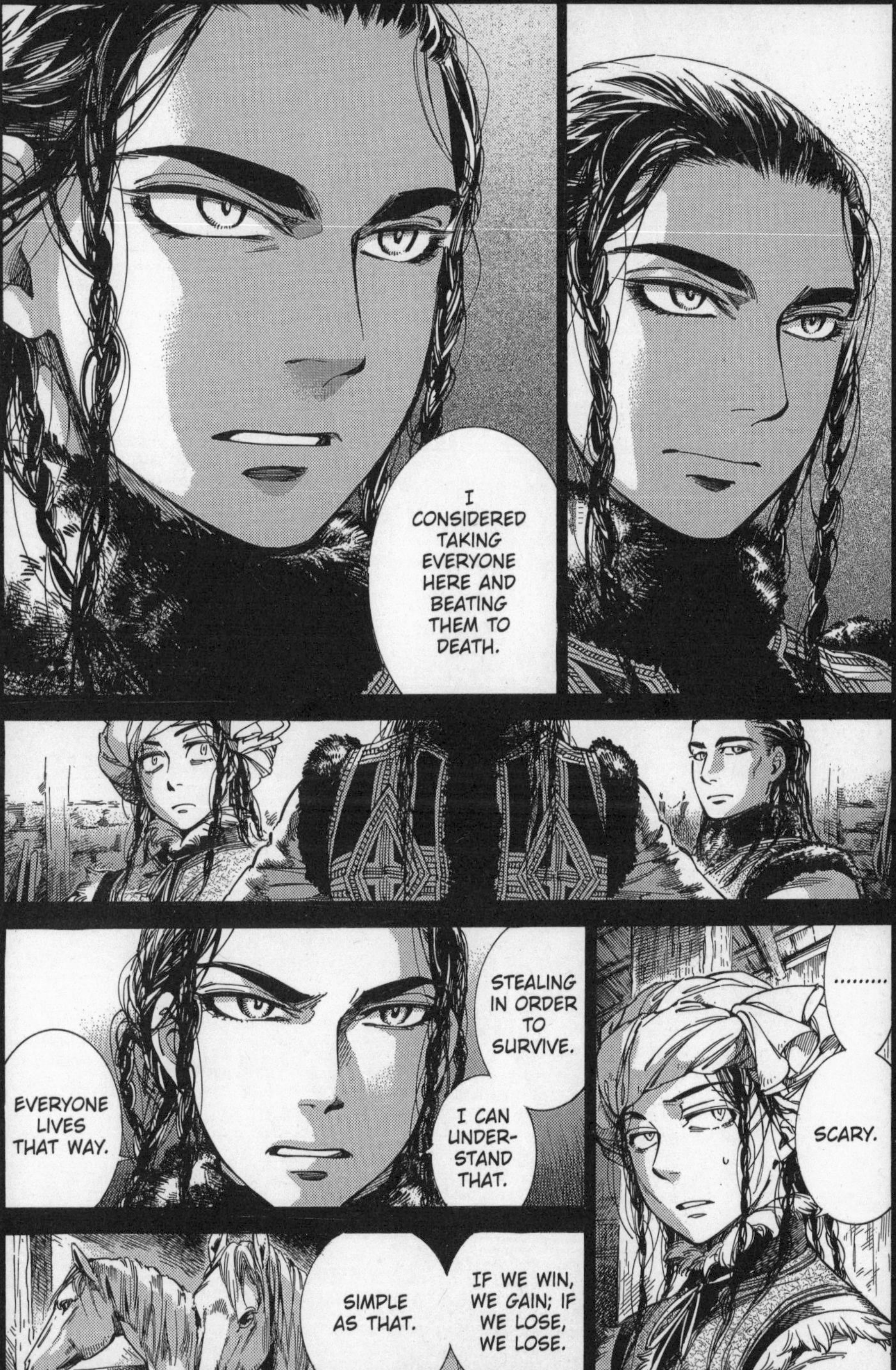
I CONSIDERED TAKING EVERYONE HERE AND BEATING THEM TO DEATH.
....
SCARY.
STEALING IN ORDER TO SURVIVE.
I CAN UNDER-STAND THAT.
EVERYONE LIVES THAT WAY.
IF WE WIN, WE GAIN; IF WE LOSE, WE LOSE.
SIMPLE AS THAT.

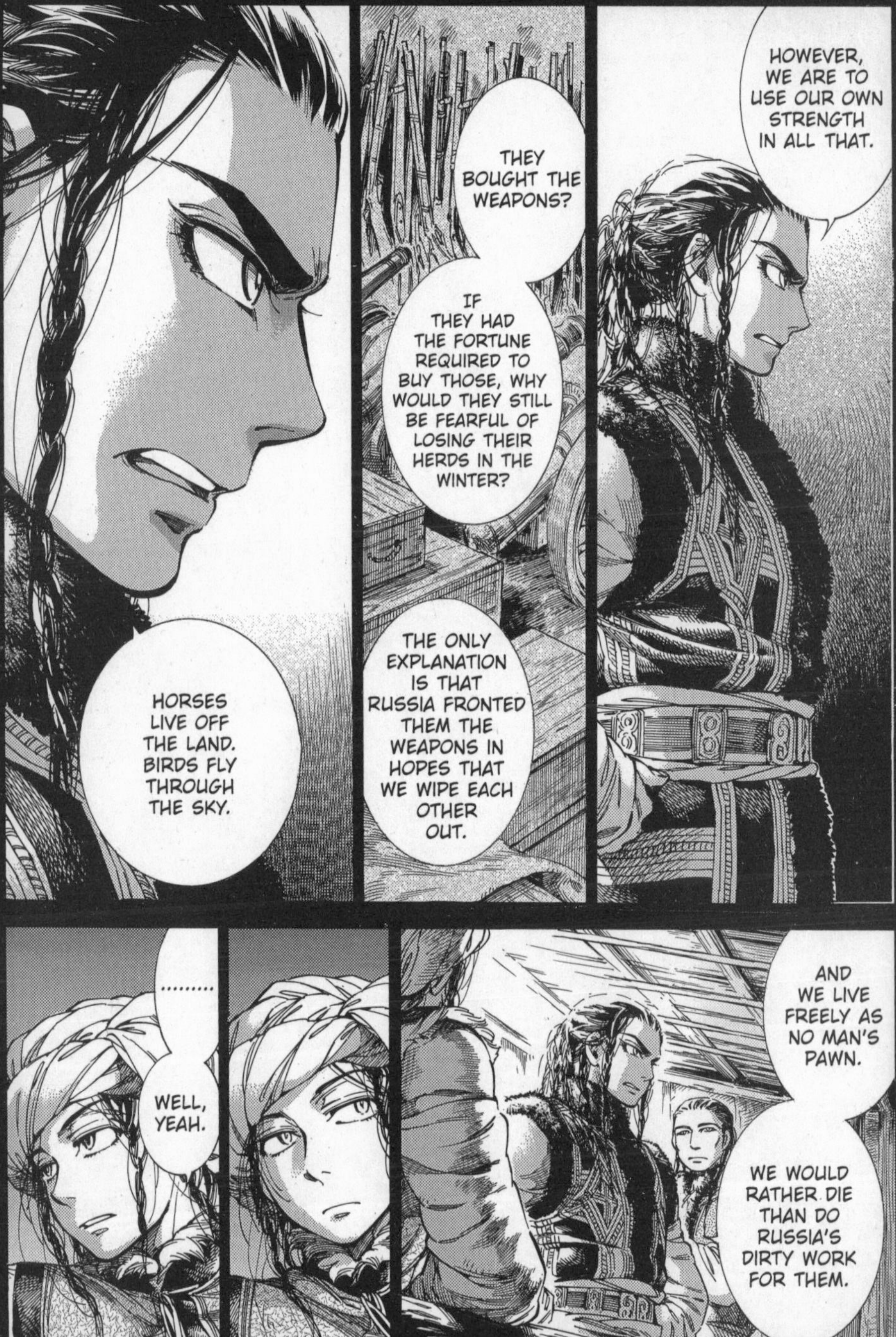
HOWEVER, WE ARE TO USE OUR OWN STRENGTH IN ALL THAT.
THEY BOUGHT THE WEAPONS?
IF THEY HAD THE FORTUNE REQUIRED TO BUY THOSE, WHY WOULD THEY STILL BE FEARFUL OF LOSING THEIR HERDS IN THE WINTER?
THE ONLY EXPLANATION IS THAT RUSSIA FRONTED THEM THE WEAPONS IN HOPES THAT WE WIPE EACH OTHER OUT.
HORSES LIVE OFF THE LAND. BIRDS FLY THROUGH THE SKY.
AND WE LIVE FREELY AS NO MAN'S PAWN.
WE WOULD RATHER DIE THAN DO RUSSIA'S DIRTY WORK FOR THEM.
....
WELL, YEAH.

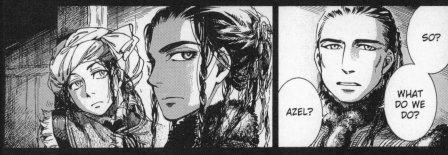

SO?

AZEL?

WHAT DO WE DO?

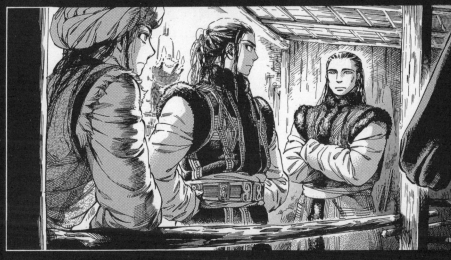

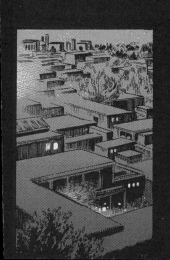

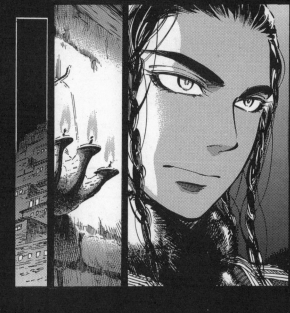

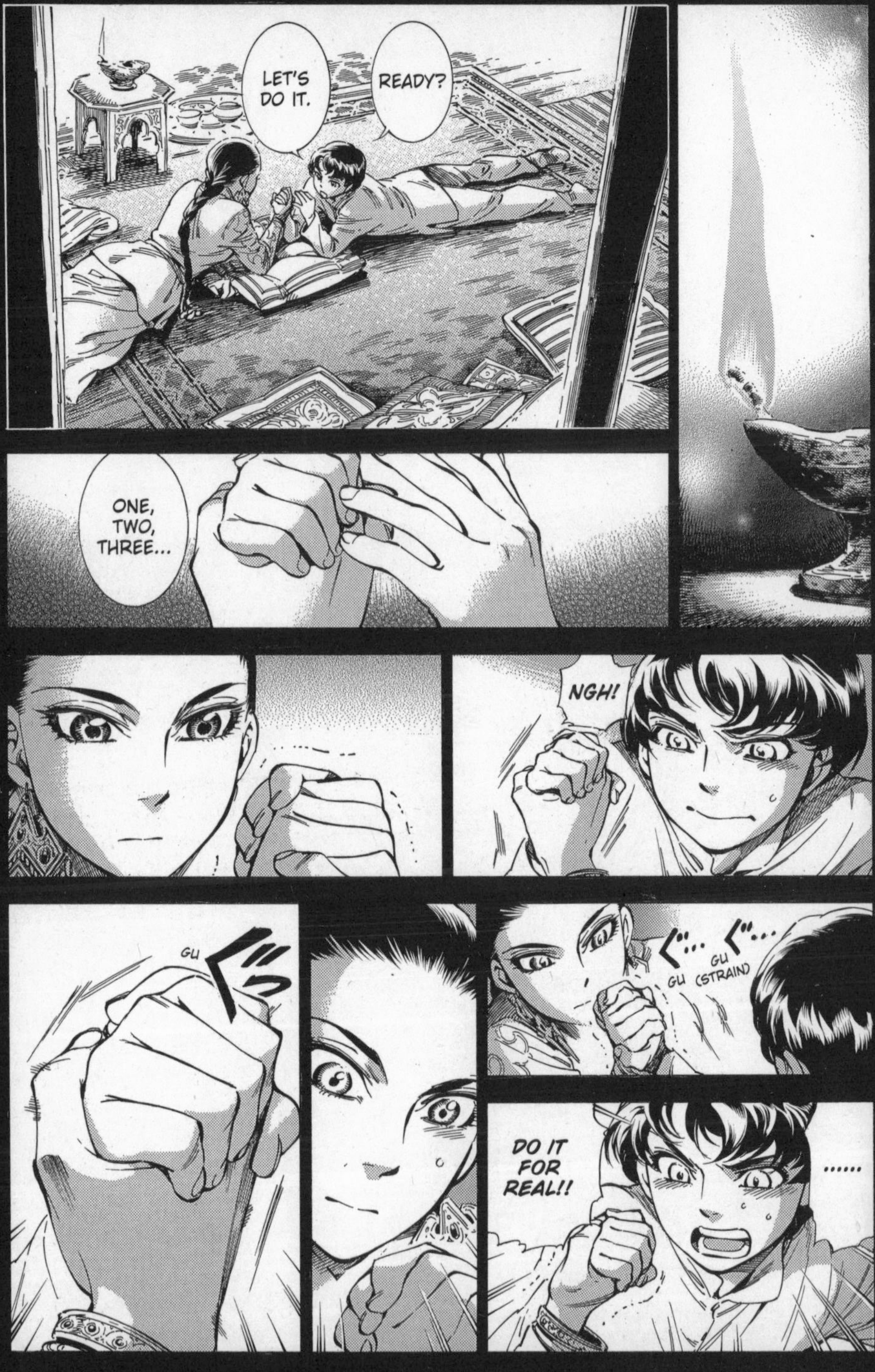
READY?
LET'S DO IT.
ONE, TWO, THREE...
NGH!
ぐ... ぐ...
GU GU (STRAIN)
......
DO IT FOR REAL!!
GU
ぐっ

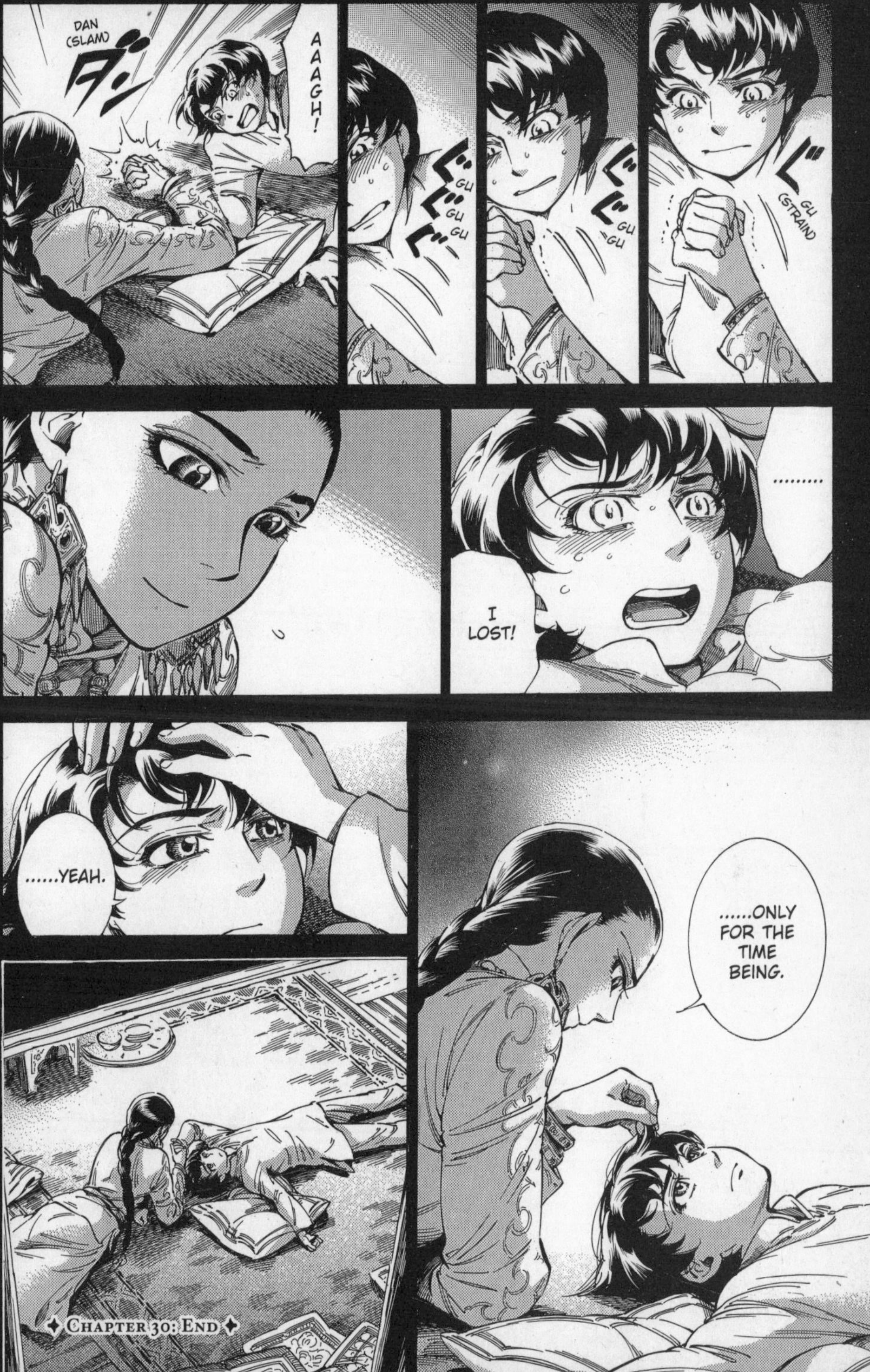
GU (STRAIN)
GU GU
GU GU GU
DAN (SLAM)
ダン
AAAGH!
....
I LOST!
......ONLY FOR THE TIME BEING.
......YEAH.
Chapter 30: End

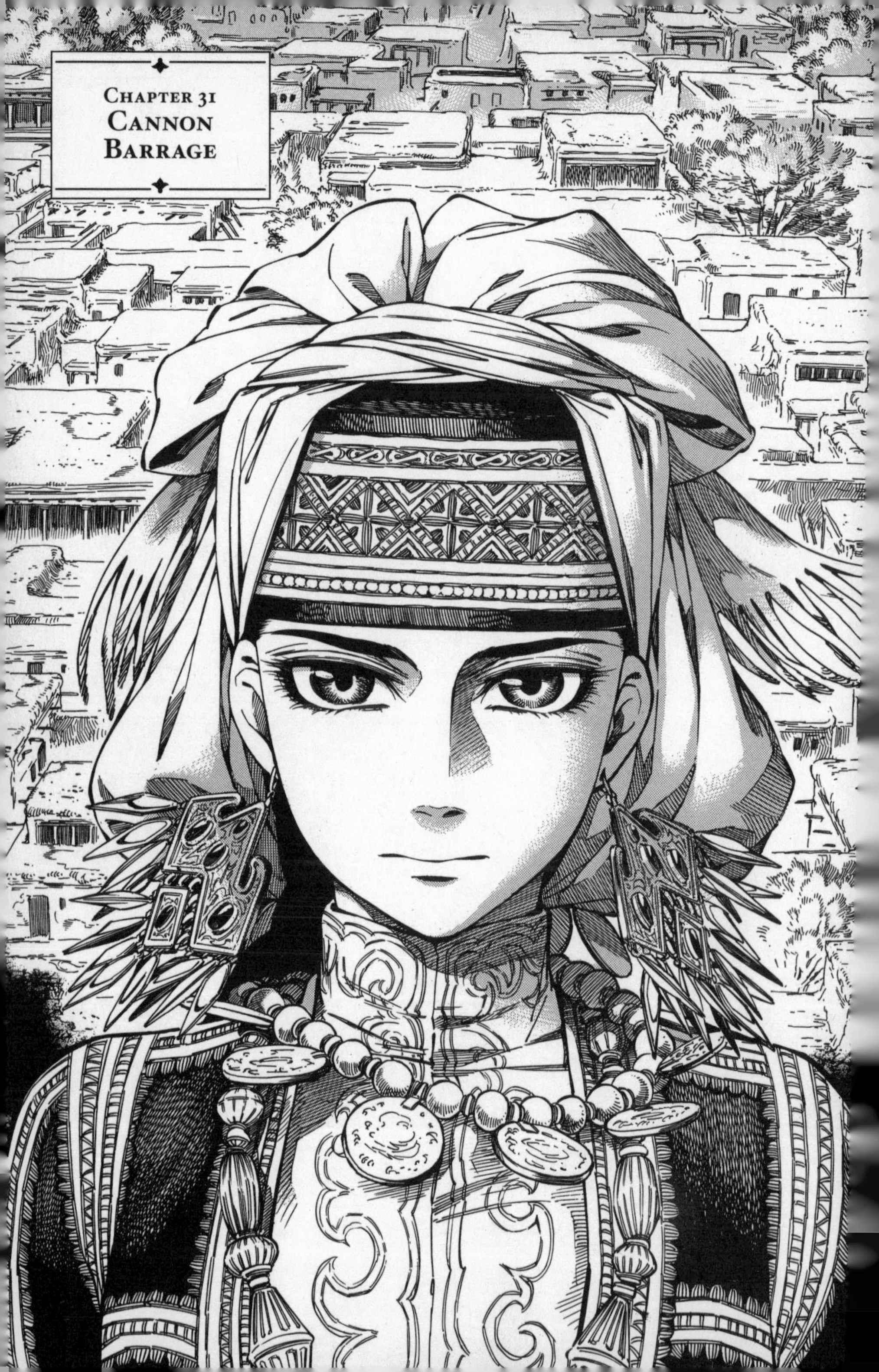
CHAPTER 31
CANNON BARRAGE

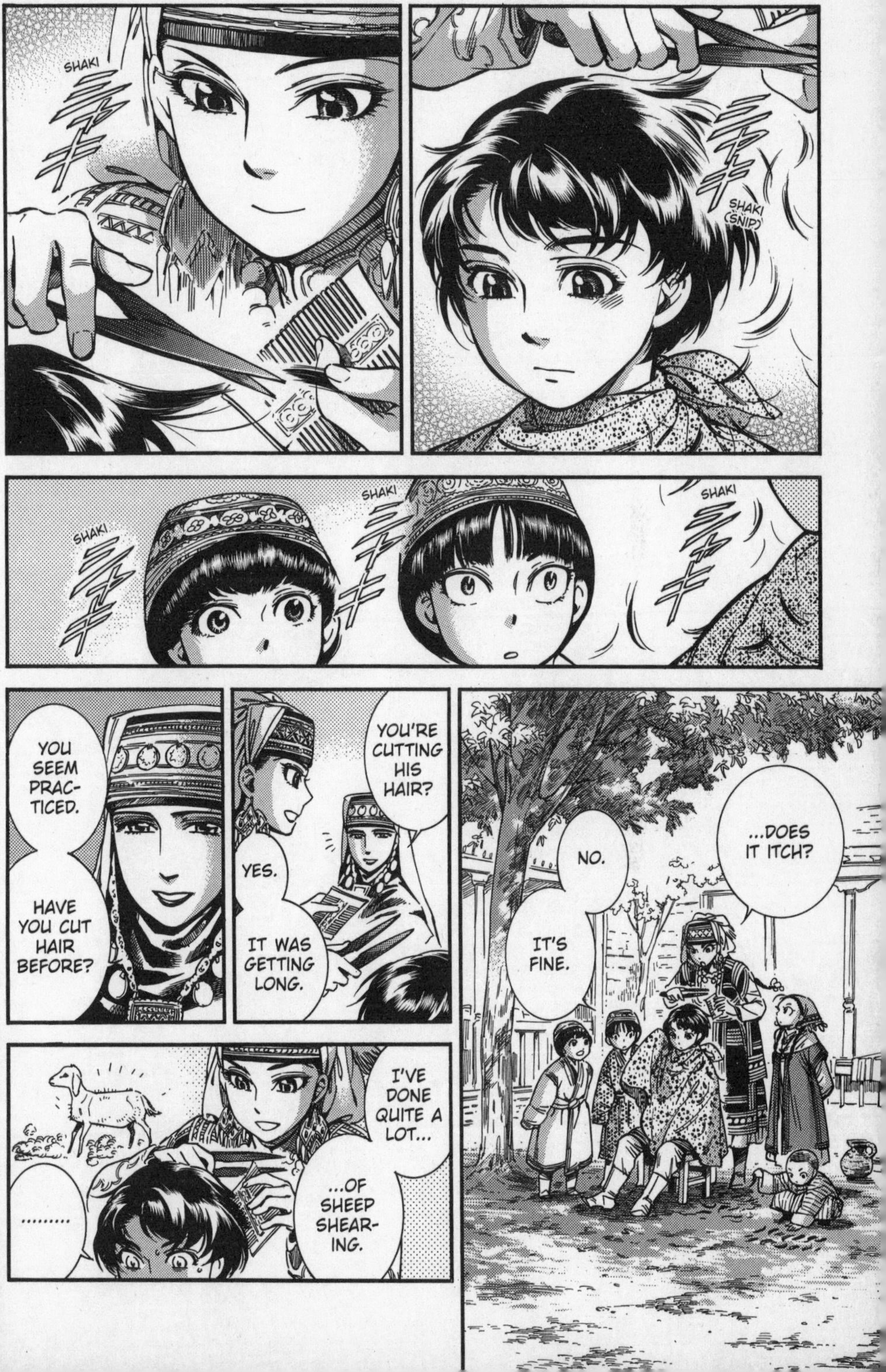
SHAKI (SNIP)
SHAKI
SHAKI
SHAKI
SHAKI
...DOES IT ITCH?
NO.
IT'S FINE.
YOU'RE CUTTING HIS HAIR?
YES.
IT WAS GETTING LONG.
YOU SEEM PRAC-TICED.
HAVE YOU CUT HAIR BEFORE?
I'VE DONE QUITE A LOT...
...OF SHEEP SHEAR-ING.
....

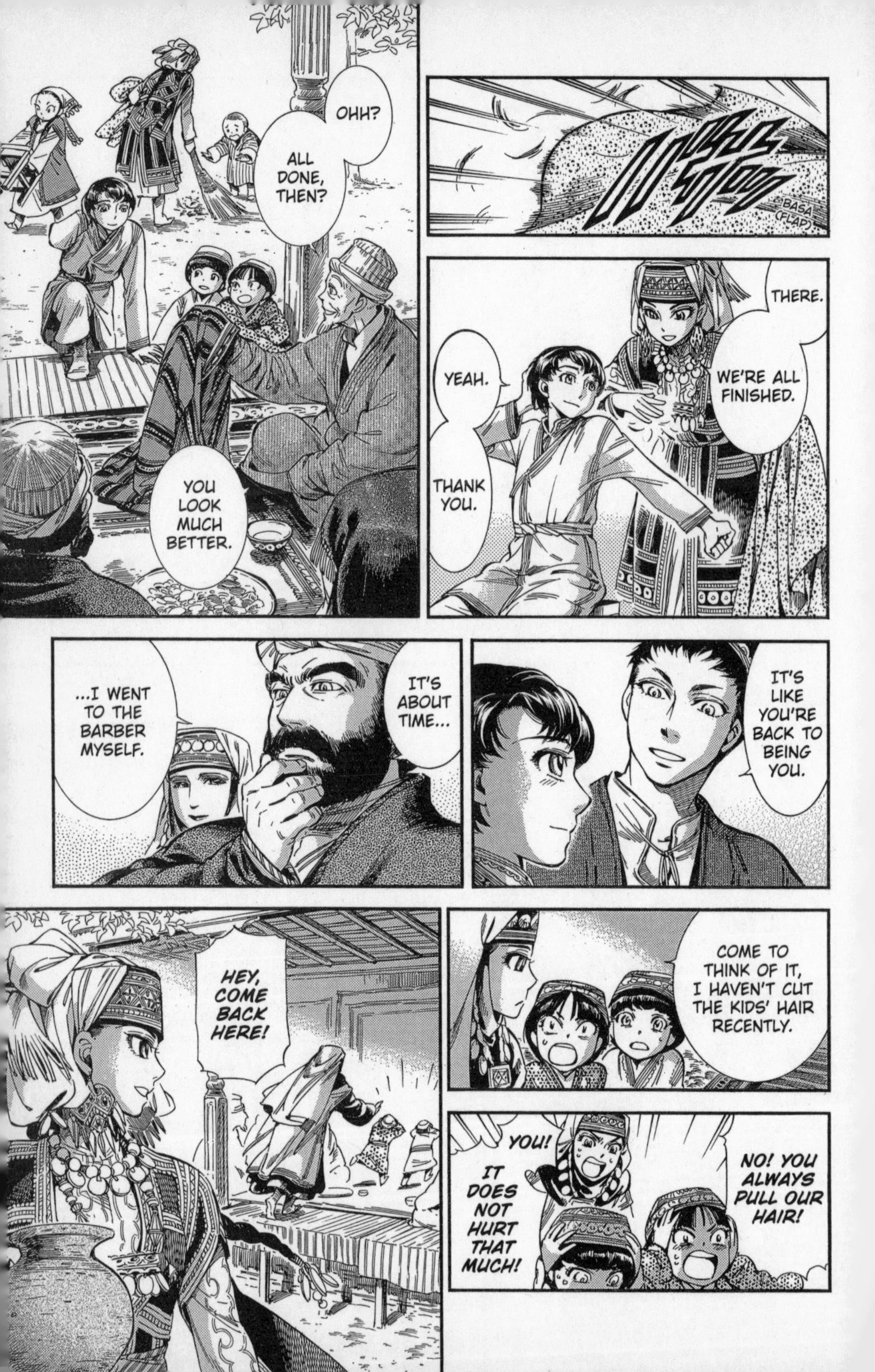
BASA (FLAP)
THERE.
WE'RE ALL FINISHED.
YEAH.
THANK YOU.
OHH?
ALL DONE, THEN?
YOU LOOK MUCH BETTER.
IT'S LIKE YOU'RE BACK TO BEING YOU.
IT'S ABOUT TIME...
...I WENT TO THE BARBER MYSELF.
COME TO THINK OF IT, I HAVEN'T CUT THE KIDS' HAIR RECENTLY.
NO! YOU ALWAYS PULL OUR HAIR!
YOU!
IT DOES NOT HURT THAT MUCH!
HEY, COME BACK HERE!

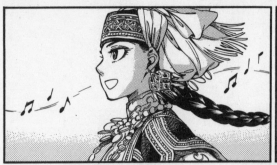
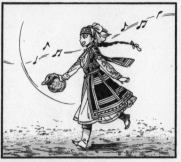
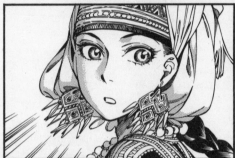
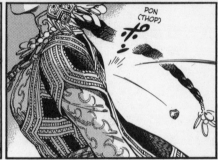

PON
(THOP)

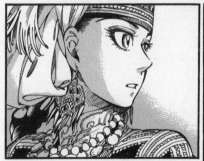
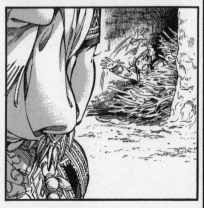
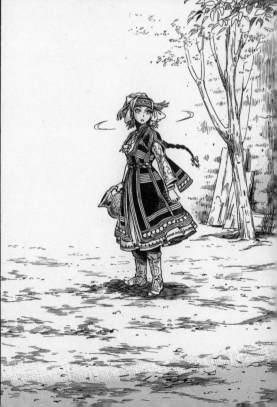

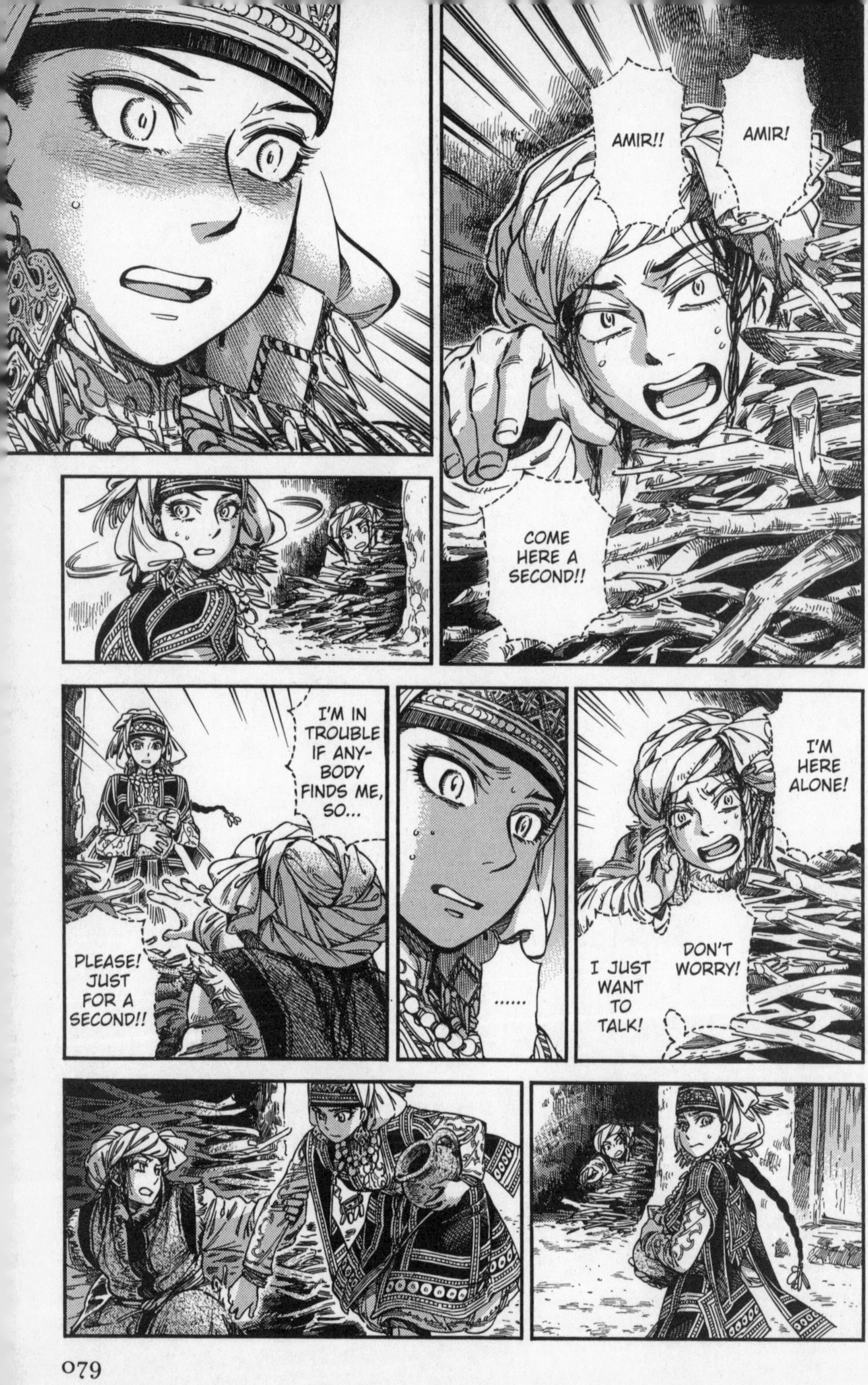
AMIR!
AMIR!!
COME HERE A SECOND!!
I'M HERE ALONE!
DON'T WORRY!
I JUST WANT TO TALK!
......
I'M IN TROUBLE IF ANYBODY FINDS ME, SO...
PLEASE! JUST FOR A SECOND!!

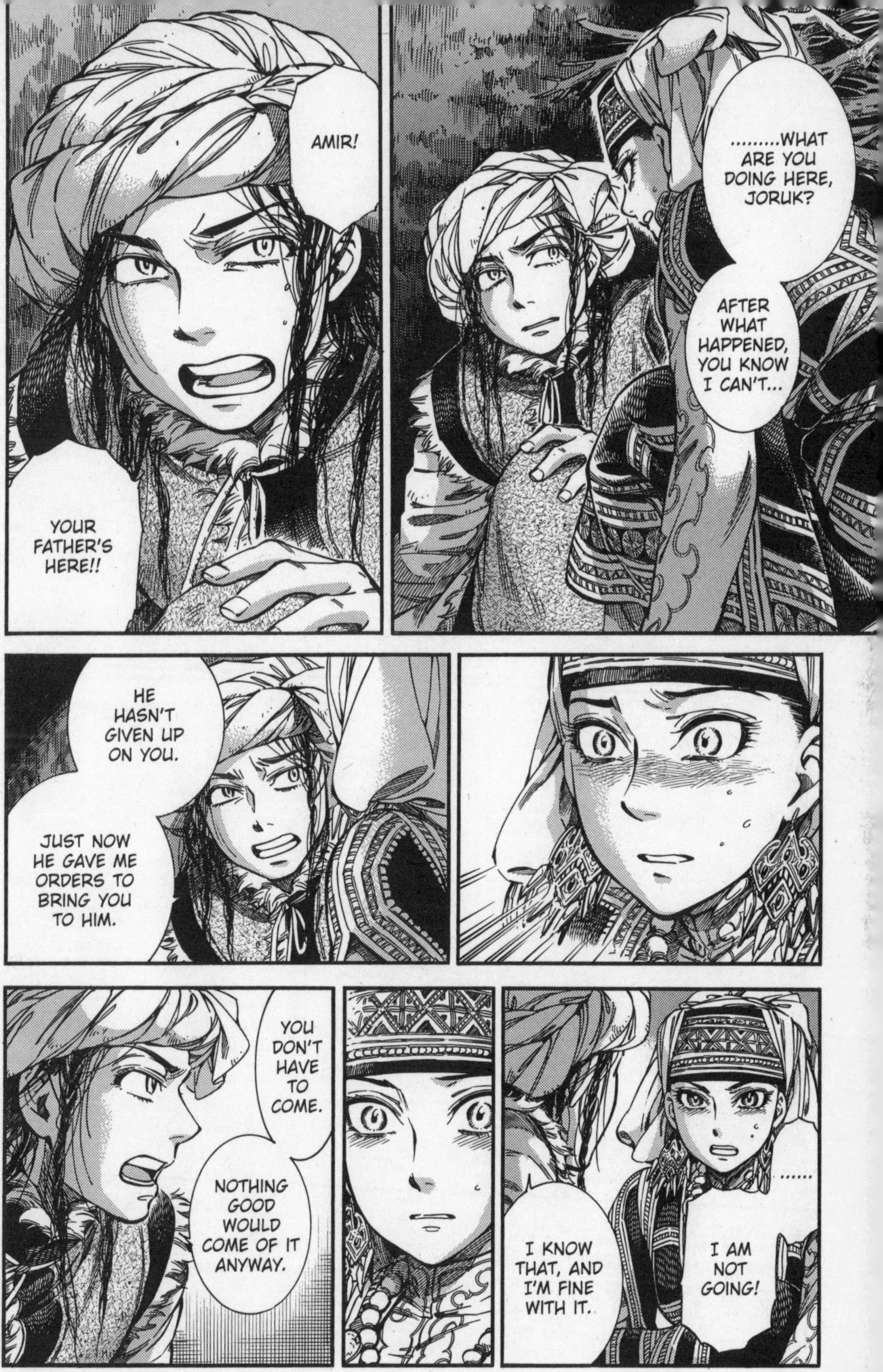

.........WHAT ARE YOU DOING HERE, JORUK?
AFTER WHAT HAPPENED, YOU KNOW I CAN'T...
AMIR!
YOUR FATHER'S HERE!!
HE HASN'T GIVEN UP ON YOU.
JUST NOW HE GAVE ME ORDERS TO BRING YOU TO HIM.
......
I AM NOT GOING!
I KNOW THAT, AND I'M FINE WITH IT.
YOU DON'T HAVE TO COME.
NOTHING GOOD WOULD COME OF IT ANYWAY.

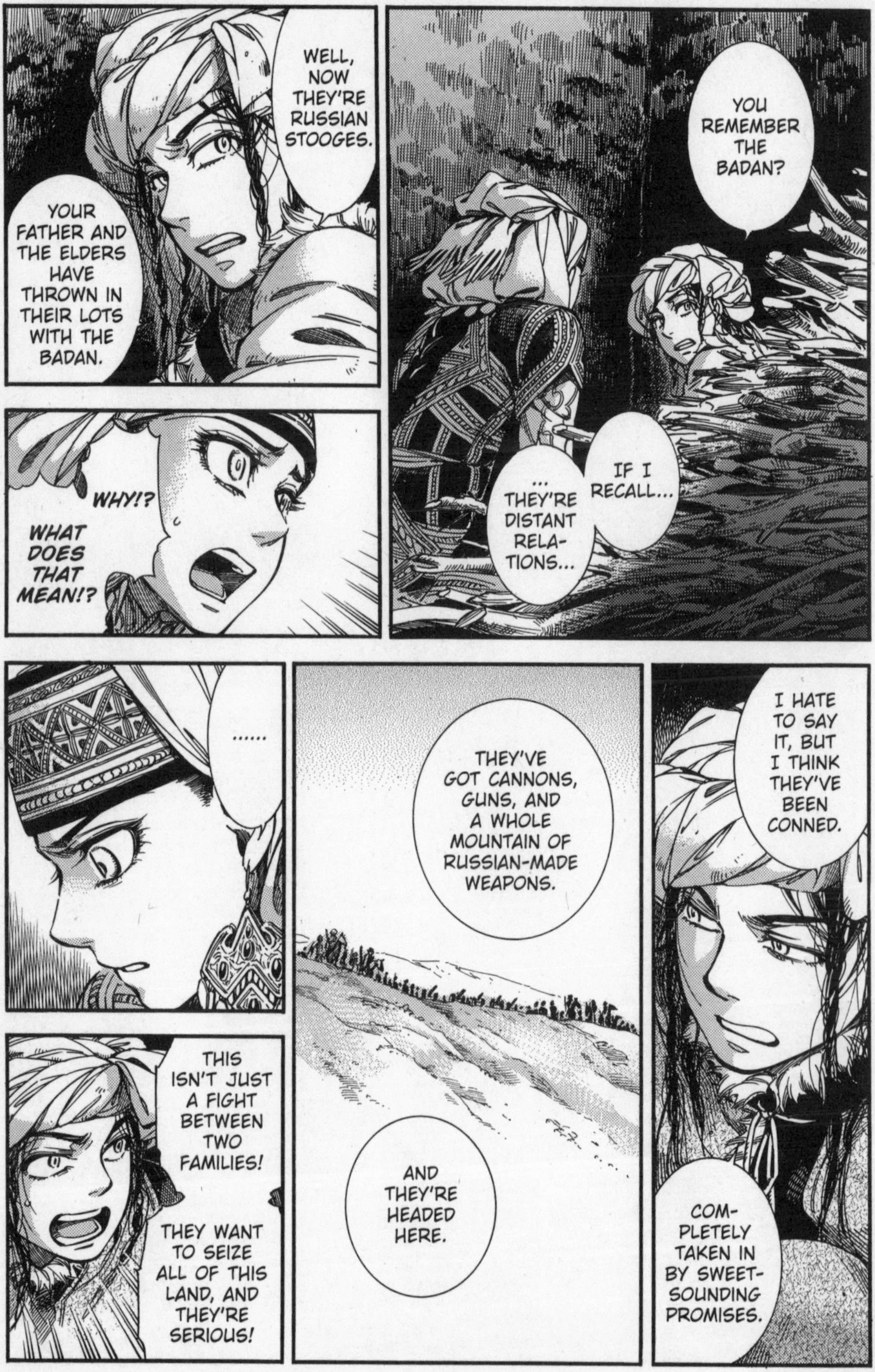
YOU REMEMBER THE BADAN?
IF I RECALL...
...THEY'RE DISTANT RELATIONS...
WELL, NOW THEY'RE RUSSIAN STOOGES.
YOUR FATHER AND THE ELDERS HAVE THROWN IN THEIR LOTS WITH THE BADAN.
WHY!?
WHAT DOES THAT MEAN!?
I HATE TO SAY IT, BUT I THINK THEY'VE BEEN CONNED.
COMPLETELY TAKEN IN BY SWEET-SOUNDING PROMISES.
THEY'VE GOT CANNONS, GUNS, AND A WHOLE MOUNTAIN OF RUSSIAN-MADE WEAPONS.
AND THEY'RE HEADED HERE.
......
THIS ISN'T JUST A FIGHT BETWEEN TWO FAMILIES!
THEY WANT TO SEIZE ALL OF THIS LAND, AND THEY'RE SERIOUS!

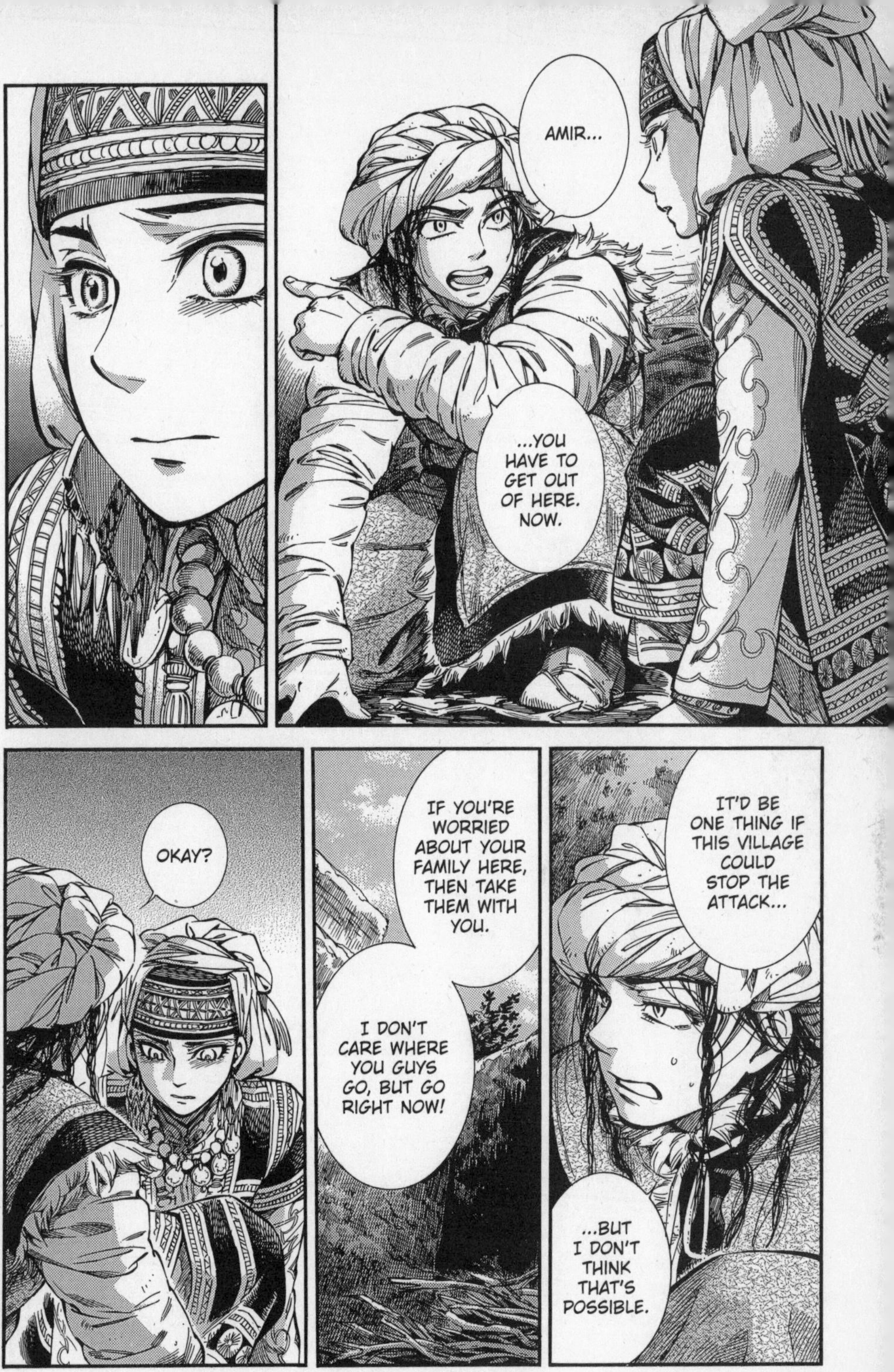
AMIR...
...YOU HAVE TO GET OUT OF HERE. NOW.
IT'D BE ONE THING IF THIS VILLAGE COULD STOP THE ATTACK...
...BUT I DON'T THINK THAT'S POSSIBLE.
IF YOU'RE WORRIED ABOUT YOUR FAMILY HERE, THEN TAKE THEM WITH YOU.
I DON'T CARE WHERE YOU GUYS GO, BUT GO RIGHT NOW!
OKAY?

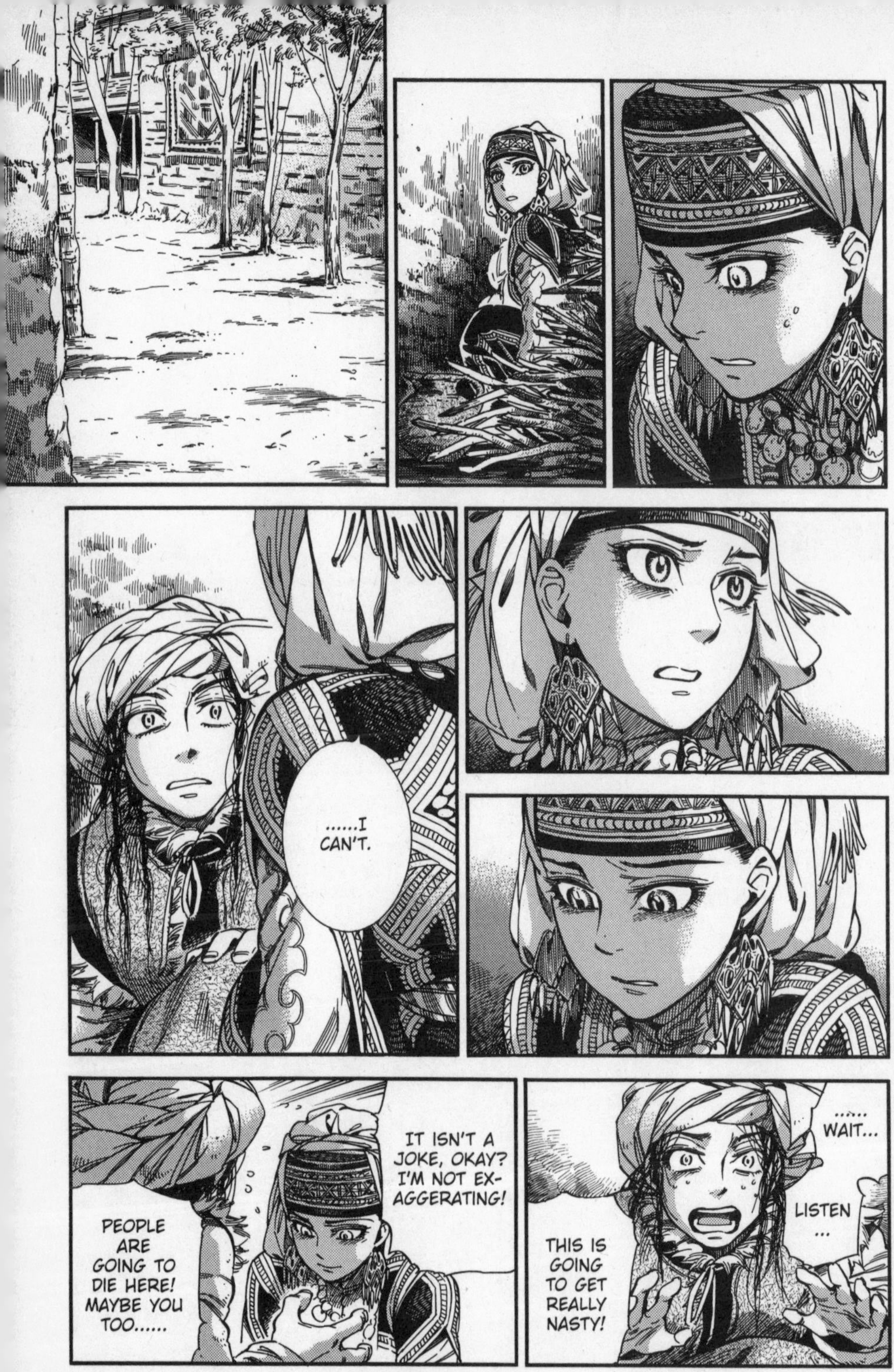
......I CAN'T.
...... WAIT...
LISTEN ...
THIS IS GOING TO GET REALLY NASTY!
IT ISN'T A JOKE, OKAY? I'M NOT EX-AGGERATING!
PEOPLE ARE GOING TO DIE HERE! MAYBE YOU TOO......

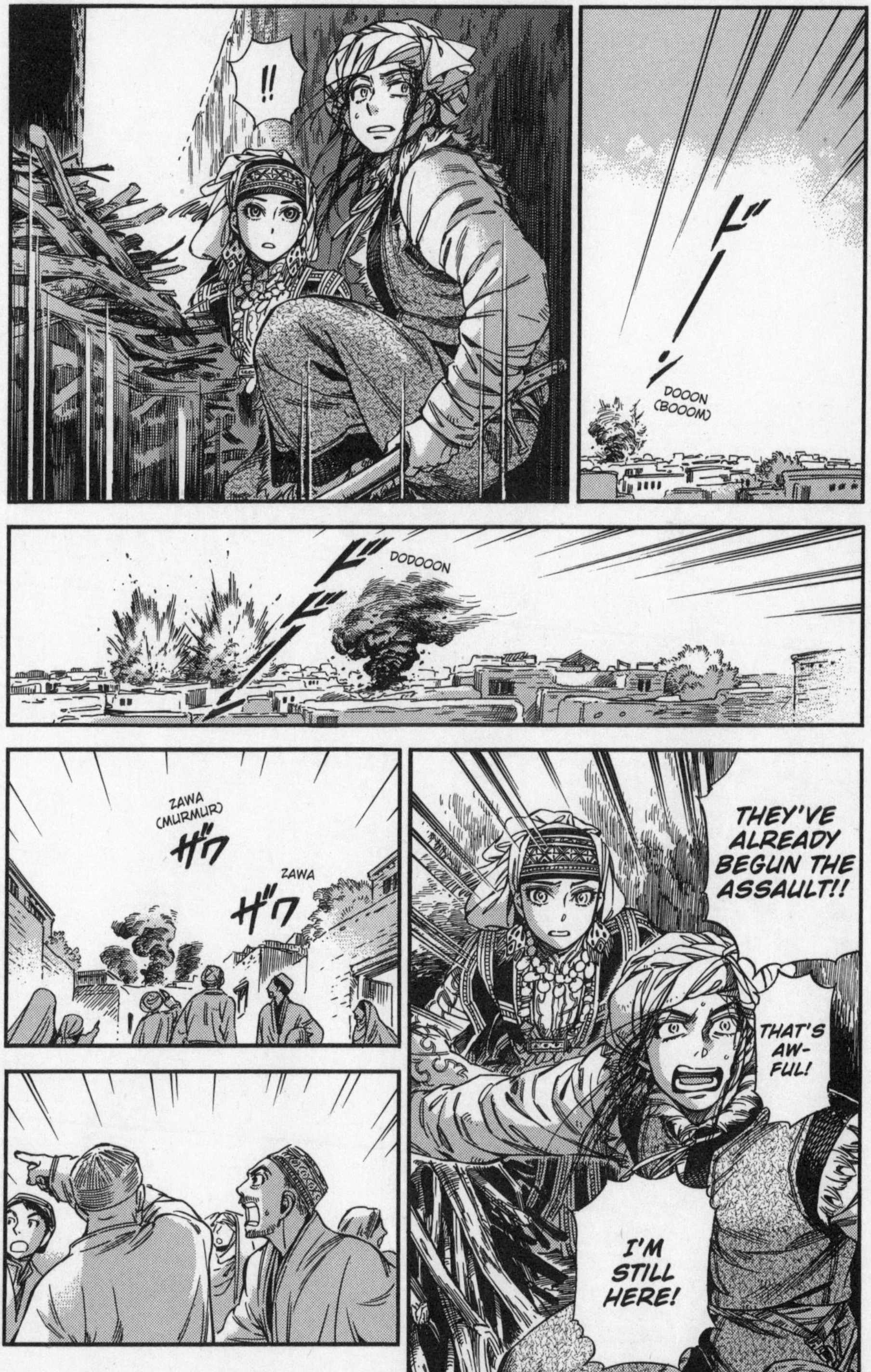
ドーン
DOOON (BOOOM)
!!
ドド
DODOOON
THEY'VE ALREADY BEGUN THE ASSAULT!!
THAT'S AW-FUL!
I'M STILL HERE!
ZAWA (MURMUR)
ザワ
ZAWA
ザワ

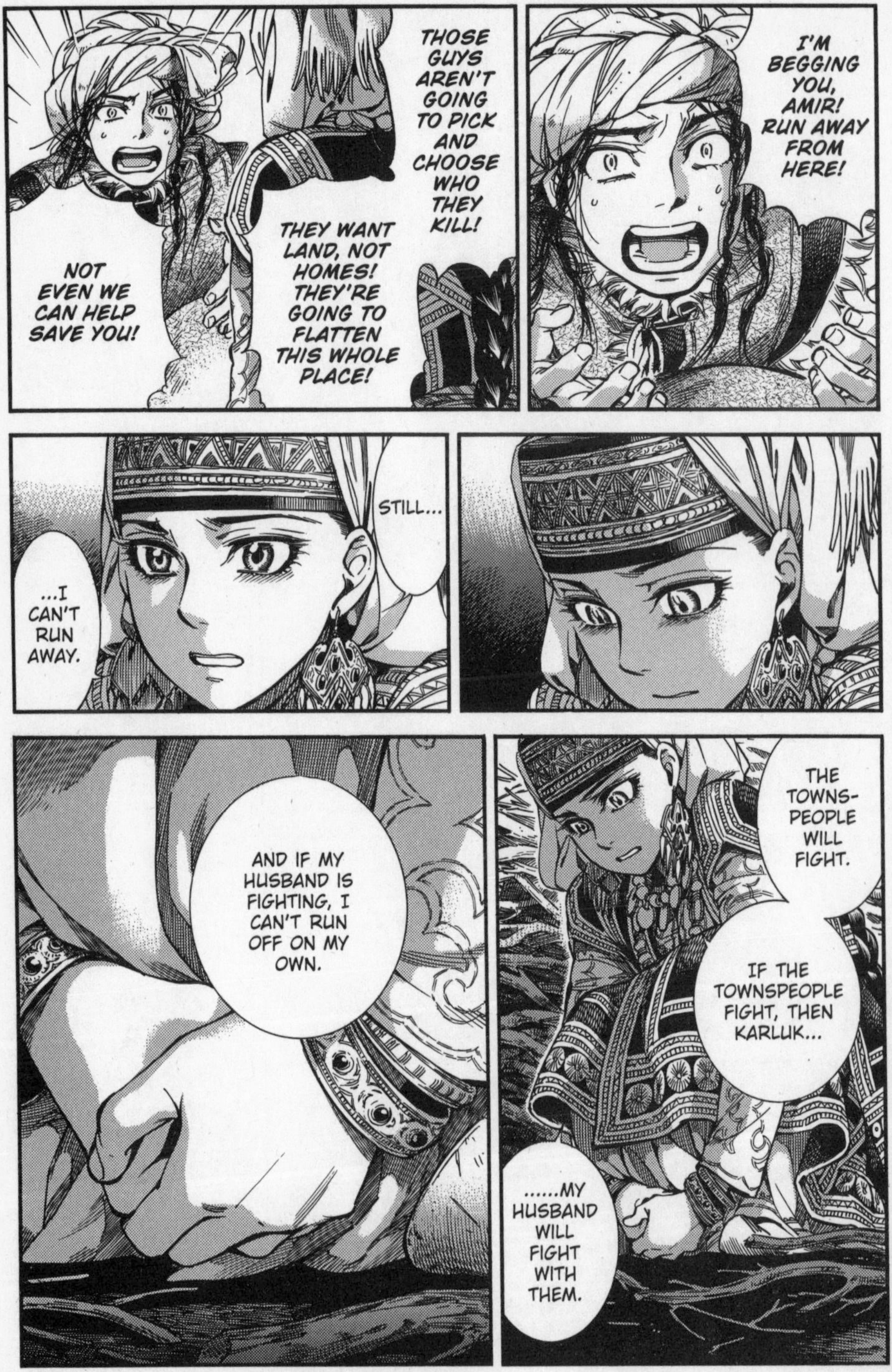
I'M BEGGING YOU, AMIR! RUN AWAY FROM HERE!
THOSE GUYS AREN'T GOING TO PICK AND CHOOSE WHO THEY KILL!
THEY WANT LAND, NOT HOMES! THEY'RE GOING TO FLATTEN THIS WHOLE PLACE!
NOT EVEN WE CAN HELP SAVE YOU!
STILL...
...I CAN'T RUN AWAY.
THE TOWNS-PEOPLE WILL FIGHT.
IF THE TOWNSPEOPLE FIGHT, THEN KARLUK...
......MY HUSBAND WILL FIGHT WITH THEM.
AND IF MY HUSBAND IS FIGHTING, I CAN'T RUN OFF ON MY OWN.

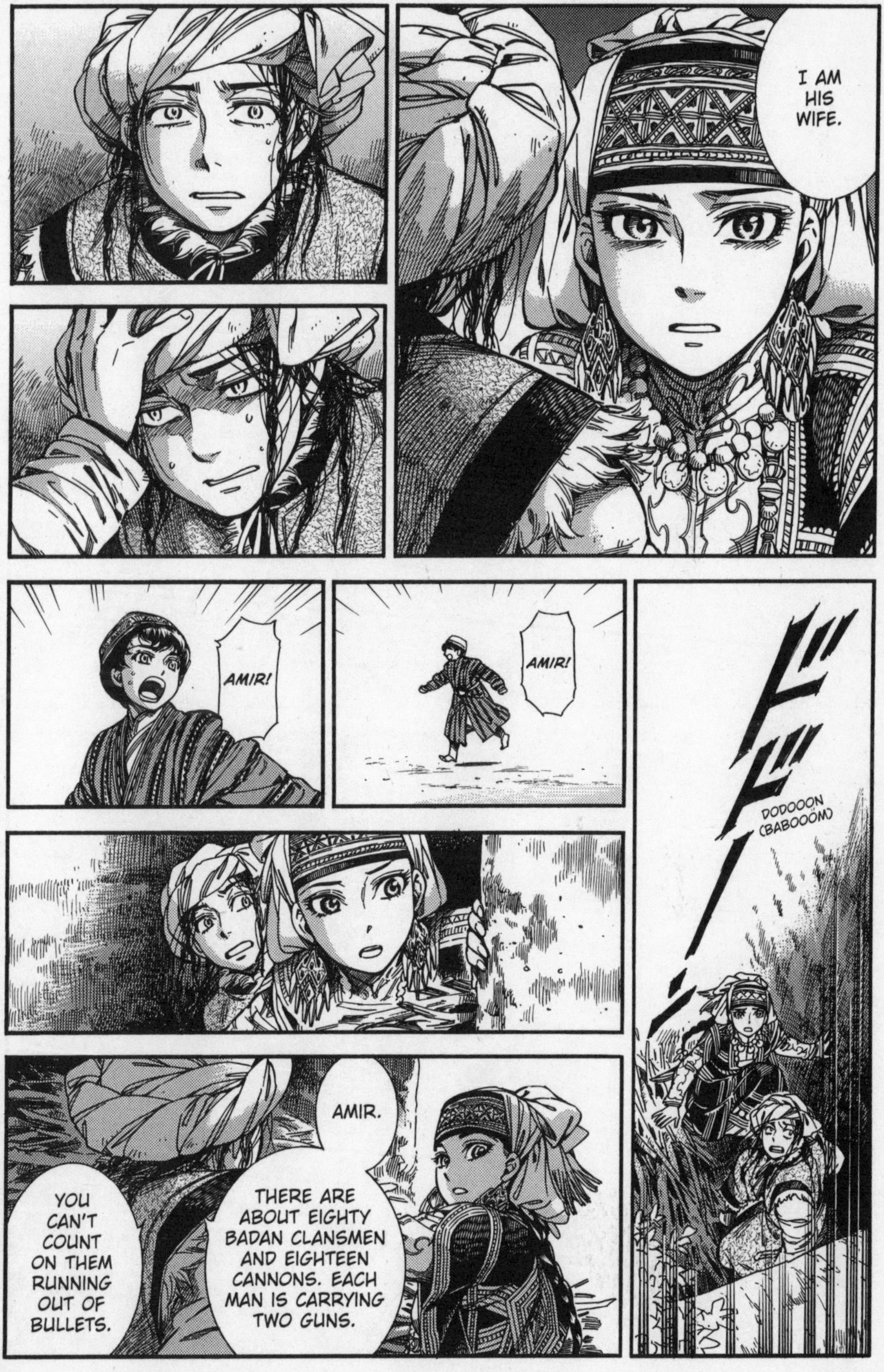
I AM HIS WIFE.
DODOOON (BABOOÖM)
AMIR!
AMIR!
AMIR.
THERE ARE ABOUT EIGHTY BADAN CLANSMEN AND EIGHTEEN CANNONS. EACH MAN IS CARRYING TWO GUNS.
YOU CAN'T COUNT ON THEM RUNNING OUT OF BULLETS.

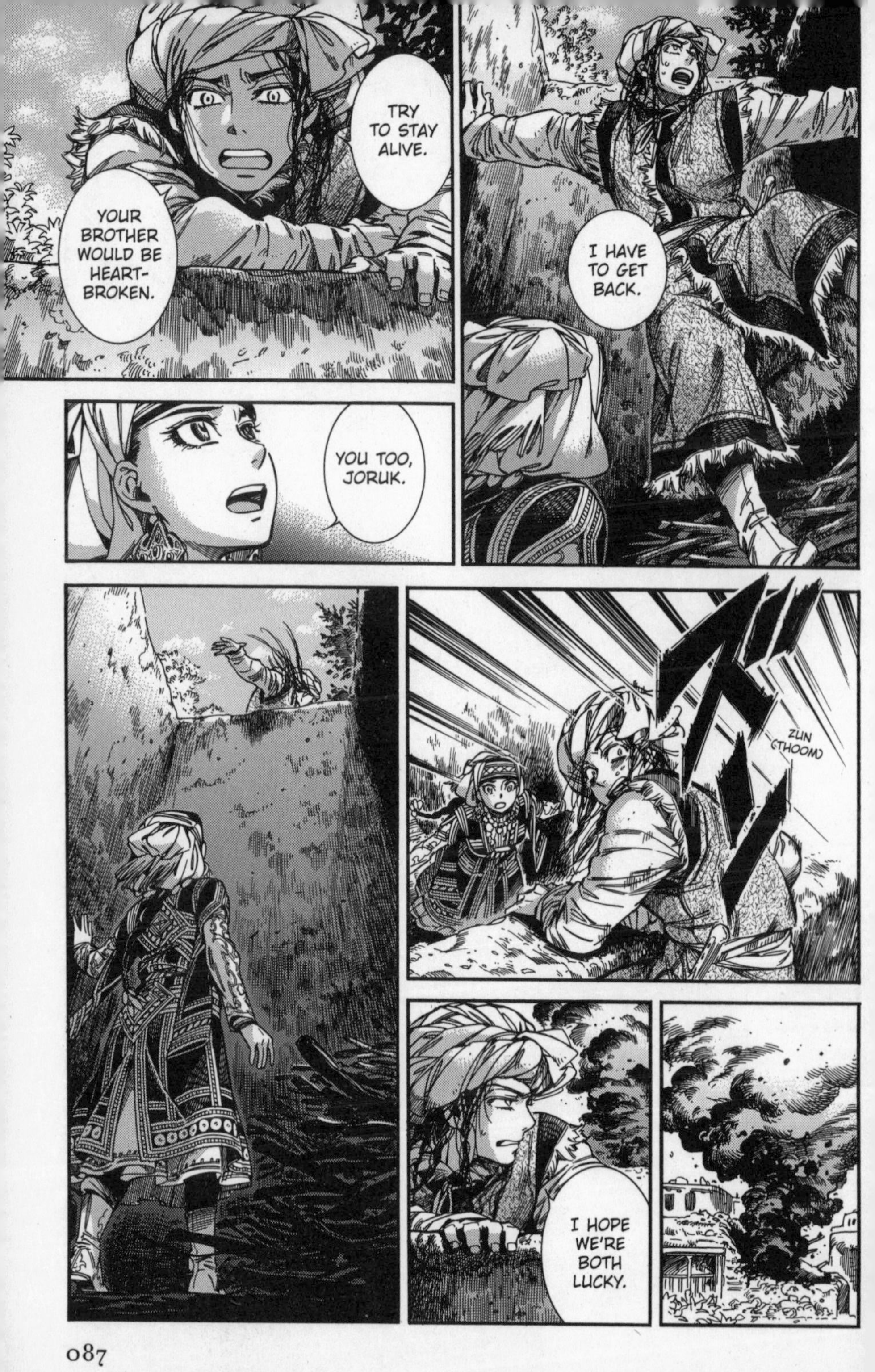
I HAVE TO GET BACK.
TRY TO STAY ALIVE.
YOUR BROTHER WOULD BE HEART-BROKEN.
YOU TOO, JORUK.
ZUN (THOOM)
I HOPE WE'RE BOTH LUCKY.

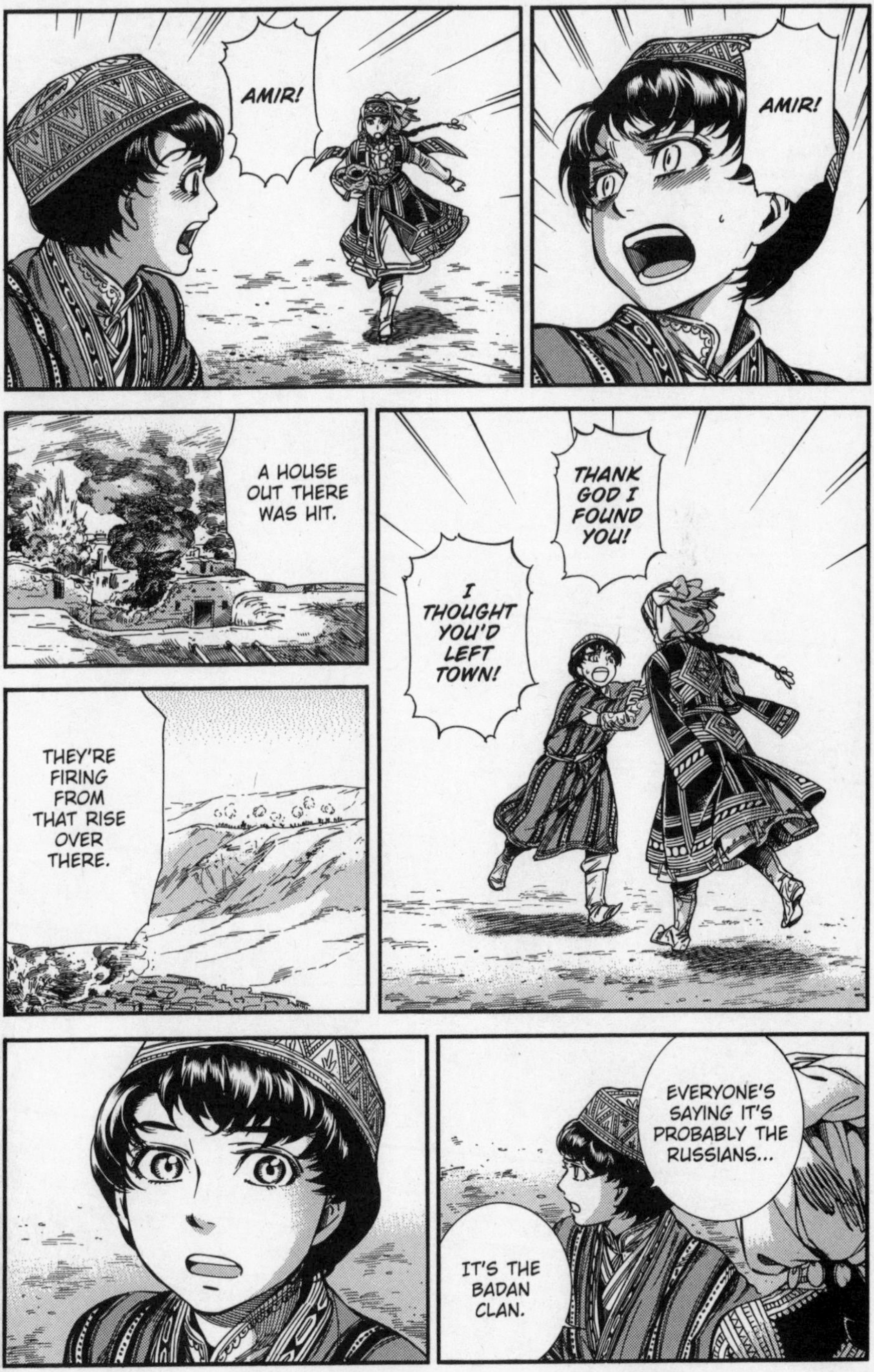
AMIR!
AMIR!
THANK GOD I FOUND YOU!
I THOUGHT YOU'D LEFT TOWN!
A HOUSE OUT THERE WAS HIT.
THEY'RE FIRING FROM THAT RISE OVER THERE.
EVERYONE'S SAYING IT'S PROBABLY THE RUSSIANS...
IT'S THE BADAN CLAN.

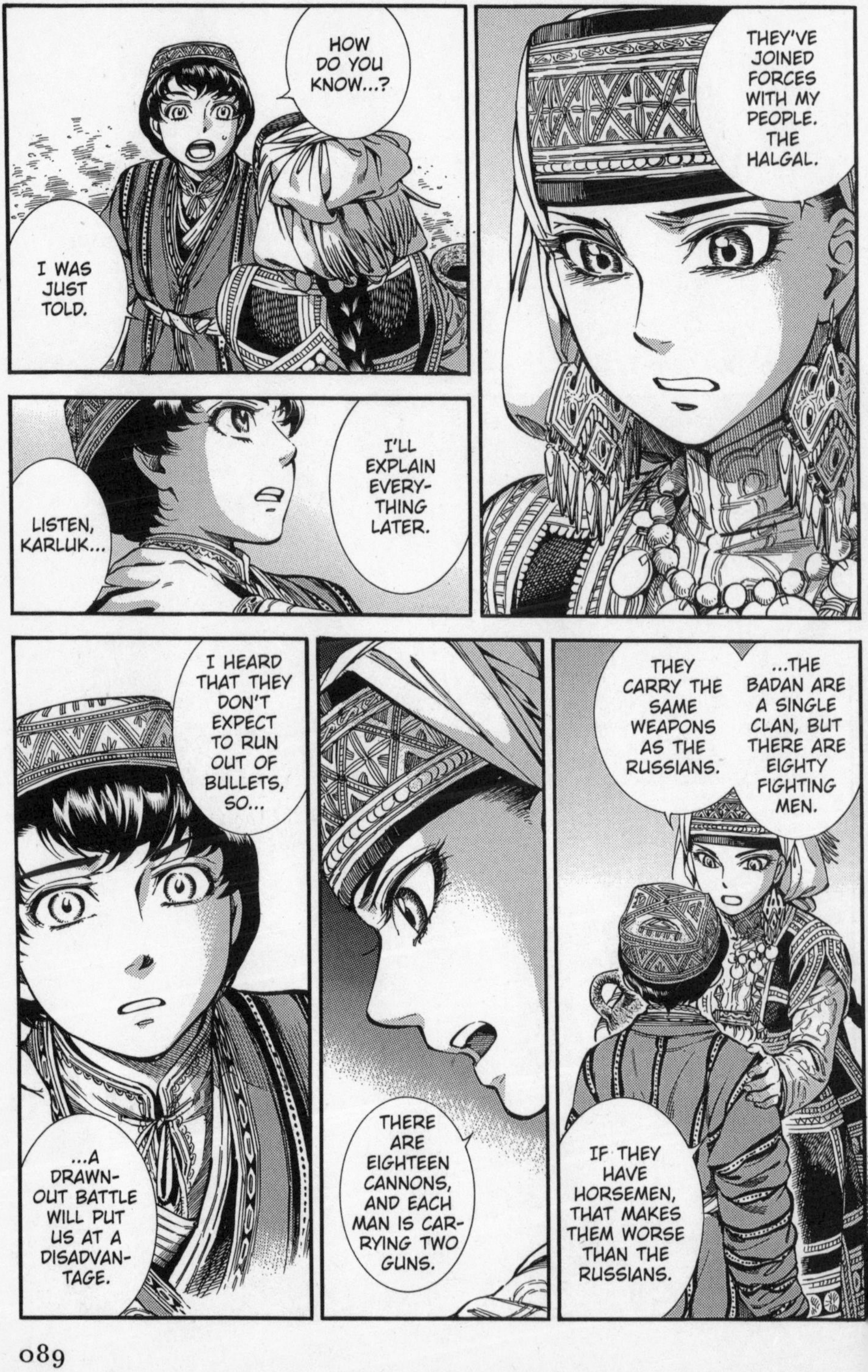
THEY'VE JOINED FORCES WITH MY PEOPLE. THE HALGAL.
HOW DO YOU KNOW...?
I WAS JUST TOLD.
I'LL EXPLAIN EVERY-THING LATER.
LISTEN, KARLUK...
...THE BADAN ARE A SINGLE CLAN, BUT THERE ARE EIGHTY FIGHTING MEN.
THEY CARRY THE SAME WEAPONS AS THE RUSSIANS.
IF THEY HAVE HORSEMEN, THAT MAKES THEM WORSE THAN THE RUSSIANS.
THERE ARE EIGHTEEN CANNONS, AND EACH MAN IS CAR-RYING TWO GUNS.
I HEARD THAT THEY DON'T EXPECT TO RUN OUT OF BULLETS, SO...
...A DRAWN-OUT BATTLE WILL PUT US AT A DISADVAN-TAGE.

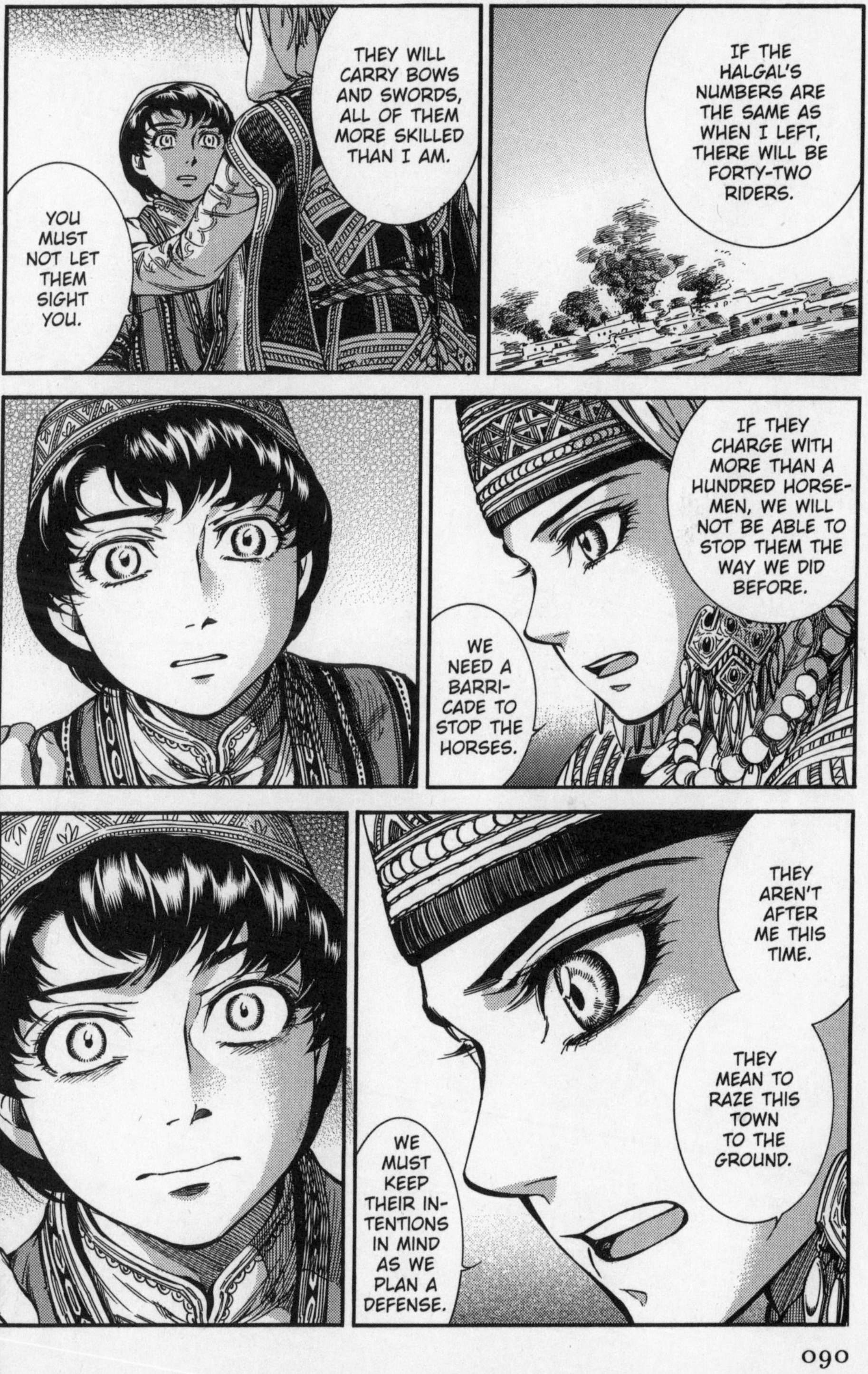
IF THE HALGAL'S NUMBERS ARE THE SAME AS WHEN I LEFT, THERE WILL BE FORTY-TWO RIDERS.
THEY WILL CARRY BOWS AND SWORDS, ALL OF THEM MORE SKILLED THAN I AM.
YOU MUST NOT LET THEM SIGHT YOU.
IF THEY CHARGE WITH MORE THAN A HUNDRED HORSE-MEN, WE WILL NOT BE ABLE TO STOP THEM THE WAY WE DID BEFORE.
WE NEED A BARRI-CADE TO STOP THE HORSES.
THEY AREN'T AFTER ME THIS TIME.
THEY MEAN TO RAZE THIS TOWN TO THE GROUND.
WE MUST KEEP THEIR IN-TENTIONS IN MIND AS WE PLAN A DEFENSE.

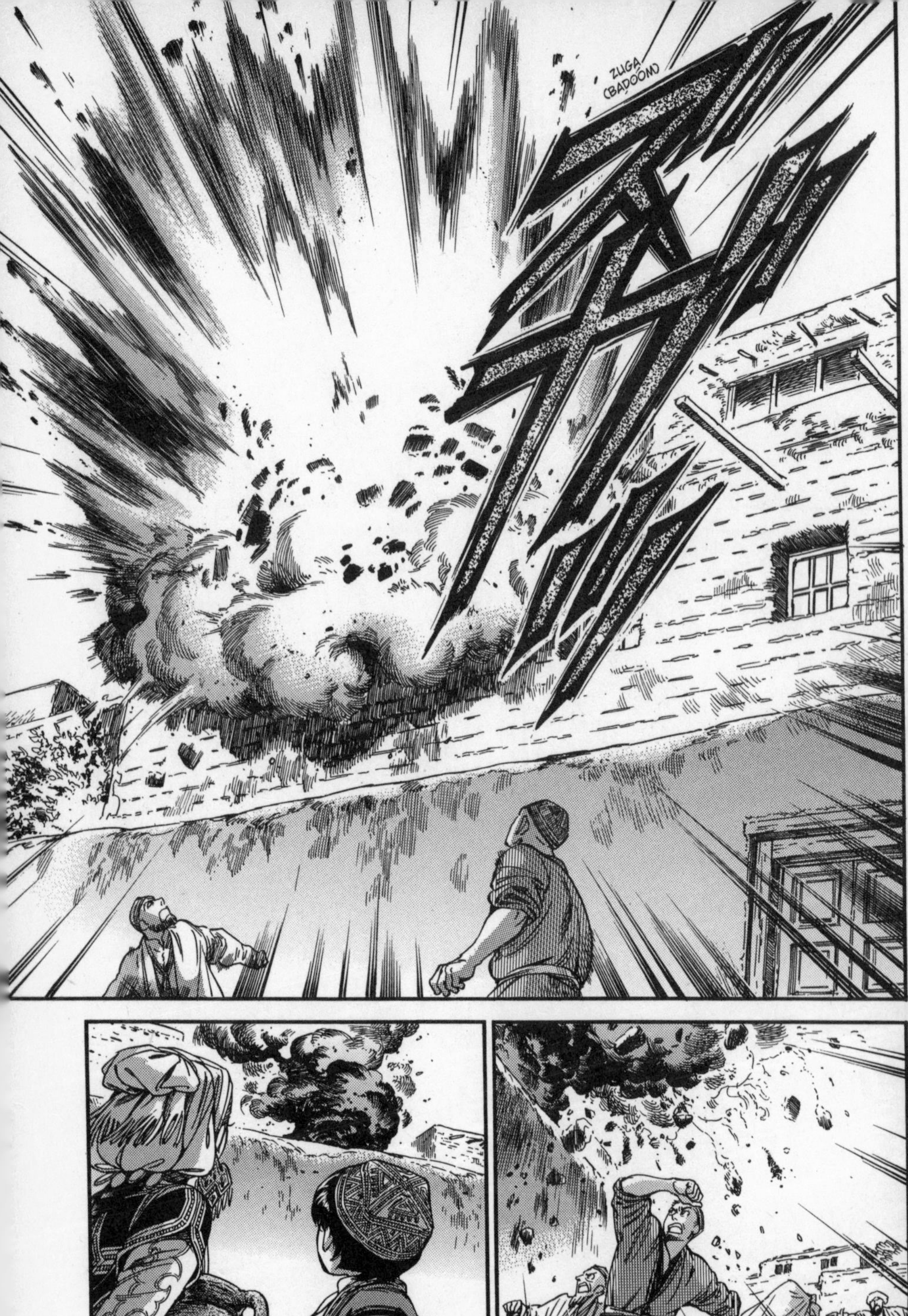
ZUGA
(BADOOM)

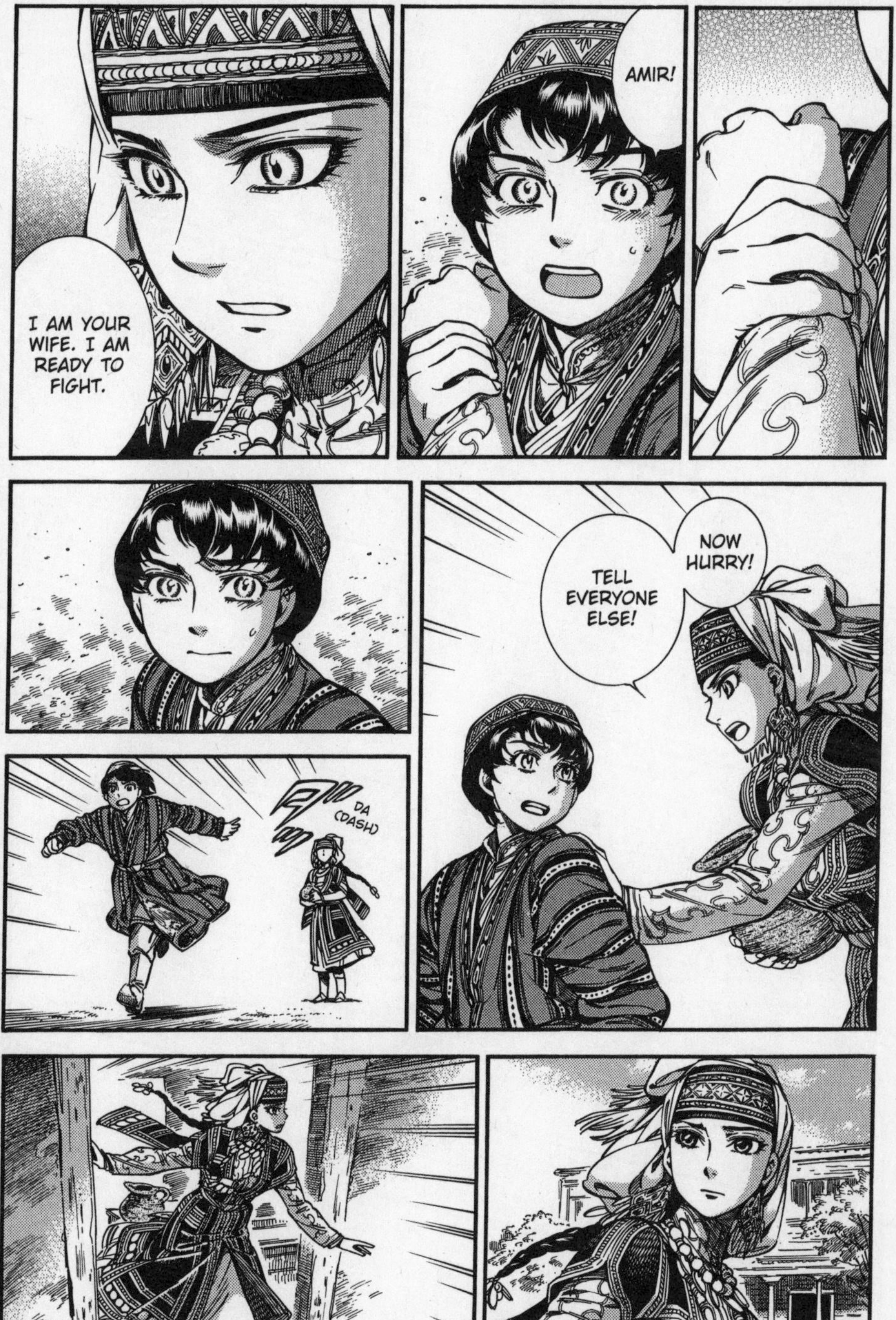
AMIR!
I AM YOUR WIFE. I AM READY TO FIGHT.
NOW HURRY!
TELL EVERYONE ELSE!
DA (DASH)

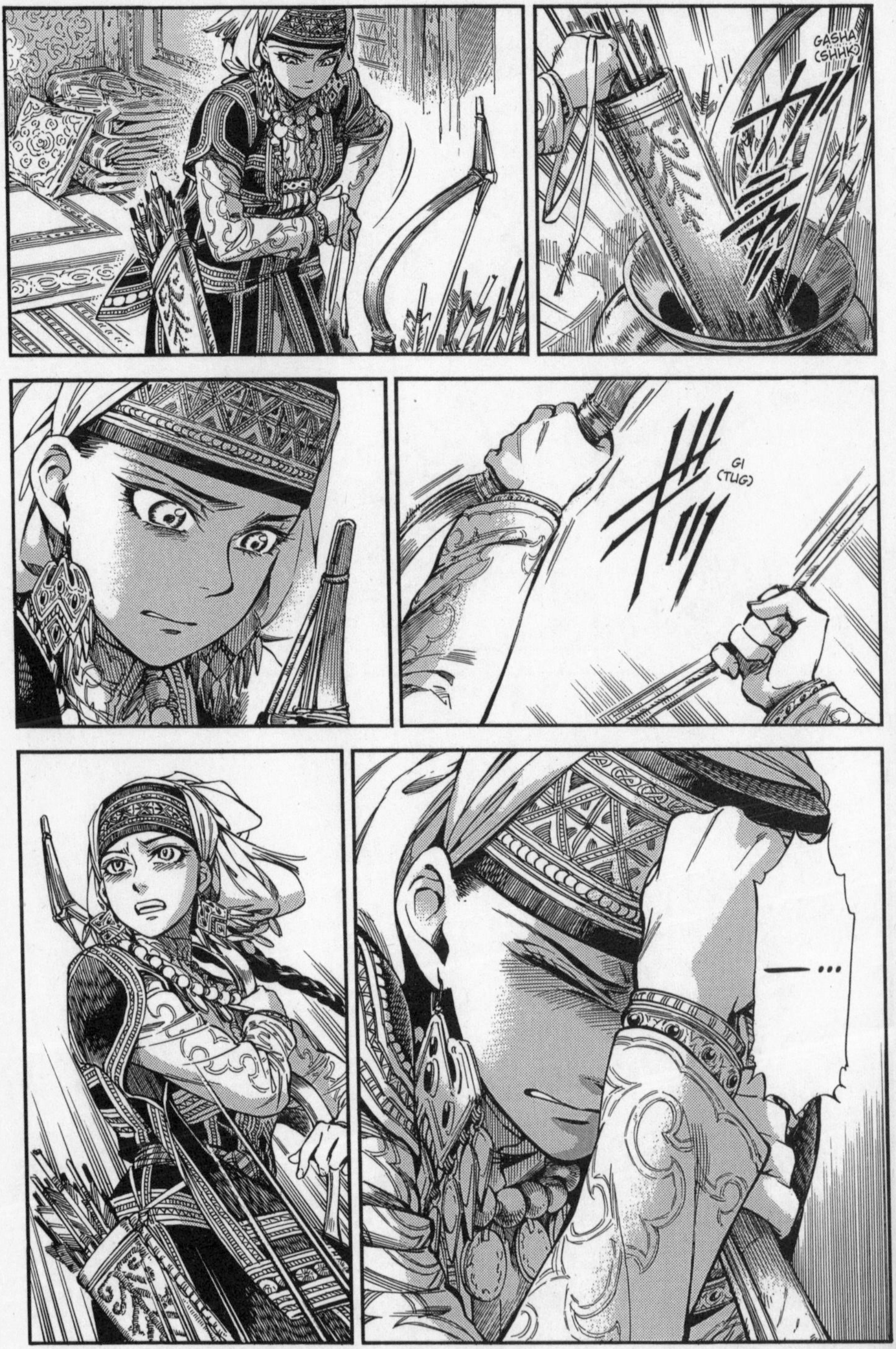
GASHA (SHHK)
GI (TUG)
—...

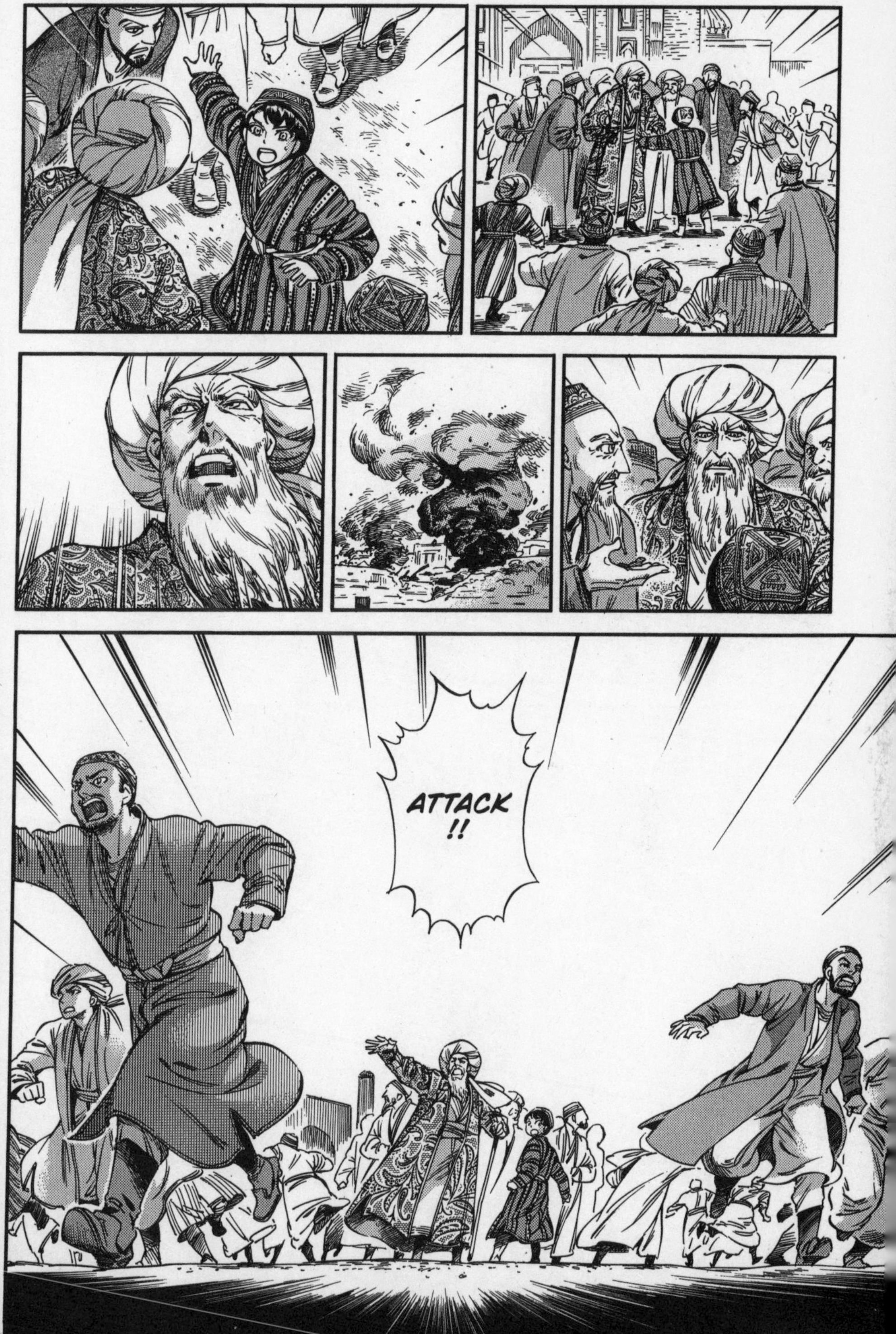
ATTACK !!

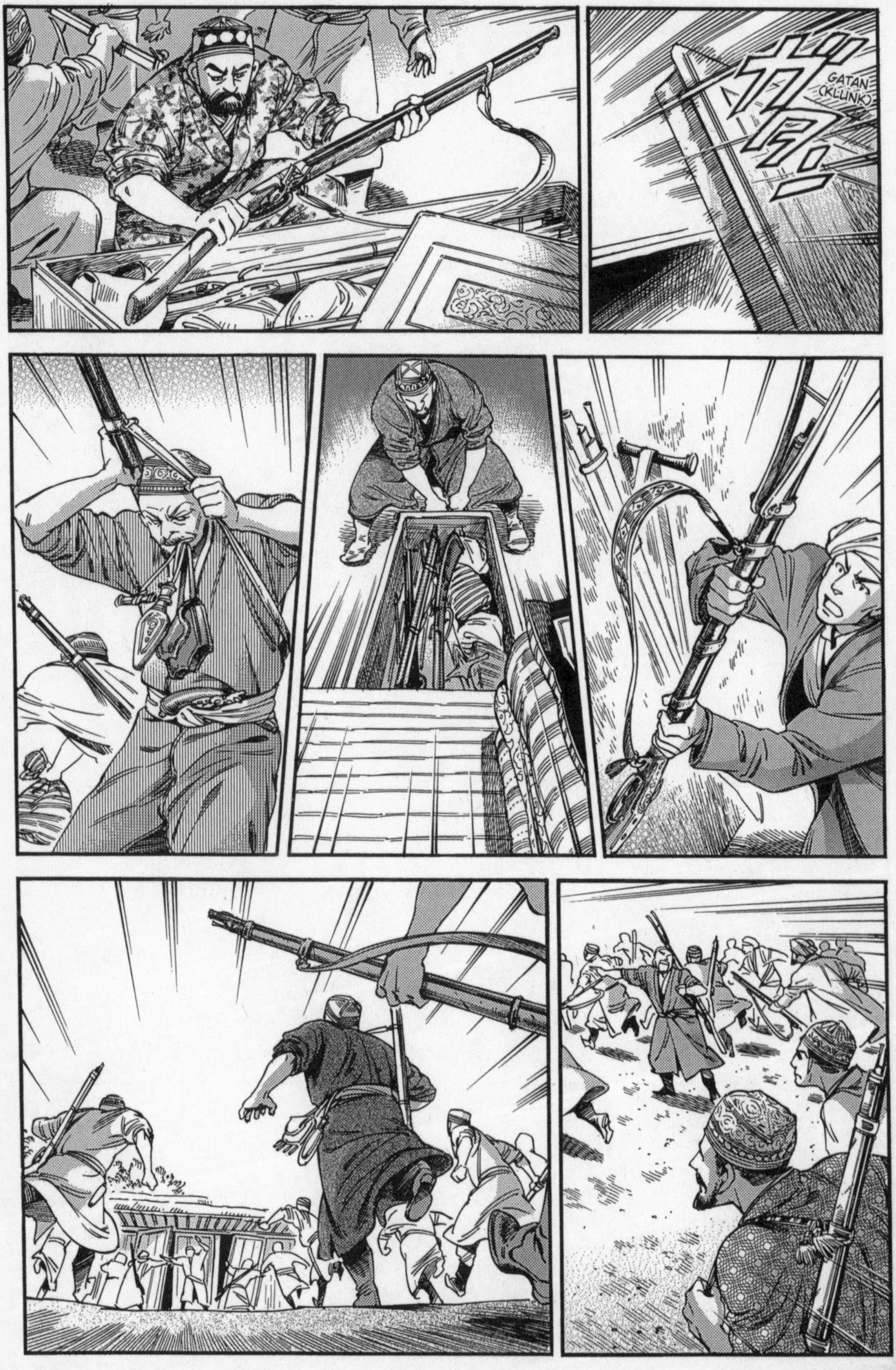
ガタ!
GATAN (KLLINK)

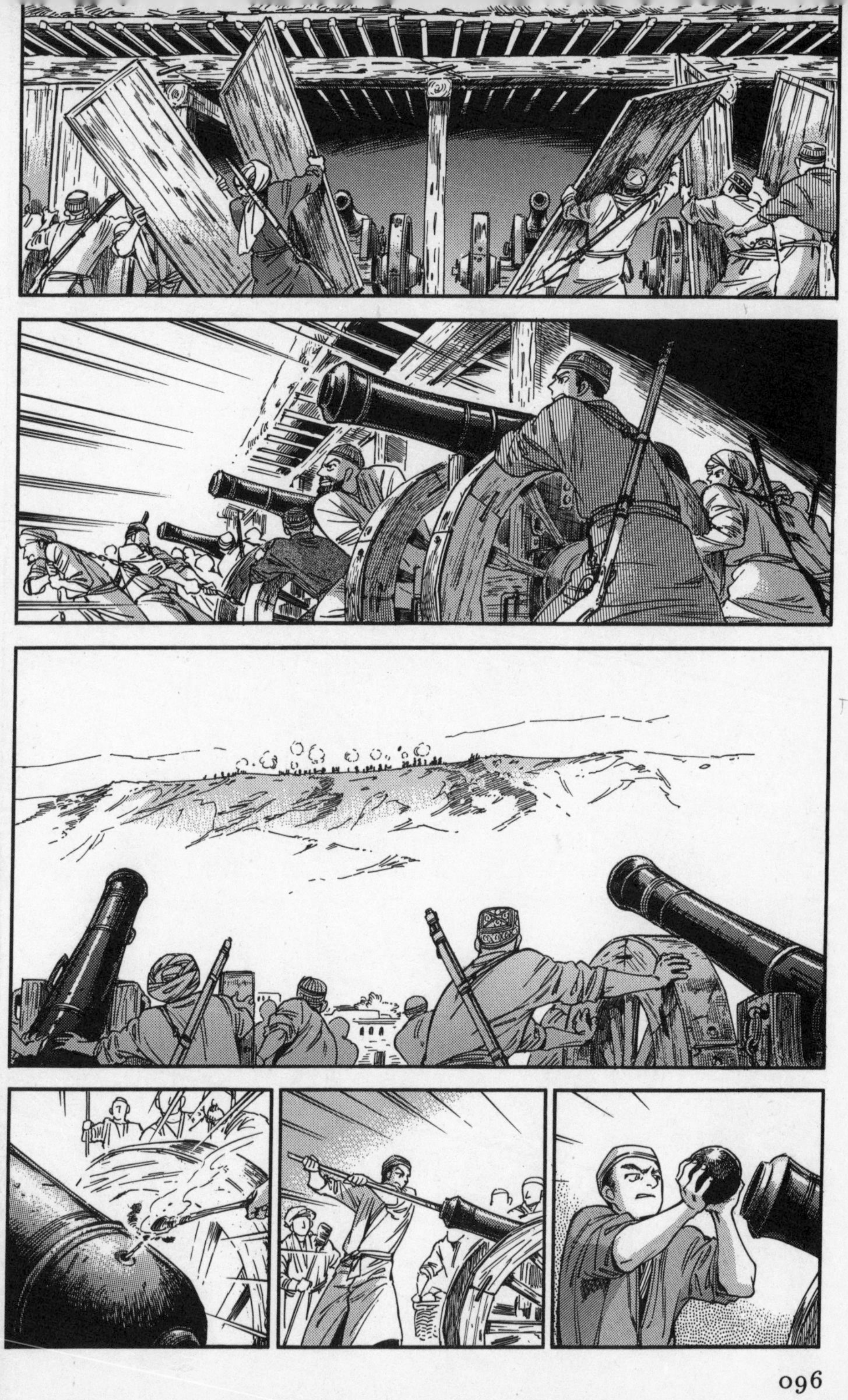

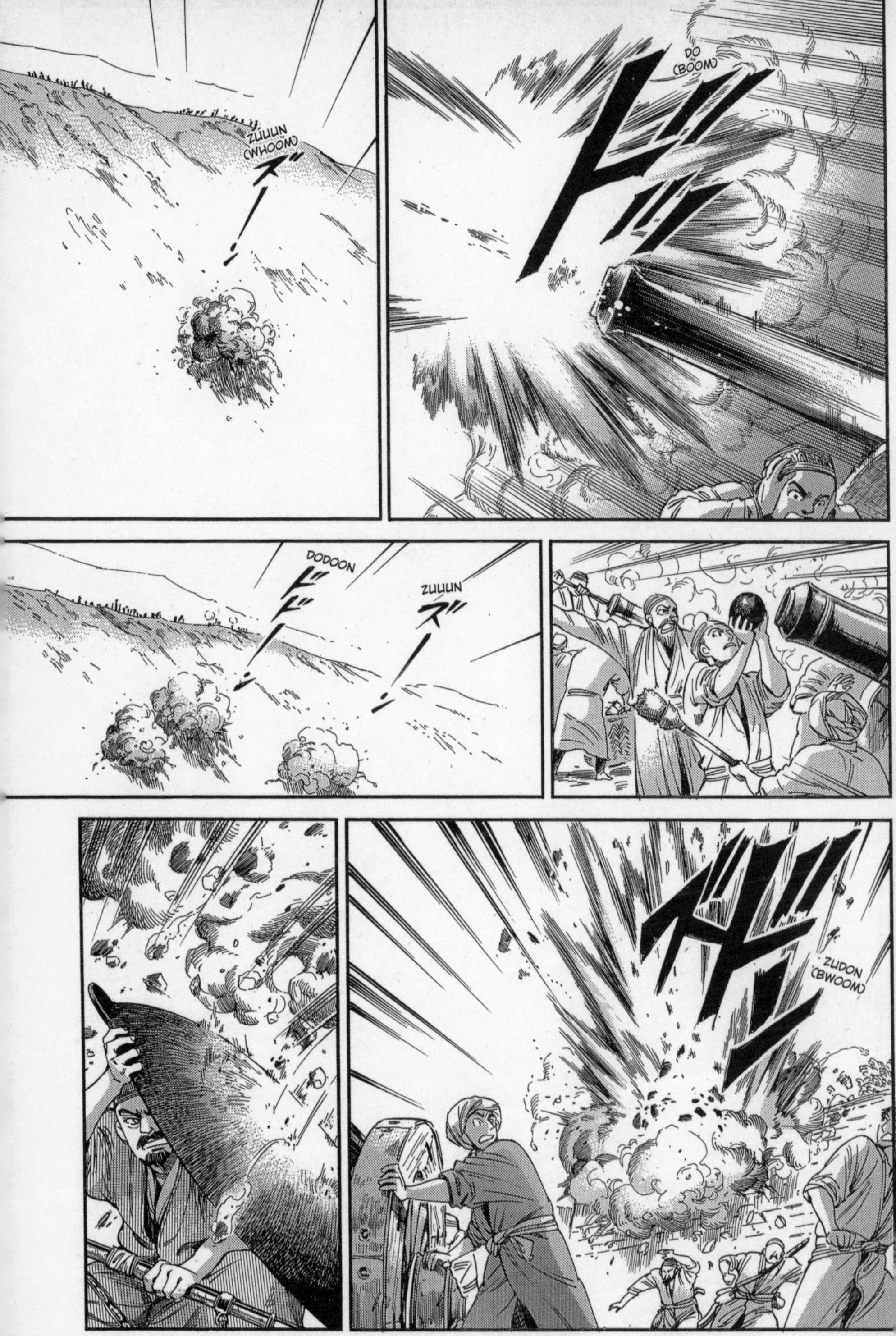
DO (BOOM)
ZUUUN (WHOOM)
ZUUUN
DODOON
ZUDON (BWOOM)

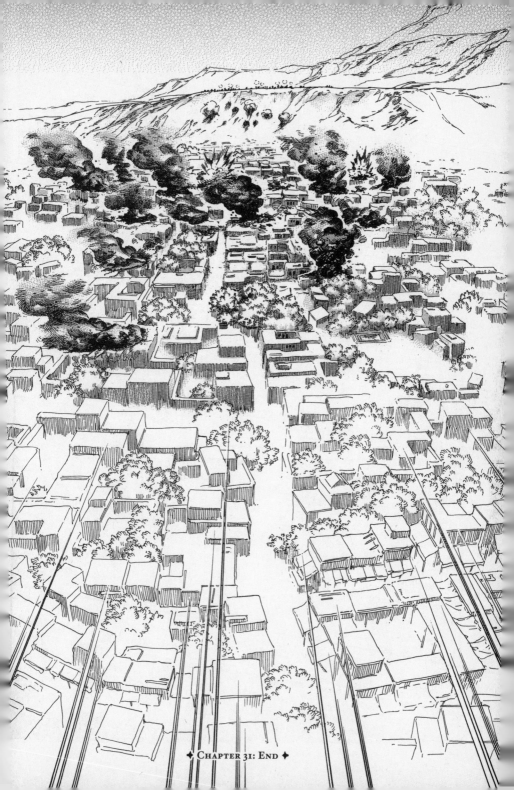

◆ CHAPTER 31: END ◆

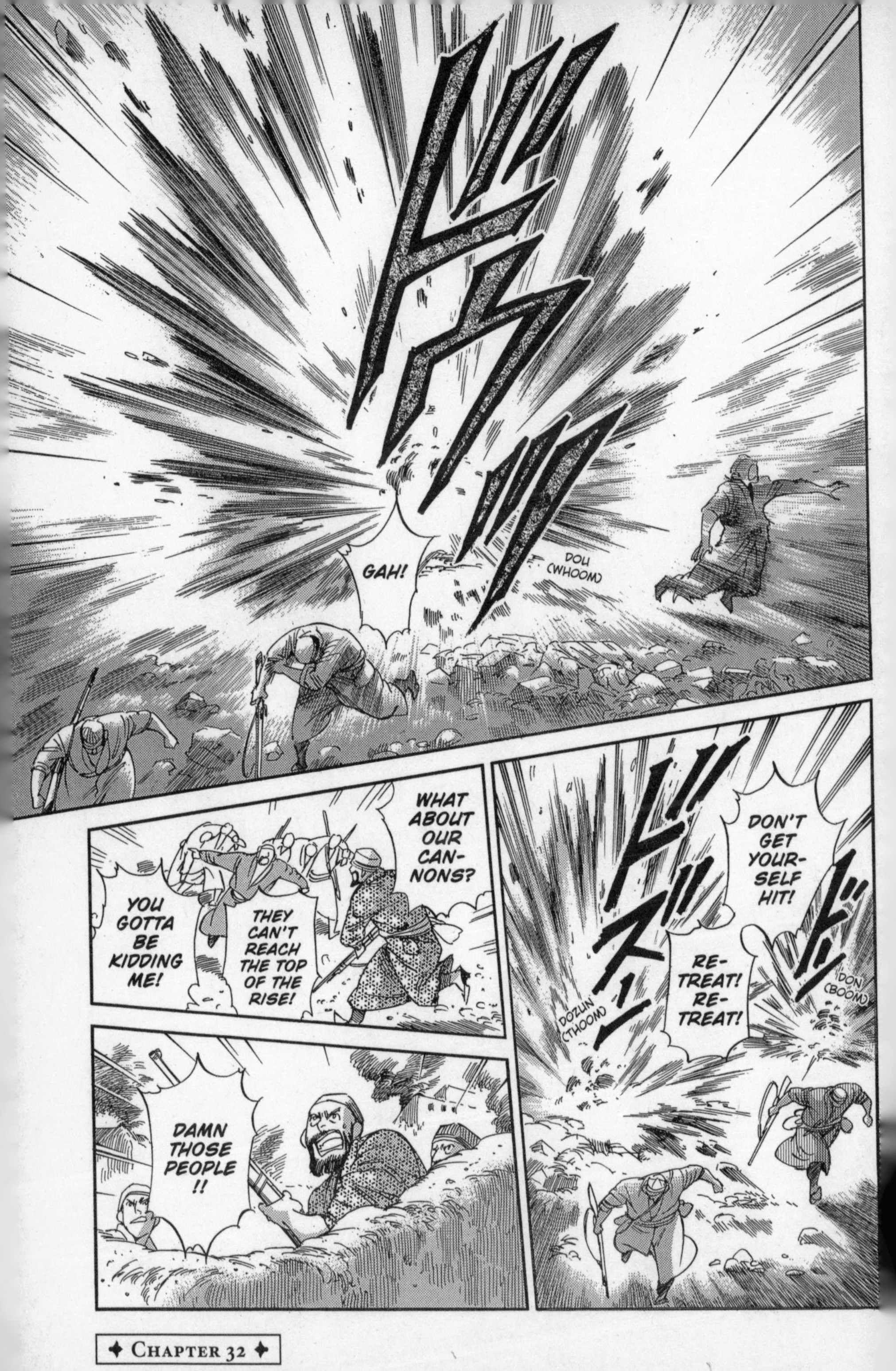
DOU (WHOOM)
GAH!
DON'T GET YOURSELF HIT!
DON (BOOM)
RE-TREAT! RE-TREAT!
DOZUN (THOOM)
WHAT ABOUT OUR CANNONS?
THEY CAN'T REACH THE TOP OF THE RISE!
YOU GOTTA BE KIDDING ME!
DAMN THOSE PEOPLE!!

✦ CHAPTER 32 ✦

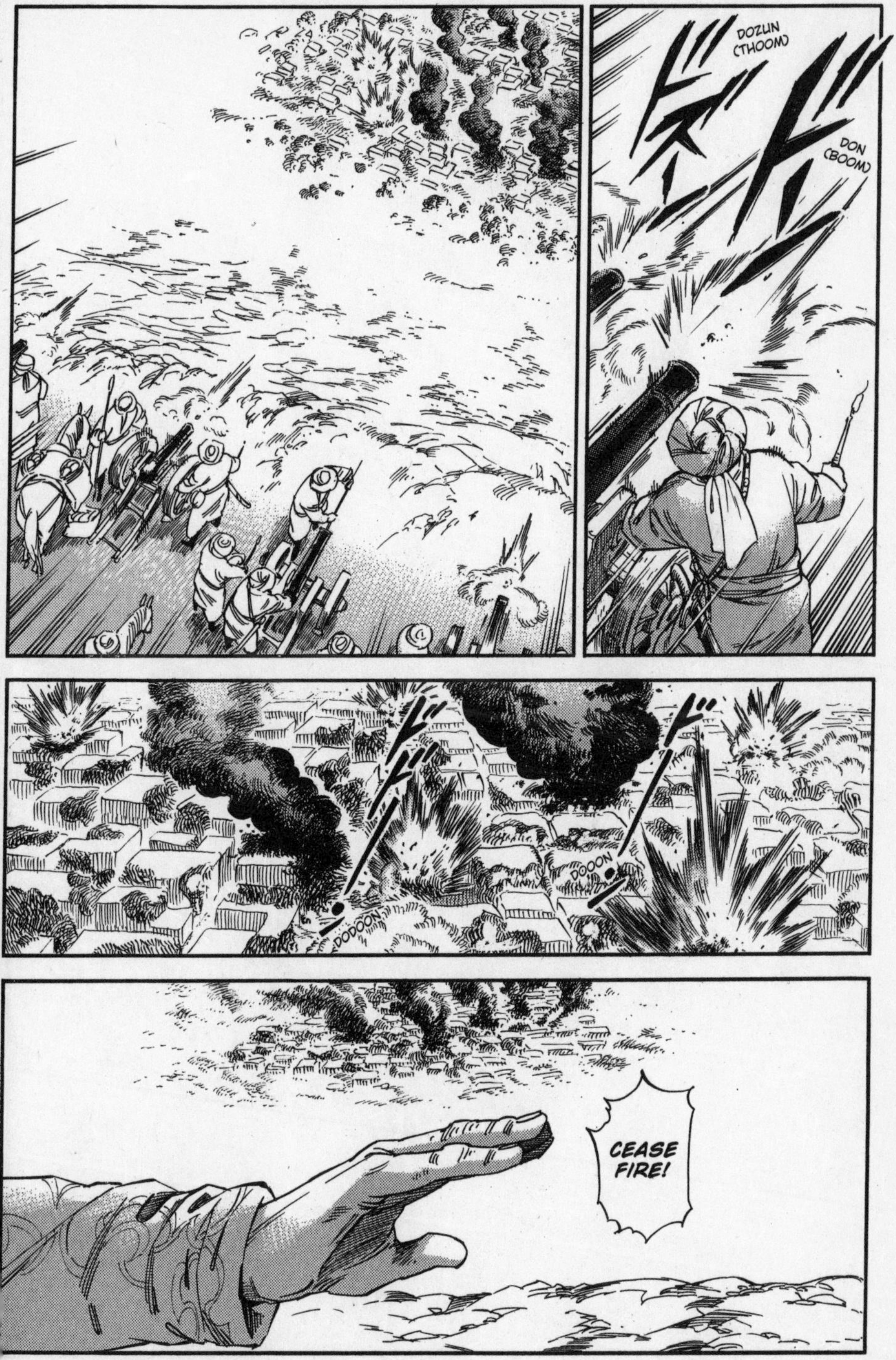
DOZUN (THOOM)
DON (BOOM)
DOOON
DODOON
CEASE FIRE!

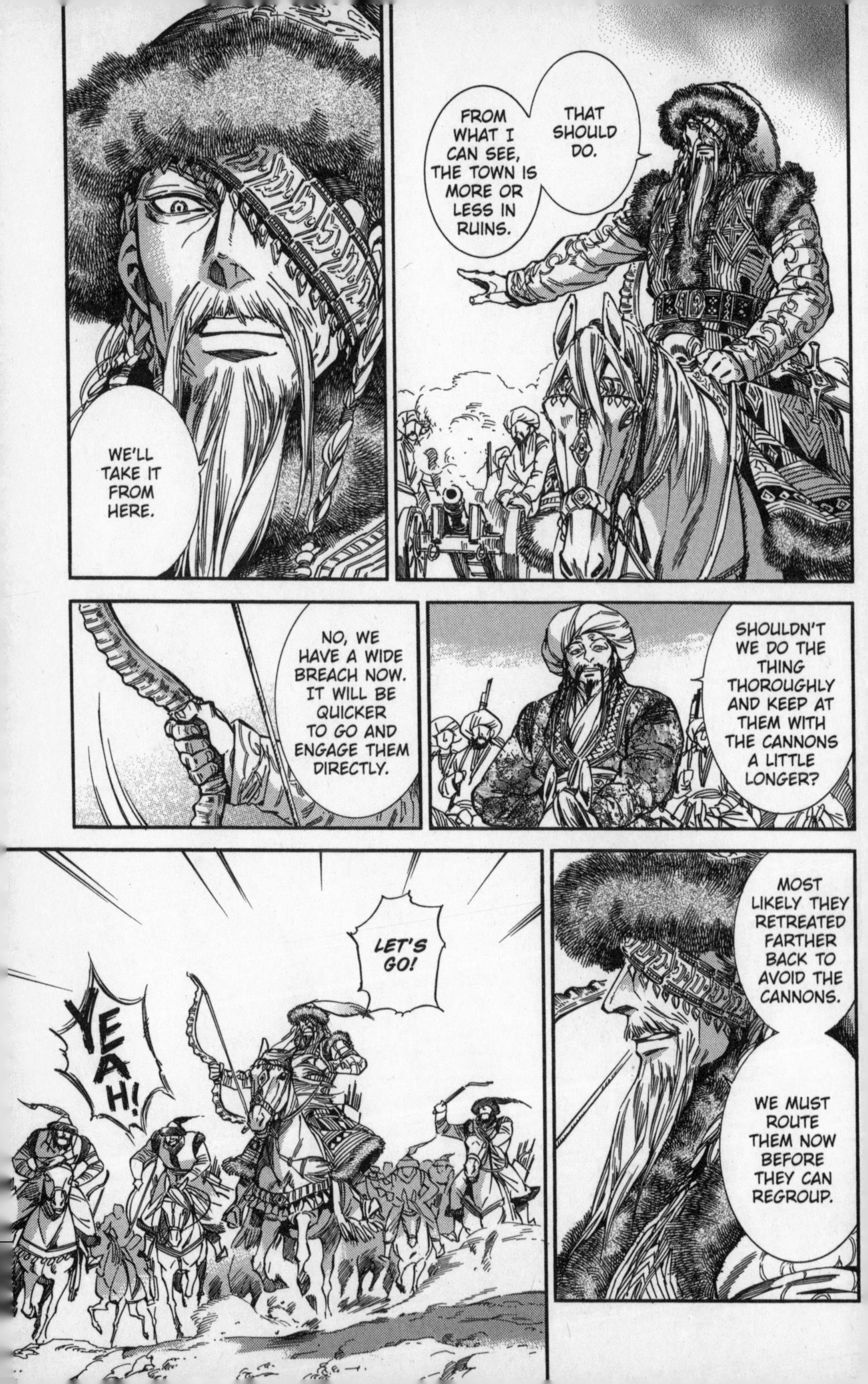
THAT SHOULD DO.
FROM WHAT I CAN SEE, THE TOWN IS MORE OR LESS IN RUINS.
WE'LL TAKE IT FROM HERE.
SHOULDN'T WE DO THE THING THOROUGHLY AND KEEP AT THEM WITH THE CANNONS A LITTLE LONGER?
NO, WE HAVE A WIDE BREACH NOW. IT WILL BE QUICKER TO GO AND ENGAGE THEM DIRECTLY.
MOST LIKELY THEY RETREATED FARTHER BACK TO AVOID THE CANNONS.
WE MUST ROUTE THEM NOW BEFORE THEY CAN REGROUP.
LET'S GO!
YEAH!

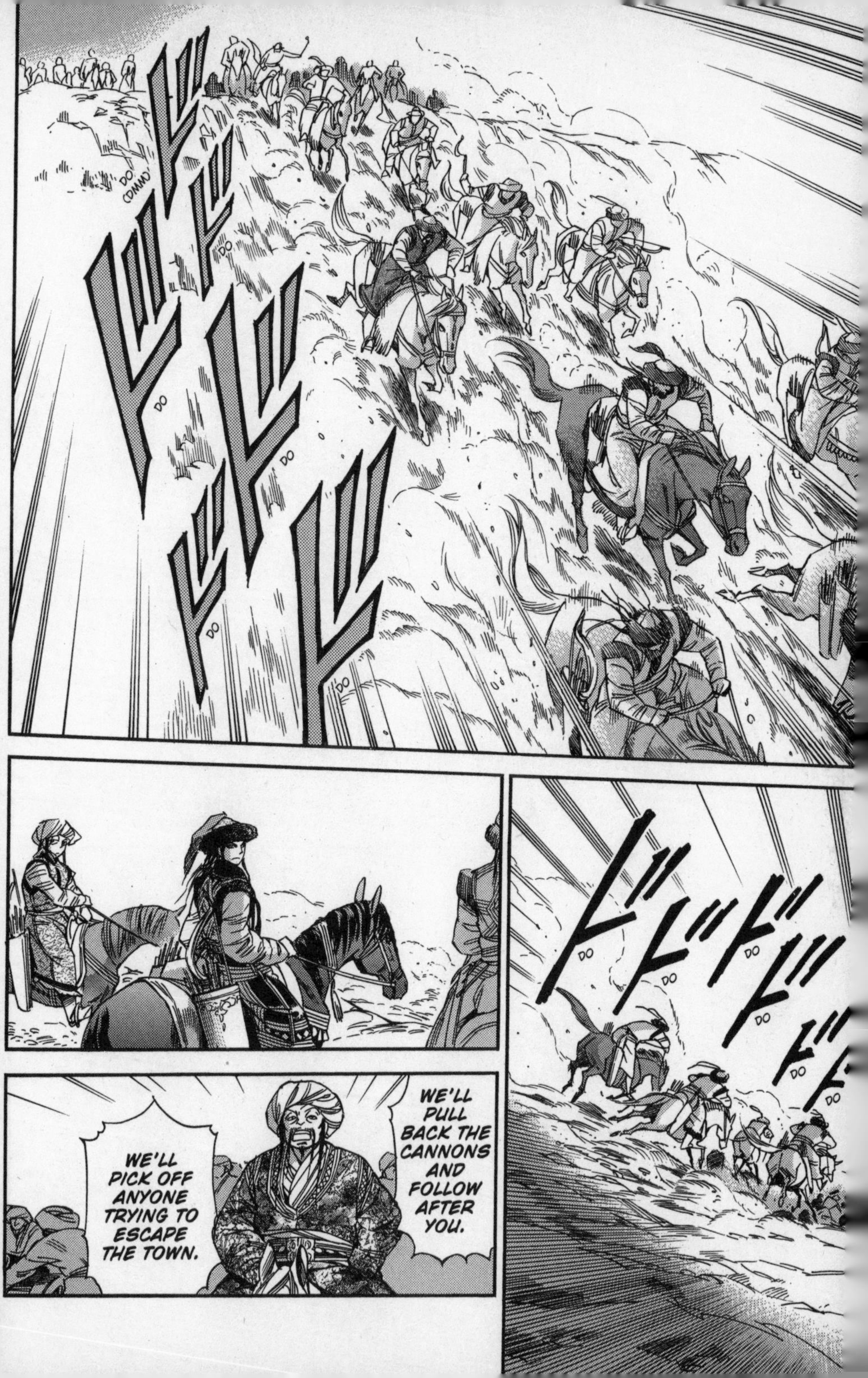
DO (DMM)
DO
DO
DO
DO
DO
DO
DO
DO
DO
DO
DO
WE'LL PULL BACK THE CANNONS AND FOLLOW AFTER YOU.
WE'LL PICK OFF ANYONE TRYING TO ESCAPE THE TOWN.

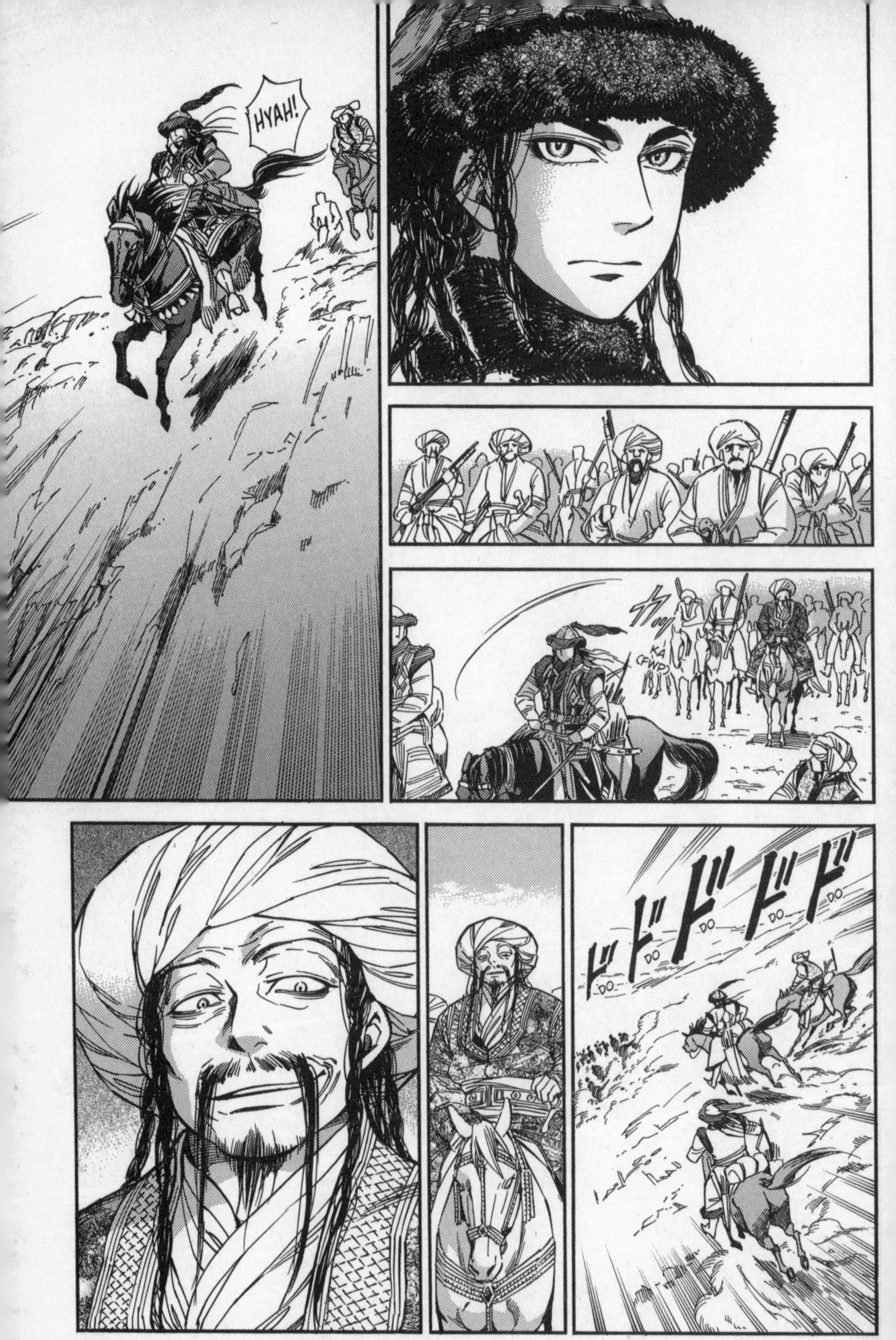
KA (FWP)
HYAH!
ドドドドド
DO DO DO DO DO

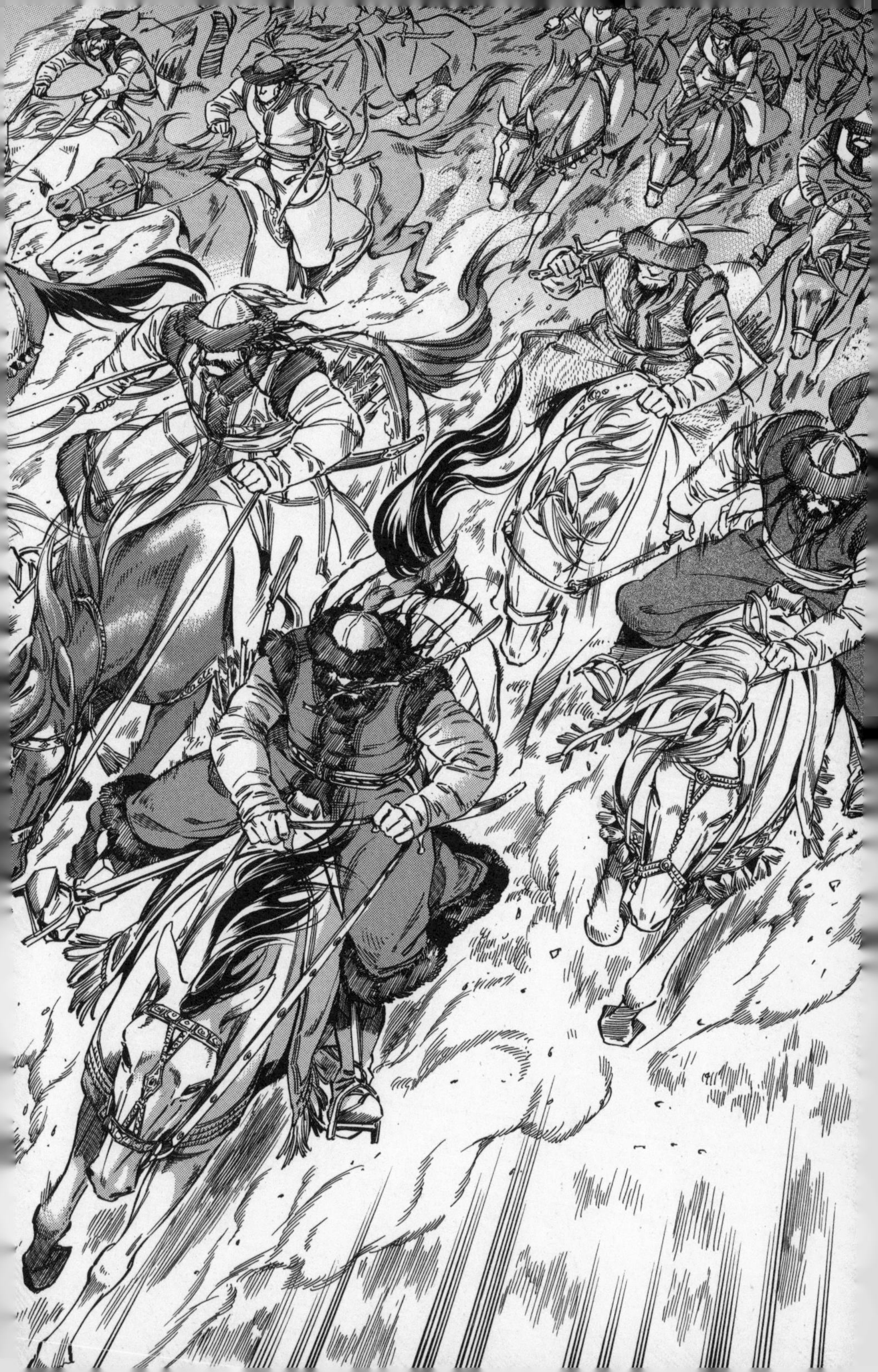

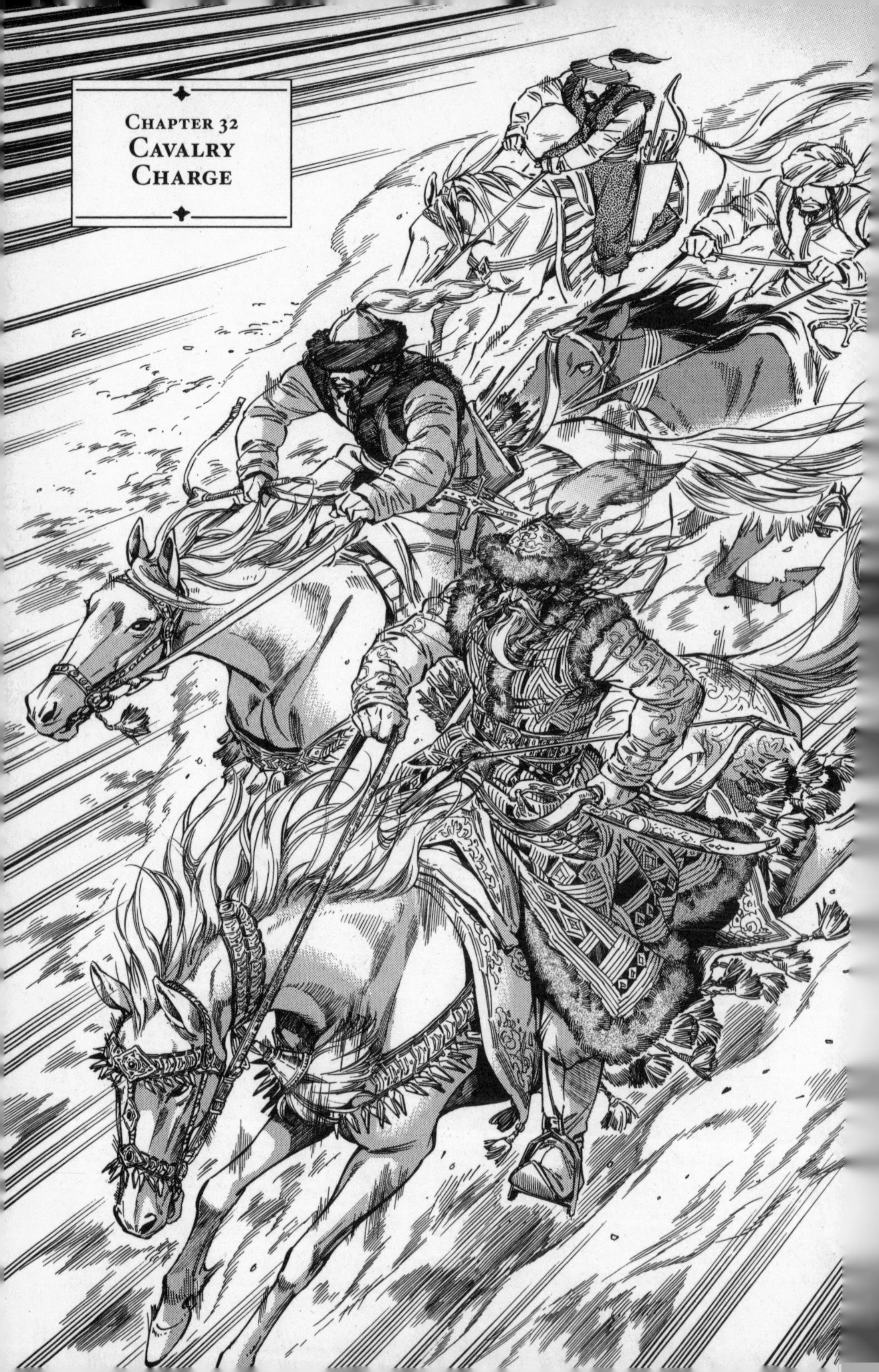
Chapter 32
Cavalry Charge

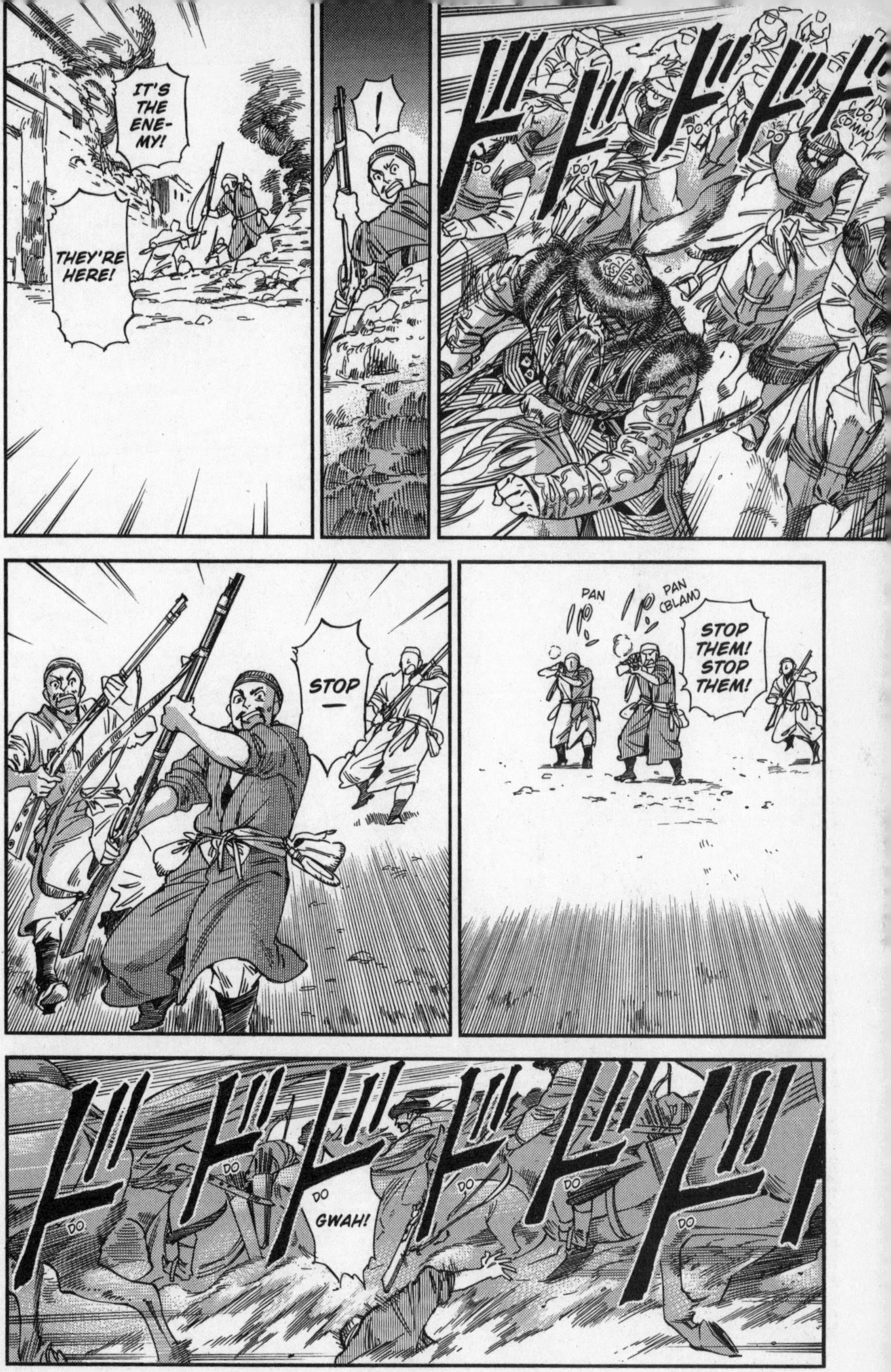
DO DO DO DO
DO (DMM)
!
IT'S THE ENEMY!
THEY'RE HERE!
PAN PAN (BLAM)
STOP THEM! STOP THEM!
STOP—
DO DO DO
DO
GWAH!
DO DO

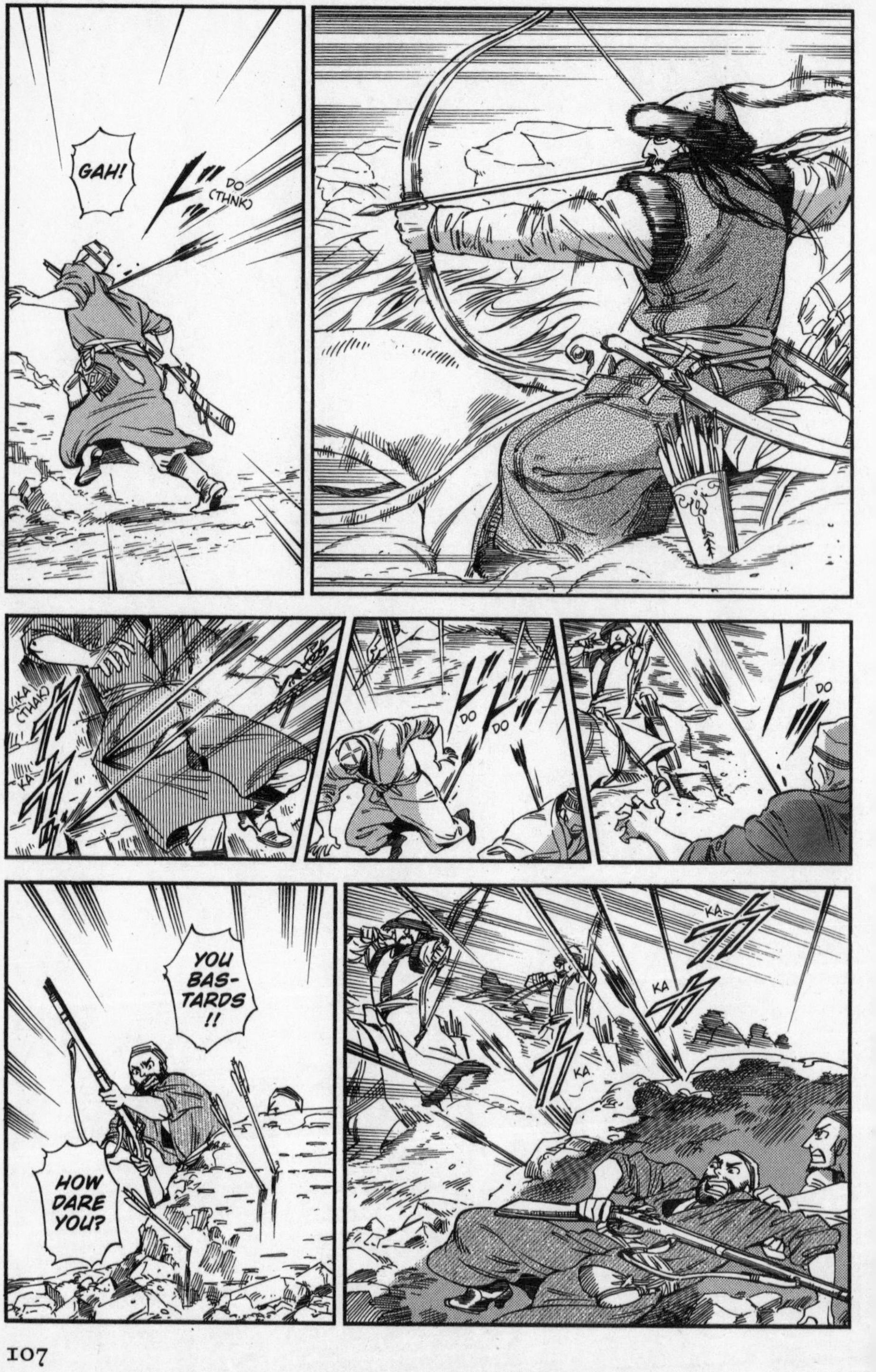
GAH!
DO (THNK)
DO
DO
DO
KA (THAK)
KA
KA
KA
KA
YOU BAS-TARDS!!
HOW DARE YOU?

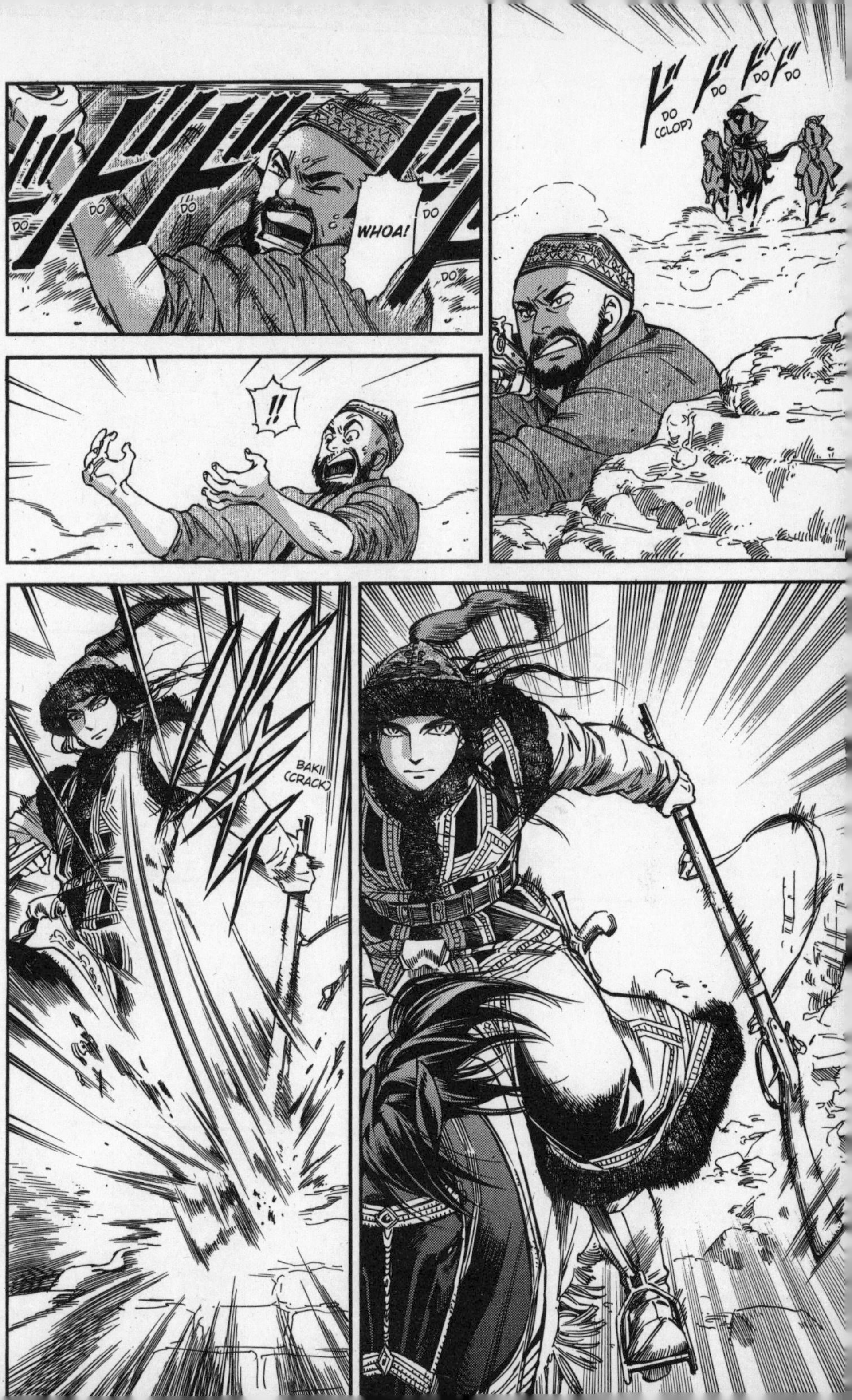
DO (CLOP)
DO
DO
DO
DO
DO
DO
WHOA!
DO
DO
!!
BAKII (CRACK)

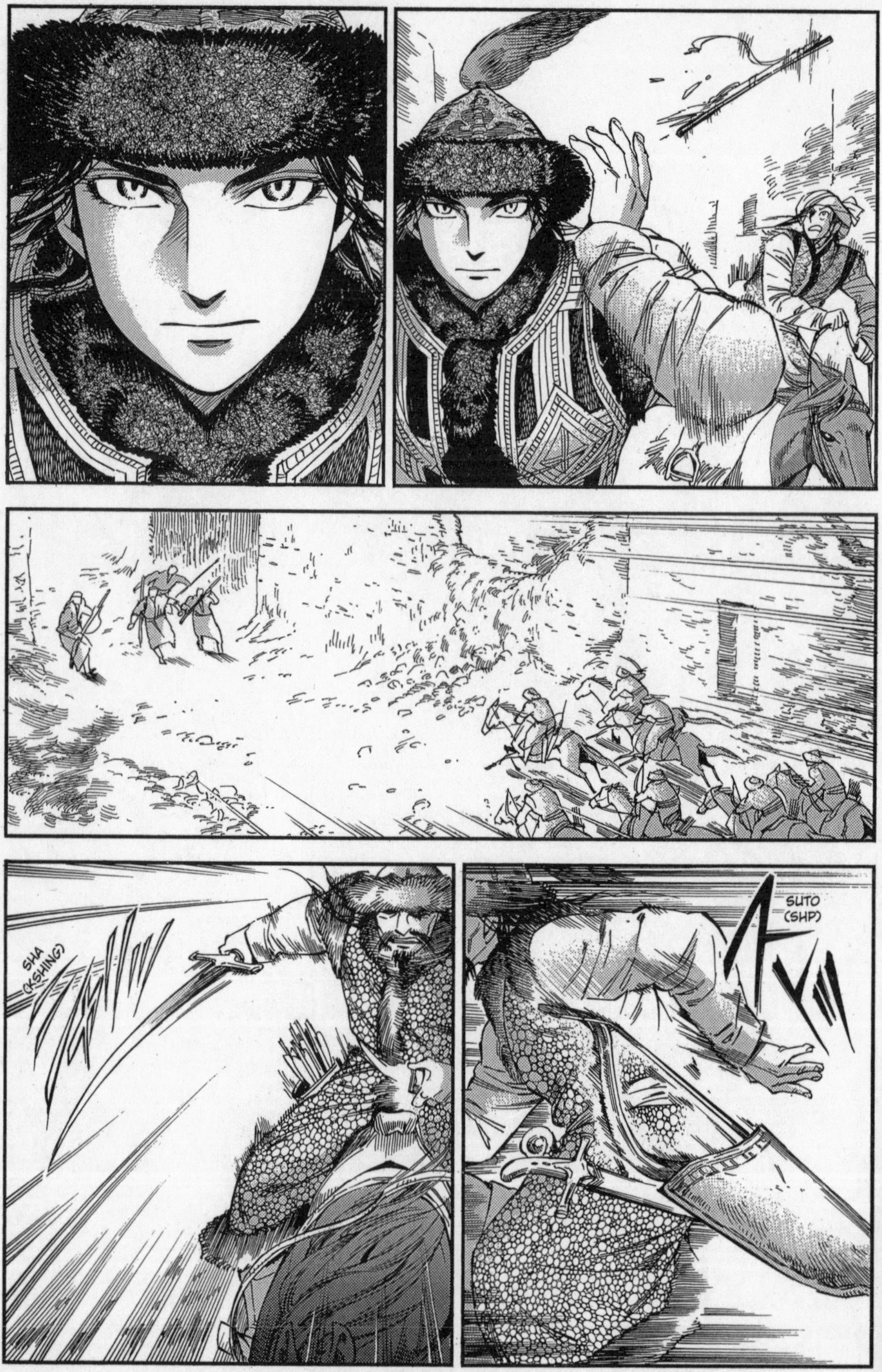
SUTO (SHP)
SHA (KSHING)

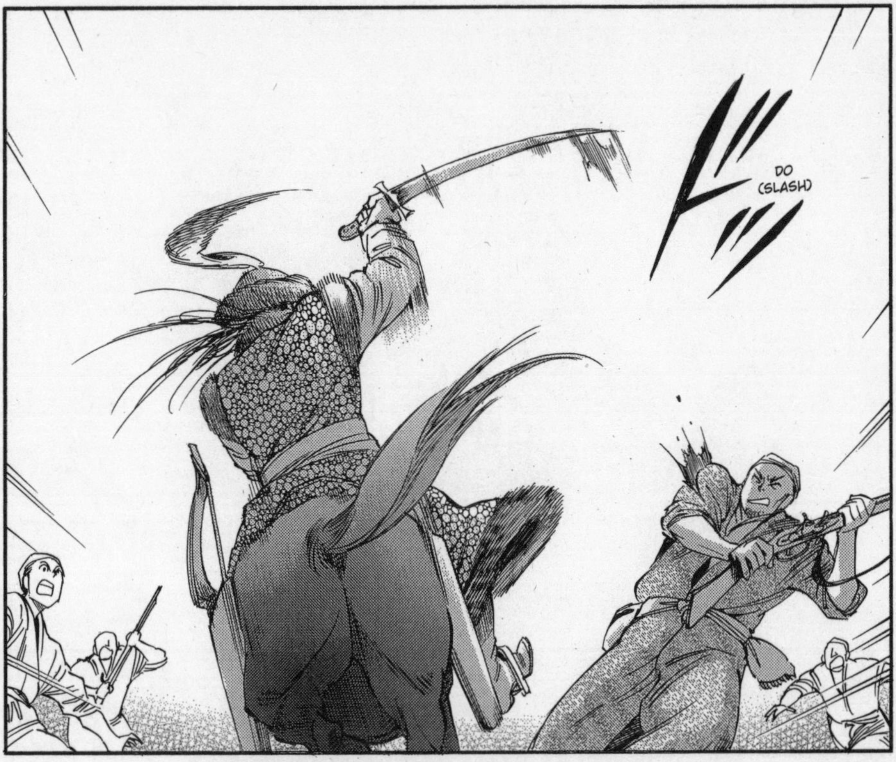
DO
(SLASH)
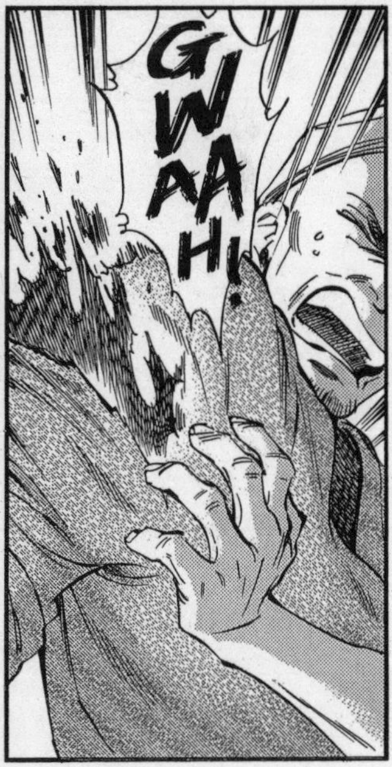
GWAAH!
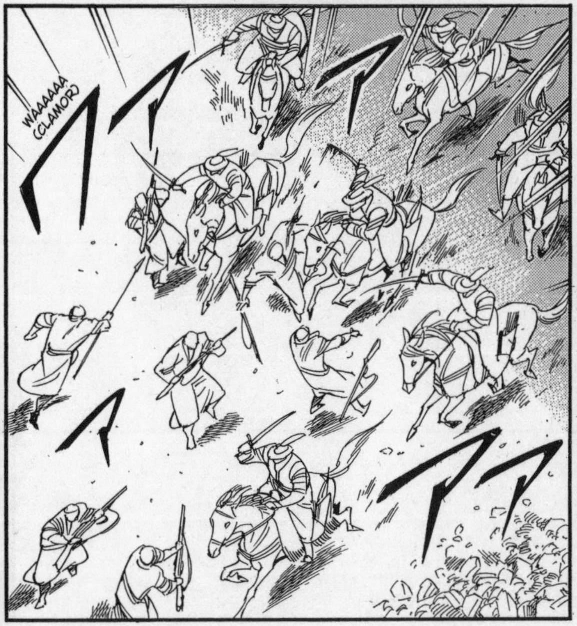
WAAAAAA
(CLAMOR)

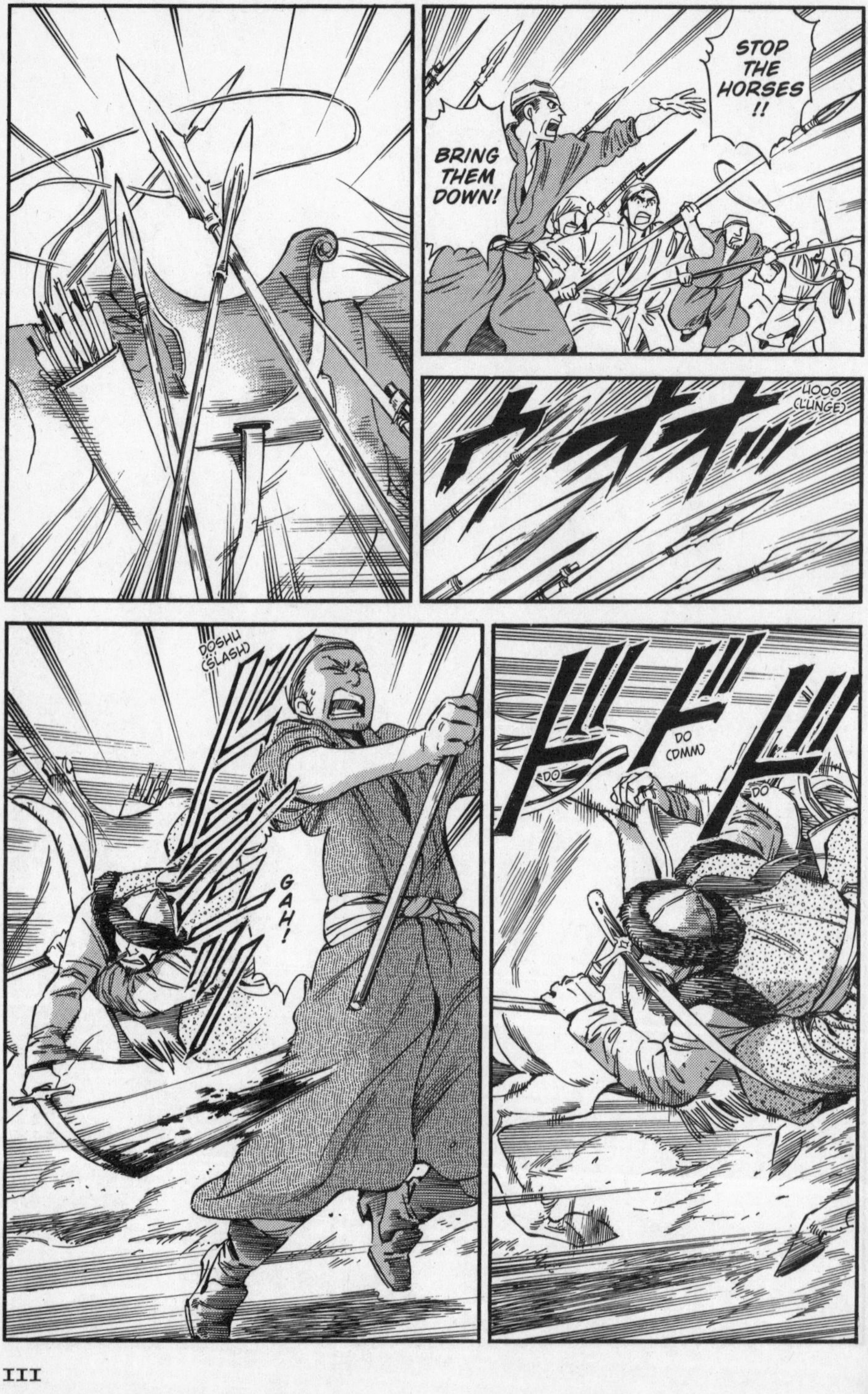
STOP THE HORSES !!
BRING THEM DOWN!
UOOO (LUNGE)
DO (DMM)
DO
DO
DOSHU (SLASH)
GAH!

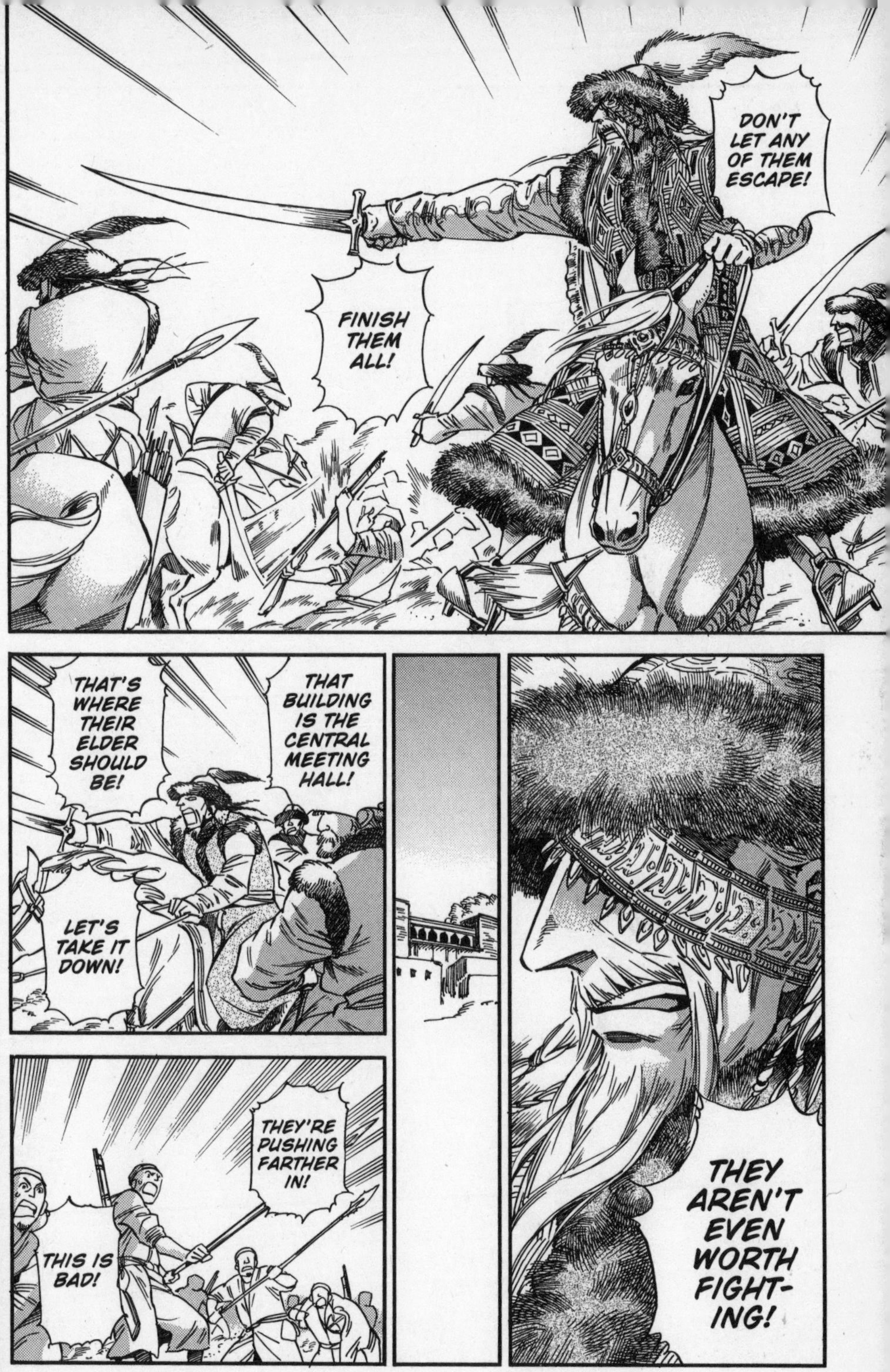
DON'T LET ANY OF THEM ESCAPE!
FINISH THEM ALL!
THEY AREN'T EVEN WORTH FIGHTING!
THAT BUILDING IS THE CENTRAL MEETING HALL!
THAT'S WHERE THEIR ELDER SHOULD BE!
LET'S TAKE IT DOWN!
THEY'RE PUSHING FARTHER IN!
THIS IS BAD!

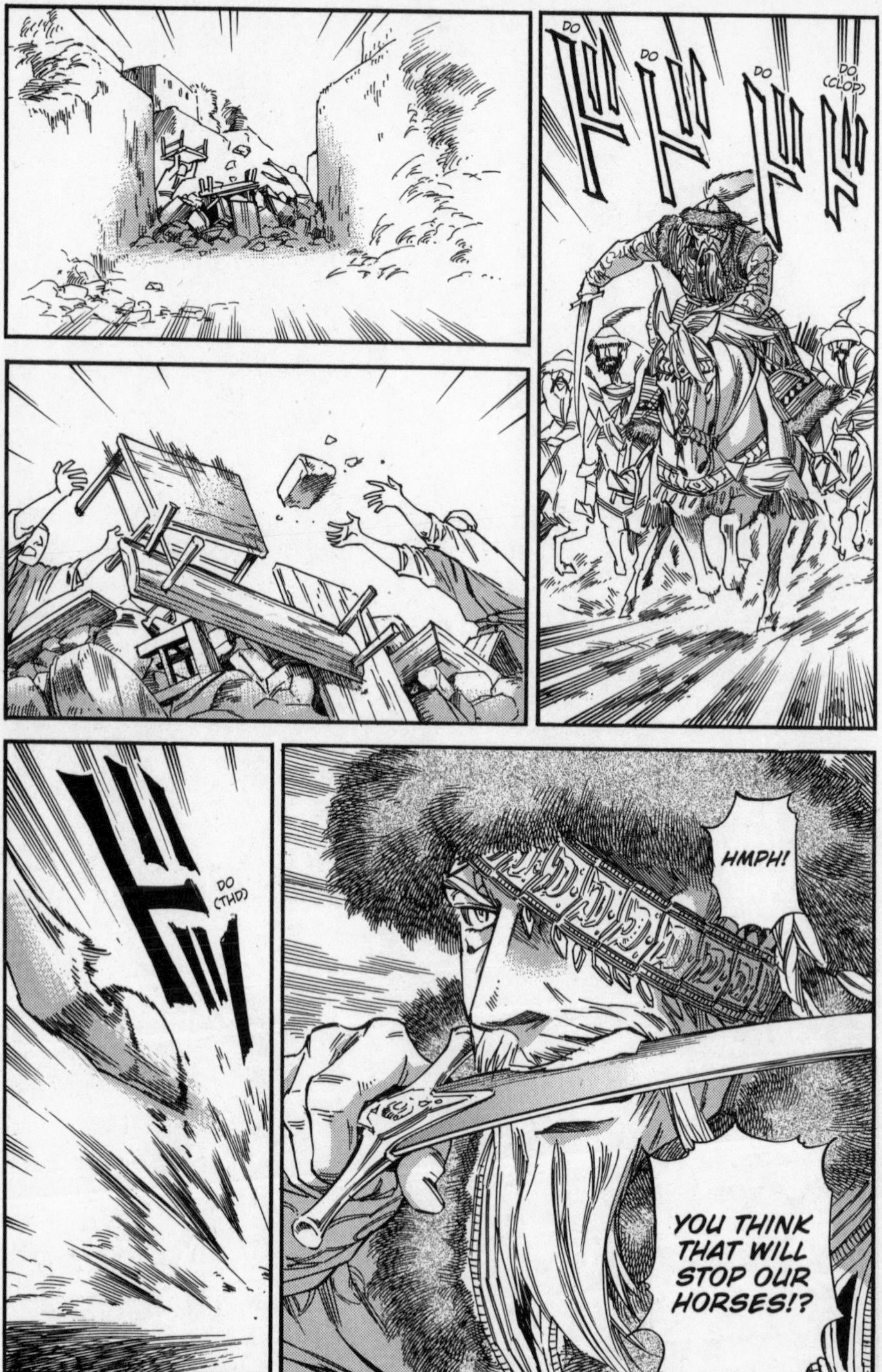
DO
DO
DO
DO
(CLOP)
HMPH!
YOU THINK THAT WILL STOP OUR HORSES!?
DO
(THD)

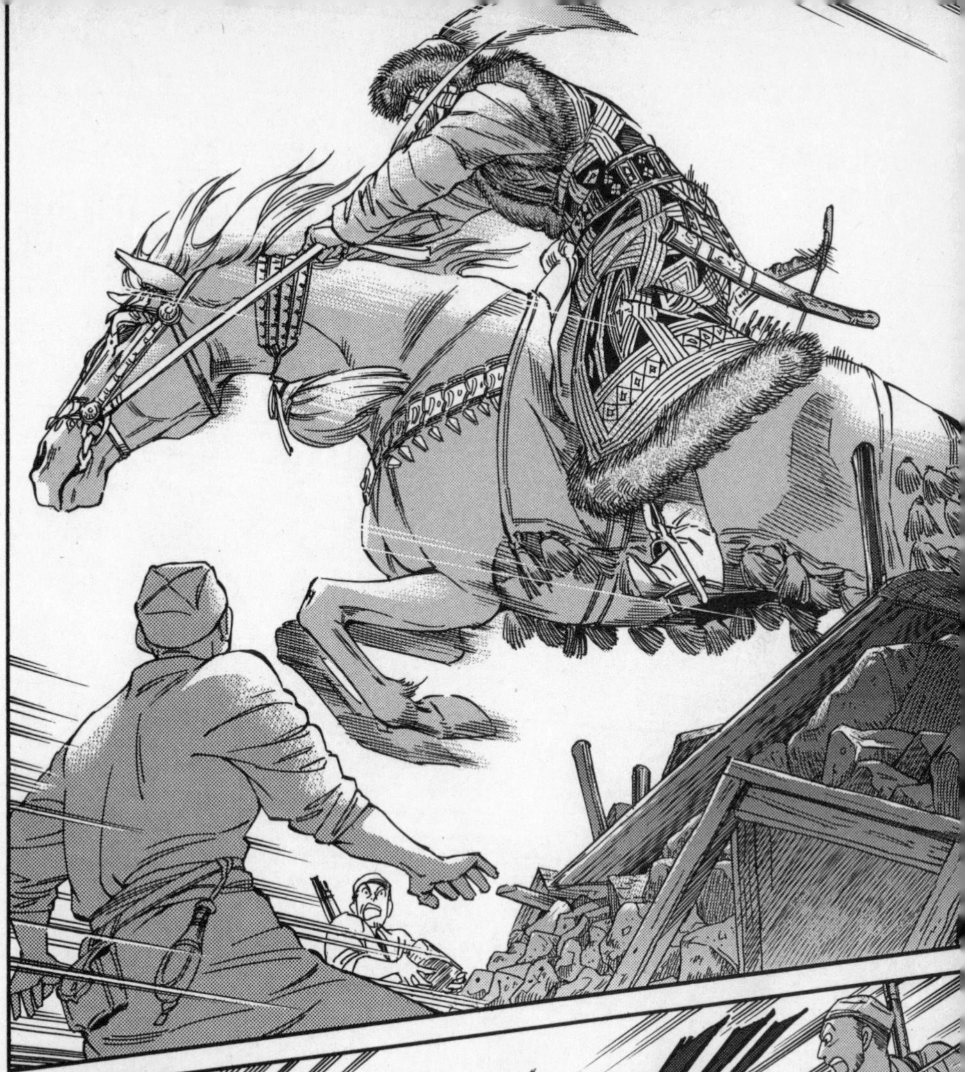

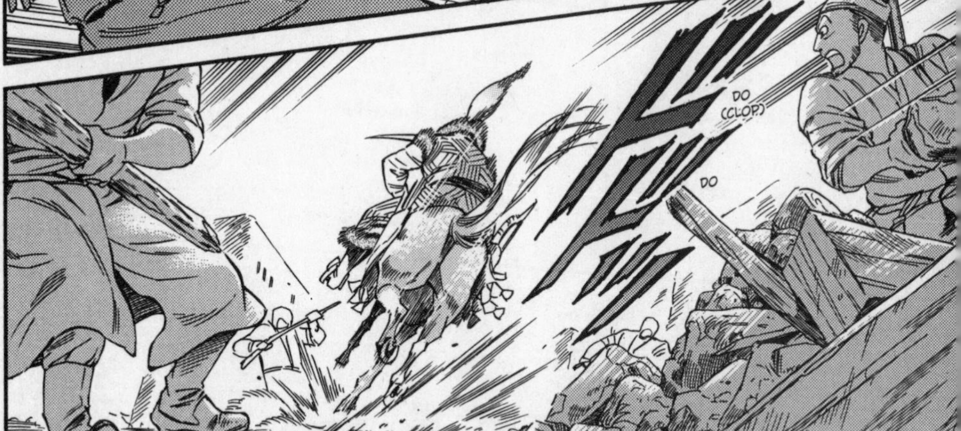

DO
(CLOP)
DO

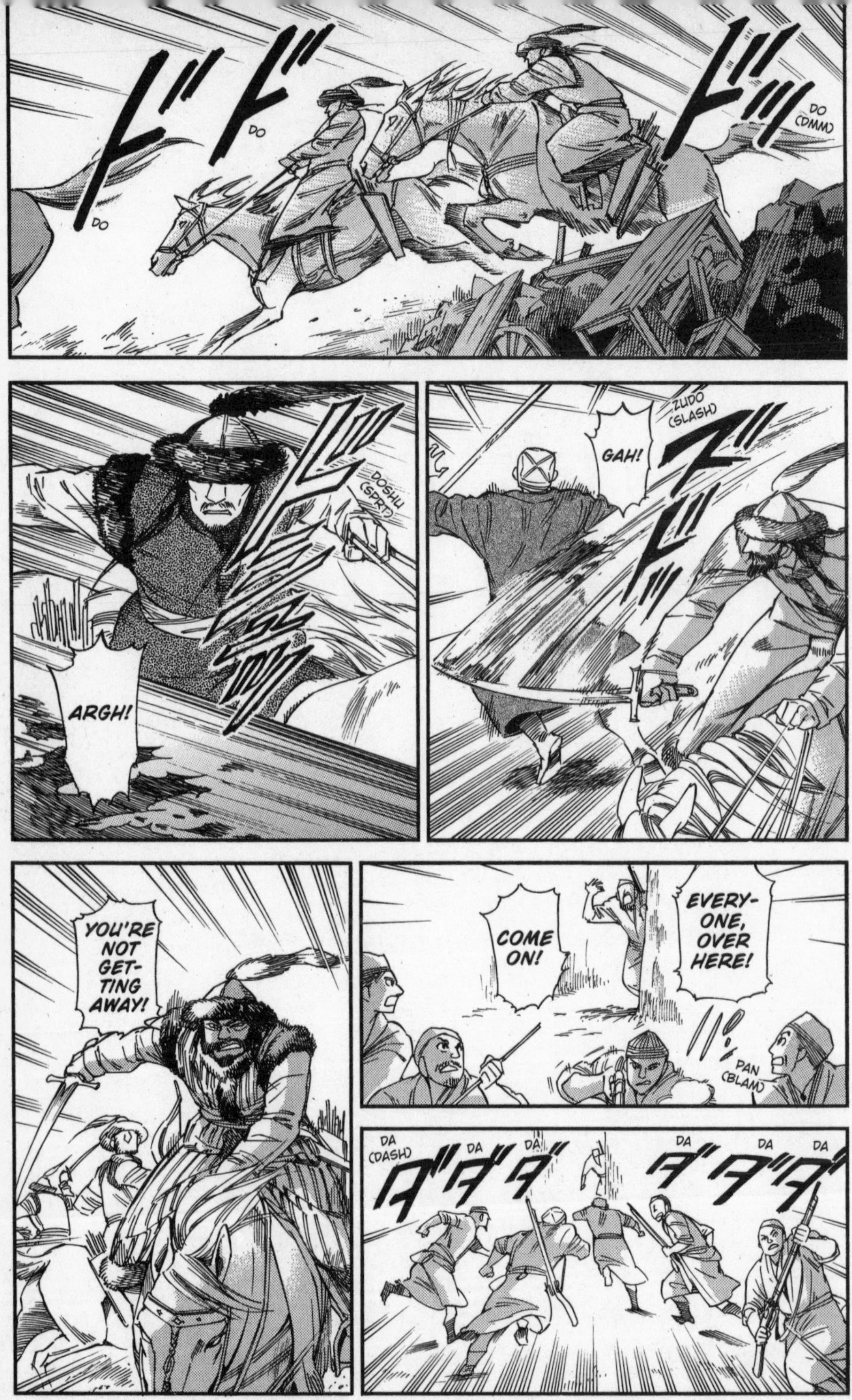
DO (DMM)
DO
DO
ZUDO (SLASH)
GAH!
DOSHU (SPRT)
ARGH!
EVERY-ONE, OVER HERE!
COME ON!
PAN (BLAM)
DA
DA
DA
DA
DA
DA (DASH)
YOU'RE NOT GET-TING AWAY!

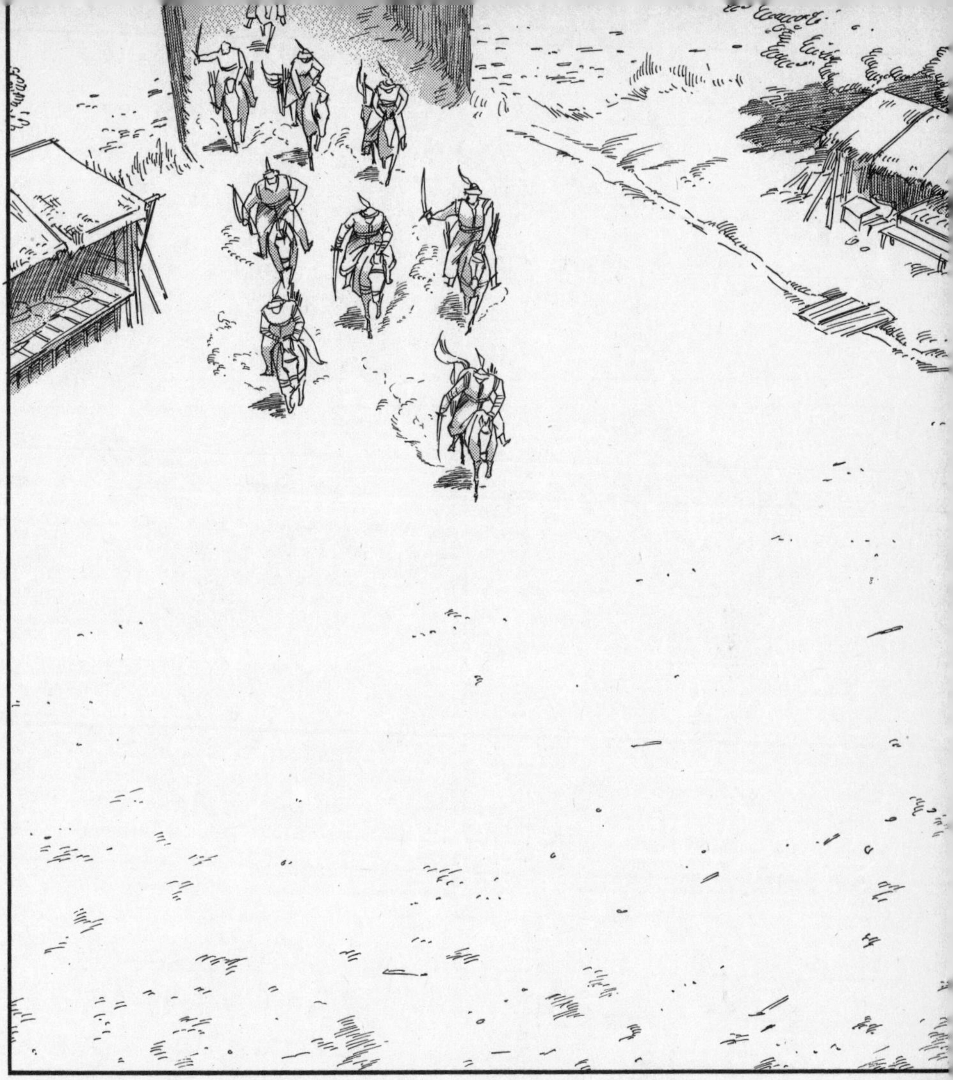

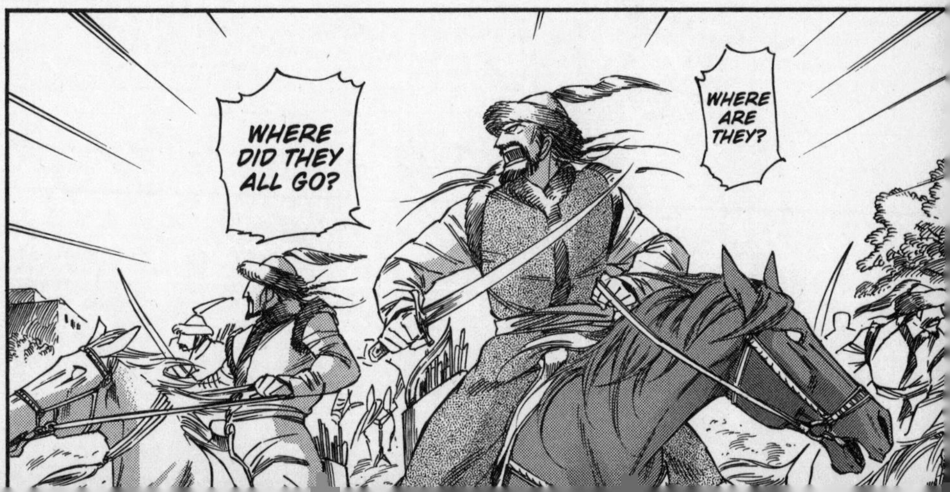

WHERE ARE THEY?
WHERE DID THEY ALL GO?

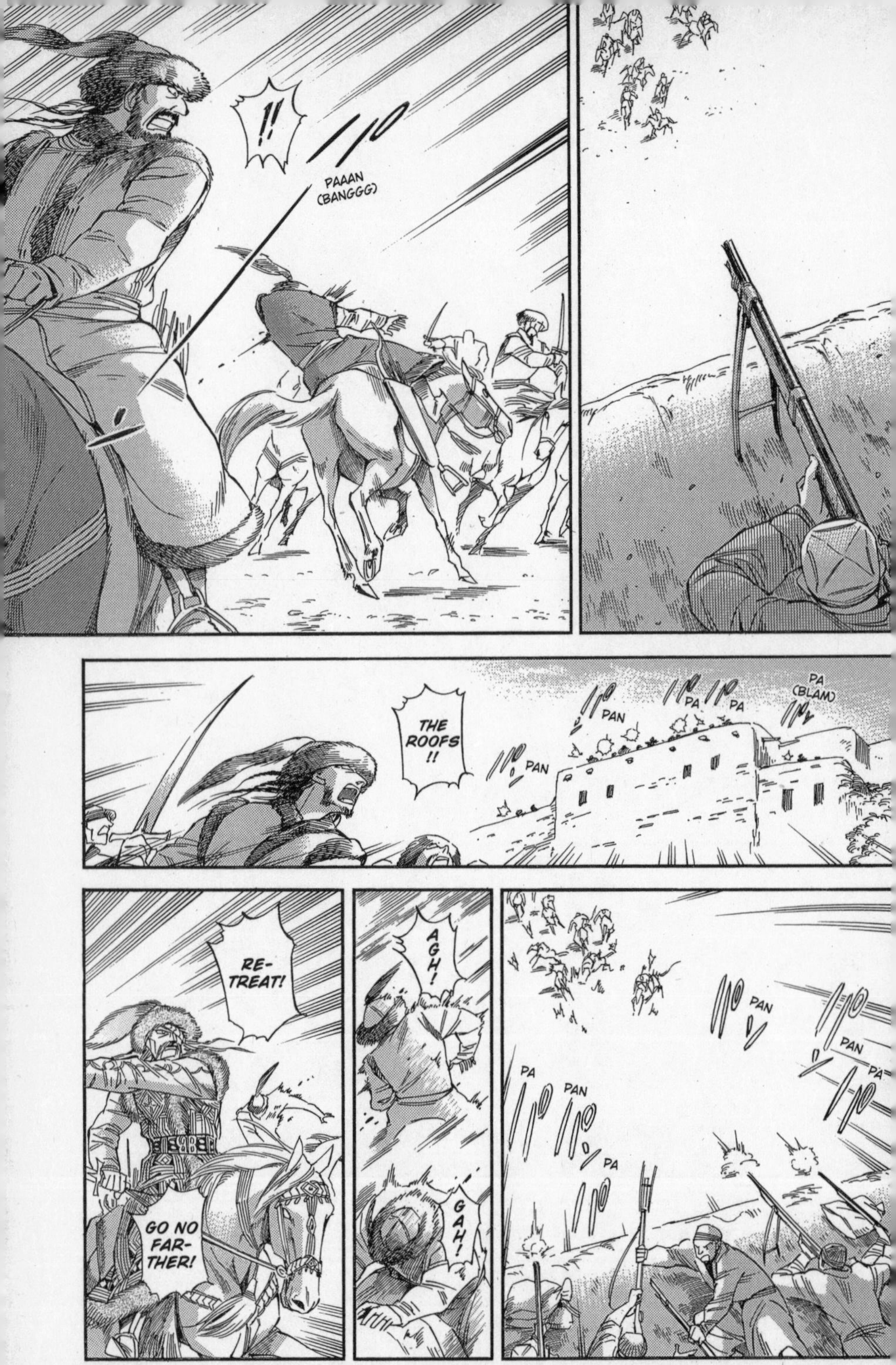
!!
PAAAN (BANGGG)
PA (BLAM)
PA
PA
PAN
PAN
THE ROOFS !!
PAN
PAN
PA
PA
PAN
PA
AGH!
GAH!
RE-TREAT!
GO NO FARTHER!

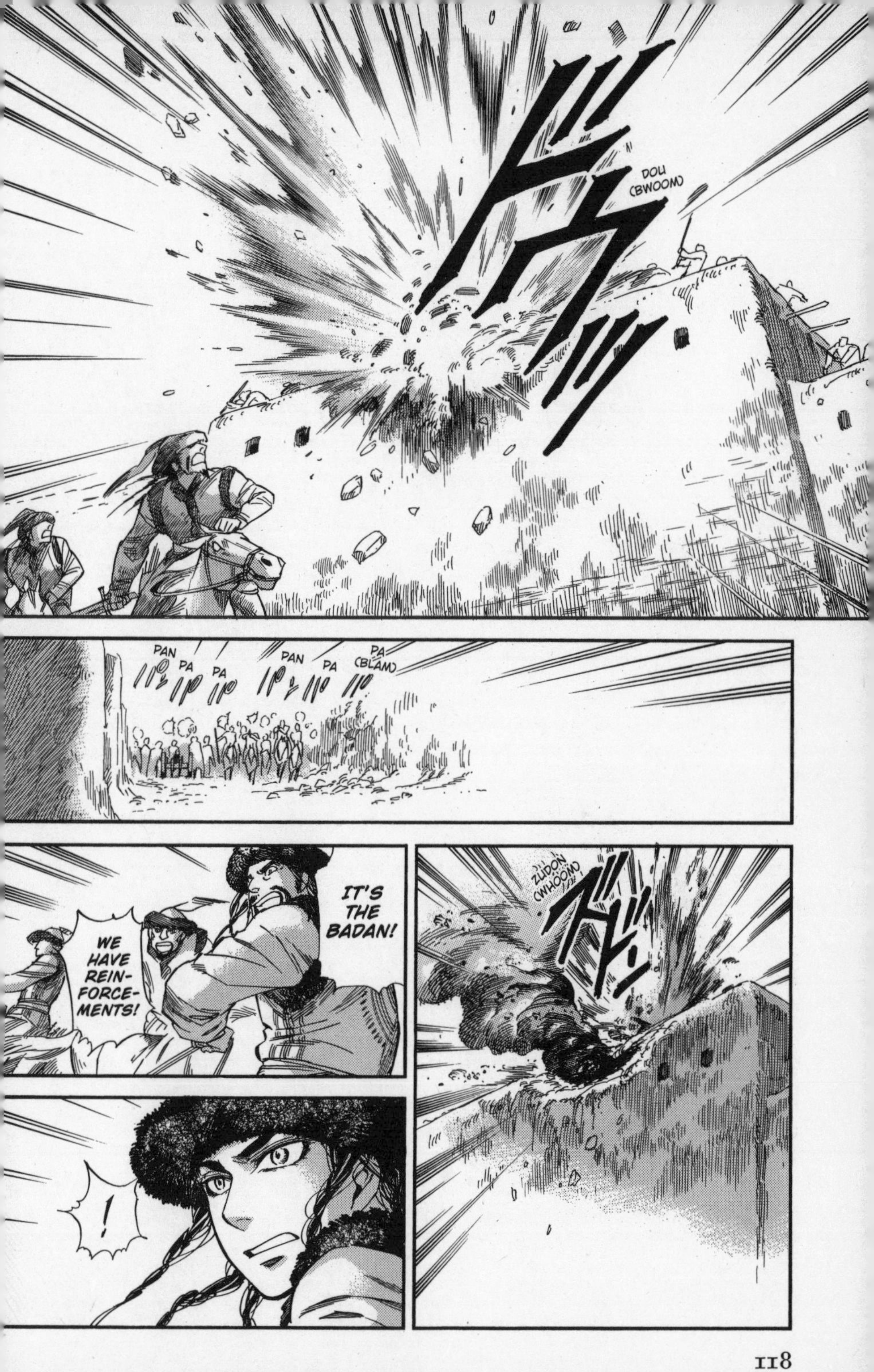
DOU (BWOOM)
PAN PA PA PAN PA PA (BLAM)
ZUDON (WHOOM)
IT'S THE BADAN!
WE HAVE REIN-FORCE-MENTS!
!

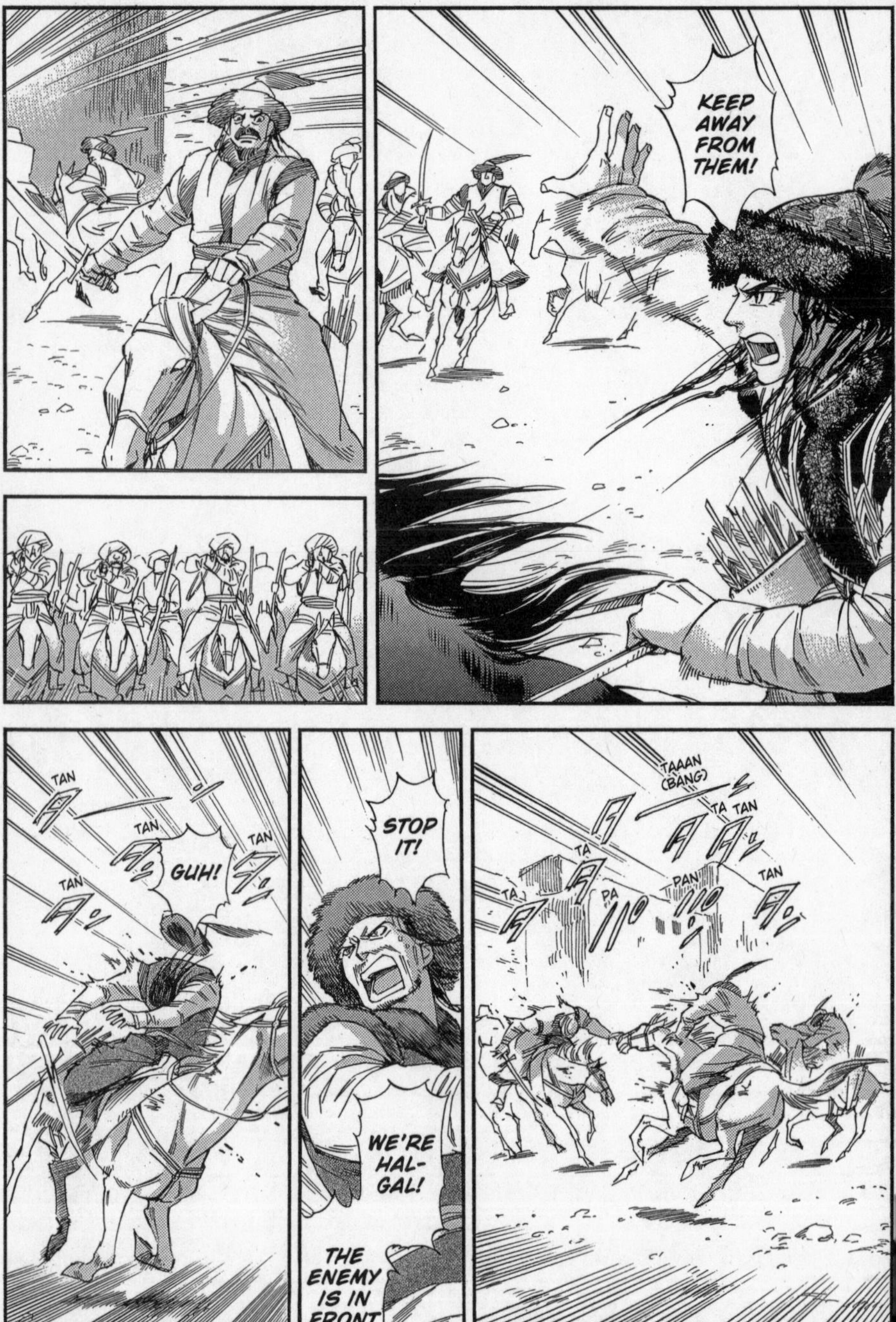
KEEP AWAY FROM THEM!
TAAAN (BANG)
TA TAN
TAN
TA
PAN
PA
TA
STOP IT!
WE'RE HAL-GAL!
THE ENEMY IS IN FRONT —
TAN
TAN
GUH!
TAN
TAN

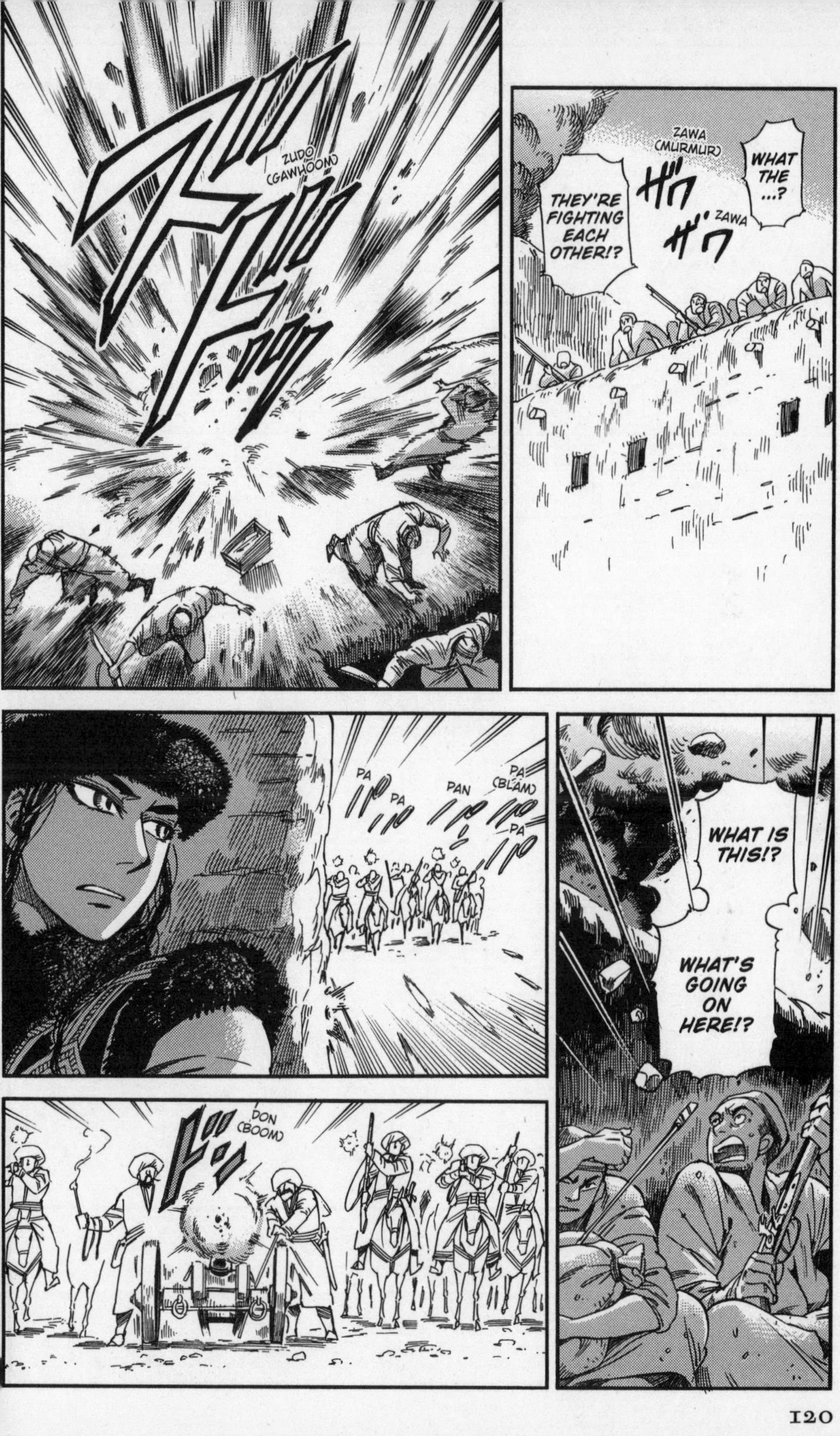
WHAT THE ...?
ZAWA (MURMUR)
ザワ
THEY'RE FIGHTING EACH OTHER!?
ザワ
ZAWA
ZUDO (GAWHOOM)
WHAT IS THIS!?
WHAT'S GOING ON HERE!?
PA (BLAM)
PAN
PA
PA
PA
DON (BOOM)

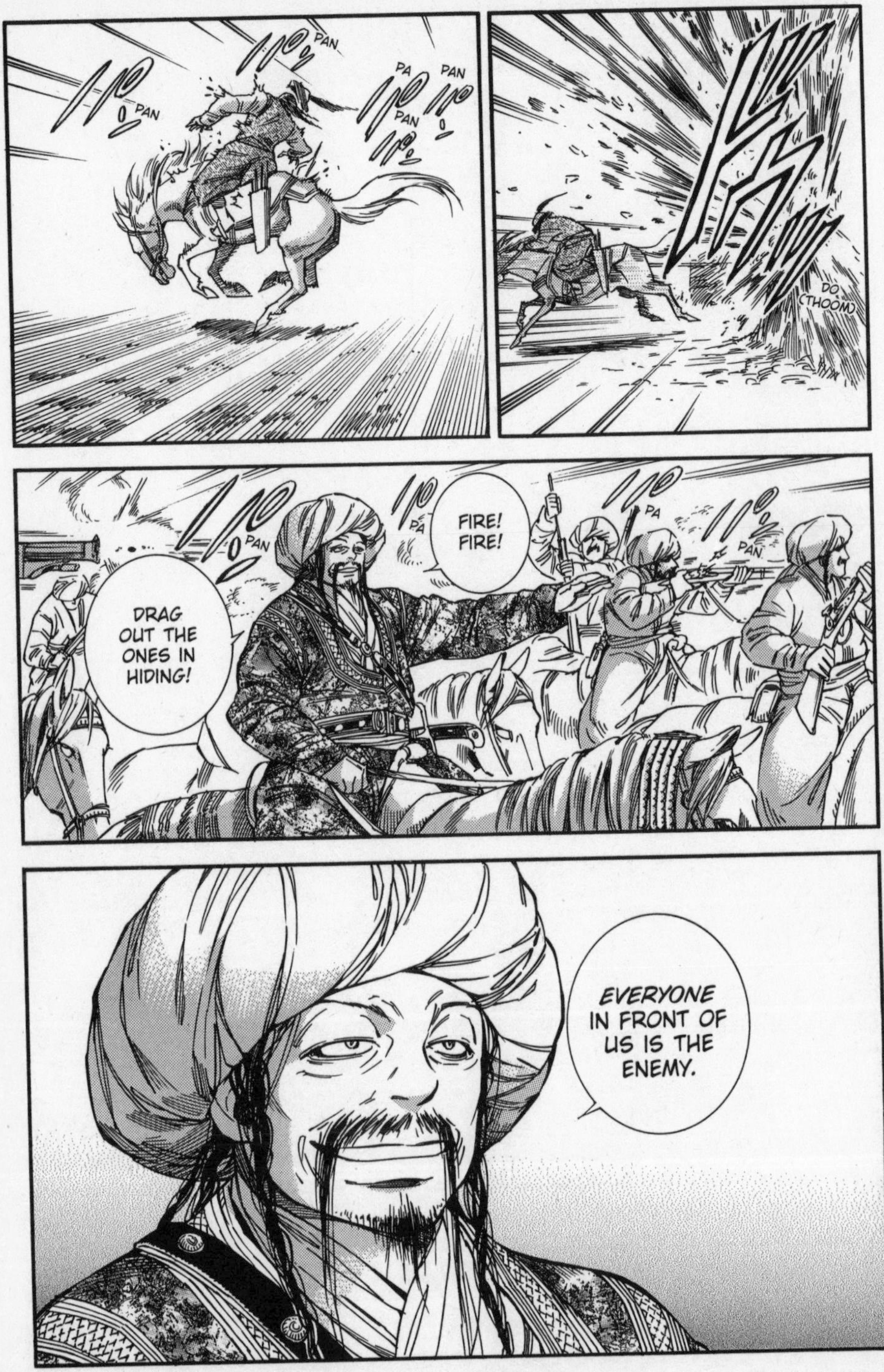
DO (THOOM)
PAN
PA
PAN
PAN
PAN
PA
PAN
FIRE! FIRE!
PA
PAN
DRAG OUT THE ONES IN HIDING!
EVERYONE IN FRONT OF US IS THE ENEMY.

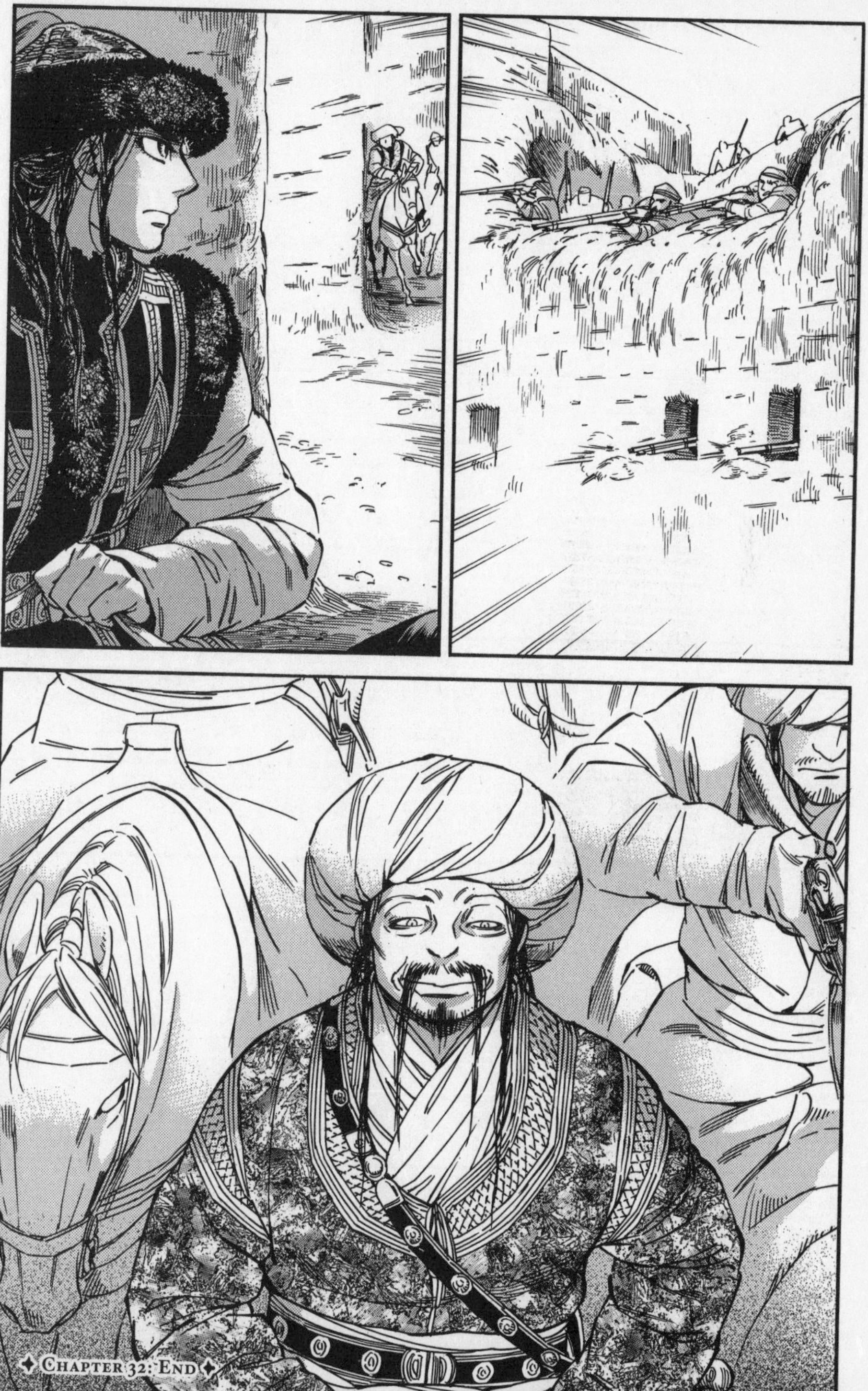
CHAPTER 32: END

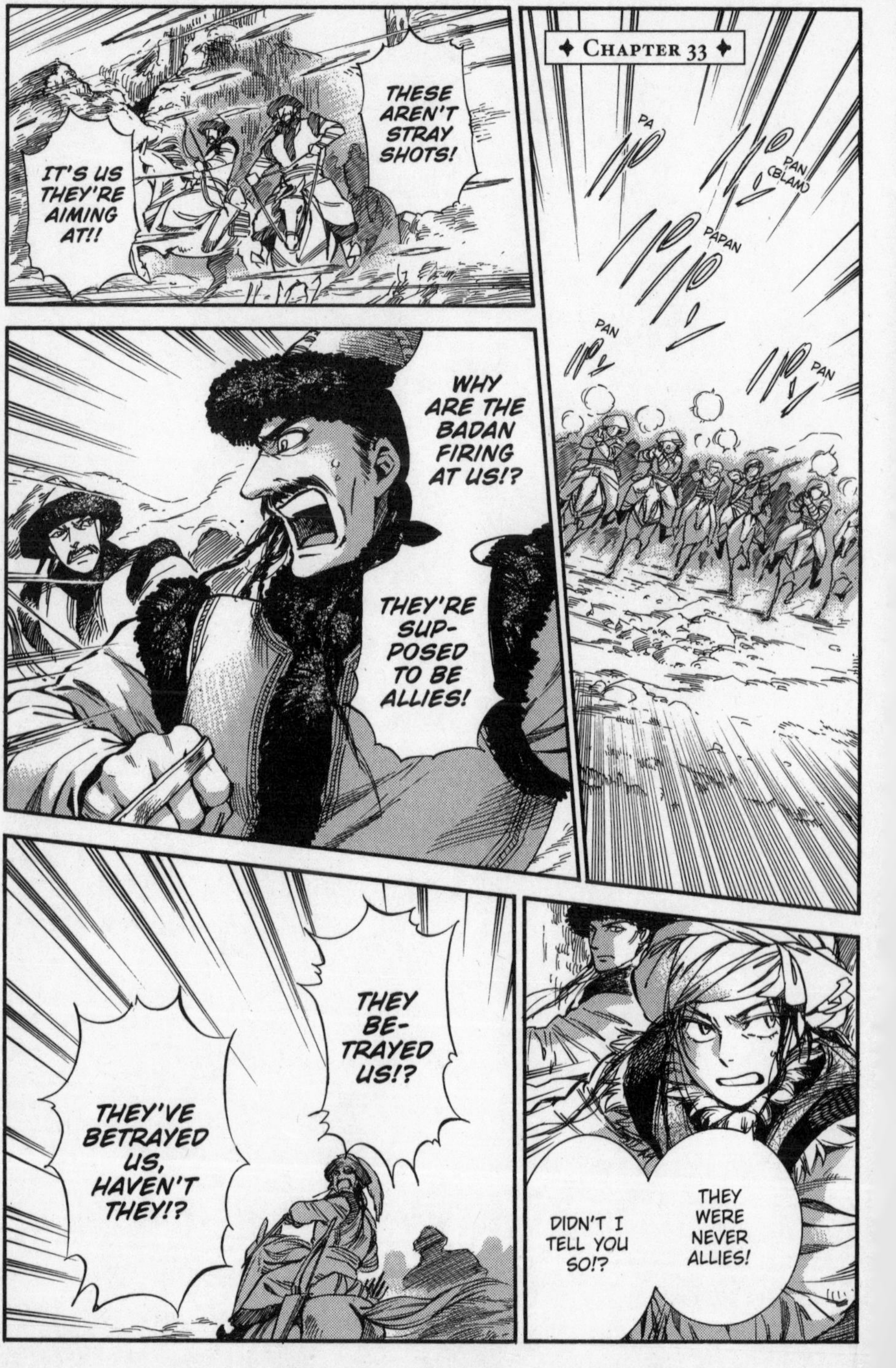

✦ CHAPTER 33 ✦
PAN (BLAM)
PA
PAPAN
PAN
PAN
THESE AREN'T STRAY SHOTS!
IT'S US THEY'RE AIMING AT!!
WHY ARE THE BADAN FIRING AT US!?
THEY'RE SUP-POSED TO BE ALLIES!
THEY WERE NEVER ALLIES!
DIDN'T I TELL YOU SO!?
THEY BE-TRAYED US!?
THEY'VE BETRAYED US, HAVEN'T THEY!?

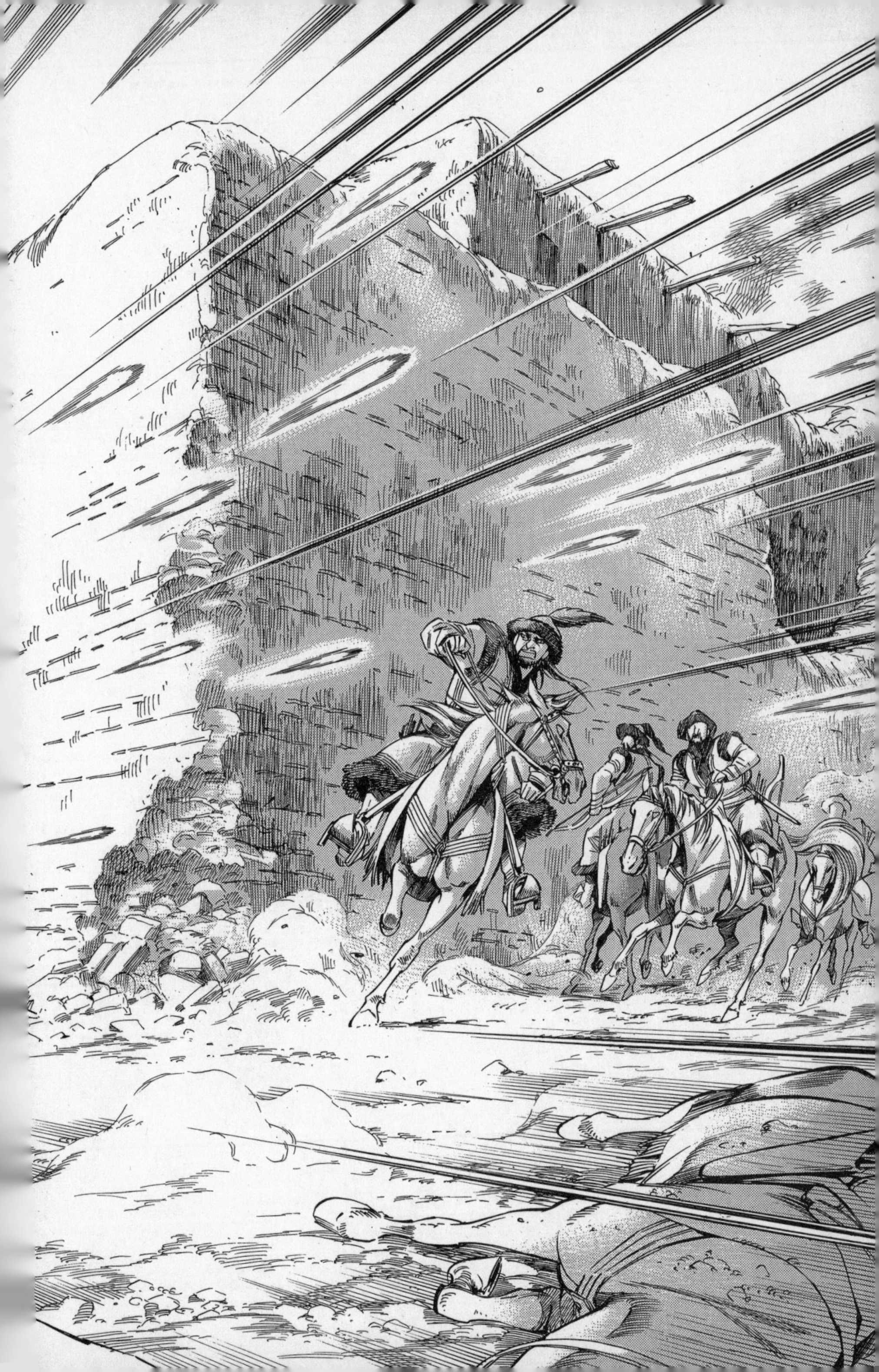

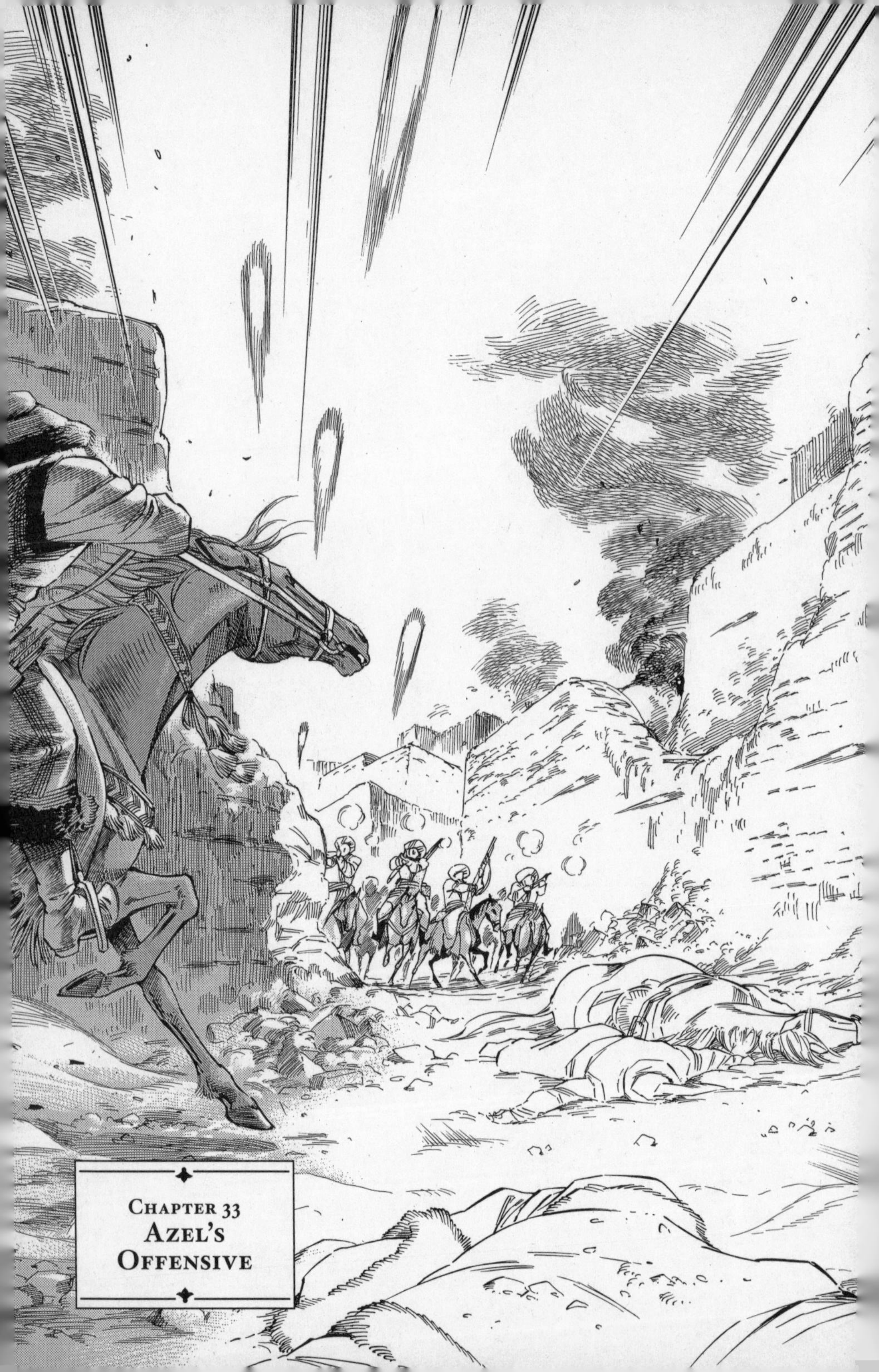
CHAPTER 33
AZEL'S
OFFENSIVE

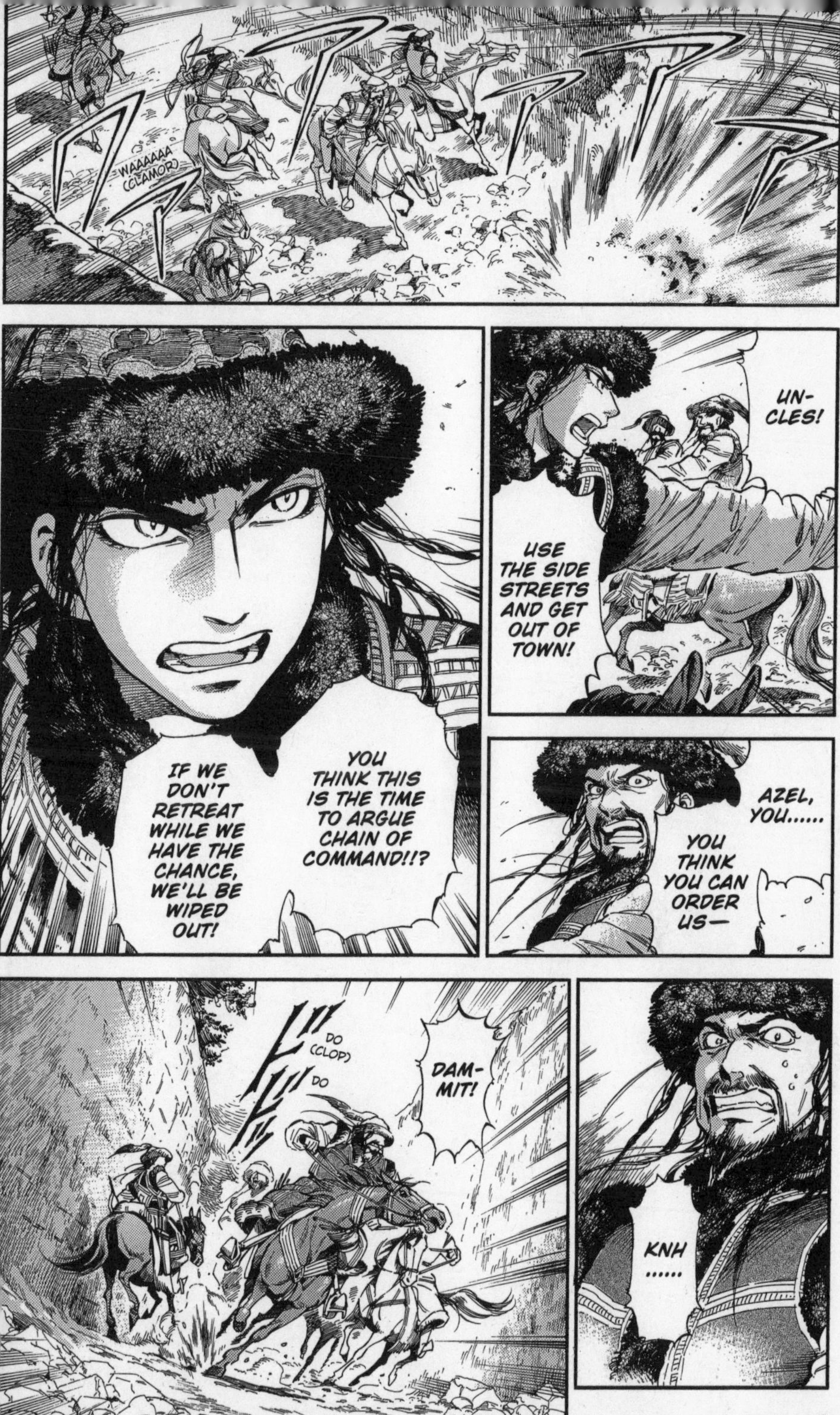
WAAAAAA (CLAMOR)
UN-CLES!
USE THE SIDE STREETS AND GET OUT OF TOWN!
AZEL, YOU......
YOU THINK YOU CAN ORDER US—
YOU THINK THIS IS THE TIME TO ARGUE CHAIN OF COMMAND!!?
IF WE DON'T RETREAT WHILE WE HAVE THE CHANCE, WE'LL BE WIPED OUT!
KNH ......
DAM-MIT!
DO (CLOP)
DO

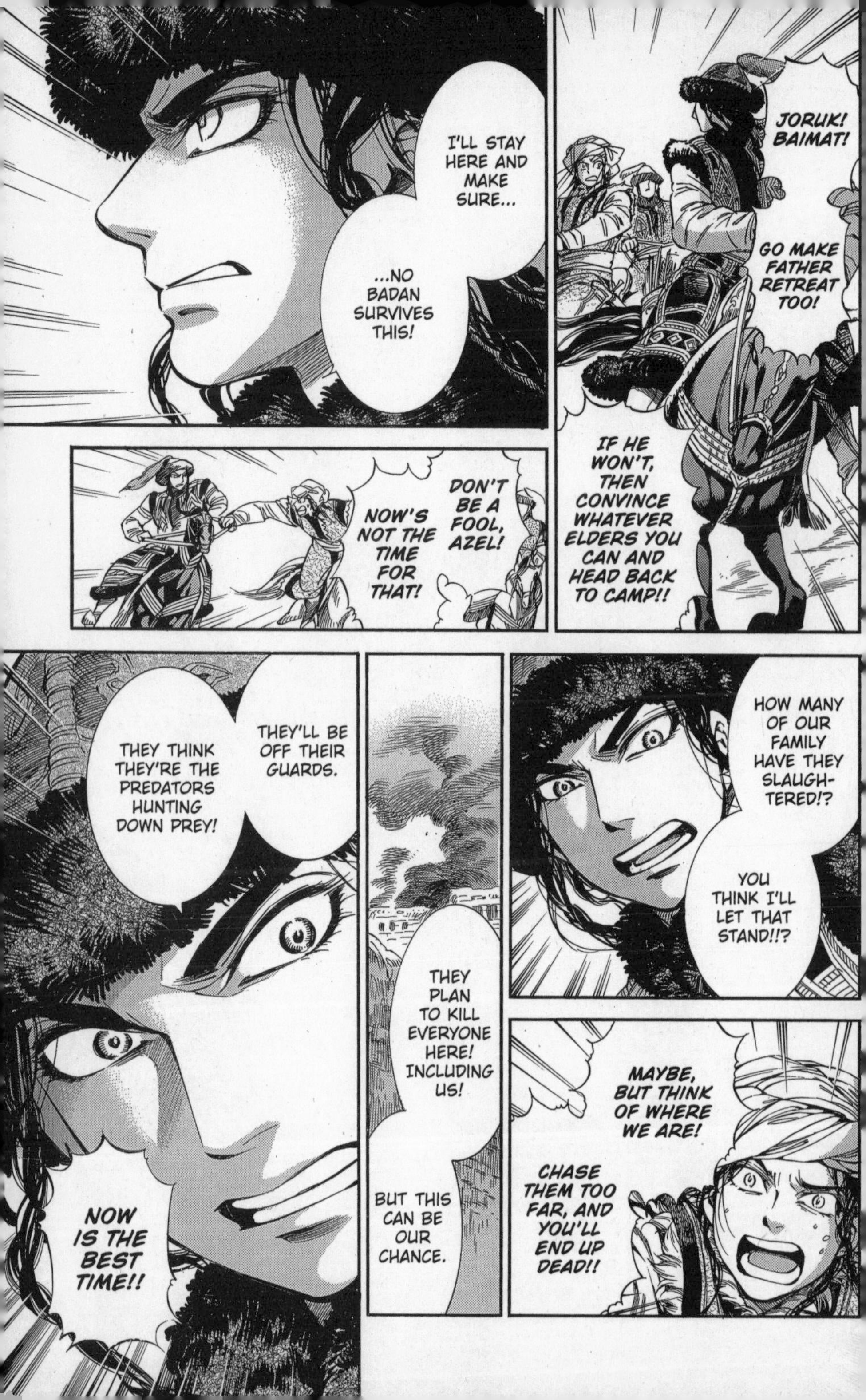
JORUK! BAIMAT!
GO MAKE FATHER RETREAT TOO!
IF HE WON'T, THEN CONVINCE WHATEVER ELDERS YOU CAN AND HEAD BACK TO CAMP!!
I'LL STAY HERE AND MAKE SURE...
...NO BADAN SURVIVES THIS!
DON'T BE A FOOL, AZEL!
NOW'S NOT THE TIME FOR THAT!
HOW MANY OF OUR FAMILY HAVE THEY SLAUGHTERED!?
YOU THINK I'LL LET THAT STAND!!?
MAYBE, BUT THINK OF WHERE WE ARE!
CHASE THEM TOO FAR, AND YOU'LL END UP DEAD!!
THEY PLAN TO KILL EVERYONE HERE! INCLUDING US!
BUT THIS CAN BE OUR CHANCE.
THEY'LL BE OFF THEIR GUARDS.
THEY THINK THEY'RE THE PREDATORS HUNTING DOWN PREY!
NOW IS THE BEST TIME!!

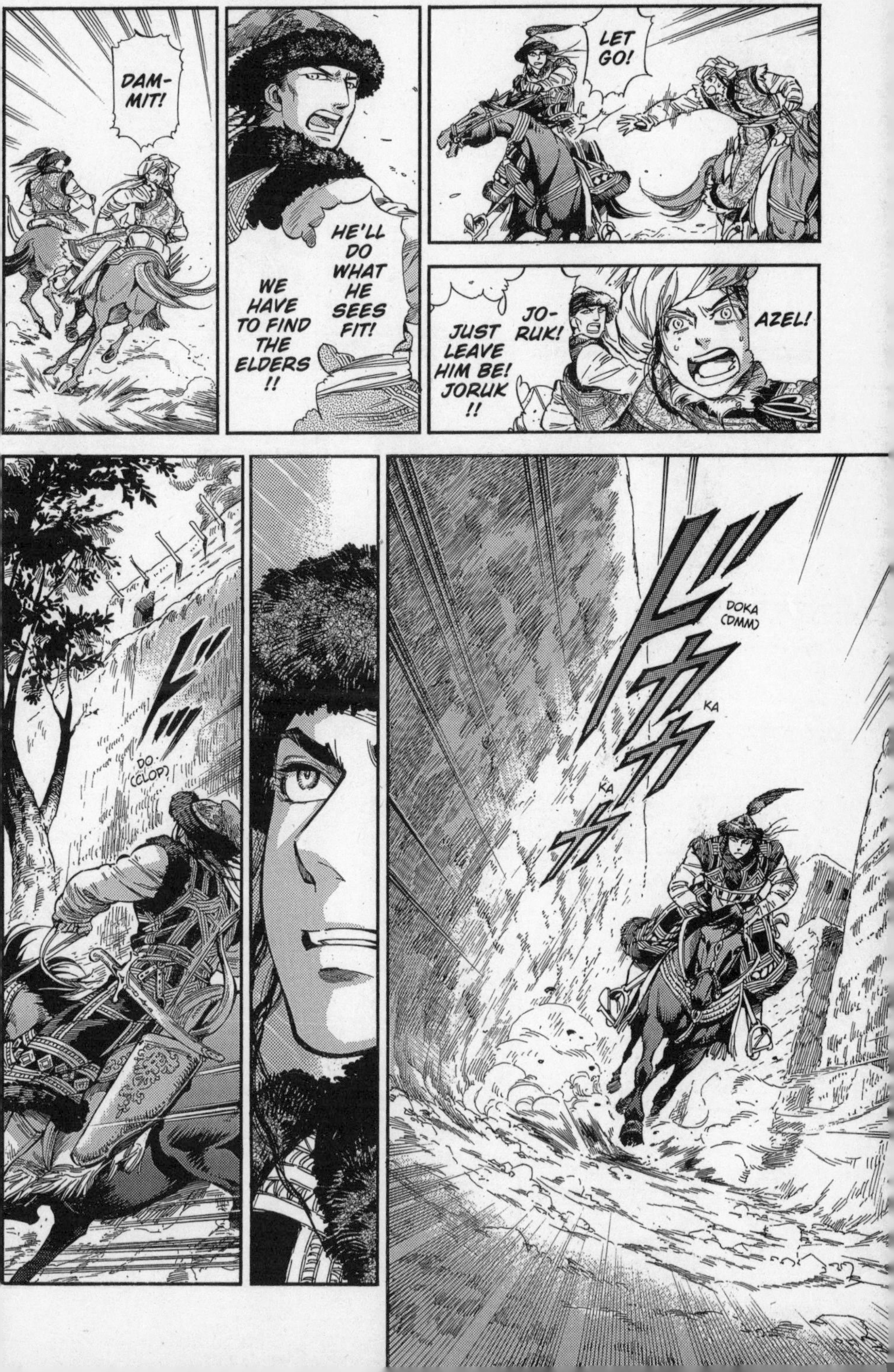
LET GO!
AZEL!
JO-RUK!
JUST LEAVE HIM BE! JORUK !!
HE'LL DO WHAT HE SEES FIT!
WE HAVE TO FIND THE ELDERS !!
DAM-MIT!
DOKA (DMM)
KA
KA
DO (CLOP)

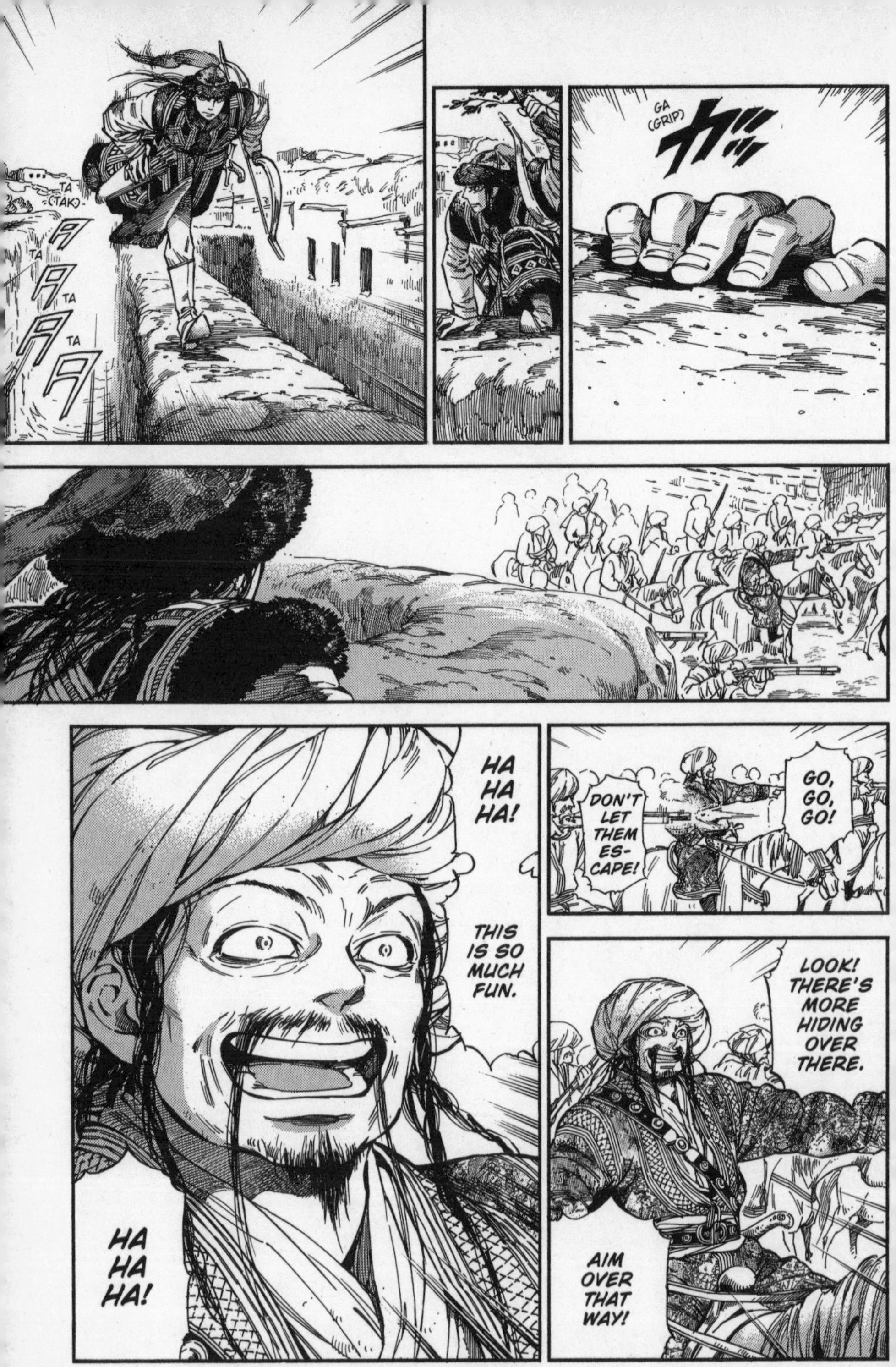
GA (GRIP)
TA (TAK)
TA
TA
TA
GO, GO, GO!
DON'T LET THEM ES-CAPE!
LOOK! THERE'S MORE HIDING OVER THERE.
AIM OVER THAT WAY!
HA HA HA!
THIS IS SO MUCH FUN.
HA HA HA!

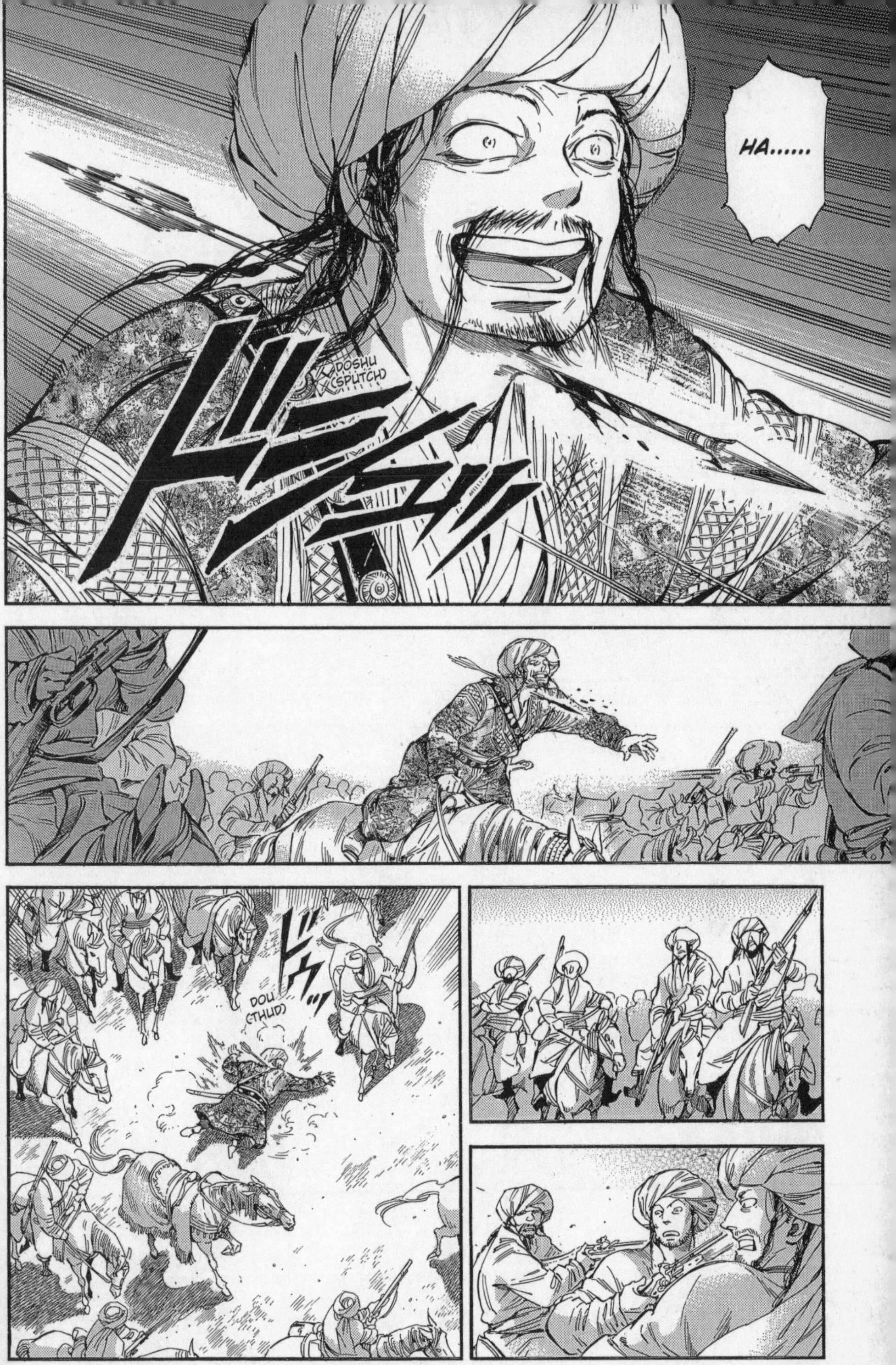
HA......
DOSHU (SPUTCH)
DOU (THUD)

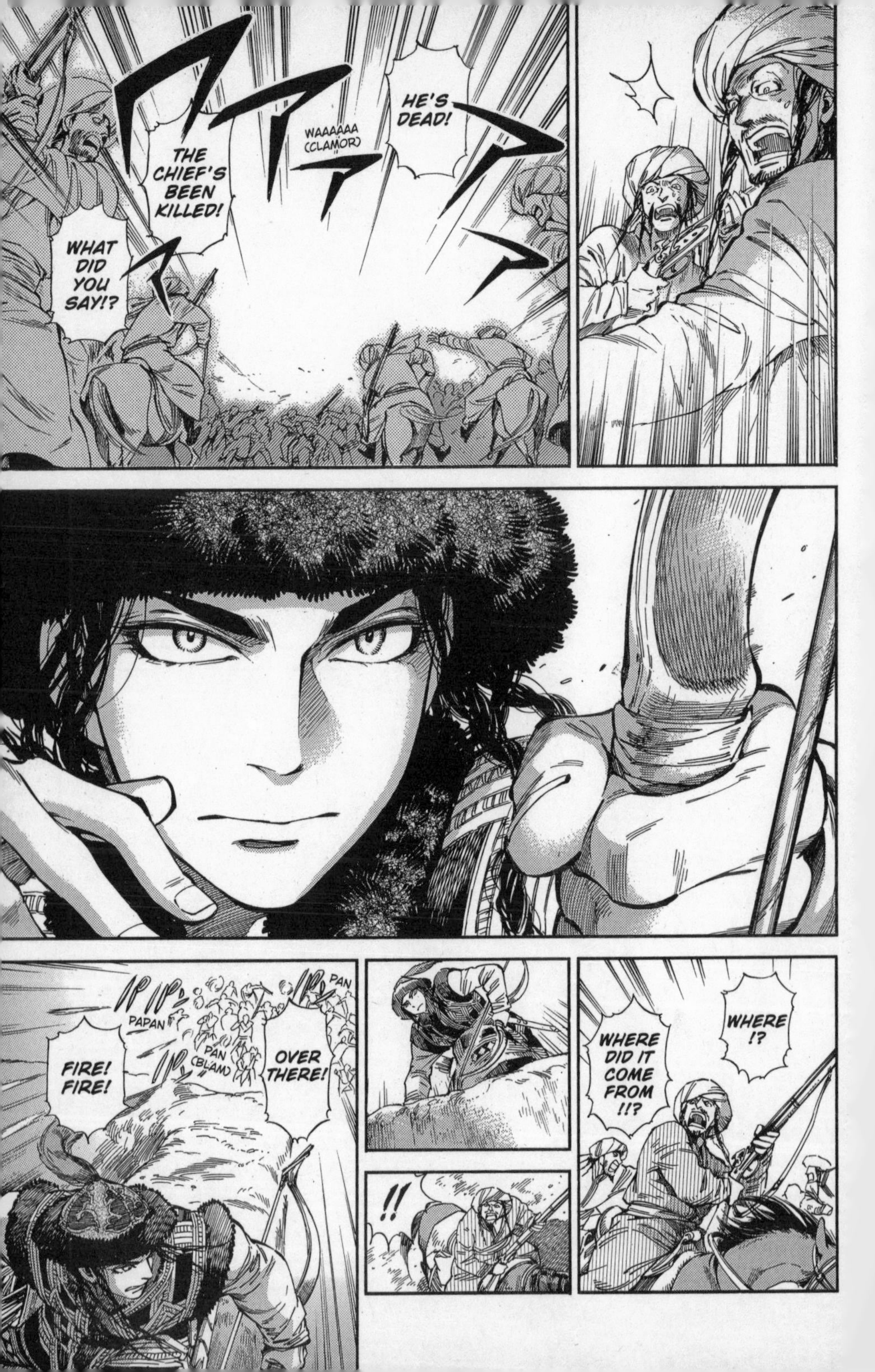
HE'S DEAD!
WAAAAAA (CLAMOR)
THE CHIEF'S BEEN KILLED!
WHAT DID YOU SAY!?
WHERE !?
WHERE DID IT COME FROM !!?
!!
PAN
OVER THERE!
PAN (BLAM)
PAPAN
FIRE! FIRE!

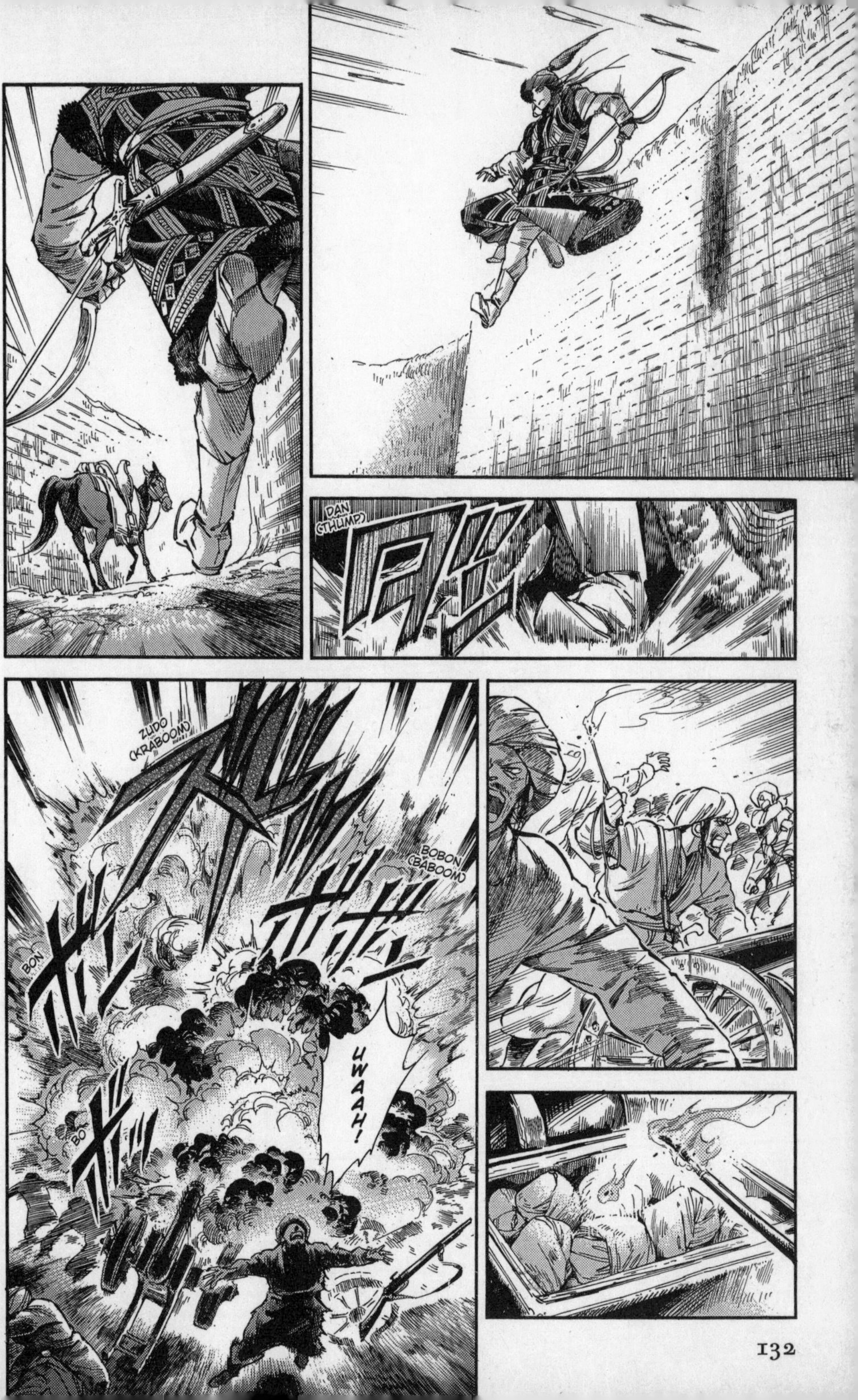
DAN (THUMP)
BOBON (BABOOM)
ZUDO (KRABOOM)
UWAAH!
BON
BO

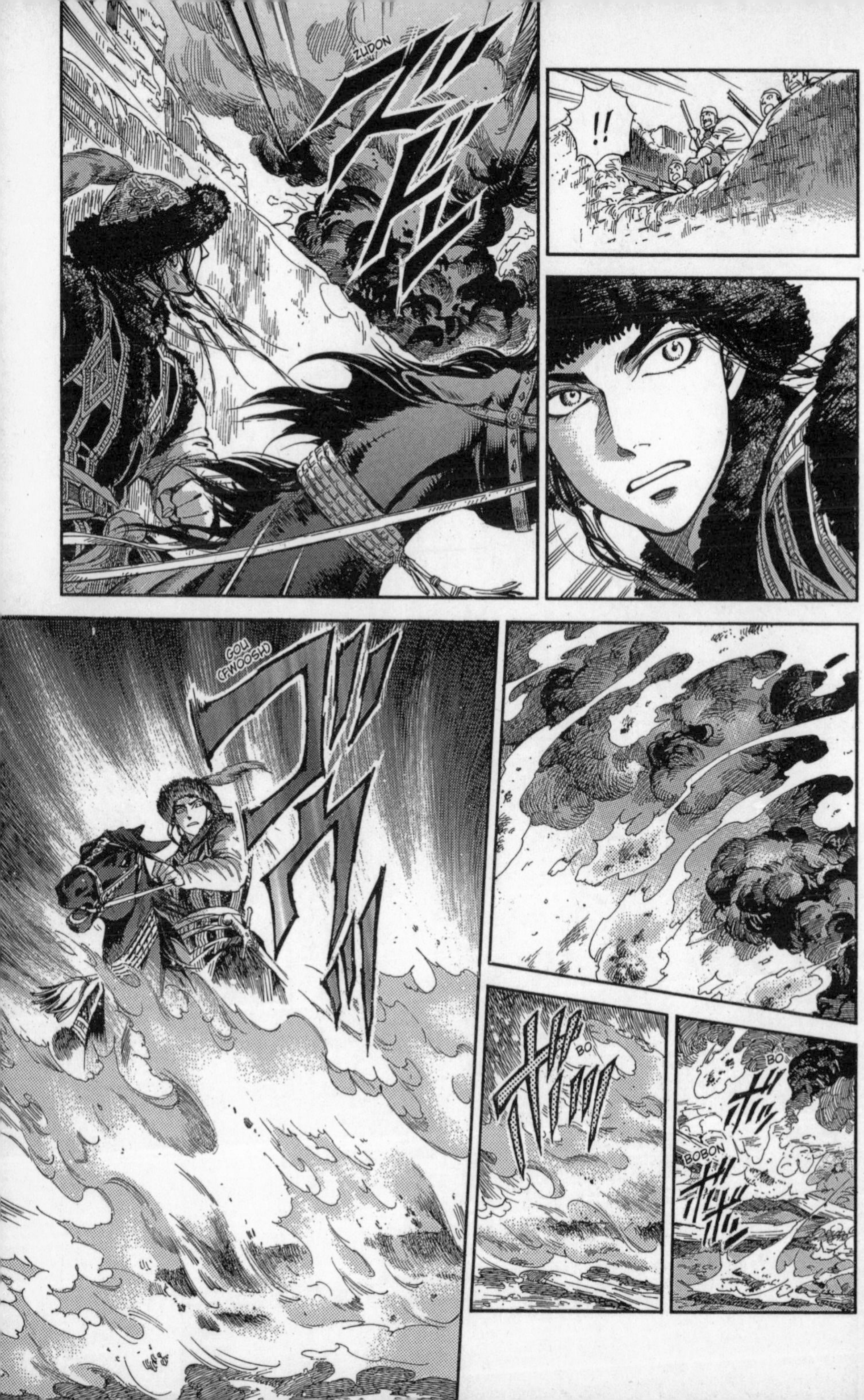
!!
ZUDON
BO
BOBON
BO
GOU (FWOOSH)

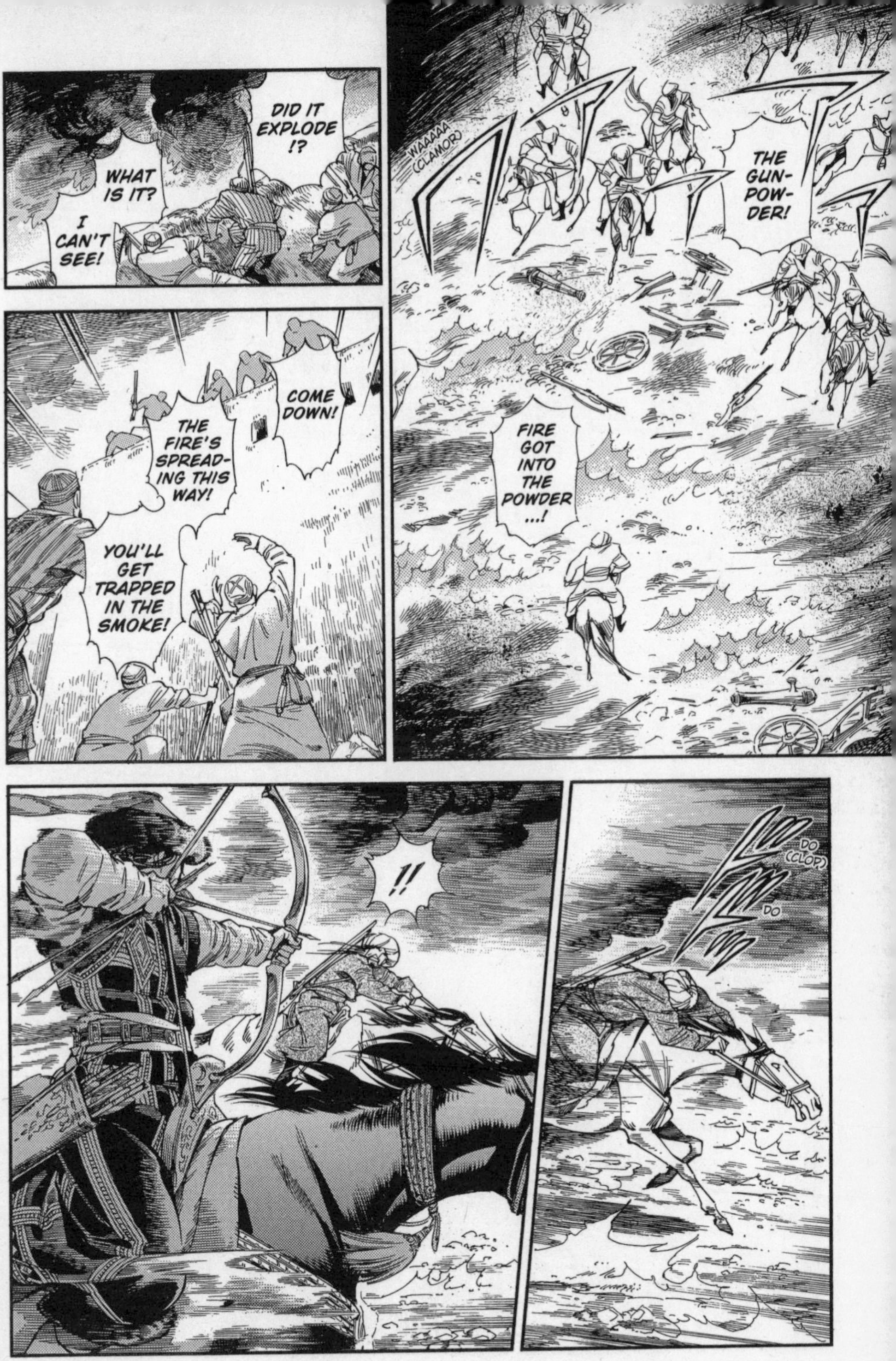
THE GUN-POWDER!
WAAAAA (CLAMOR)
FIRE GOT INTO THE POWDER ...!
DID IT EXPLODE !?
WHAT IS IT?
I CAN'T SEE!
COME DOWN!
THE FIRE'S SPREAD-ING THIS WAY!
YOU'LL GET TRAPPED IN THE SMOKE!
DO (CLOP)
DO
!!

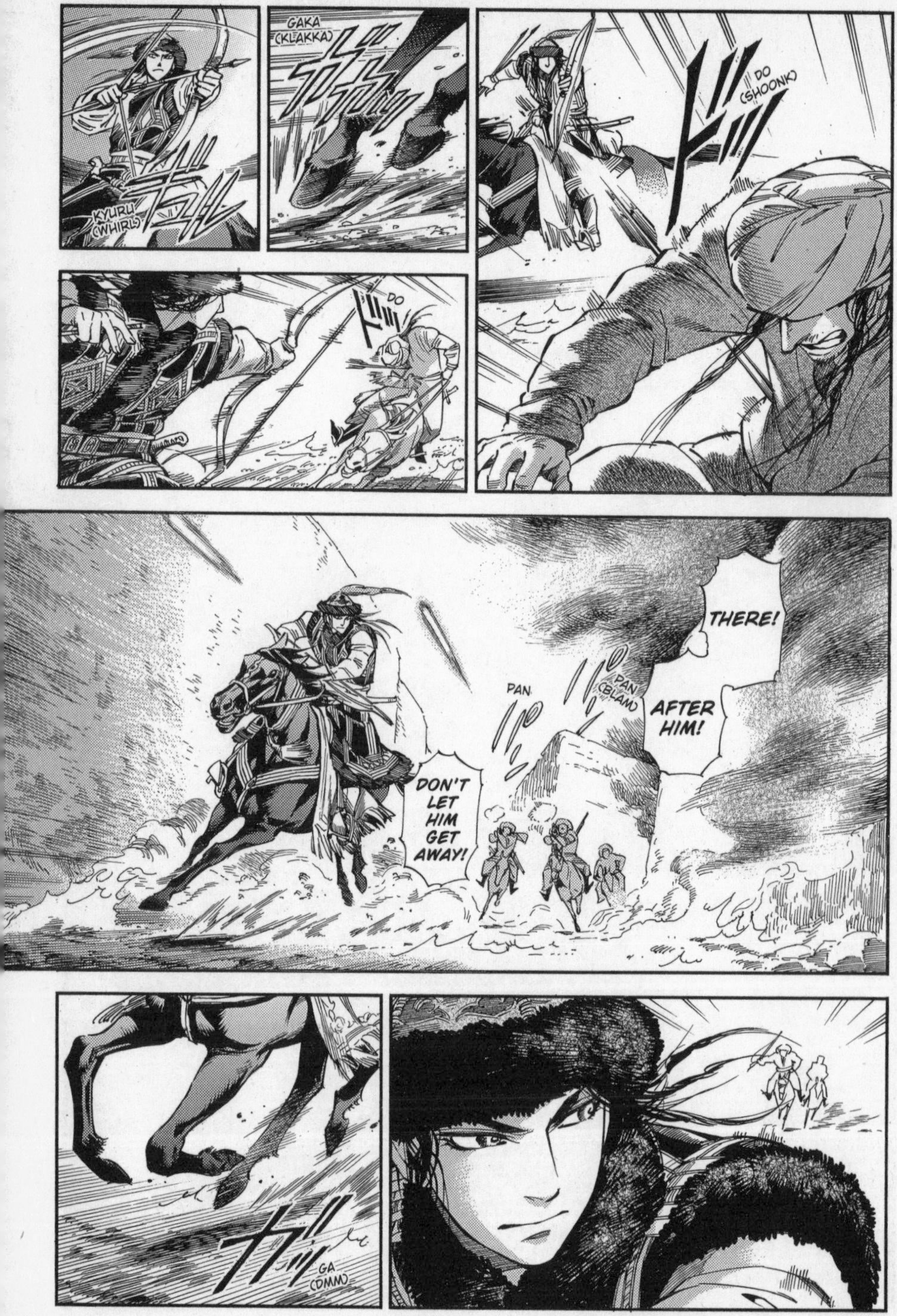

DO (SHOONK)
GAKA (KLAKKA)
KYURU (WHIRL)
DO
THERE!
PAN (BLAM)
AFTER HIM!
PAN
DON'T LET HIM GET AWAY!
GA (DMM)

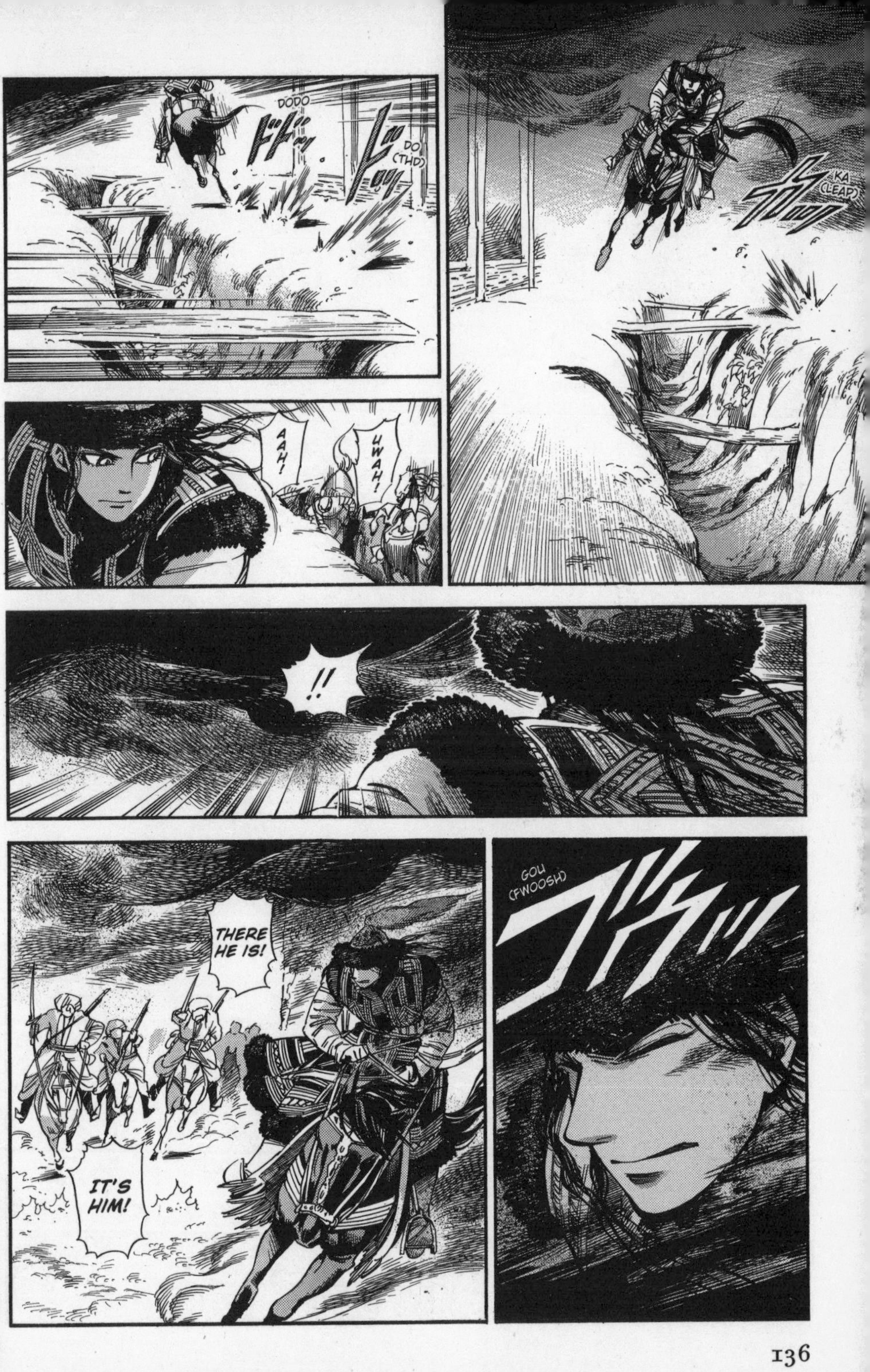
KA
(LEAP)
DODO
DO
(THD)
UWAH!
AAH!
!!
GOU
(FWOOSH)
THERE HE IS!
IT'S HIM!

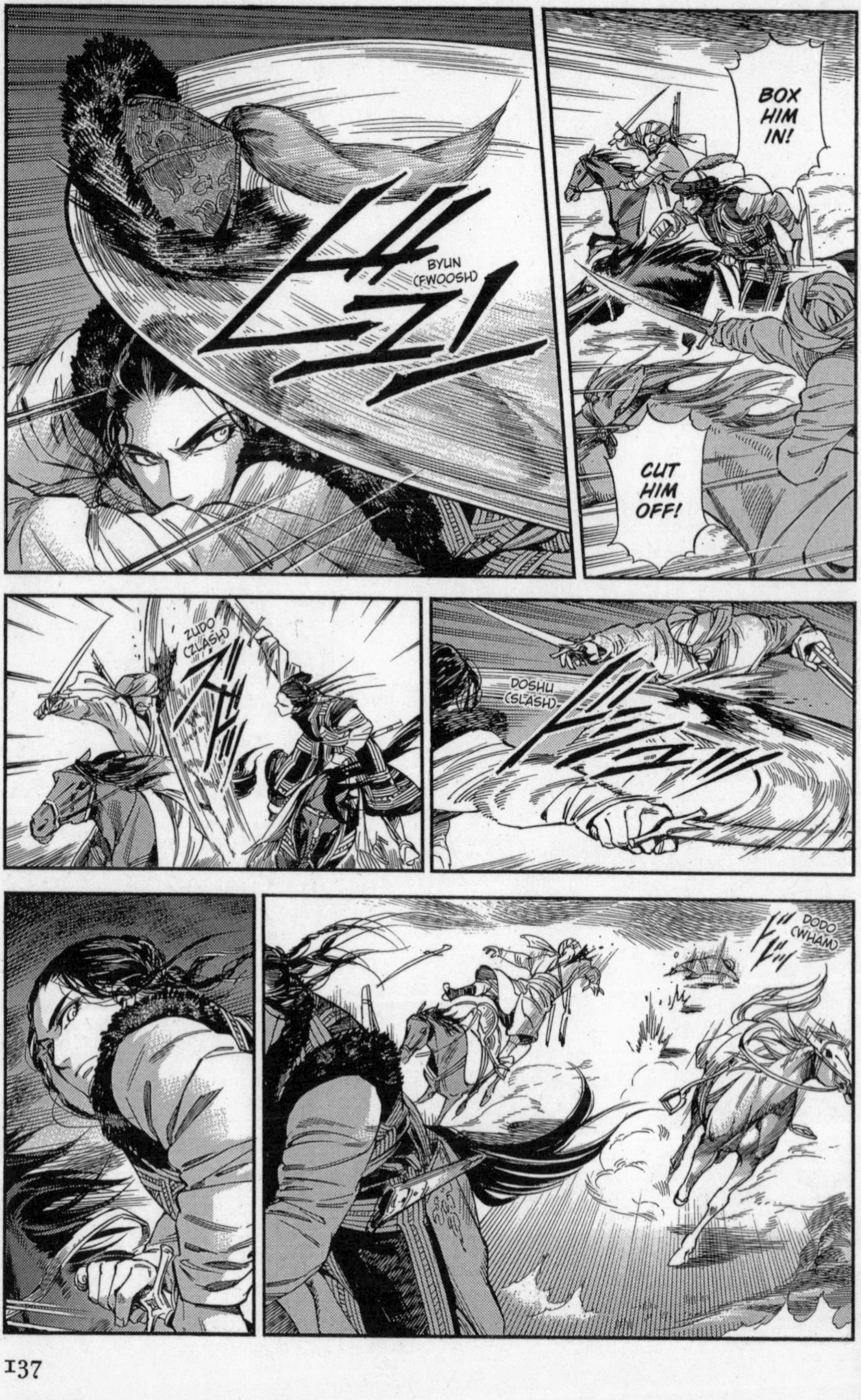
BOX HIM IN!
CUT HIM OFF!
BYUN (FWOOSH)
DOSHU (SLASH)
ZUDO (ZLASH)
DODO (WHAM)

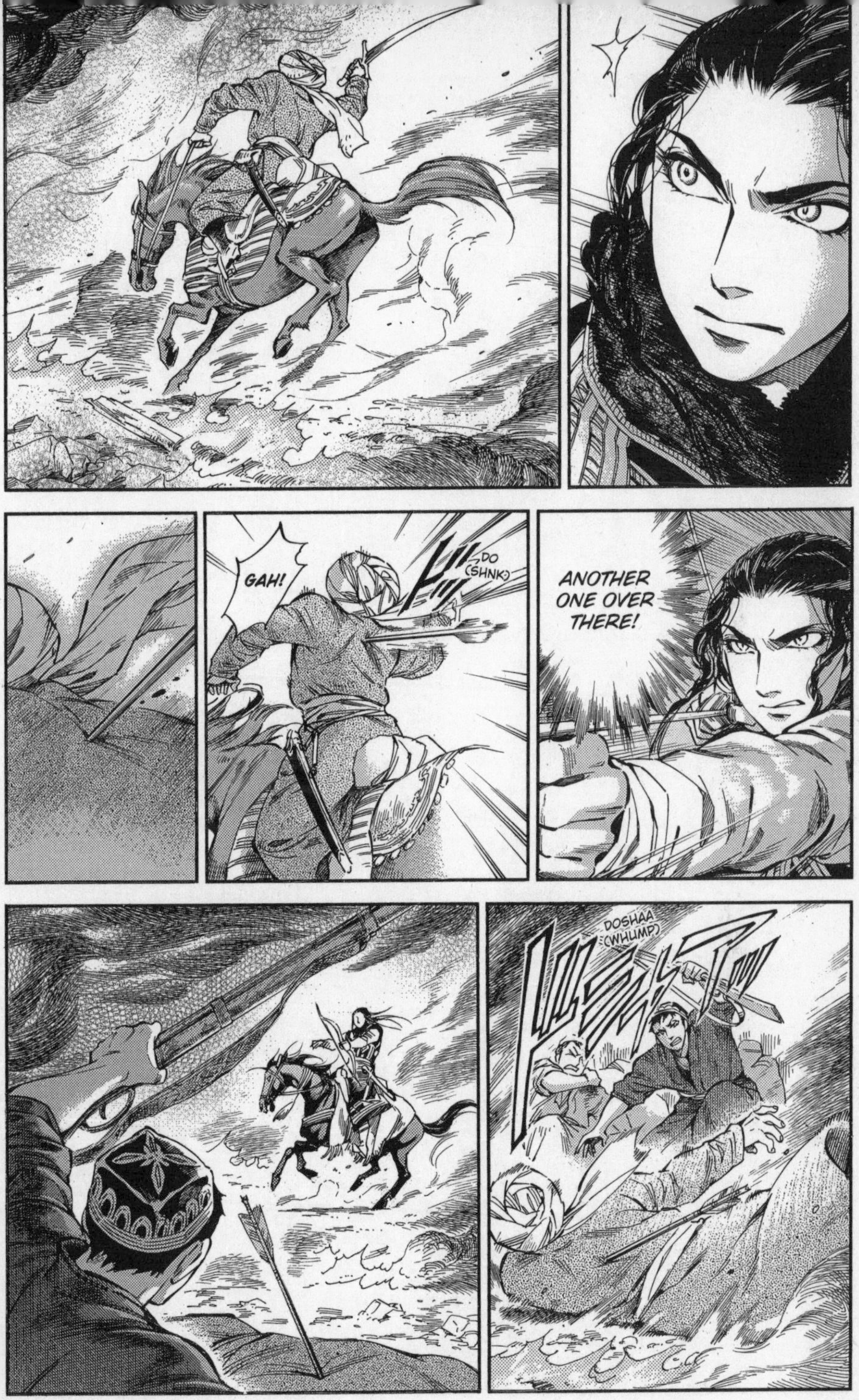
ANOTHER ONE OVER THERE!
GAH!
DO (SHNK)
DOSHAA (WHUMP)

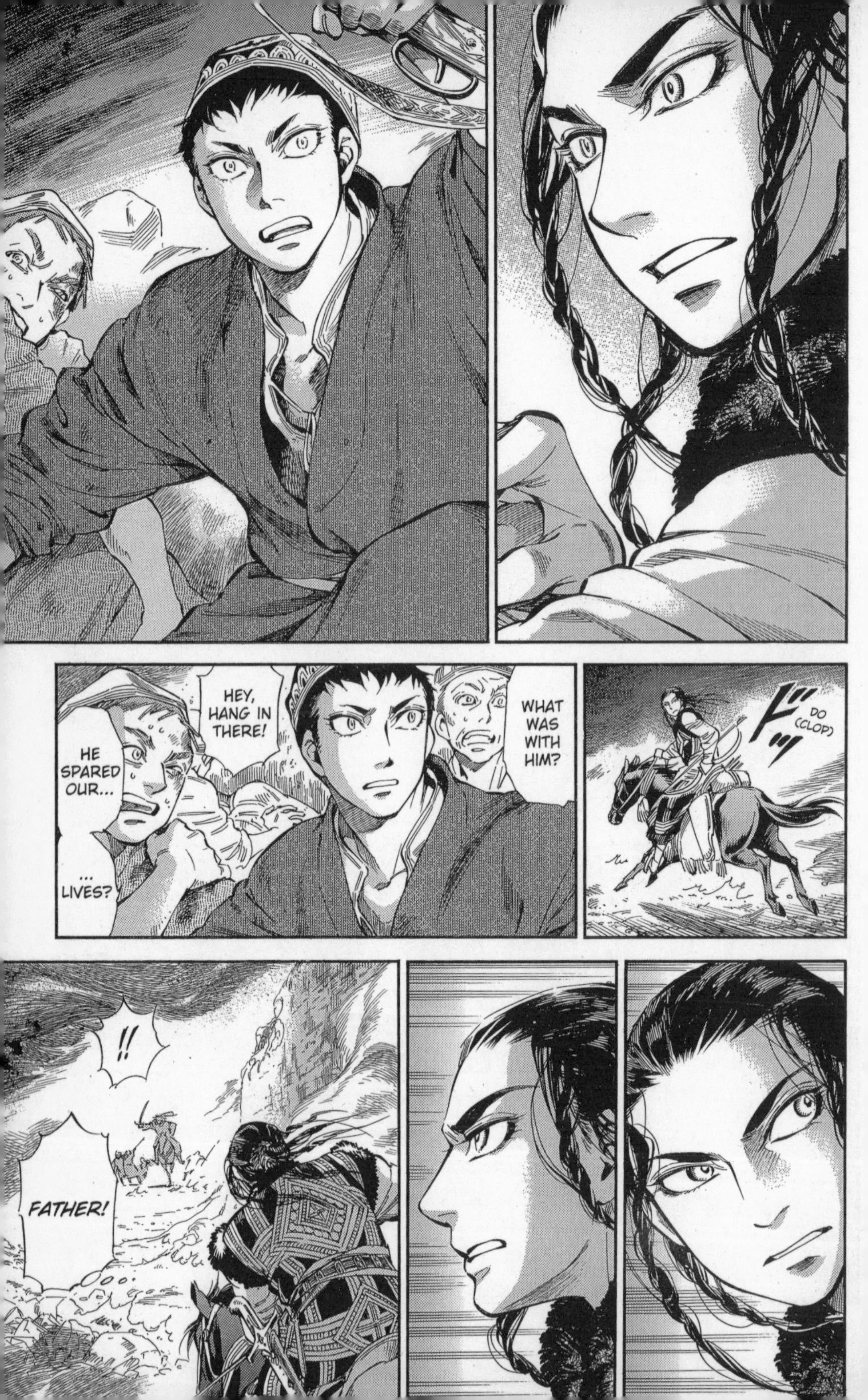
DO (CLOP)
WHAT WAS WITH HIM?
HEY, HANG IN THERE!
HE SPARED OUR...
... LIVES?
!!
... FATHER!

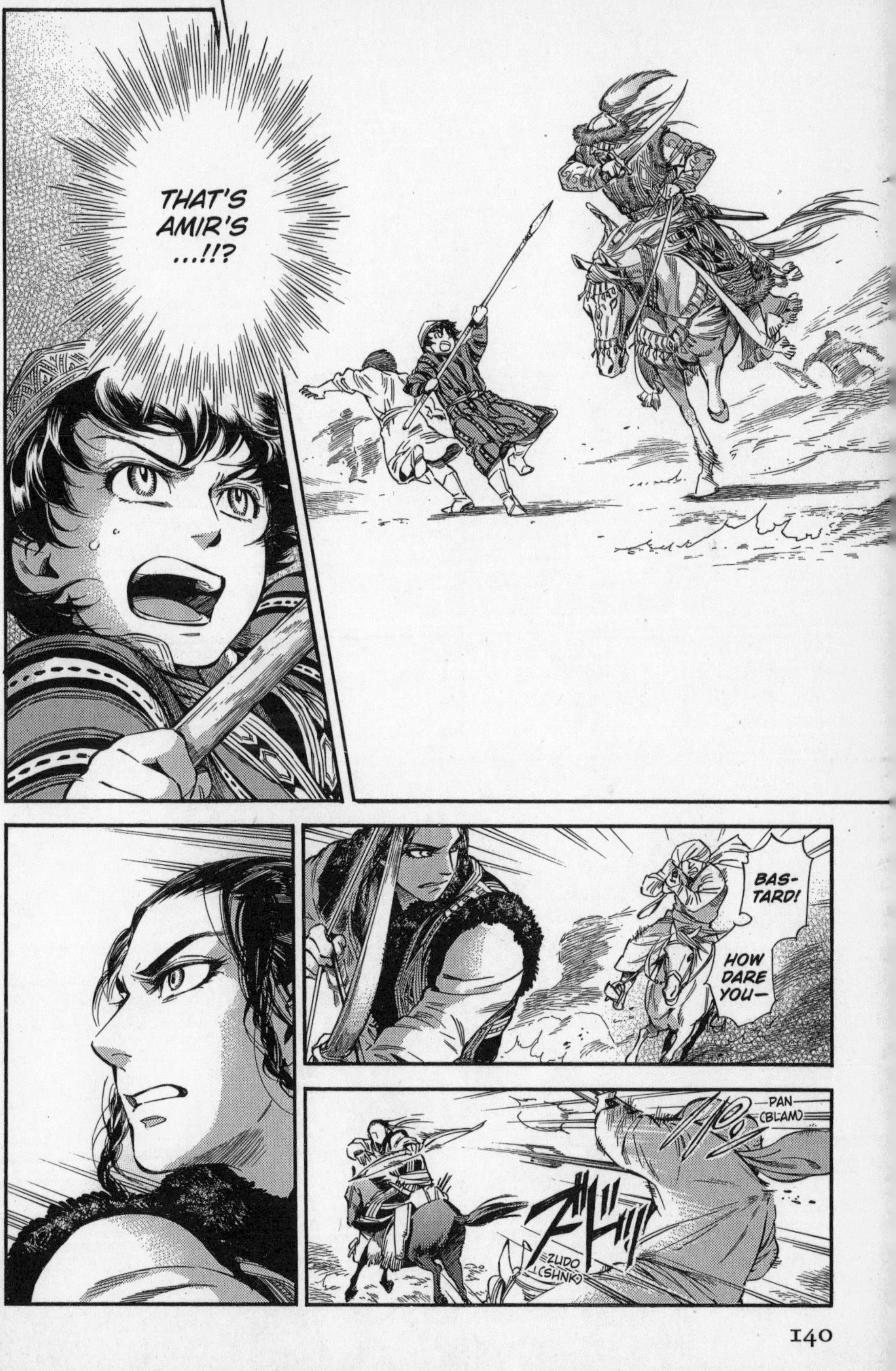
THAT'S AMIR'S ...!!?
BAS-TARD!
HOW DARE YOU—
PAN (BLAM)
ズドッ
ZUDO (SHNK)

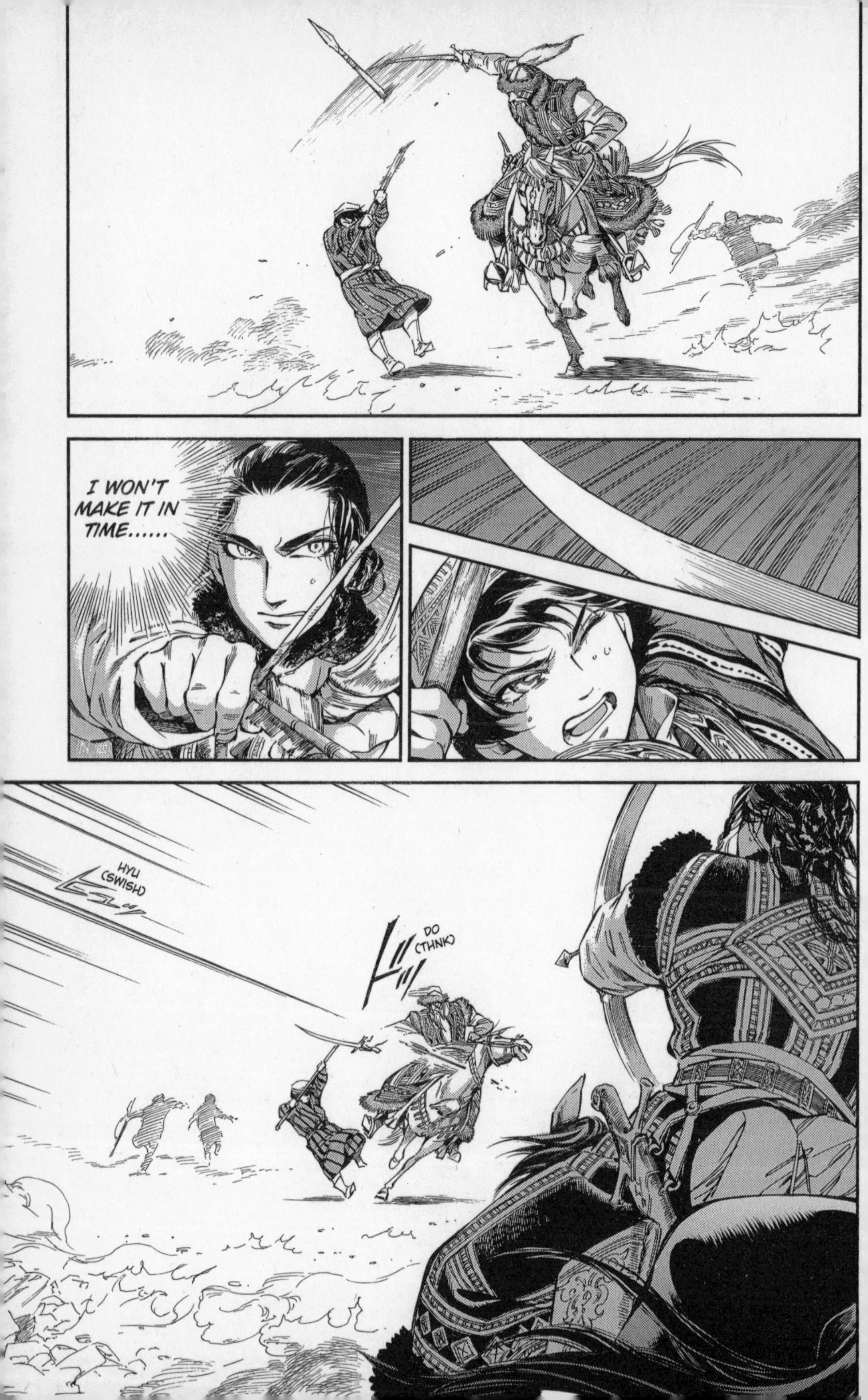
I WON'T MAKE IT IN TIME......
HYU (SWISH)
DO (THINK)

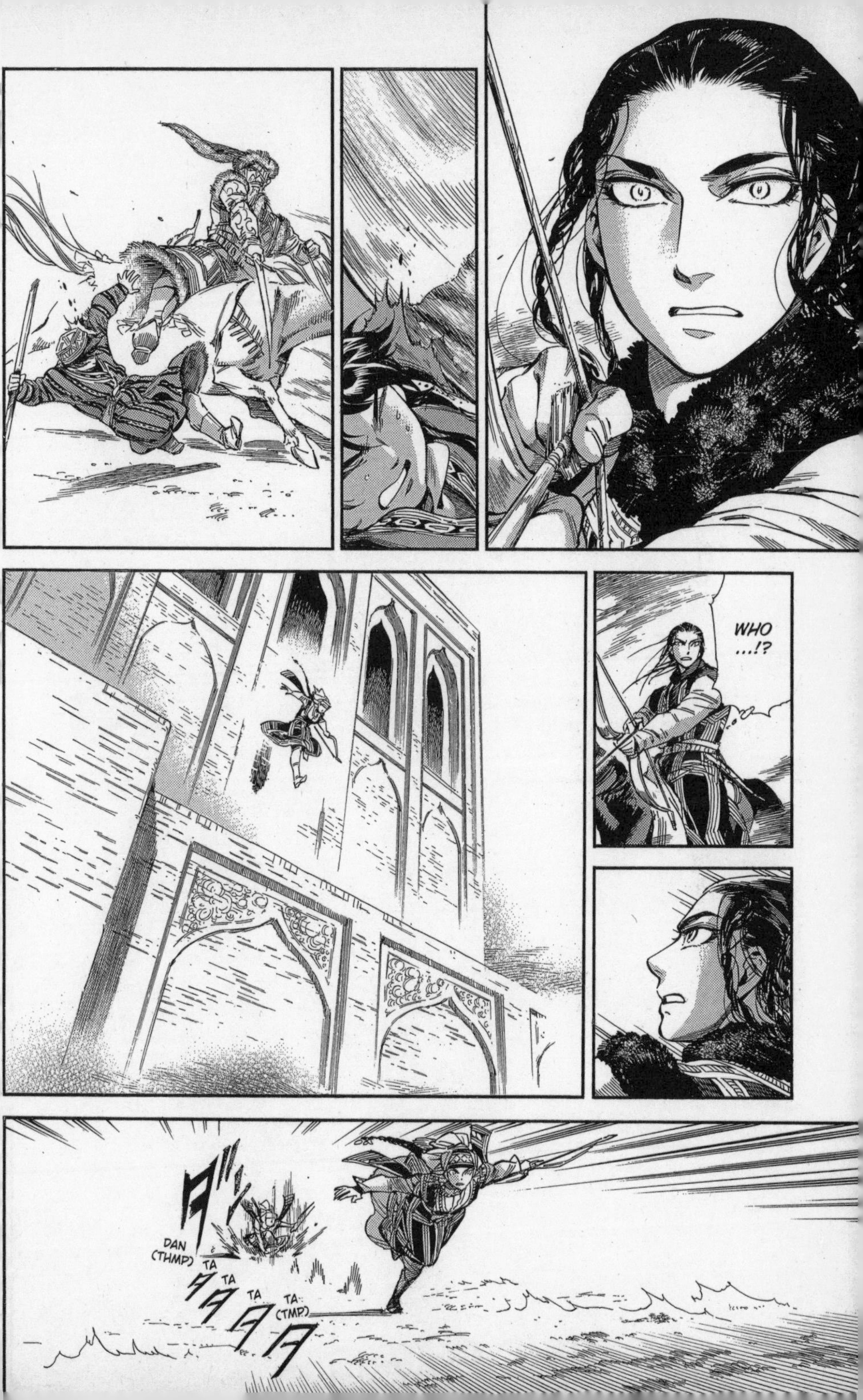
WHO ...!?
DAN (THMP)
TA TA TA TA (TMP)

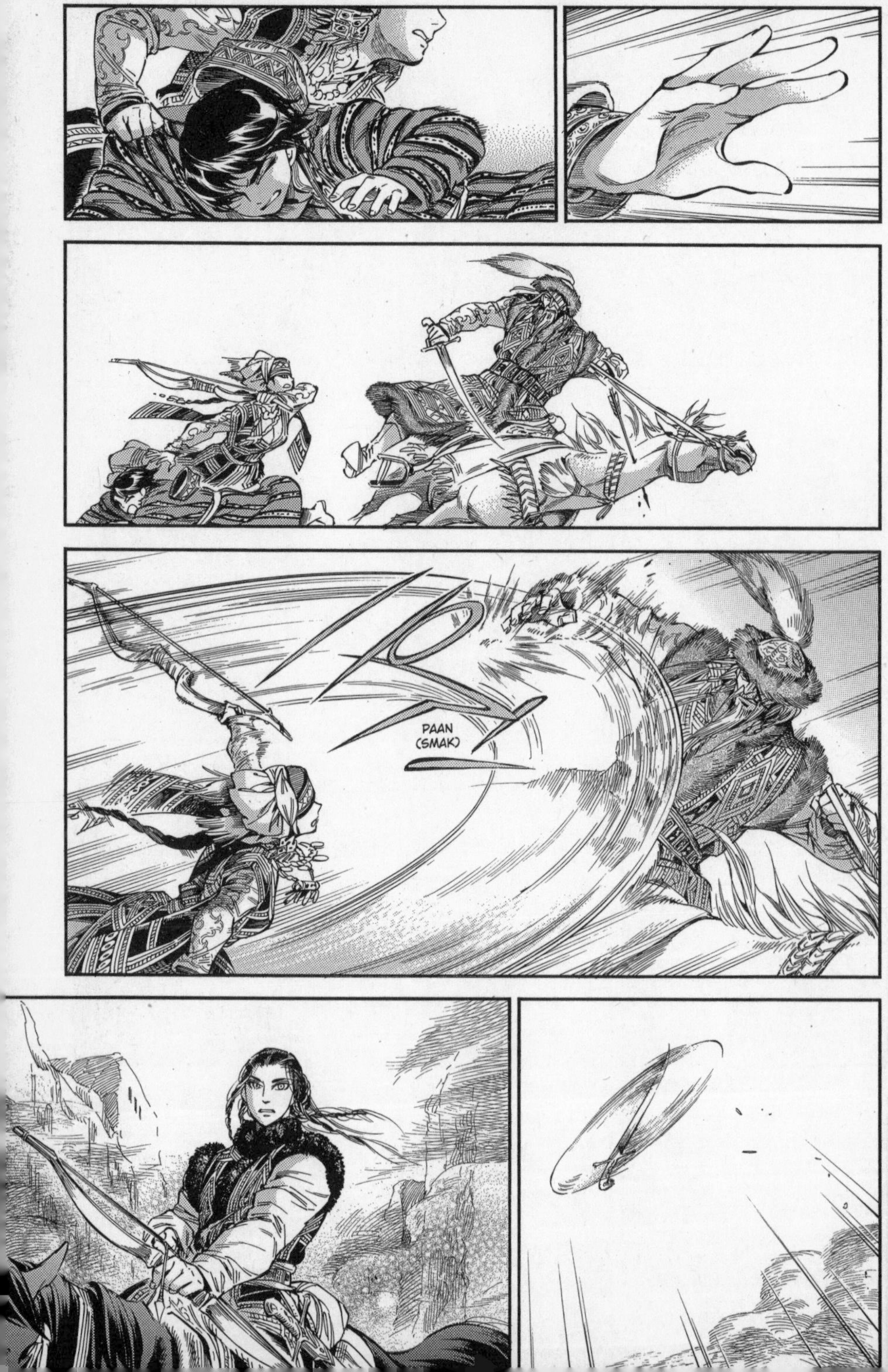
PAAN
(SMAK)

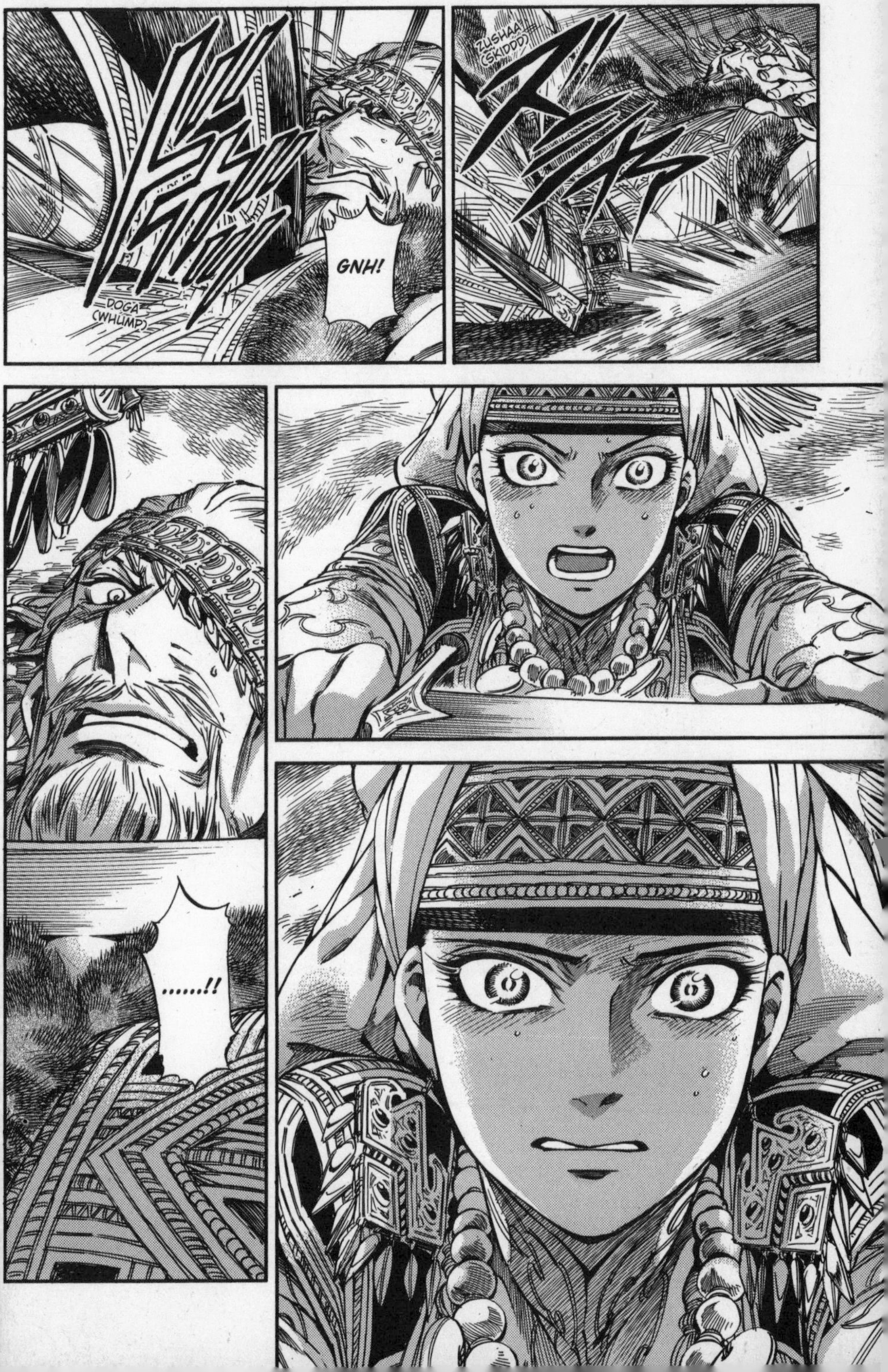
ZUSHAA (SKIDDD)
GNH!
DOGA (WHUMP)
......!!

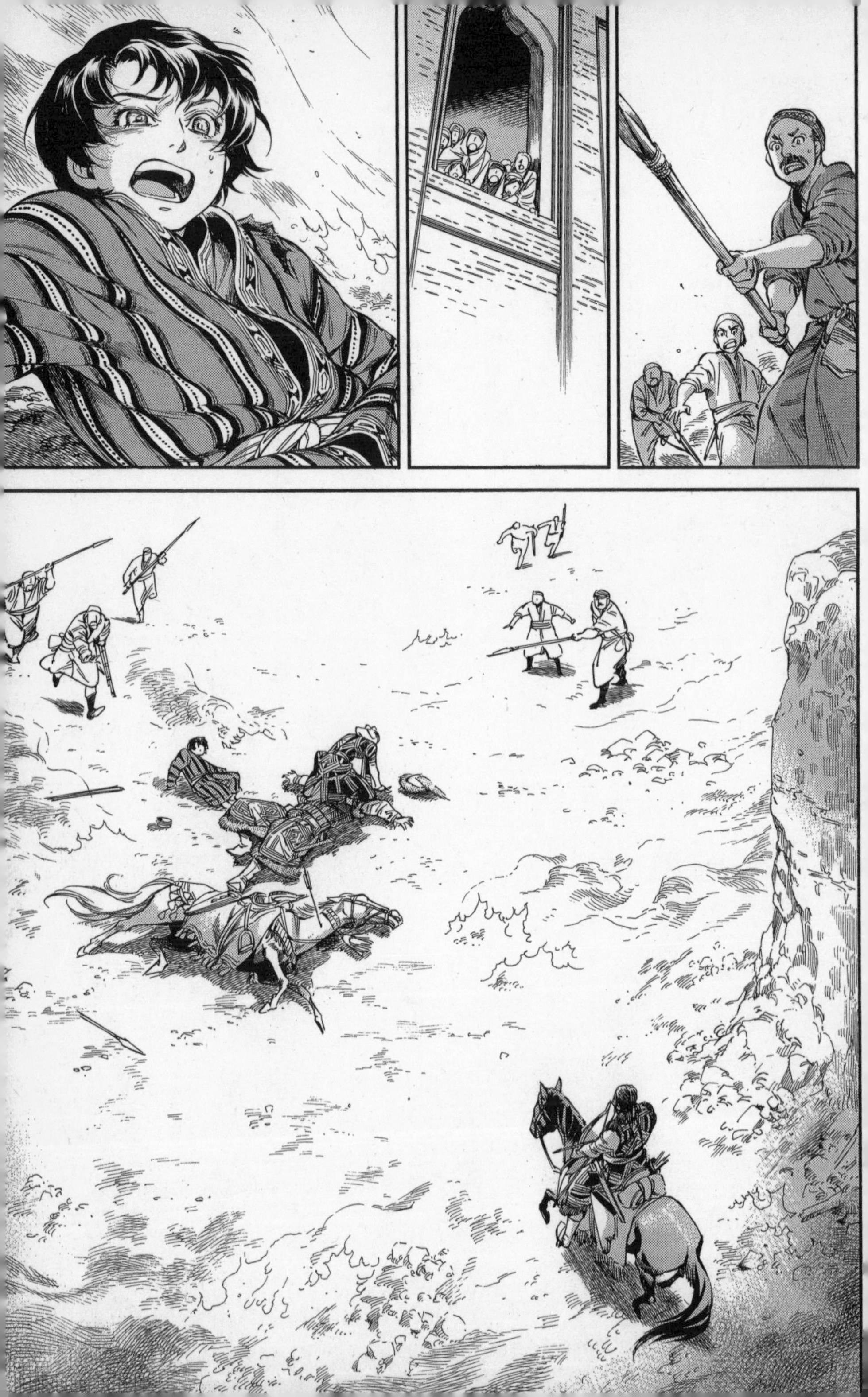

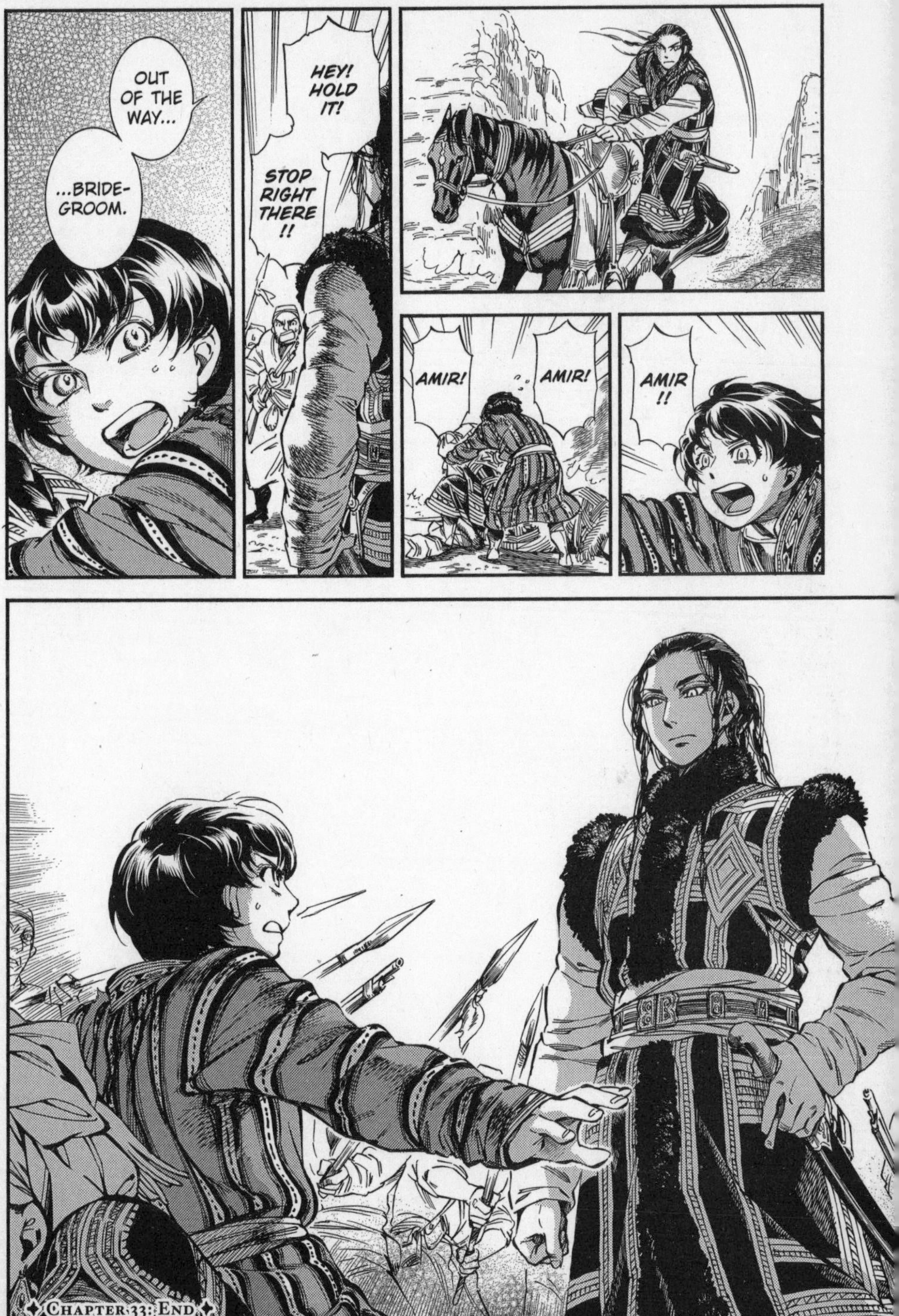
AMIR !!
AMIR!
AMIR!
HEY! HOLD IT!
STOP RIGHT THERE !!
OUT OF THE WAY...
...BRIDE-GROOM.
Chapter 33: End

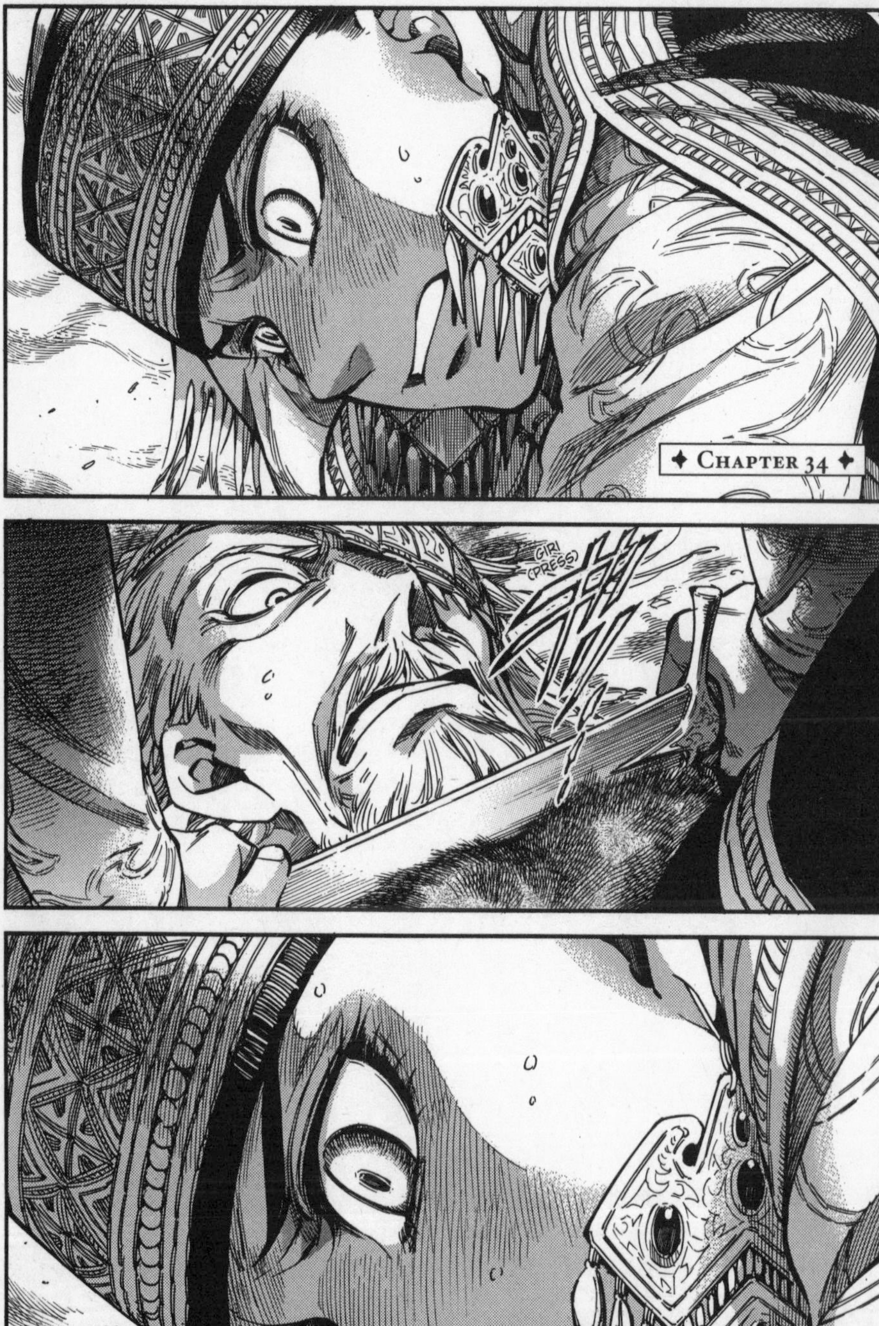
CHAPTER 34
GIRI (PRESS)

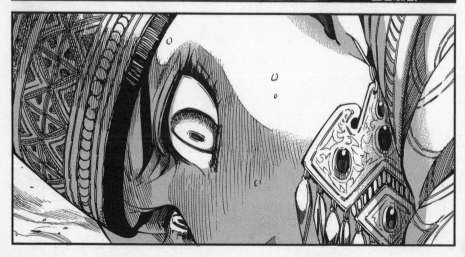

Chapter 34
Shielding You from Behind

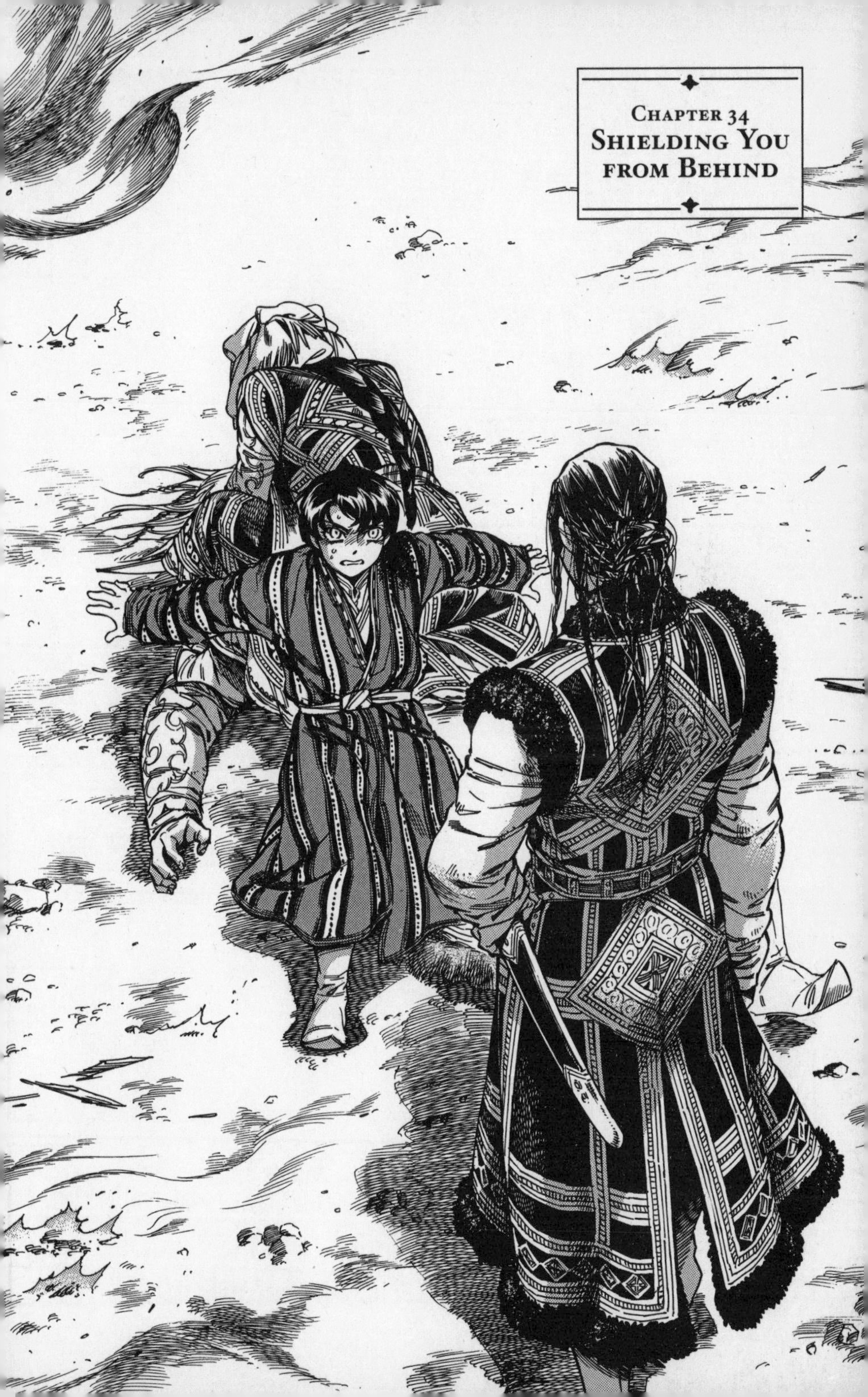

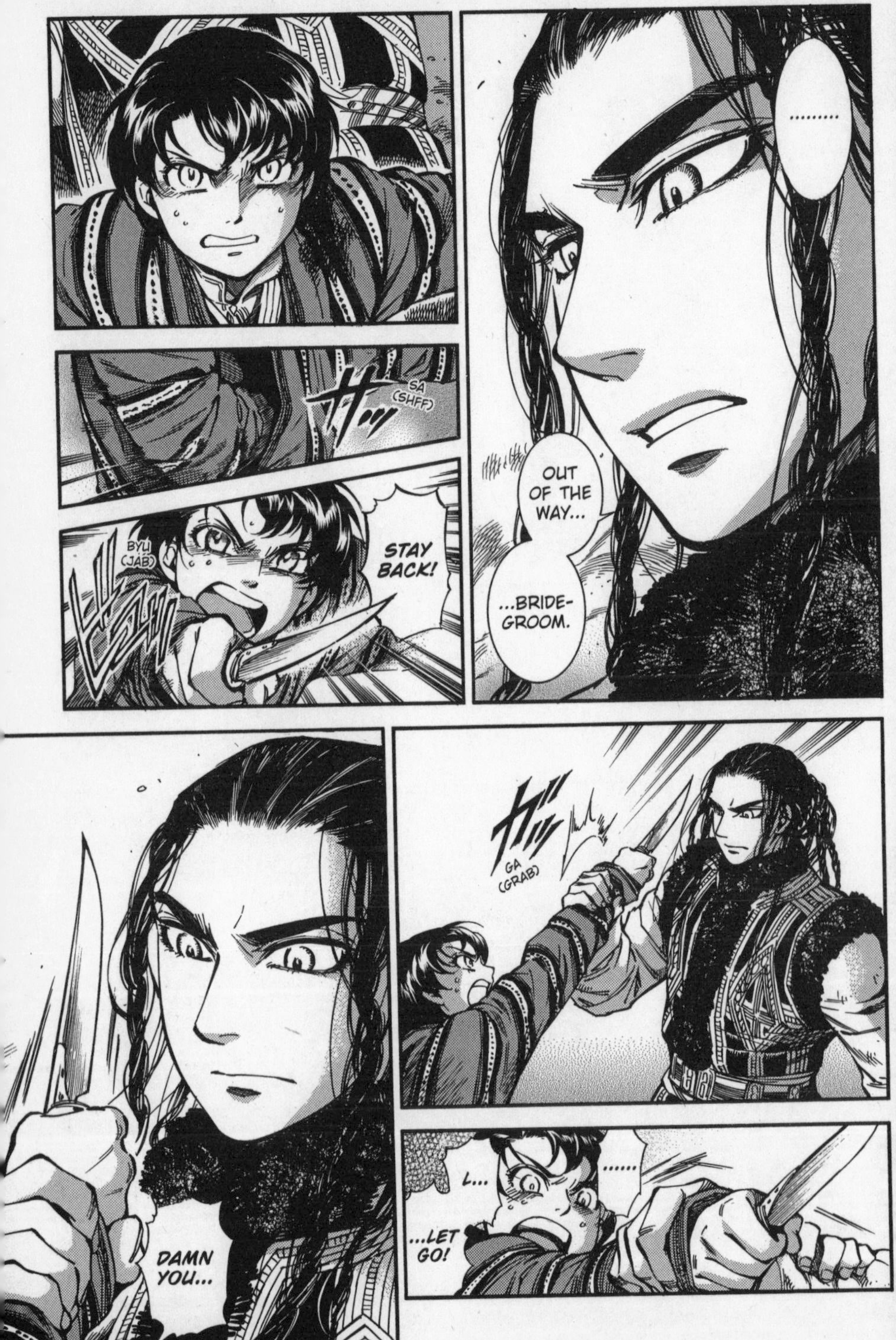

....
OUT OF THE WAY...
...BRIDE-GROOM.
SA (SHFF)
STAY BACK!
BYU (JAB)
GA (GRAB)
......
I...
...LET GO!
DAMN YOU...

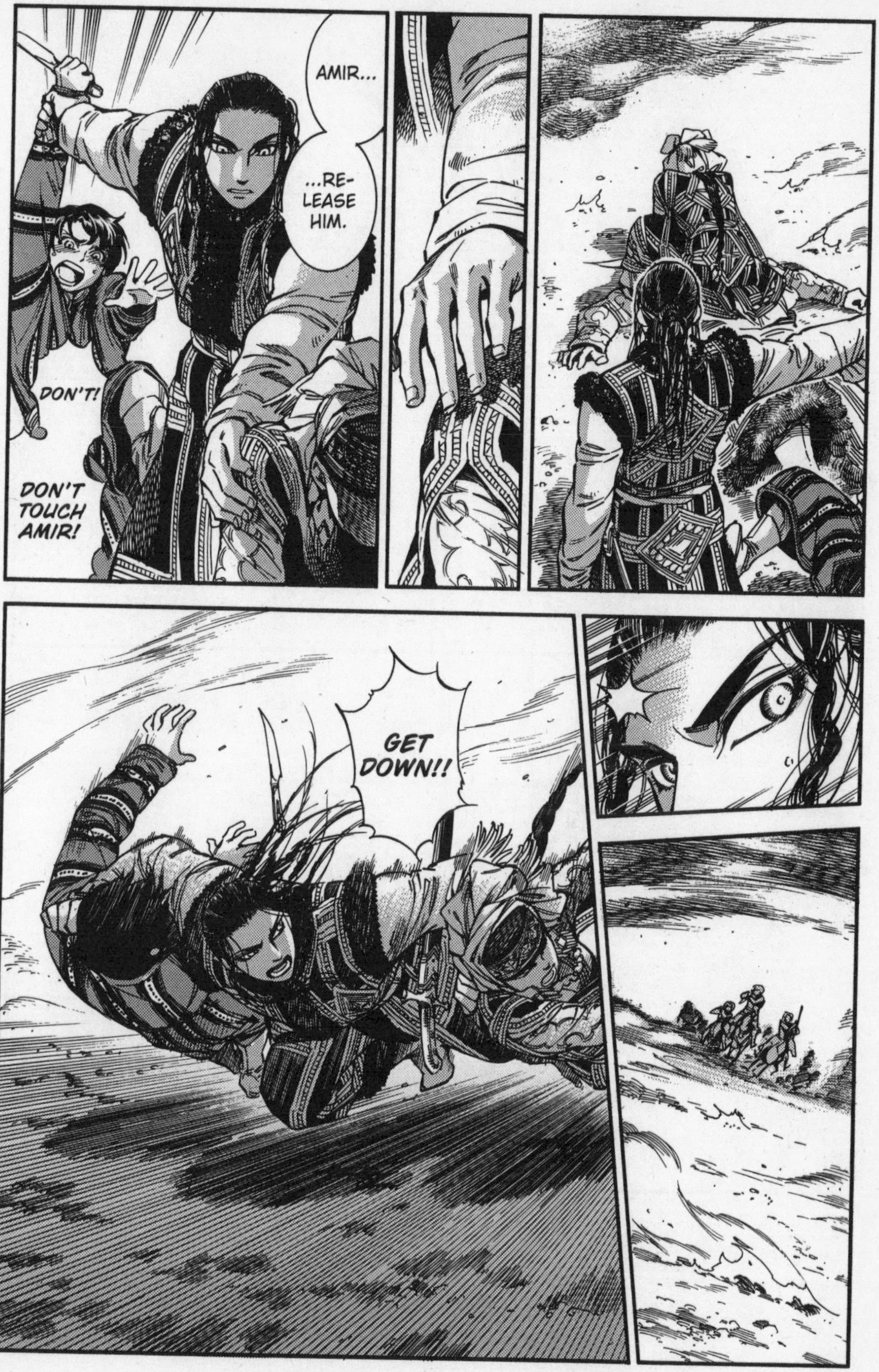
AMIR...
...RE-LEASE HIM.
DON'T!
DON'T TOUCH AMIR!
GET DOWN!!

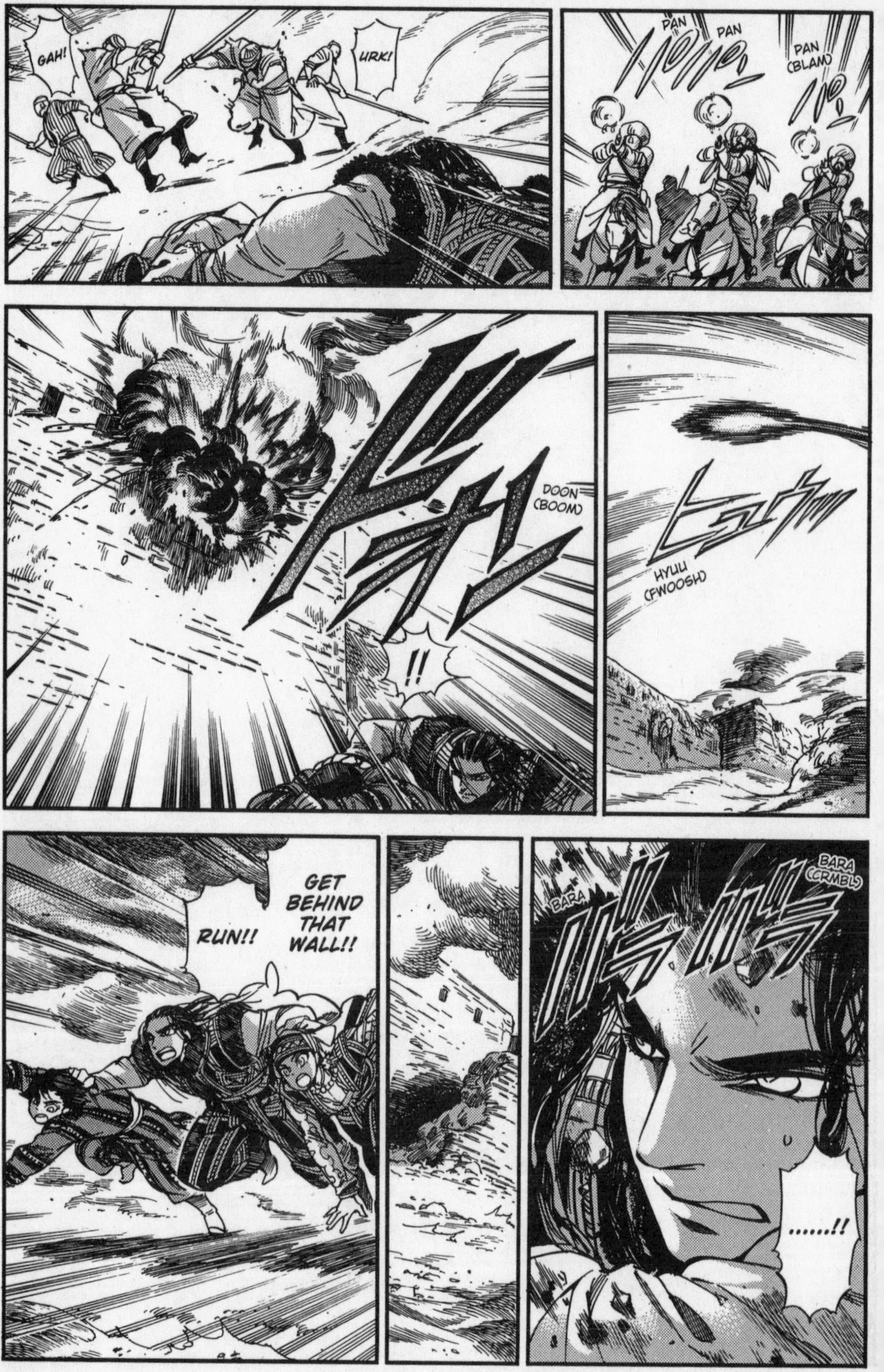

PAN
PAN
PAN (BLAM)
URK!
GAH!
HYUU (FWOOSH)
DOON (BOOM)
!!
BARA (CRMBL)
BARA
......!!
GET BEHIND THAT WALL!!
RUN!!

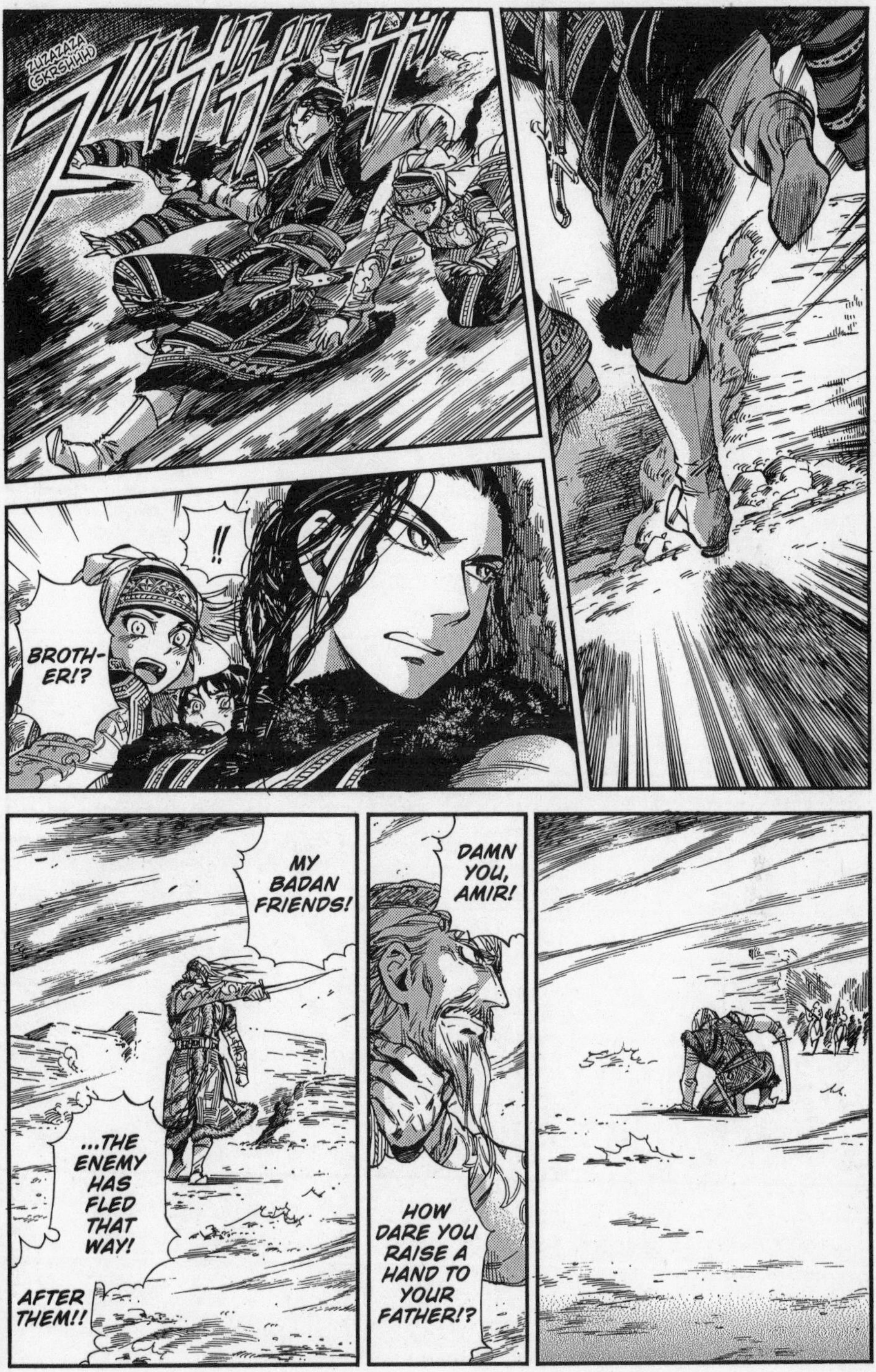
ZUZAZAZA (SKRSHHH)
!!
BROTH-ER!?
DAMN YOU, AMIR!
HOW DARE YOU RAISE A HAND TO YOUR FATHER!?
MY BADAN FRIENDS!
...THE ENEMY HAS FLED THAT WAY!
AFTER THEM!!

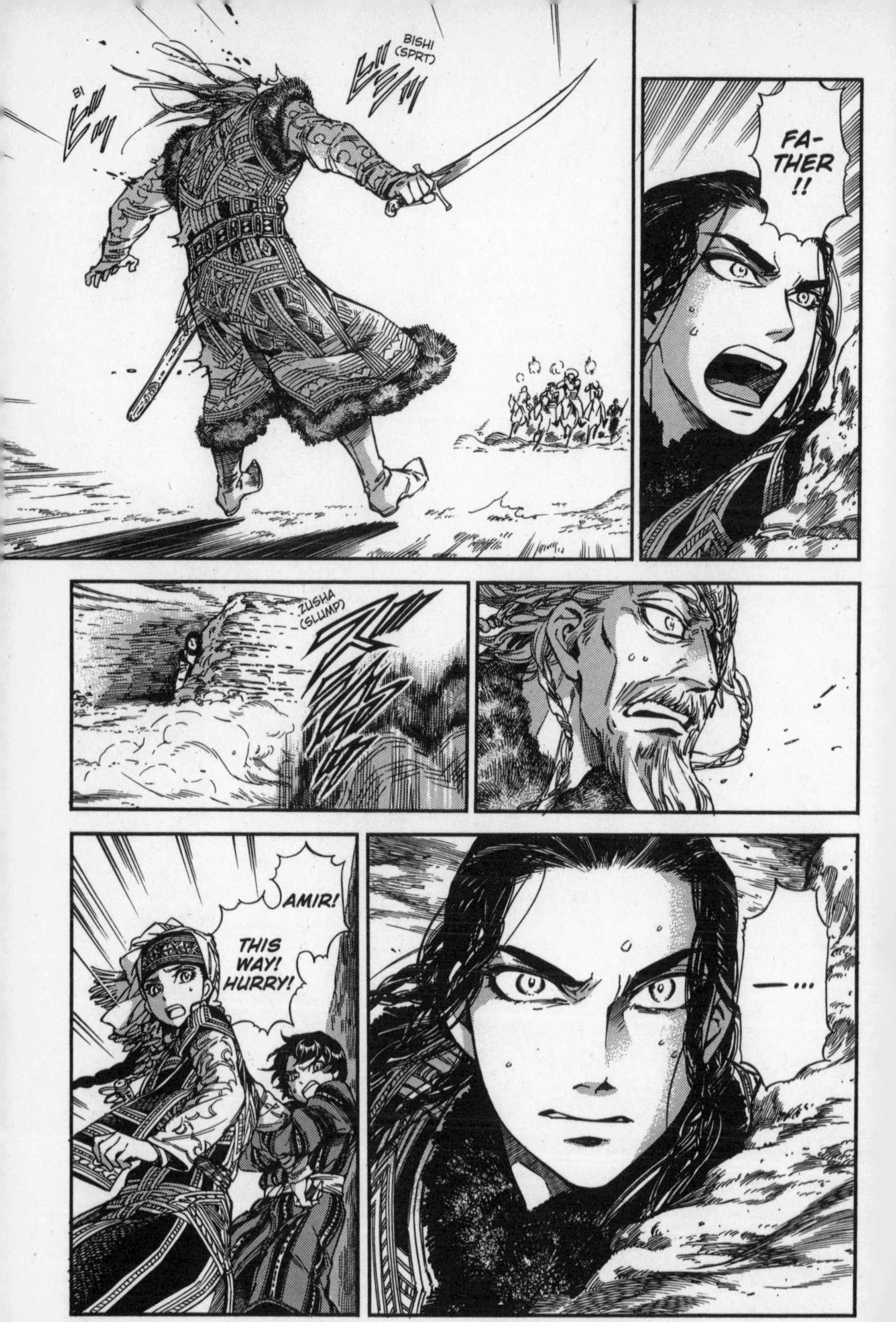
FA-THER!!
BISHI (SPRT)
BI
ZUSHA (SLUMP)
—...
AMIR!
THIS WAY! HURRY!

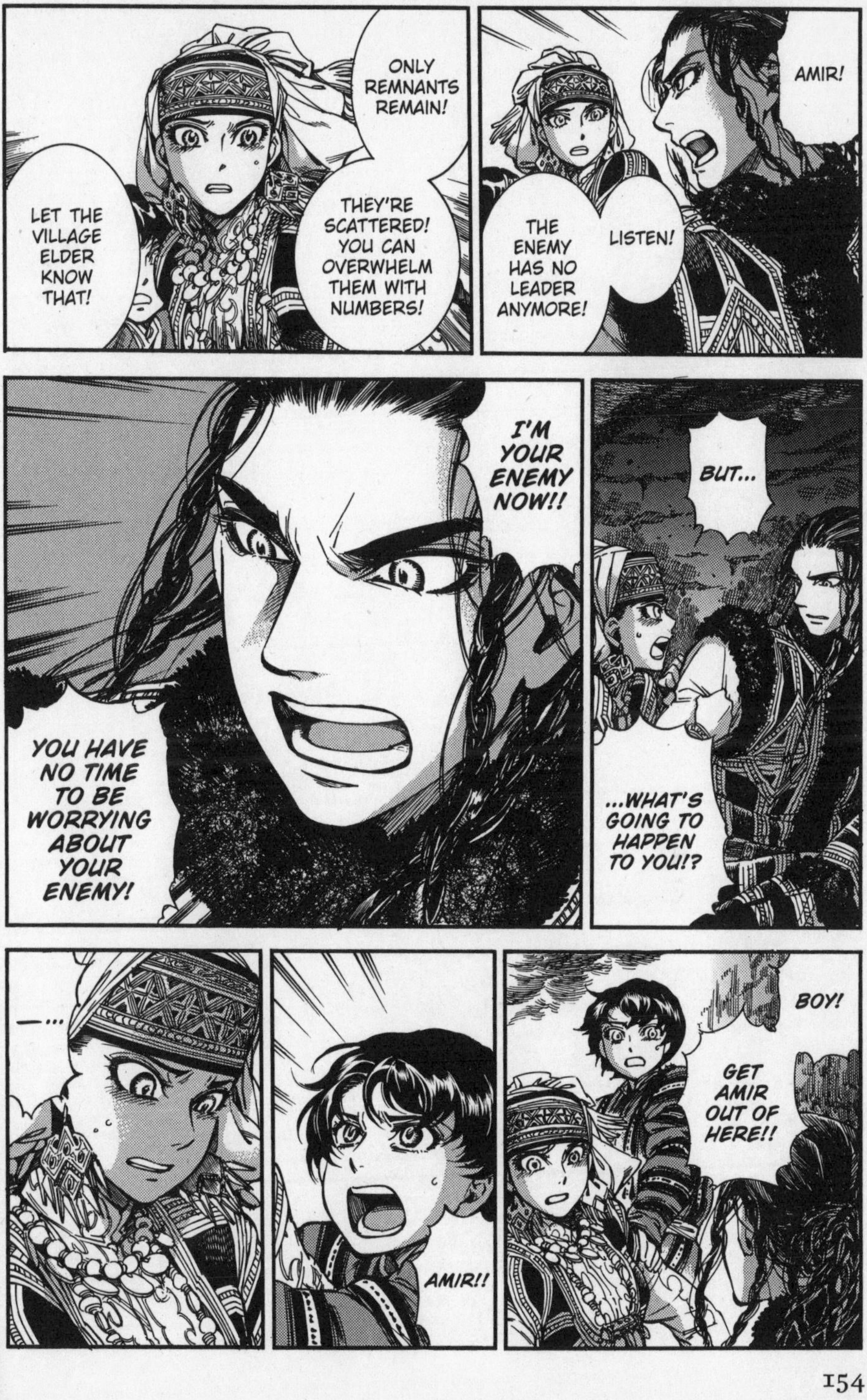
AMIR!
LISTEN!
THE ENEMY HAS NO LEADER ANYMORE!
ONLY REMNANTS REMAIN!
THEY'RE SCATTERED! YOU CAN OVERWHELM THEM WITH NUMBERS!
LET THE VILLAGE ELDER KNOW THAT!
BUT...
...WHAT'S GOING TO HAPPEN TO YOU!?
I'M YOUR ENEMY NOW!!
YOU HAVE NO TIME TO BE WORRYING ABOUT YOUR ENEMY!
BOY!
GET AMIR OUT OF HERE!!
AMIR!!
—...

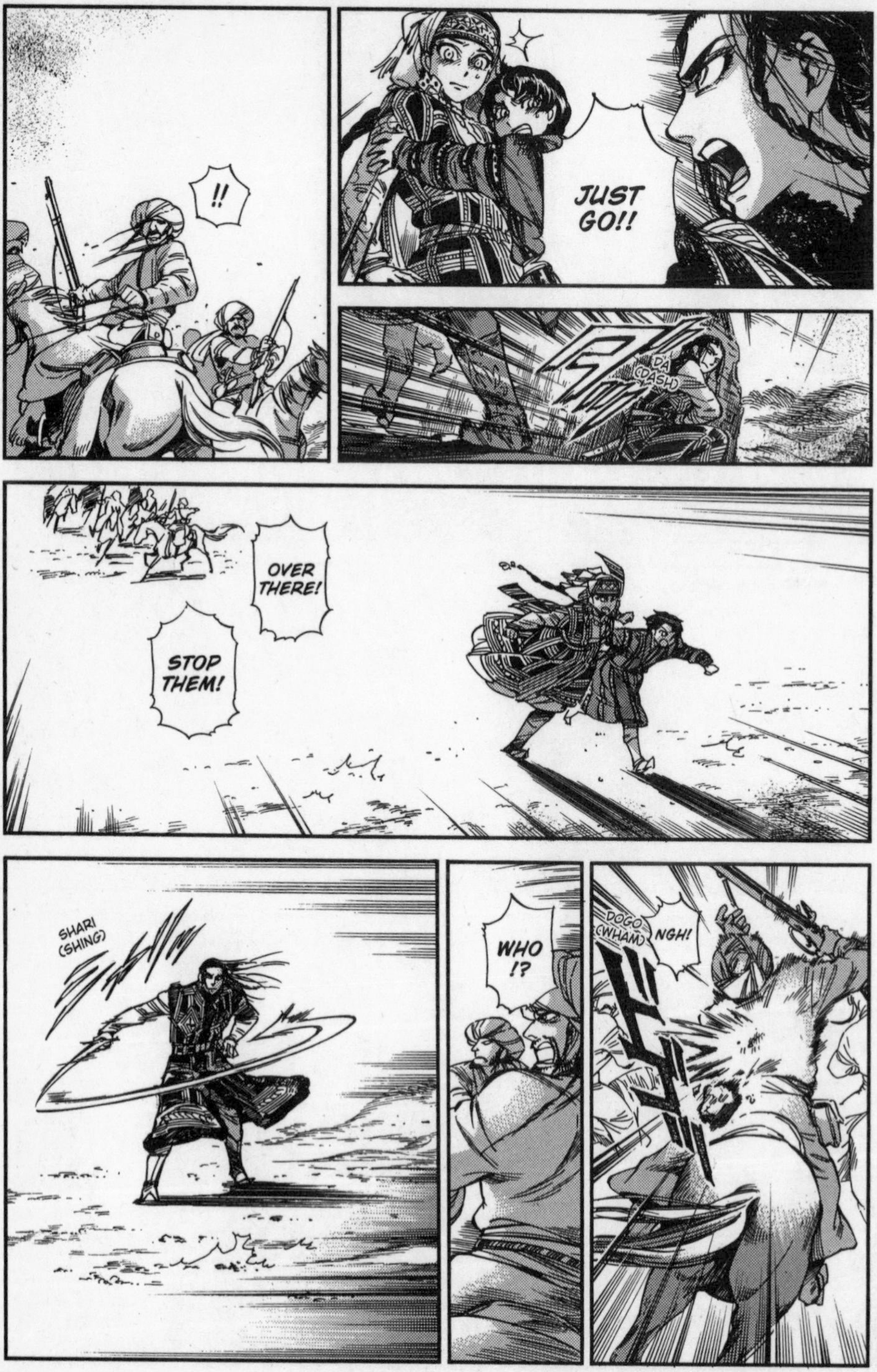
JUST GO!!
DA (DASH)
!!
OVER THERE!
STOP THEM!
NGH!
DOGO (WHAM)
WHO !?
SHARI (SHING)

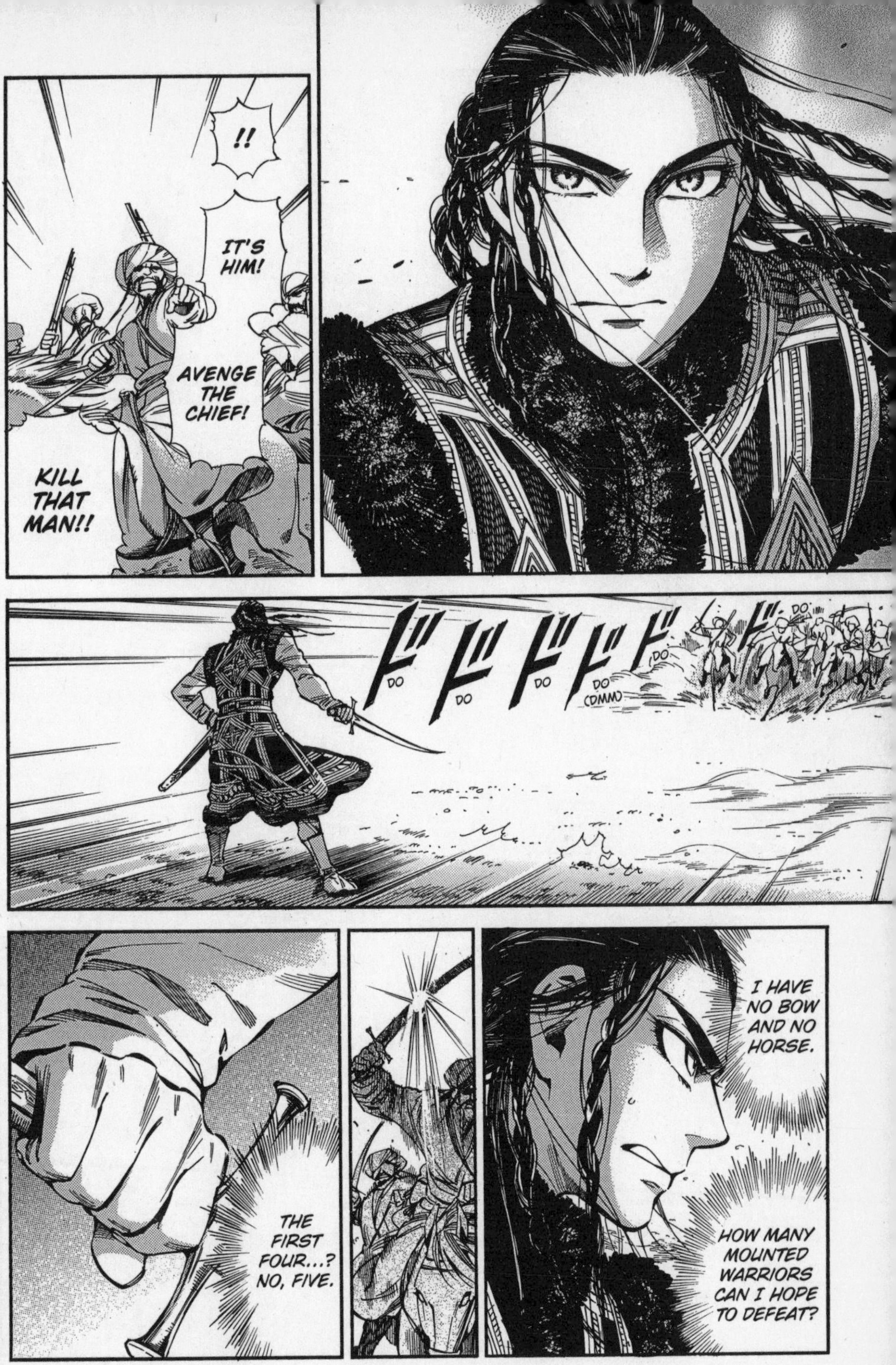
!!
IT'S HIM!
AVENGE THE CHIEF!
KILL THAT MAN!!
ドドドドドド
DO DO DO DO DO DO (DMM)
I HAVE NO BOW AND NO HORSE.
HOW MANY MOUNTED WARRIORS CAN I HOPE TO DEFEAT?
THE FIRST FOUR...? NO, FIVE.

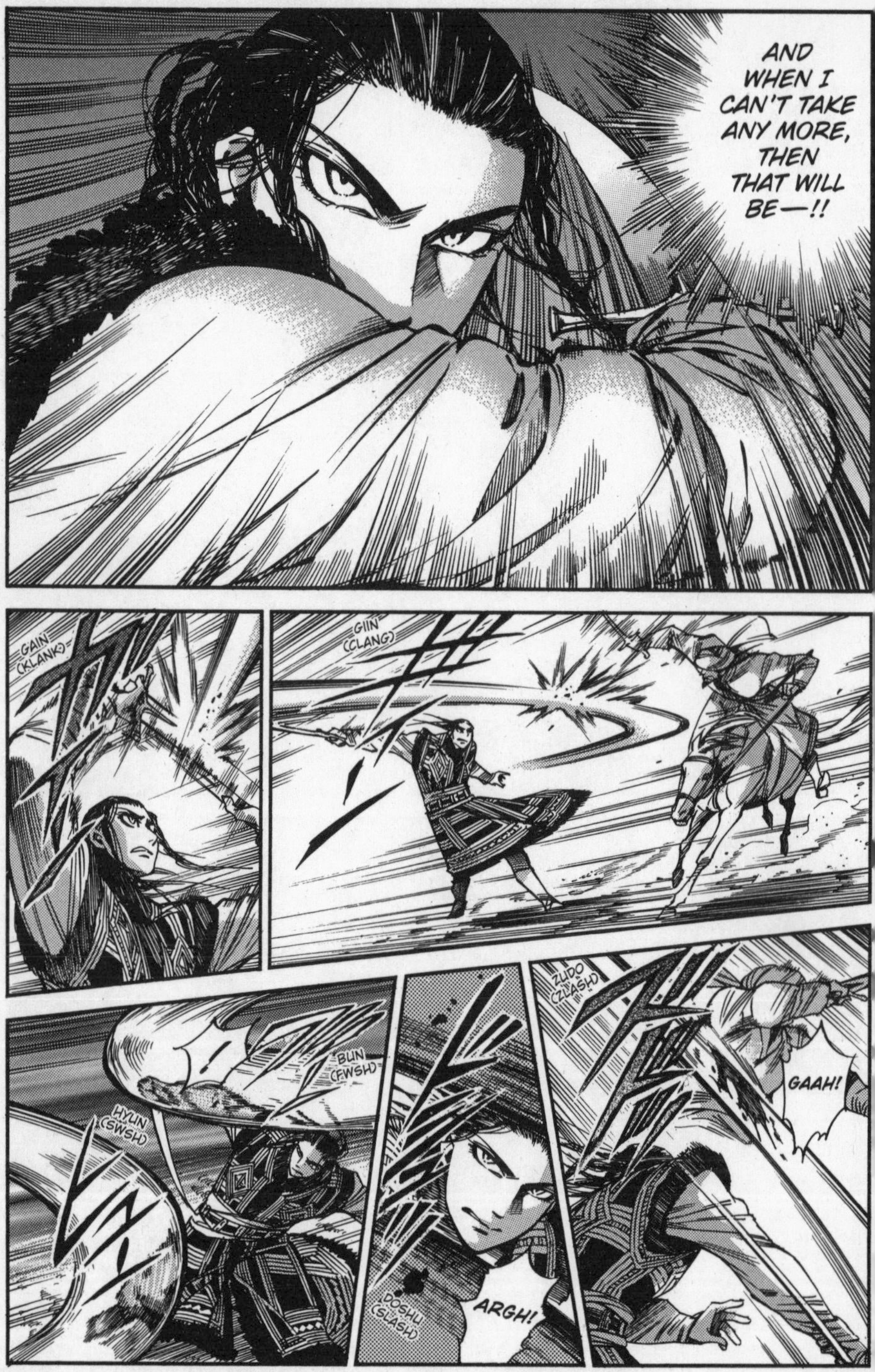
AND WHEN I CAN'T TAKE ANY MORE, THEN THAT WILL BE—!!
GIIN (CLANG)
GAIN (KLANK)
ZUDO (ZLASH)
GAAH!
DOSHU (SLASH)
ARGH!
BUN (FWSH)
HYUN (SWSH)

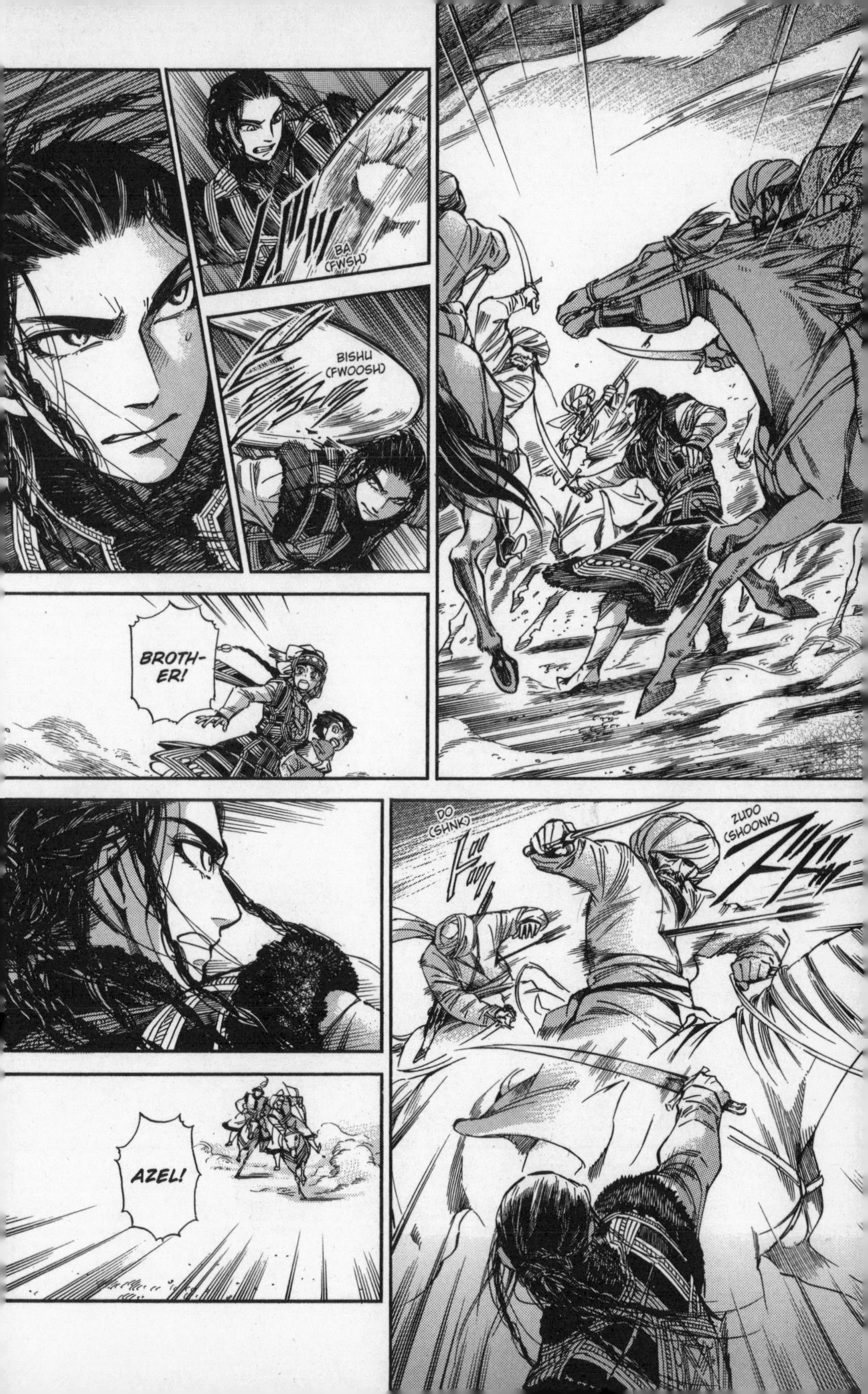
BA (FWSH)
BISHU (FWOOSH)
BROTHER!
ZUDO (SHOONK)
DO (SHNK)
AZEL!

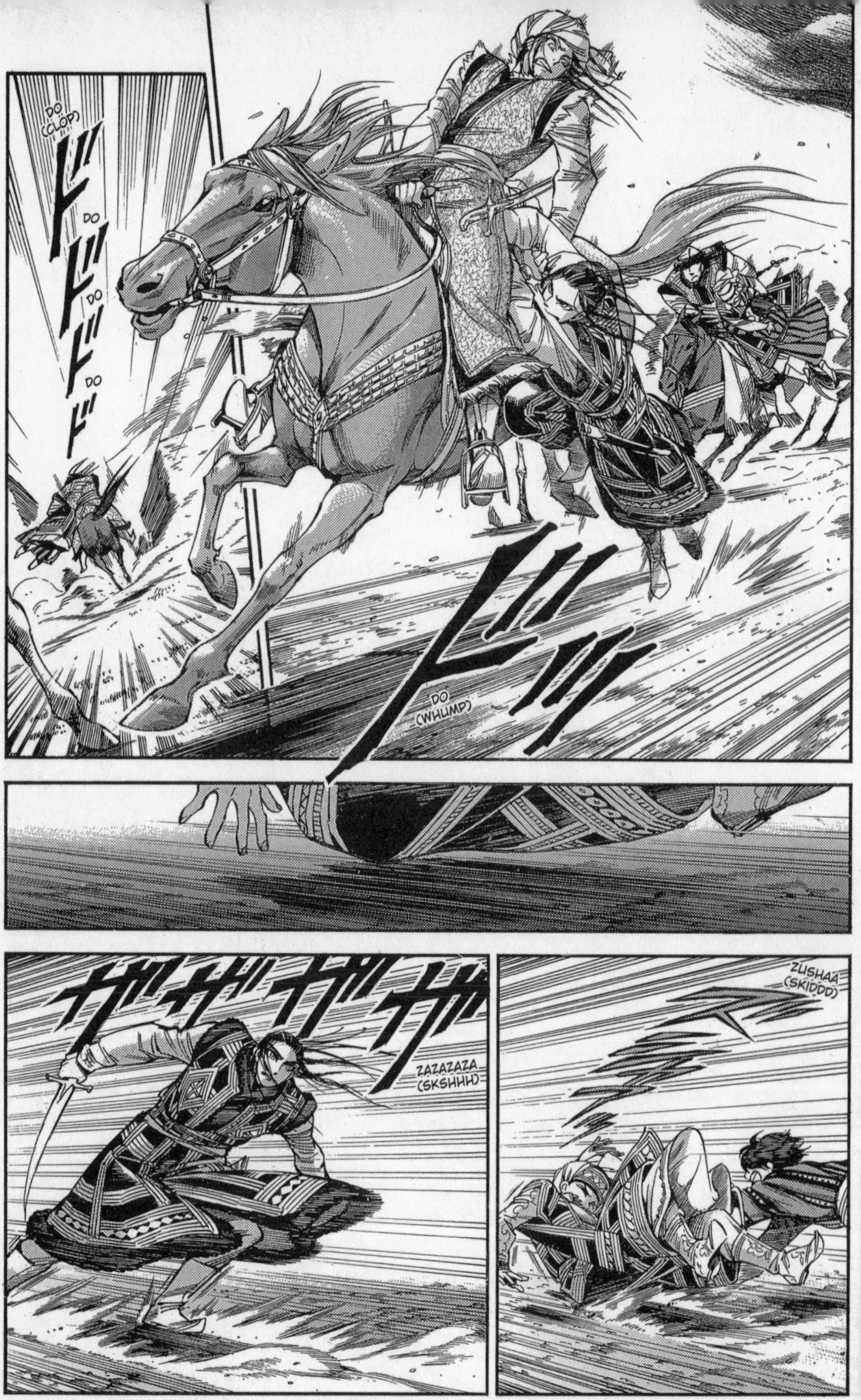
DO (CLOP)
DO
DO
DO
DO (WHUMP)
ZUSHAA (SKIDDD)
ZAZAZAZA (SKSHHH)

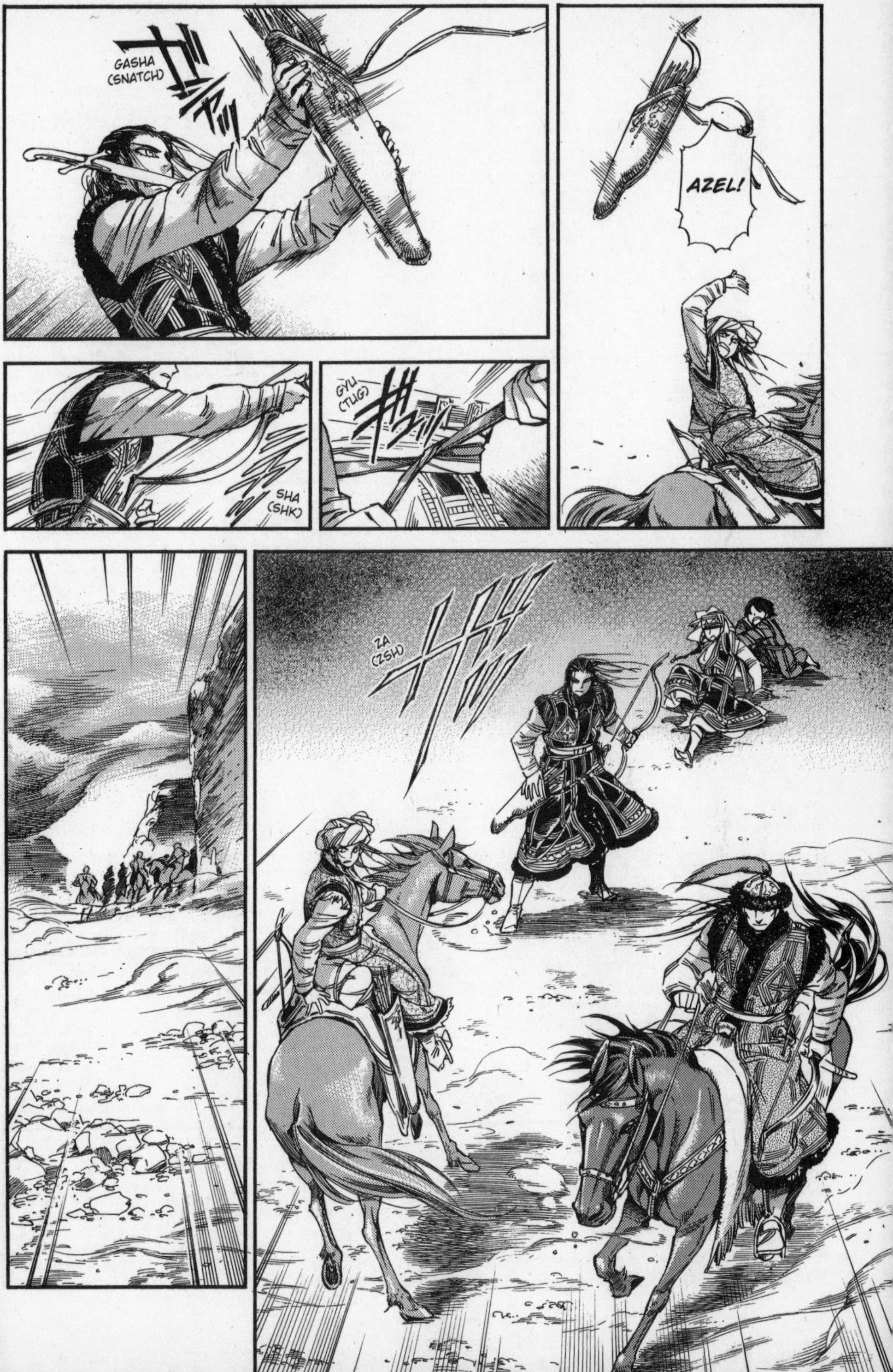
AZEL!
GASHA (SNATCH)
GYU (TUG)
SHA (SHK)
ZA (ZSH)

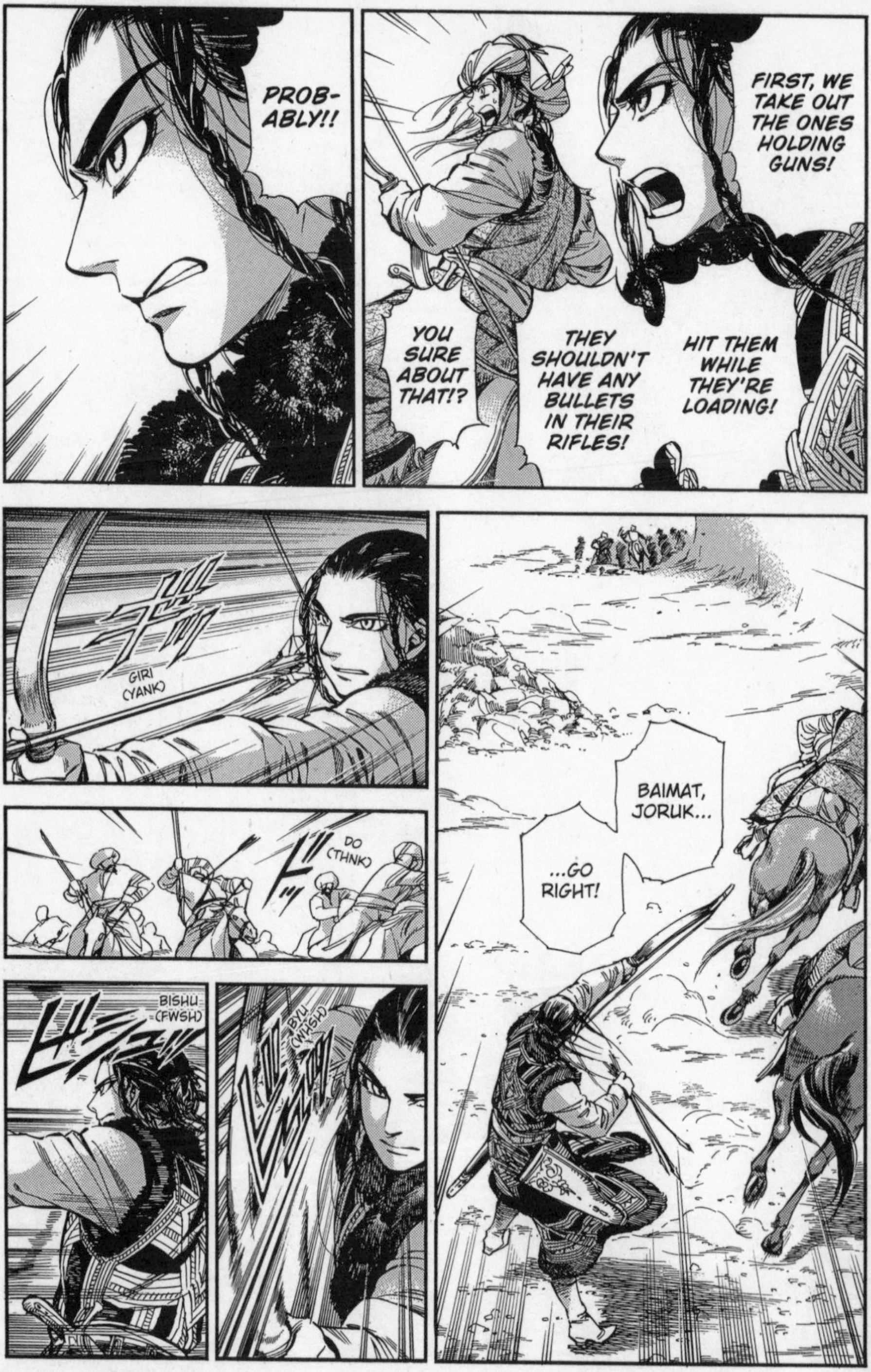
FIRST, WE TAKE OUT THE ONES HOLDING GUNS!
HIT THEM WHILE THEY'RE LOADING!
THEY SHOULDN'T HAVE ANY BULLETS IN THEIR RIFLES!
YOU SURE ABOUT THAT!?
PROB-ABLY!!
BAIMAT, JORUK...
...GO RIGHT!
GIRI (YANK)
DO (THNK)
BYU (WHSH)
BISHU (FWSH)

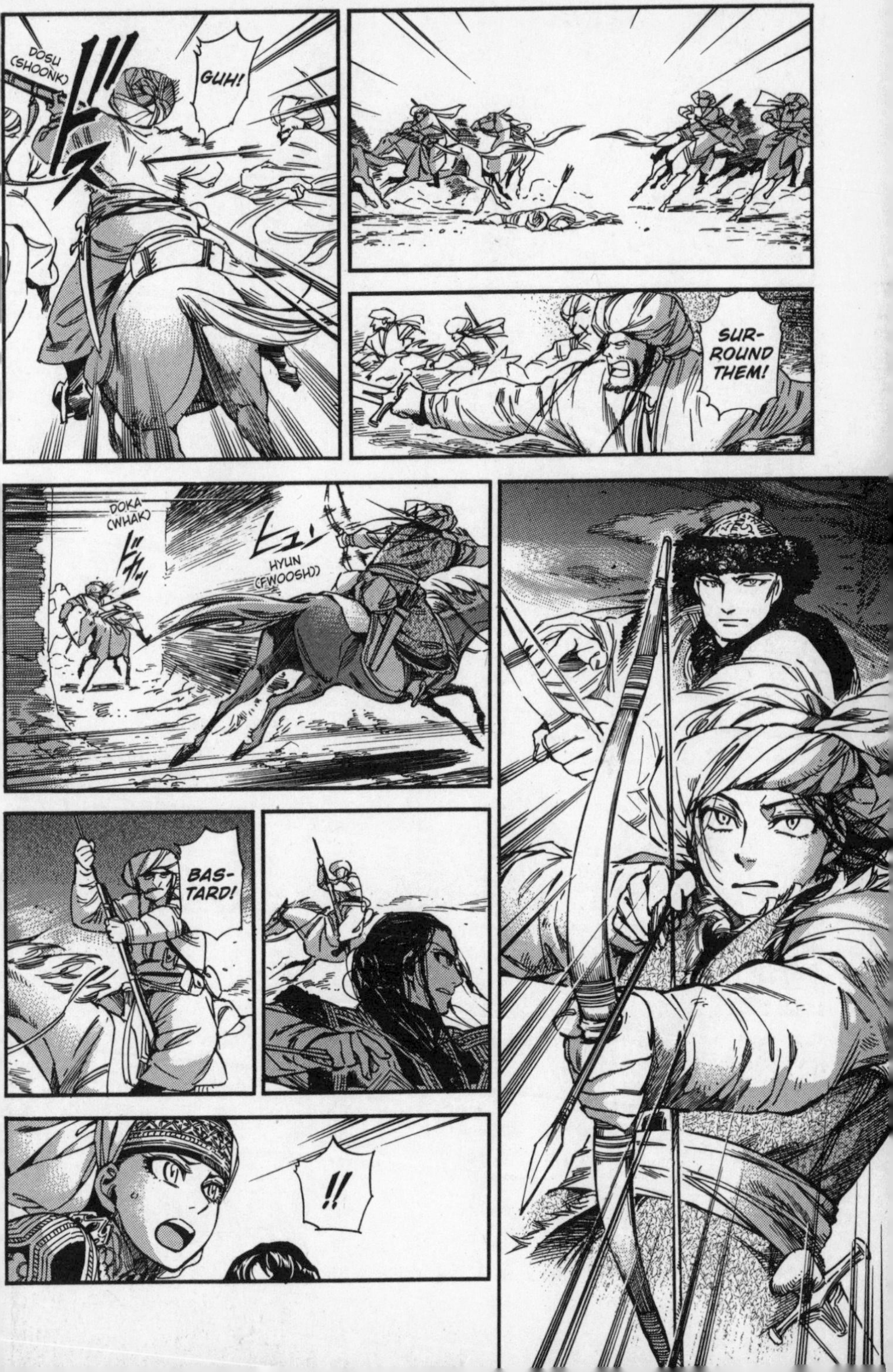
SUR-ROUND THEM!
DOSU (SHOONK)
ドス
GUH!
ヒュッ
HYUN (FWOOSH)
DOKA (WHAK)
ドカッ
BAS-TARD!
!!

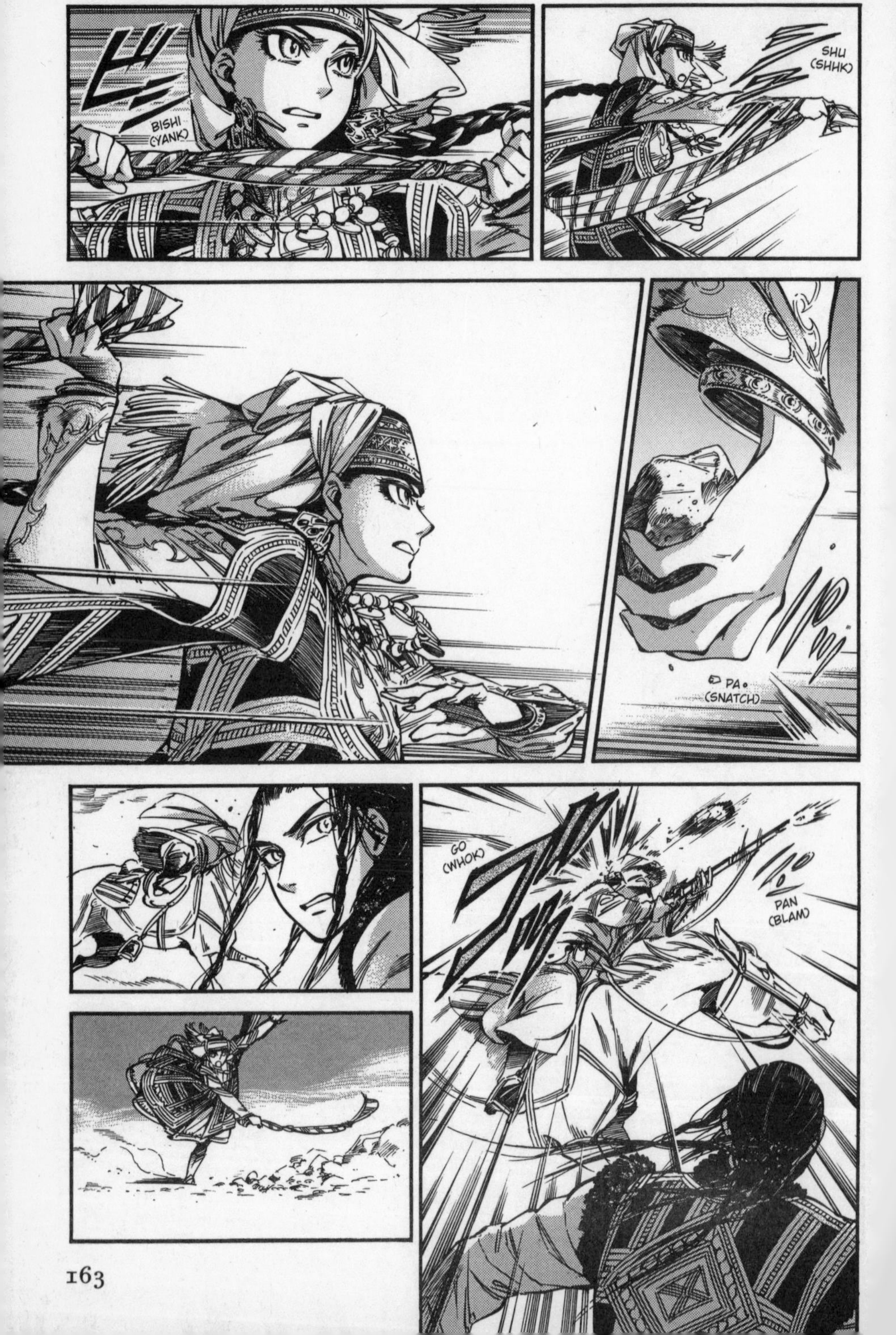
SHU
(SHHK)
BISHI
(YANK)
PA
(SNATCH)
GO
(WHOK)
PAN
(BLAM)

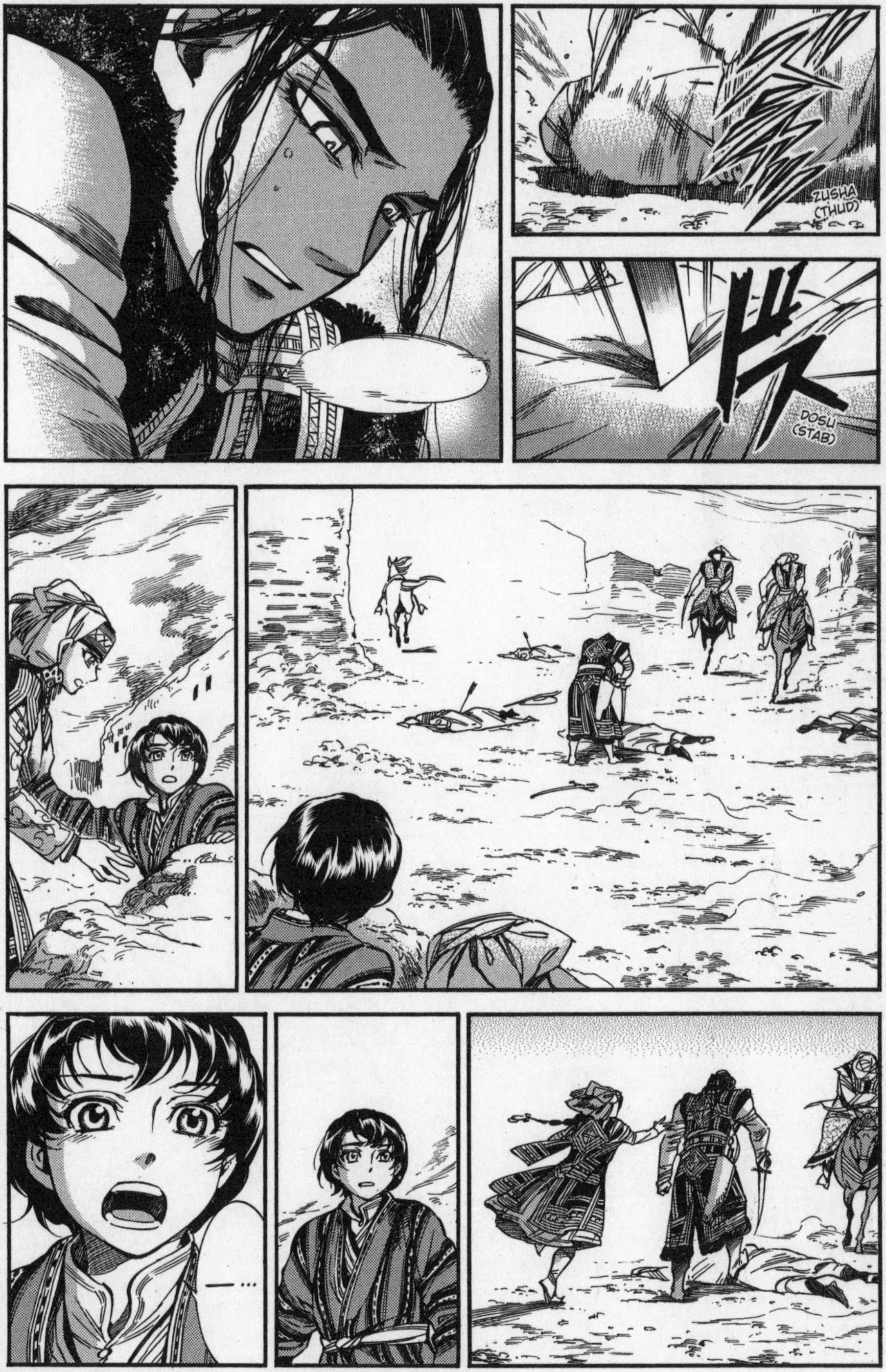
ZUSHA (THUD)
DOSU (STAB)
—...

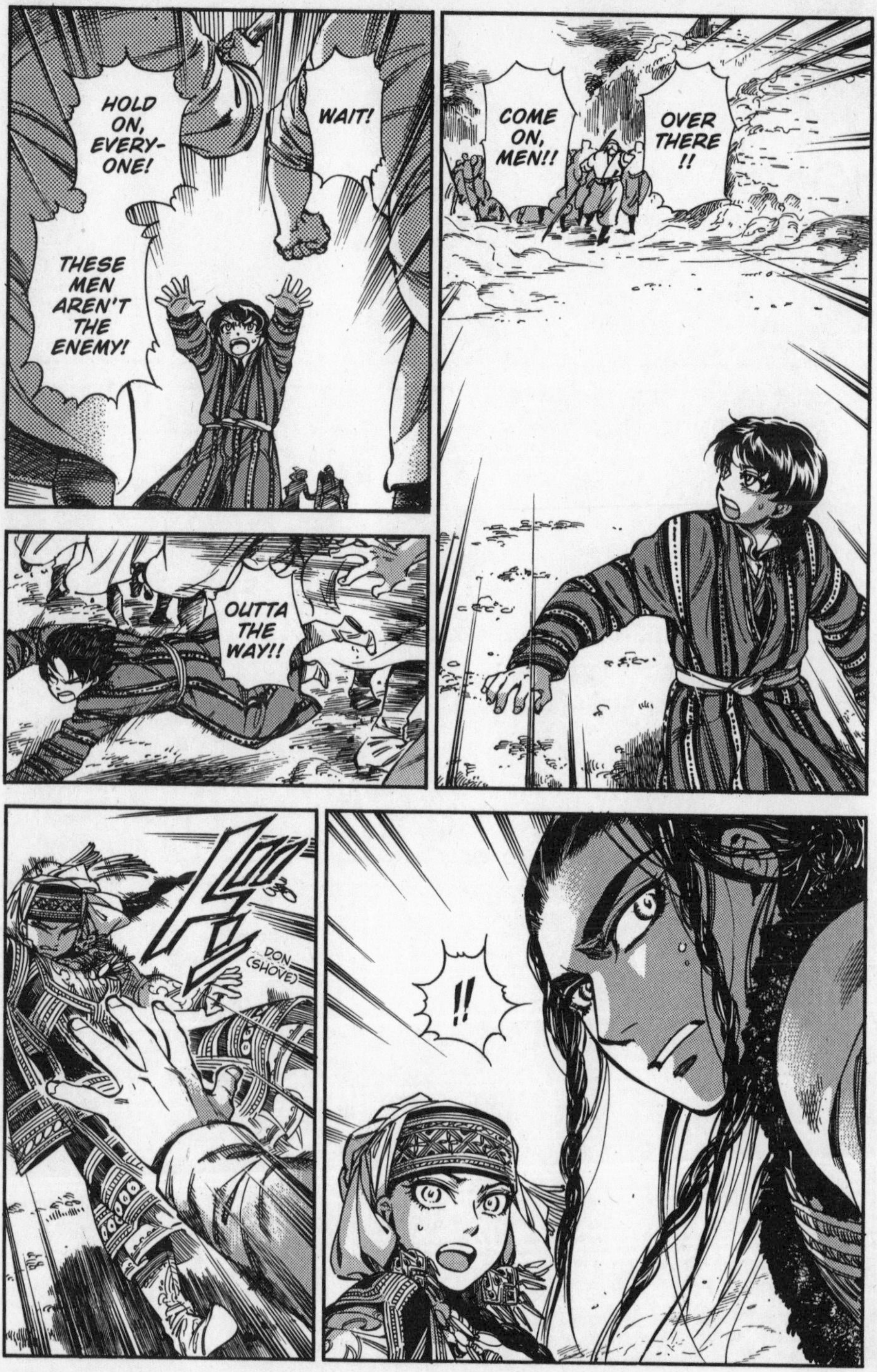
OVER THERE!!
COME ON, MEN!!
WAIT!
HOLD ON, EVERYONE!
THESE MEN AREN'T THE ENEMY!
OUTTA THE WAY!!
!!
DON (SHOVE)

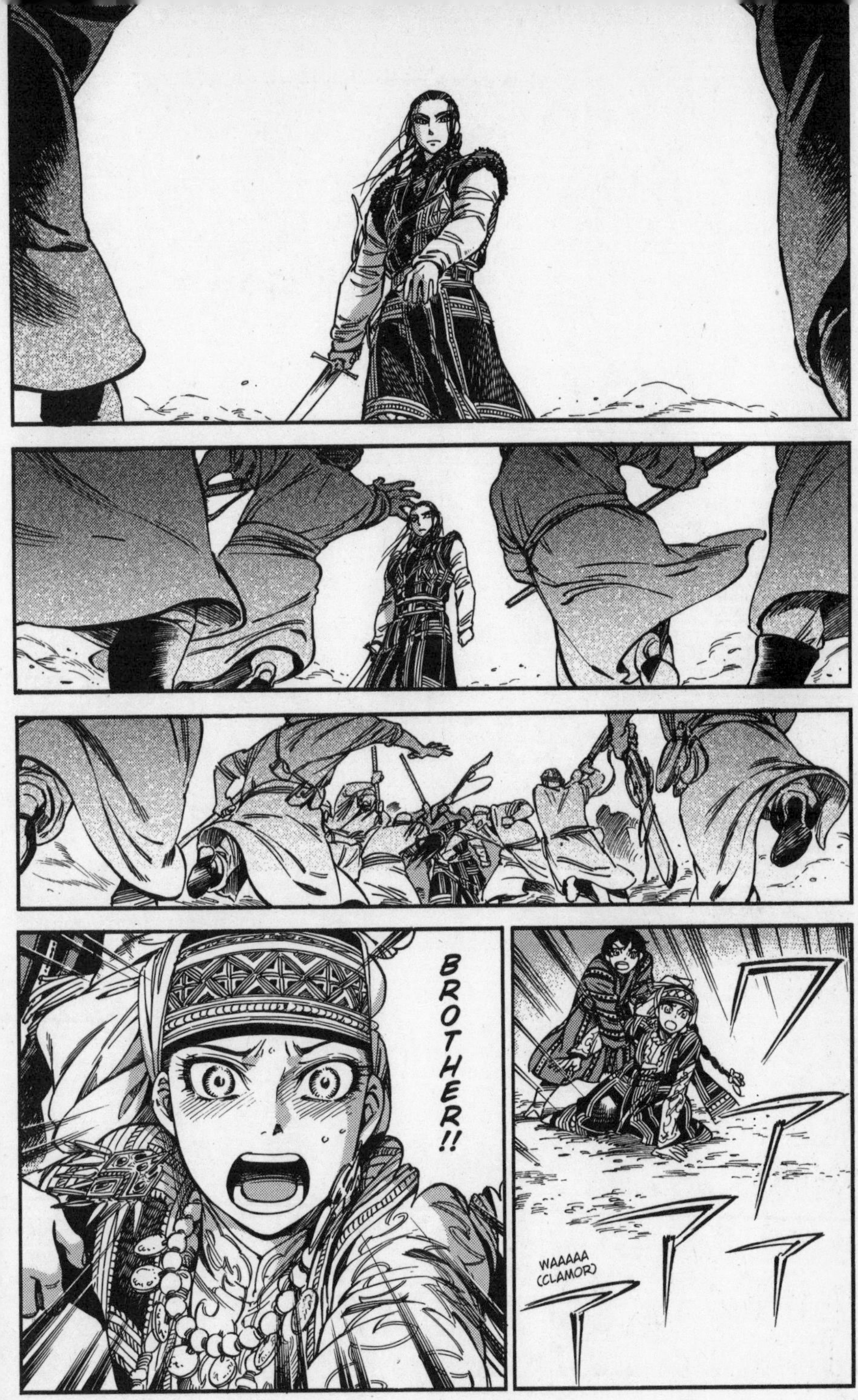
BROTHER!!
WAAAAA (CLAMOR)

♦ Chapter 34: End ♦

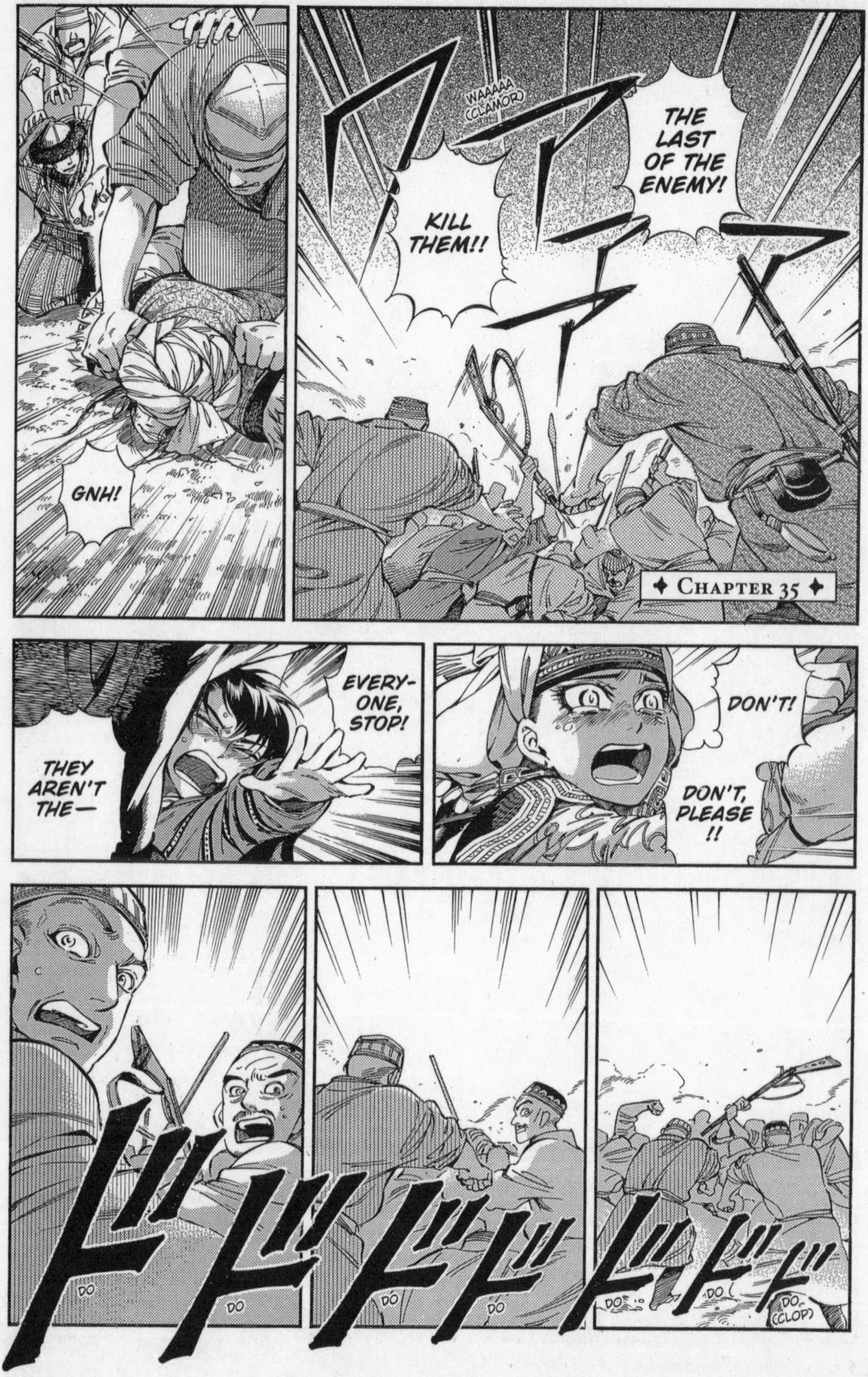
WAAAAA (CLAMOR)
THE LAST OF THE ENEMY!
KILL THEM!!
Chapter 35
GNH!
DON'T!
DON'T, PLEASE !!
EVERY-ONE, STOP!
THEY AREN'T THE—
DO
DO
DO (CLOP)
DO
DO
DO
DO

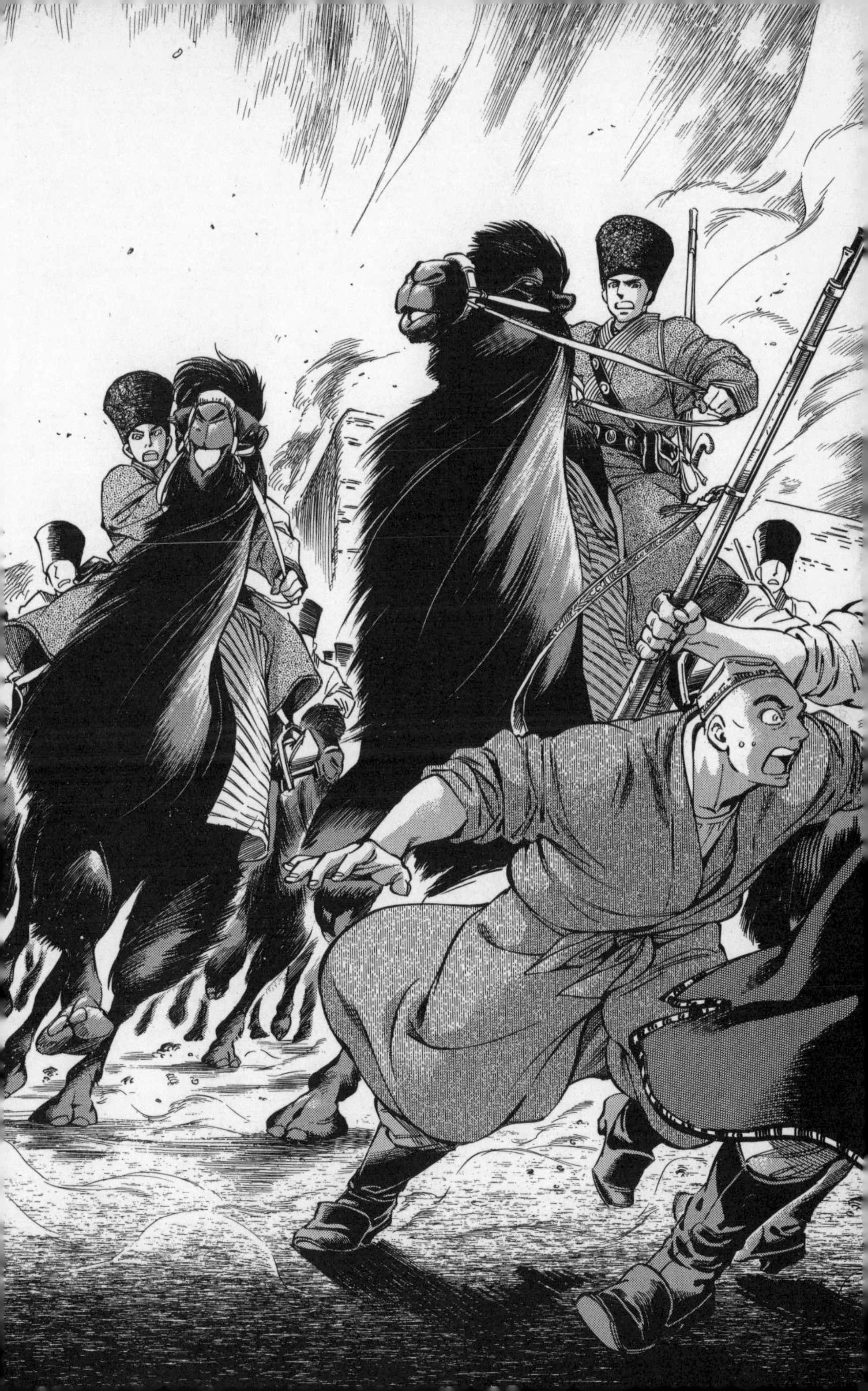

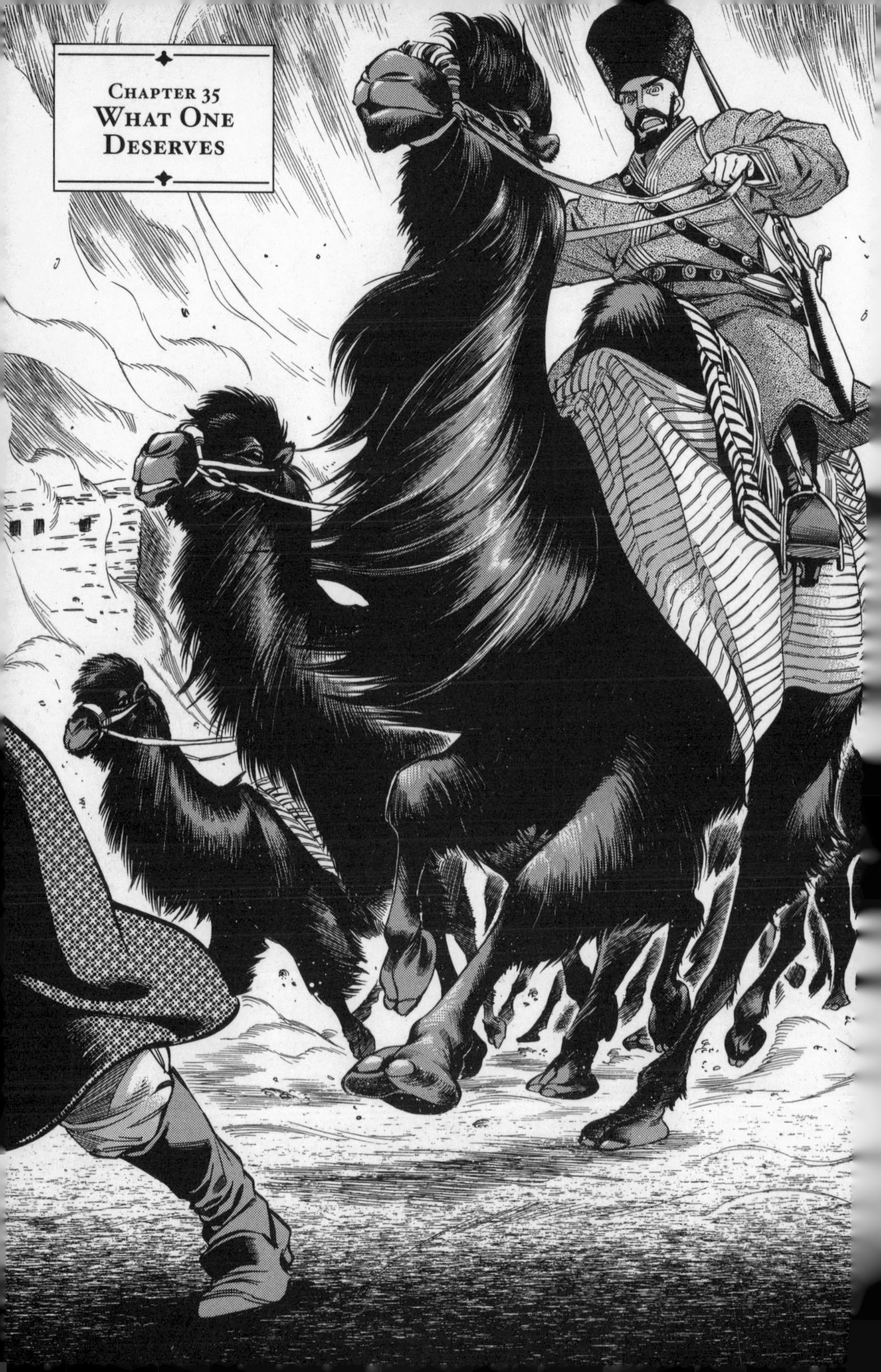
Chapter 35
What One
Deserves

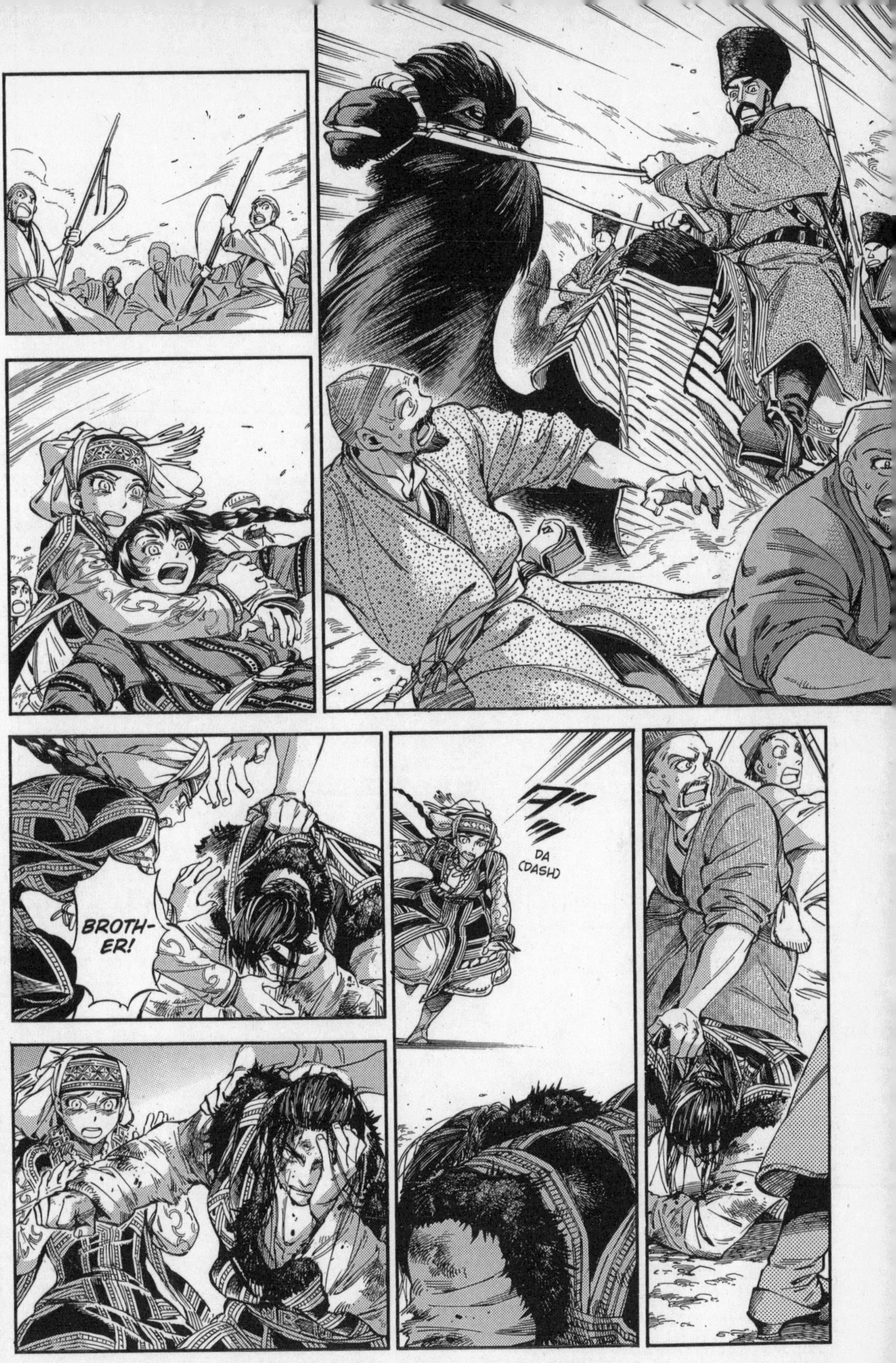
ダッ
DA (DASH)
BROTHER-ER!

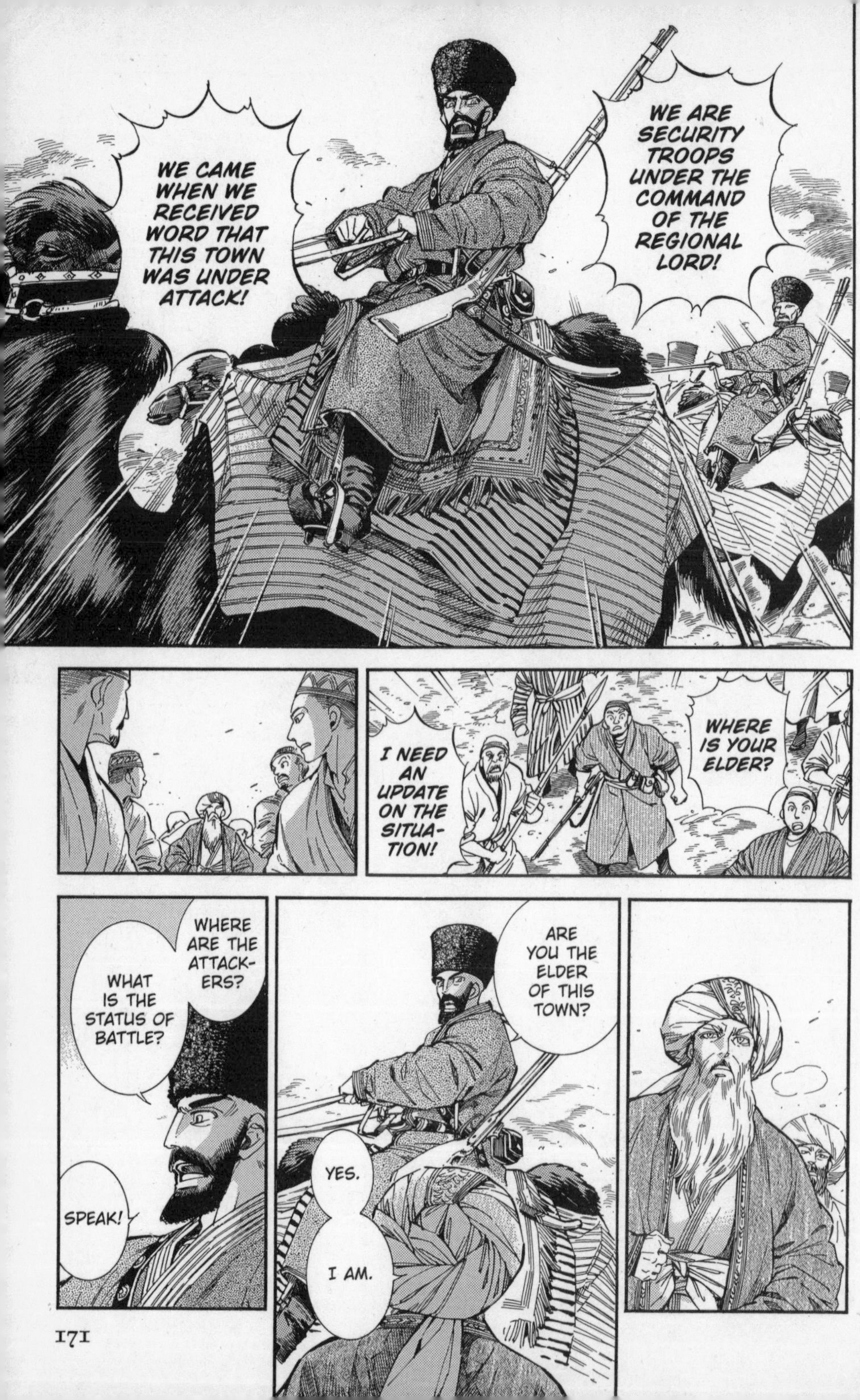
WE ARE SECURITY TROOPS UNDER THE COMMAND OF THE REGIONAL LORD!
WE CAME WHEN WE RECEIVED WORD THAT THIS TOWN WAS UNDER ATTACK!
WHERE IS YOUR ELDER?
I NEED AN UPDATE ON THE SITUA-TION!
ARE YOU THE ELDER OF THIS TOWN?
YES.
I AM.
WHERE ARE THE ATTACK-ERS?
WHAT IS THE STATUS OF BATTLE?
SPEAK!

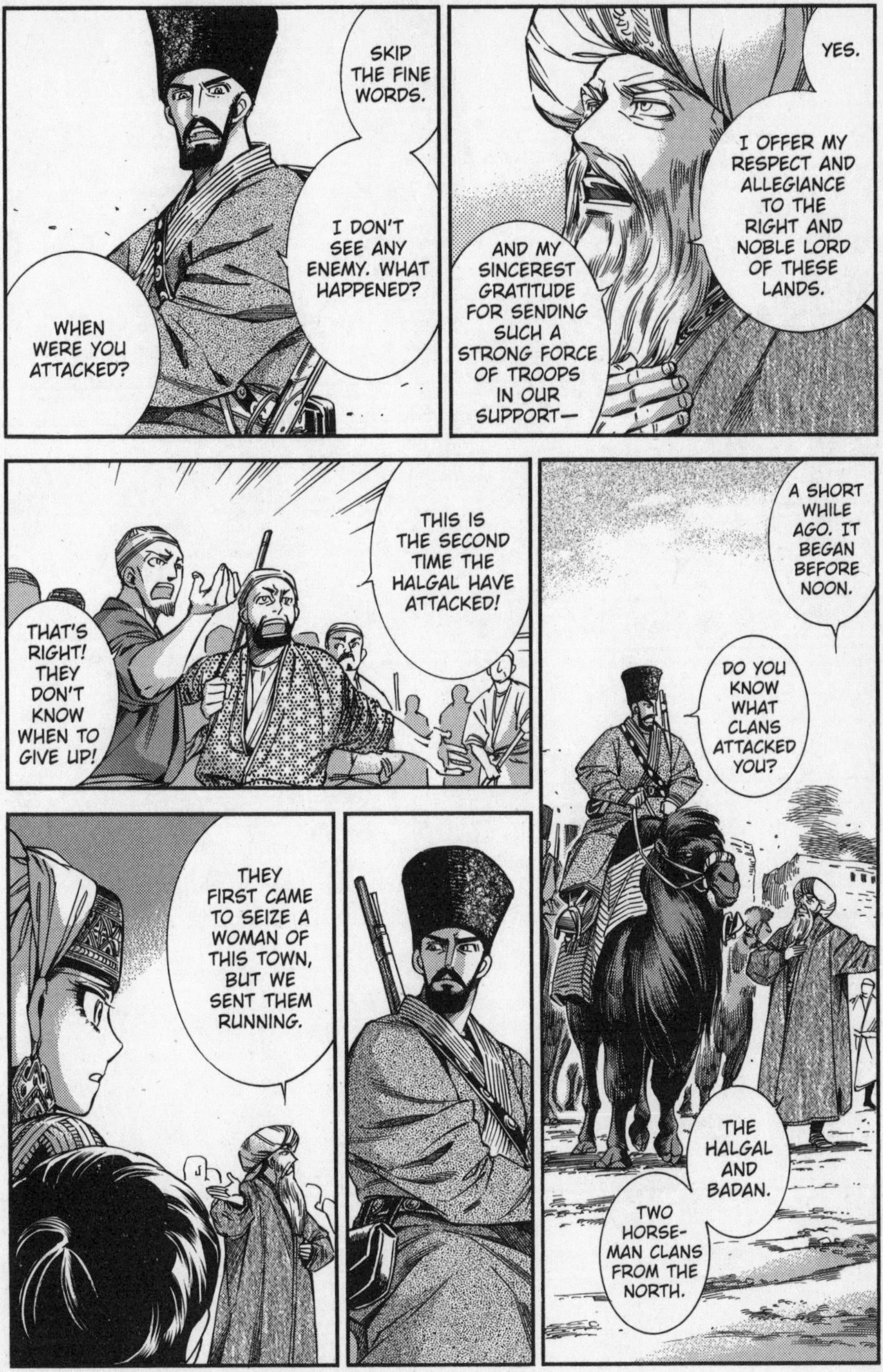
YES.
I OFFER MY RESPECT AND ALLEGIANCE TO THE RIGHT AND NOBLE LORD OF THESE LANDS.
AND MY SINCEREST GRATITUDE FOR SENDING SUCH A STRONG FORCE OF TROOPS IN OUR SUPPORT—
SKIP THE FINE WORDS.
I DON'T SEE ANY ENEMY. WHAT HAPPENED?
WHEN WERE YOU ATTACKED?
A SHORT WHILE AGO. IT BEGAN BEFORE NOON.
DO YOU KNOW WHAT CLANS ATTACKED YOU?
THE HALGAL AND BADAN.
TWO HORSEMAN CLANS FROM THE NORTH.
THIS IS THE SECOND TIME THE HALGAL HAVE ATTACKED!
THAT'S RIGHT! THEY DON'T KNOW WHEN TO GIVE UP!
THEY FIRST CAME TO SEIZE A WOMAN OF THIS TOWN, BUT WE SENT THEM RUNNING.

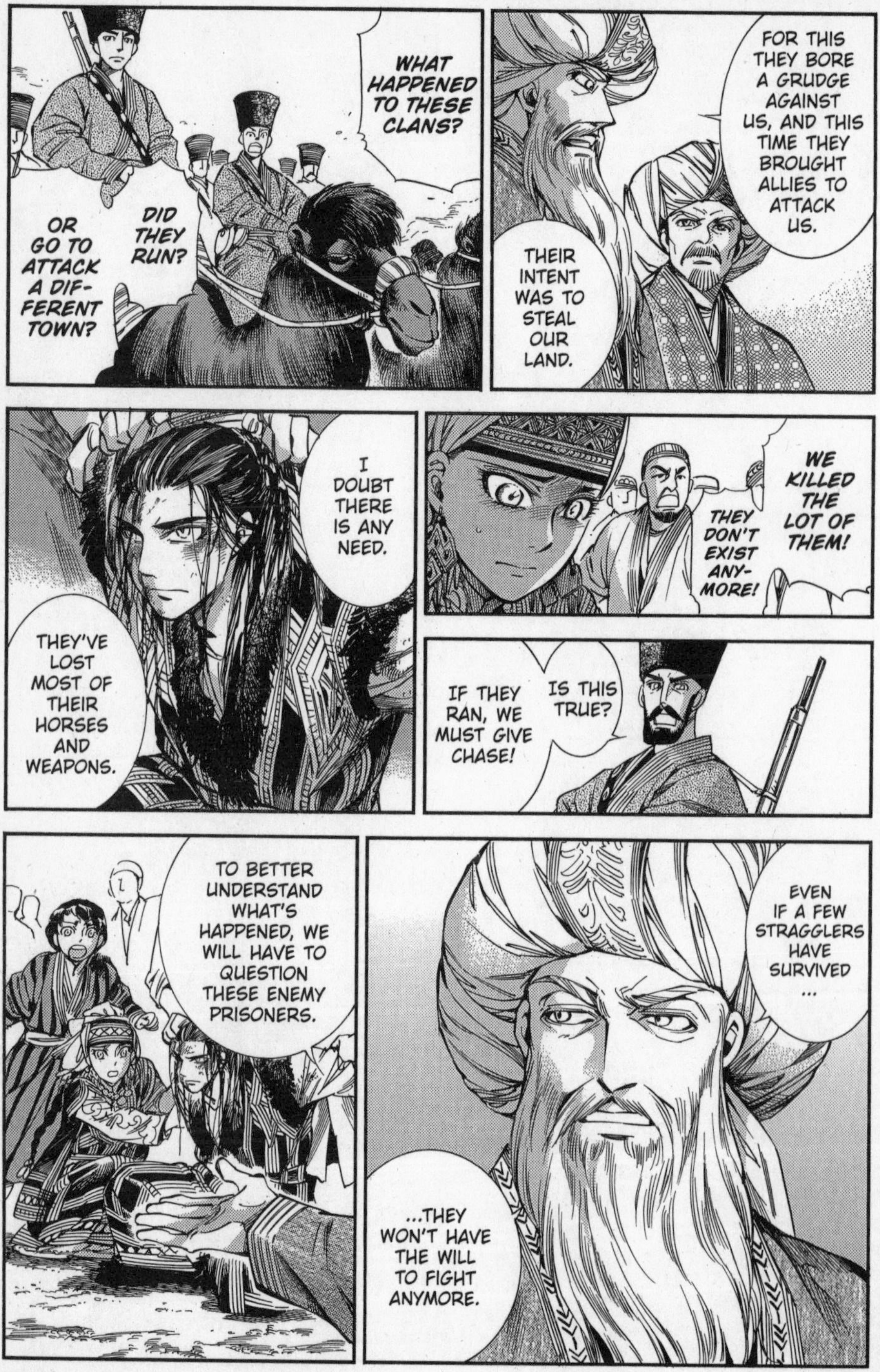
FOR THIS THEY BORE A GRUDGE AGAINST US, AND THIS TIME THEY BROUGHT ALLIES TO ATTACK US.
THEIR INTENT WAS TO STEAL OUR LAND.
WHAT HAPPENED TO THESE CLANS?
DID THEY RUN?
OR GO TO ATTACK A DIF-FERENT TOWN?
WE KILLED THE LOT OF THEM!
THEY DON'T EXIST ANY-MORE!
IS THIS TRUE?
IF THEY RAN, WE MUST GIVE CHASE!
I DOUBT THERE IS ANY NEED.
THEY'VE LOST MOST OF THEIR HORSES AND WEAPONS.
EVEN IF A FEW STRAGGLERS HAVE SURVIVED ...
...THEY WON'T HAVE THE WILL TO FIGHT ANYMORE.
TO BETTER UNDERSTAND WHAT'S HAPPENED, WE WILL HAVE TO QUESTION THESE ENEMY PRISONERS.

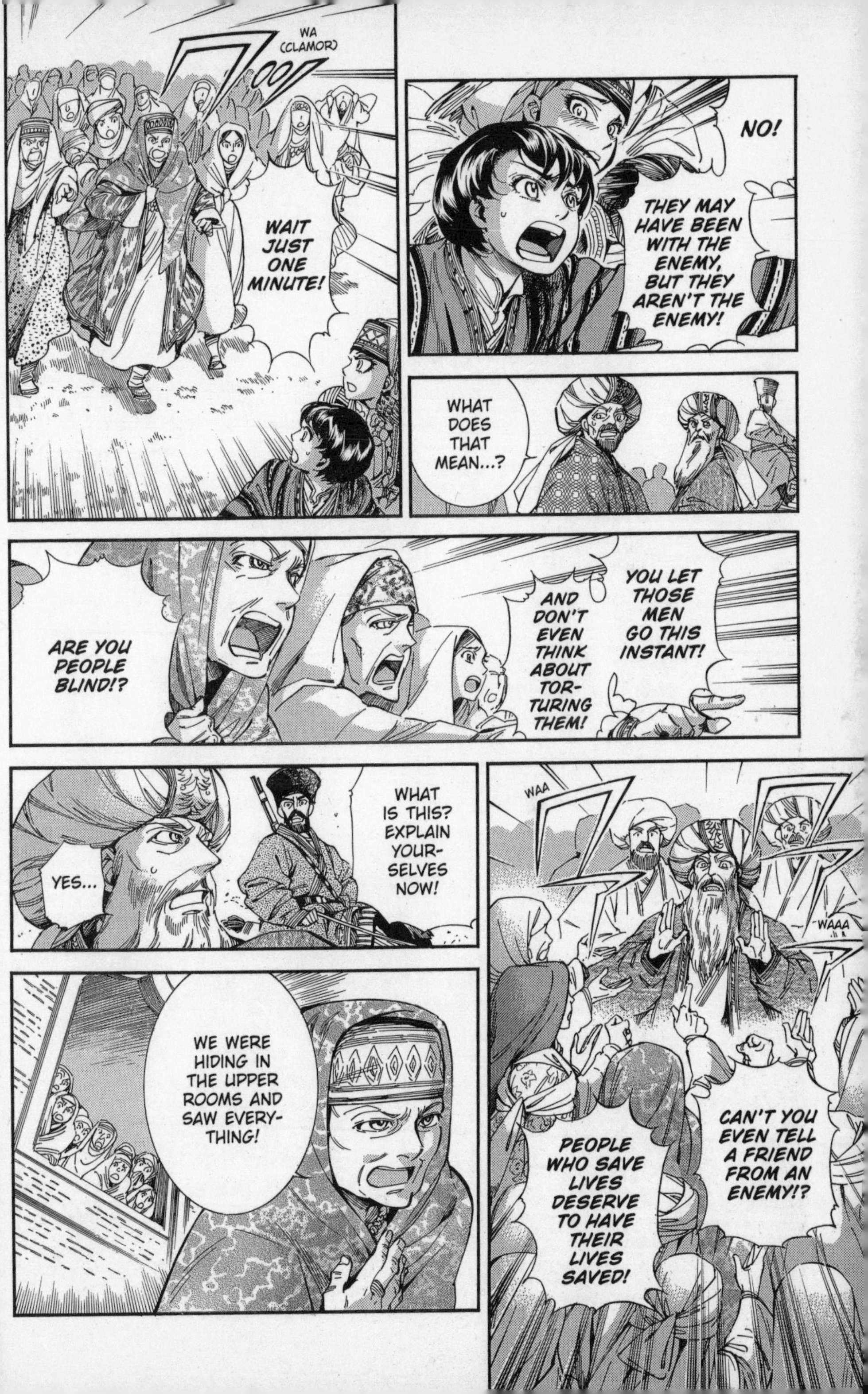
NO!
THEY MAY HAVE BEEN WITH THE ENEMY, BUT THEY AREN'T THE ENEMY!
WHAT DOES THAT MEAN...?
WA (CLAMOR)
WAIT JUST ONE MINUTE!
YOU LET THOSE MEN GO THIS INSTANT!
AND DON'T EVEN THINK ABOUT TOR-TURING THEM!
ARE YOU PEOPLE BLIND!?
WAA
WAAA
CAN'T YOU EVEN TELL A FRIEND FROM AN ENEMY!?
PEOPLE WHO SAVE LIVES DESERVE TO HAVE THEIR LIVES SAVED!
WHAT IS THIS? EXPLAIN YOUR-SELVES NOW!
YES...
WE WERE HIDING IN THE UPPER ROOMS AND SAW EVERY-THING!

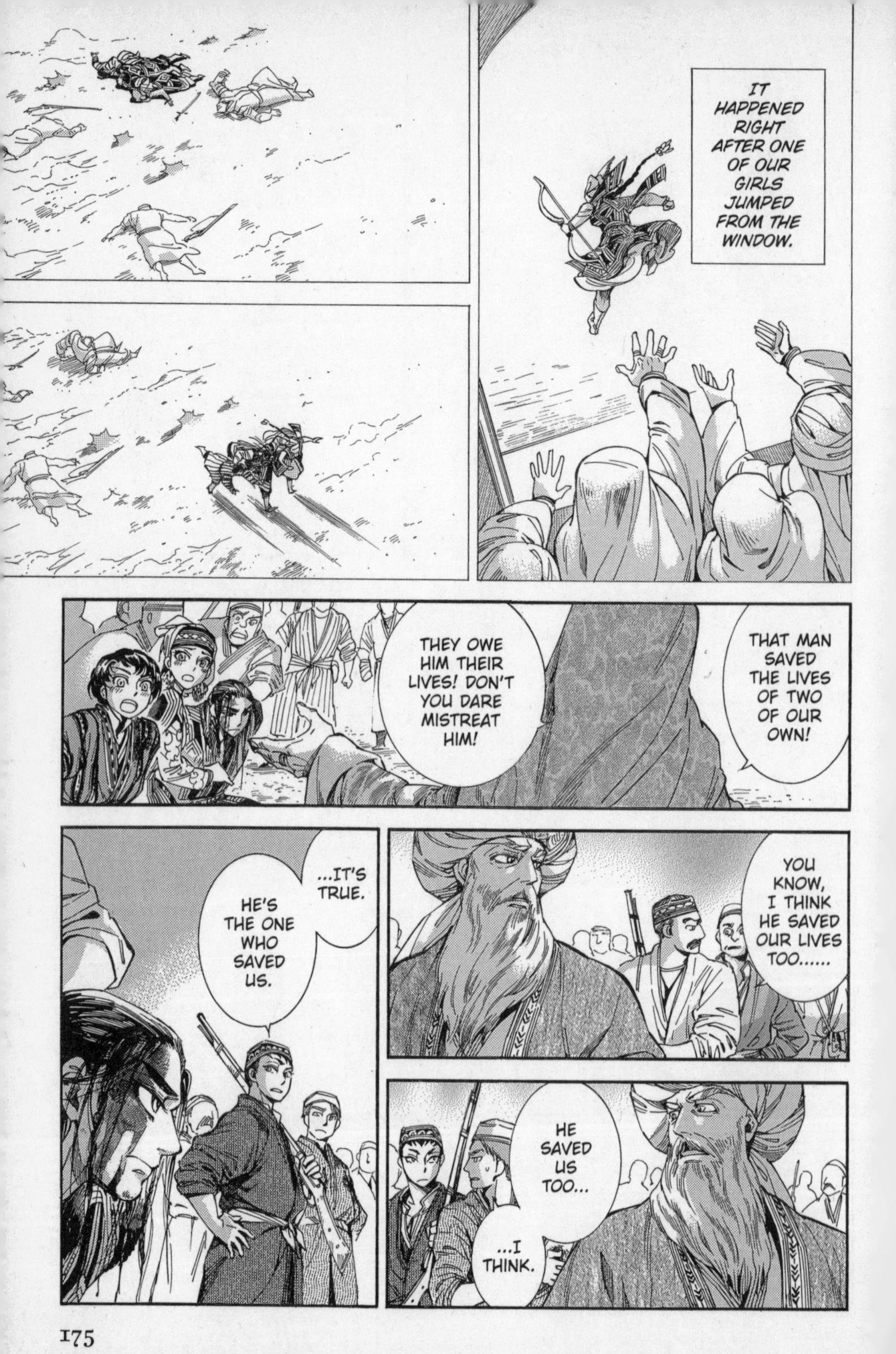
IT HAPPENED RIGHT AFTER ONE OF OUR GIRLS JUMPED FROM THE WINDOW.
THAT MAN SAVED THE LIVES OF TWO OF OUR OWN!
THEY OWE HIM THEIR LIVES! DON'T YOU DARE MISTREAT HIM!
YOU KNOW, I THINK HE SAVED OUR LIVES TOO......
HE SAVED US TOO...
...I THINK.
...IT'S TRUE.
HE'S THE ONE WHO SAVED US.

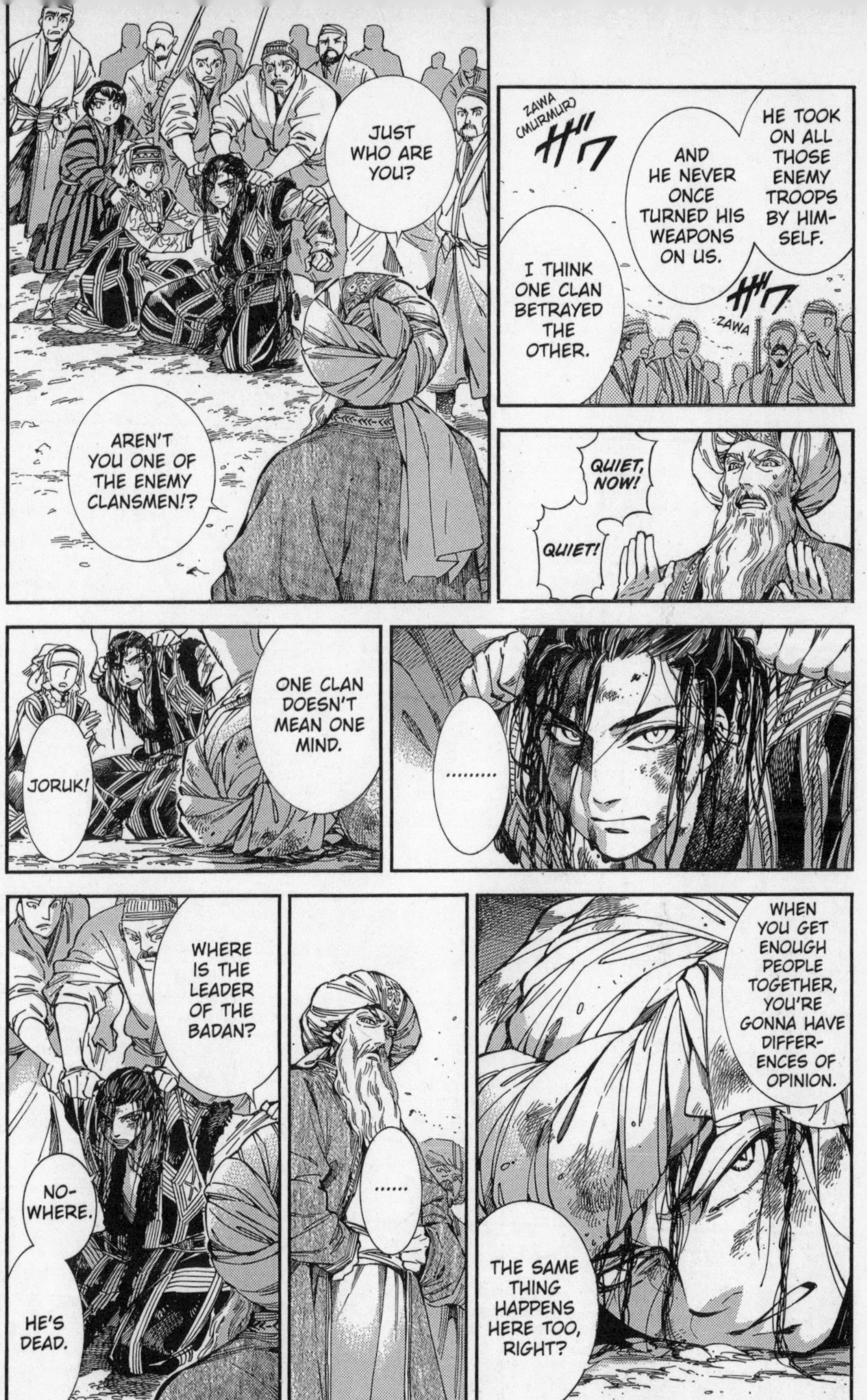
HE TOOK ON ALL THOSE ENEMY TROOPS BY HIM-SELF.
ZAWA (MURMUR)
ザワ
AND HE NEVER ONCE TURNED HIS WEAPONS ON US.
I THINK ONE CLAN BETRAYED THE OTHER.
ザワ
ZAWA
QUIET, NOW!
QUIET!
JUST WHO ARE YOU?
AREN'T YOU ONE OF THE ENEMY CLANSMEN!?
....
ONE CLAN DOESN'T MEAN ONE MIND.
JORUK!
WHEN YOU GET ENOUGH PEOPLE TOGETHER, YOU'RE GONNA HAVE DIFFER-ENCES OF OPINION.
THE SAME THING HAPPENS HERE TOO, RIGHT?
......
WHERE IS THE LEADER OF THE BADAN?
NO-WHERE.
HE'S DEAD.

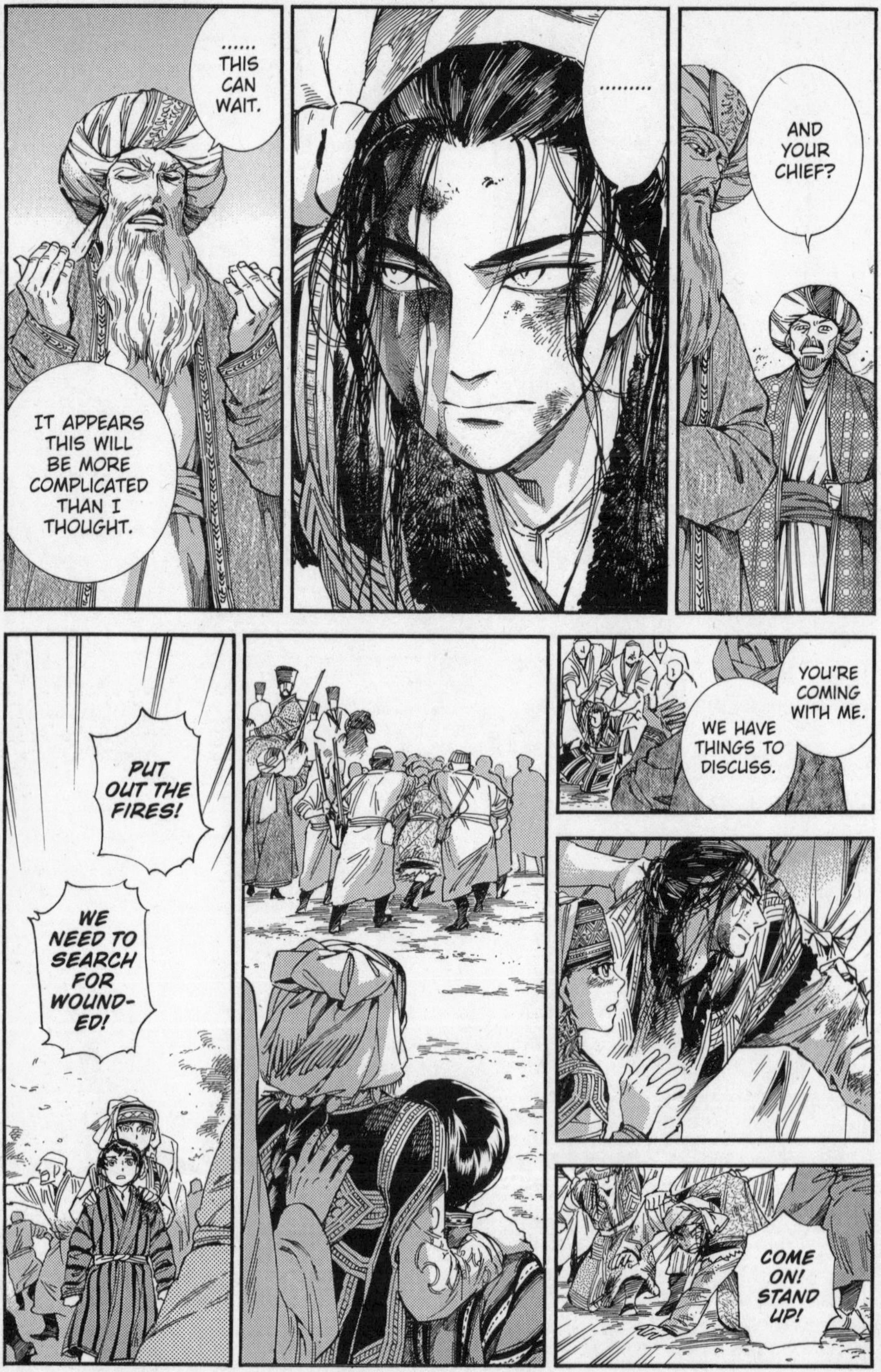
AND YOUR CHIEF?
....
...... THIS CAN WAIT.
IT APPEARS THIS WILL BE MORE COMPLICATED THAN I THOUGHT.
YOU'RE COMING WITH ME.
WE HAVE THINGS TO DISCUSS.
COME ON! STAND UP!
PUT OUT THE FIRES!
WE NEED TO SEARCH FOR WOUND-ED!

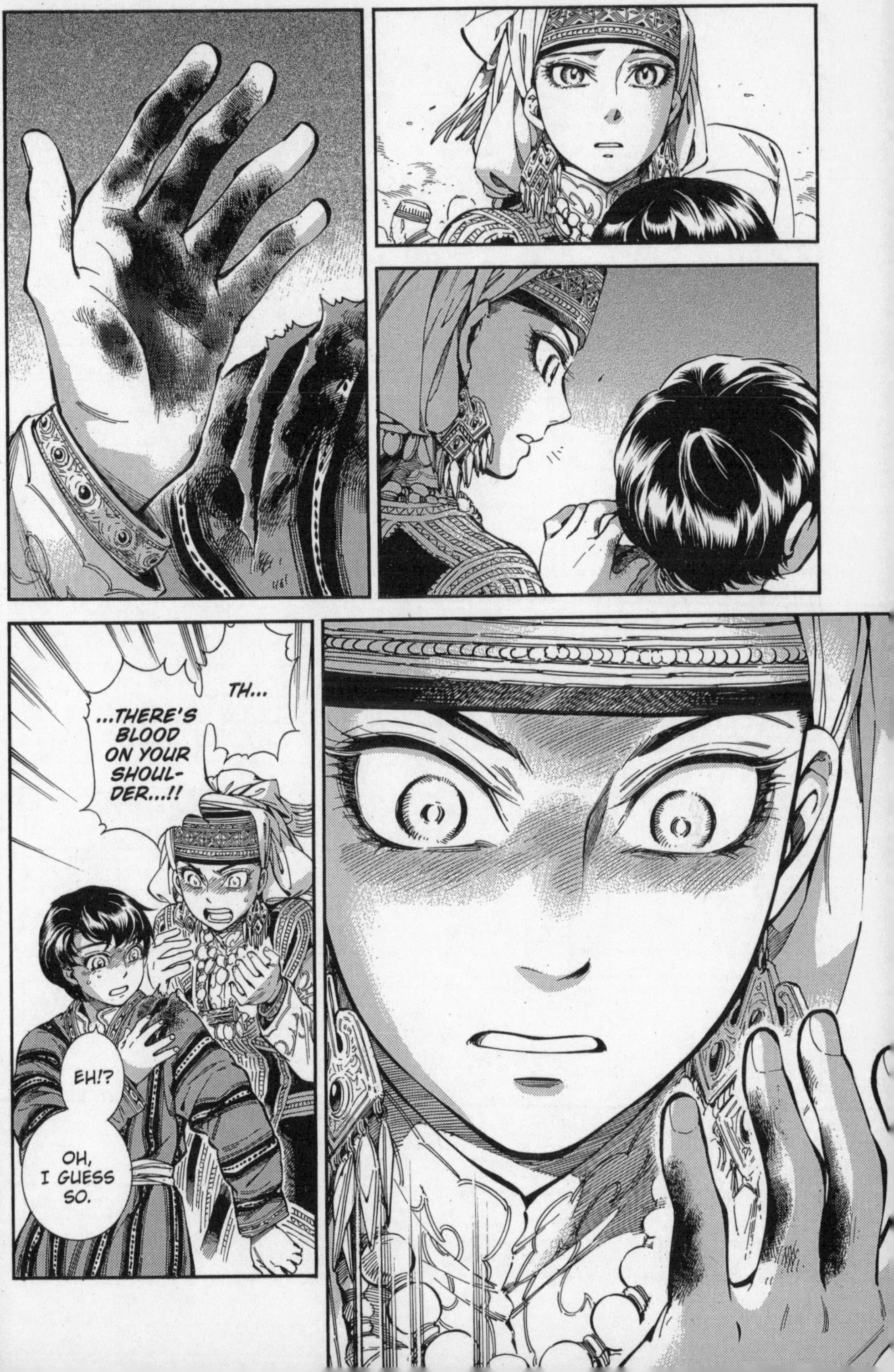
TH...
...THERE'S BLOOD ON YOUR SHOULDER...!!
EH!?
OH, I GUESS SO.

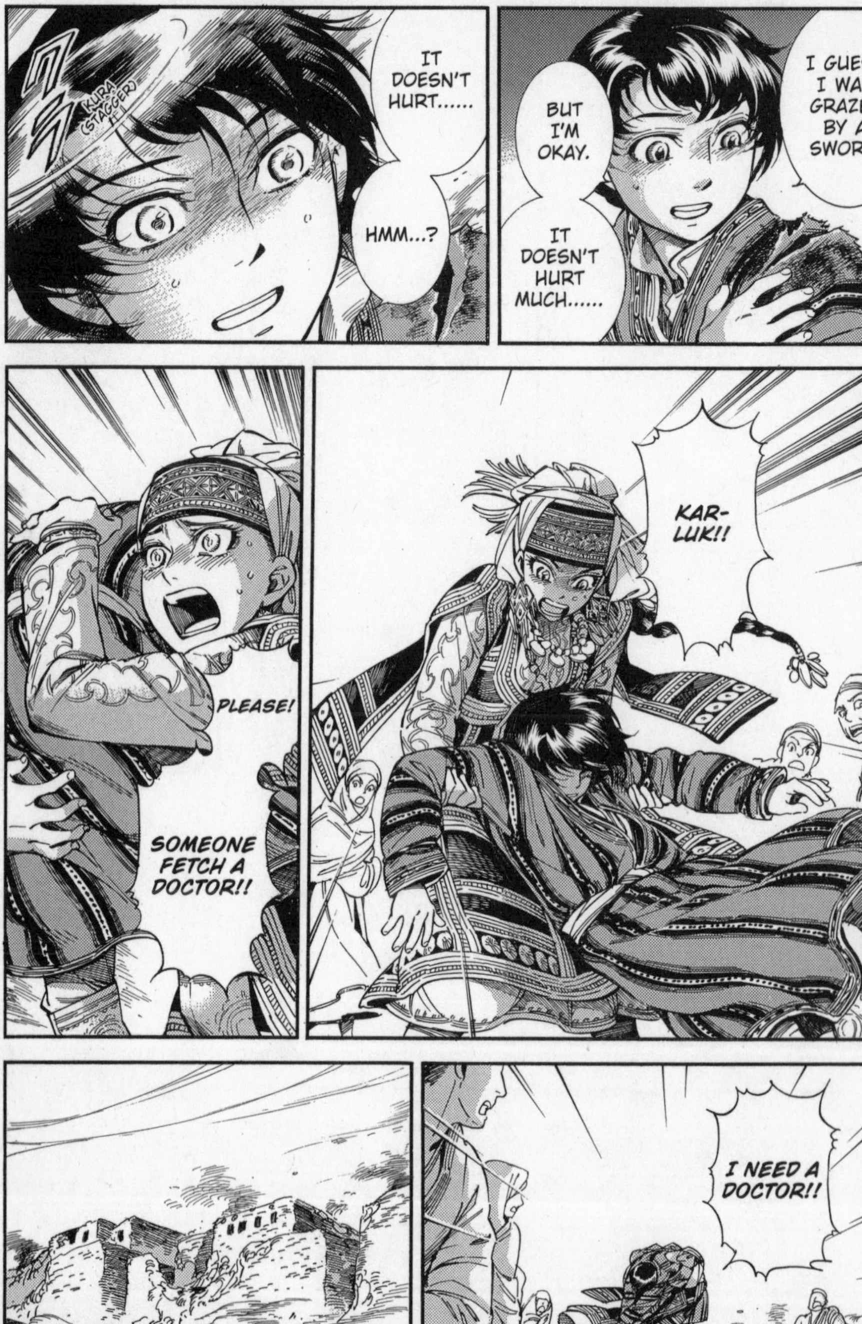
I GUESS I WAS GRAZED BY A SWORD.
BUT I'M OKAY.
IT DOESN'T HURT MUCH......
IT DOESN'T HURT......
HMM...?
KURA (STAGGER)
KAR-LUK!!
PLEASE!
SOMEONE FETCH A DOCTOR!!
I NEED A DOCTOR!!

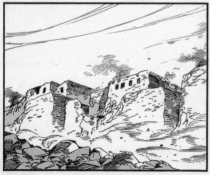

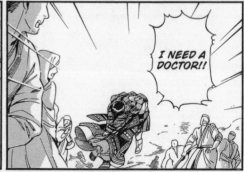

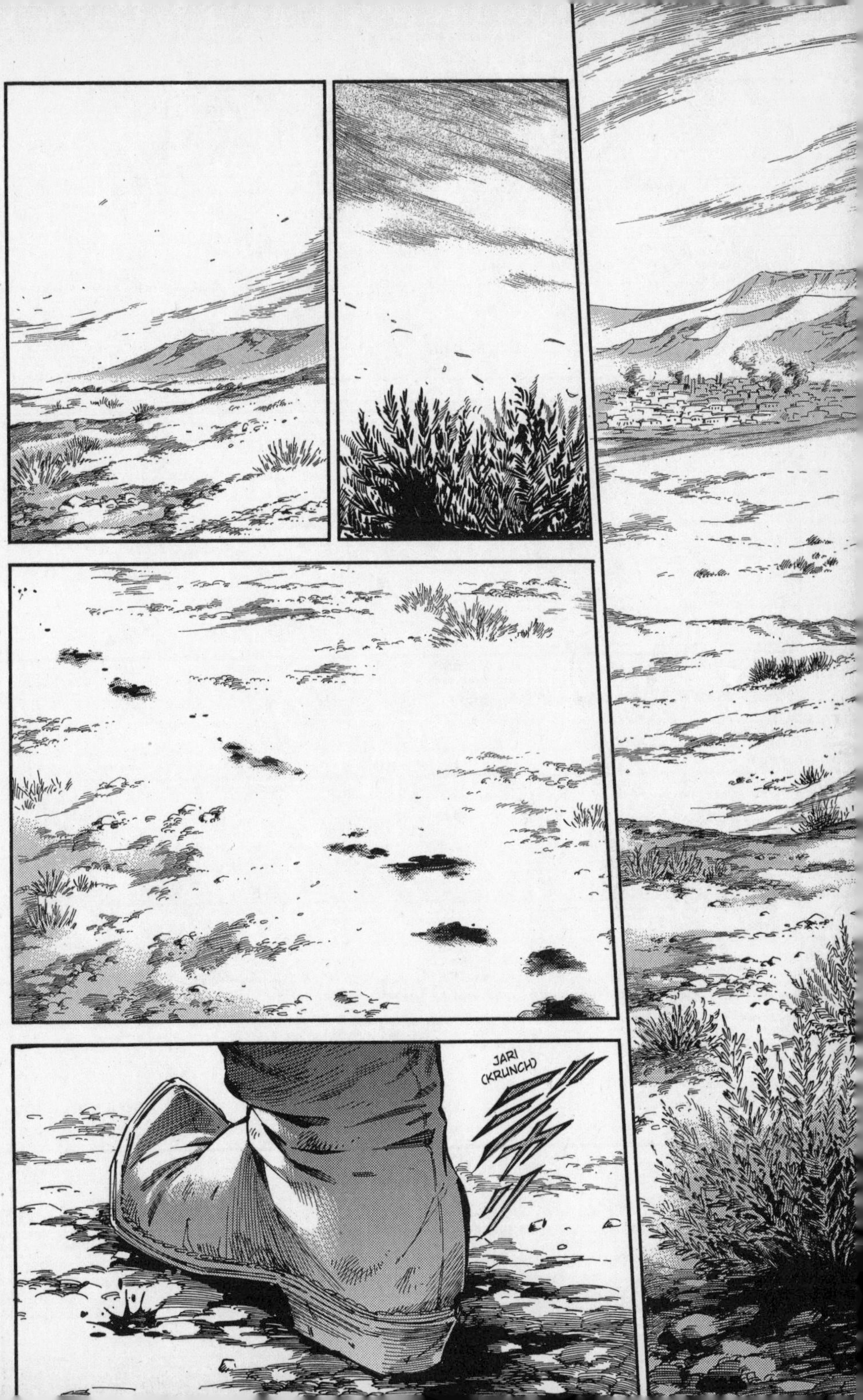
JARI
(KRUNCH)

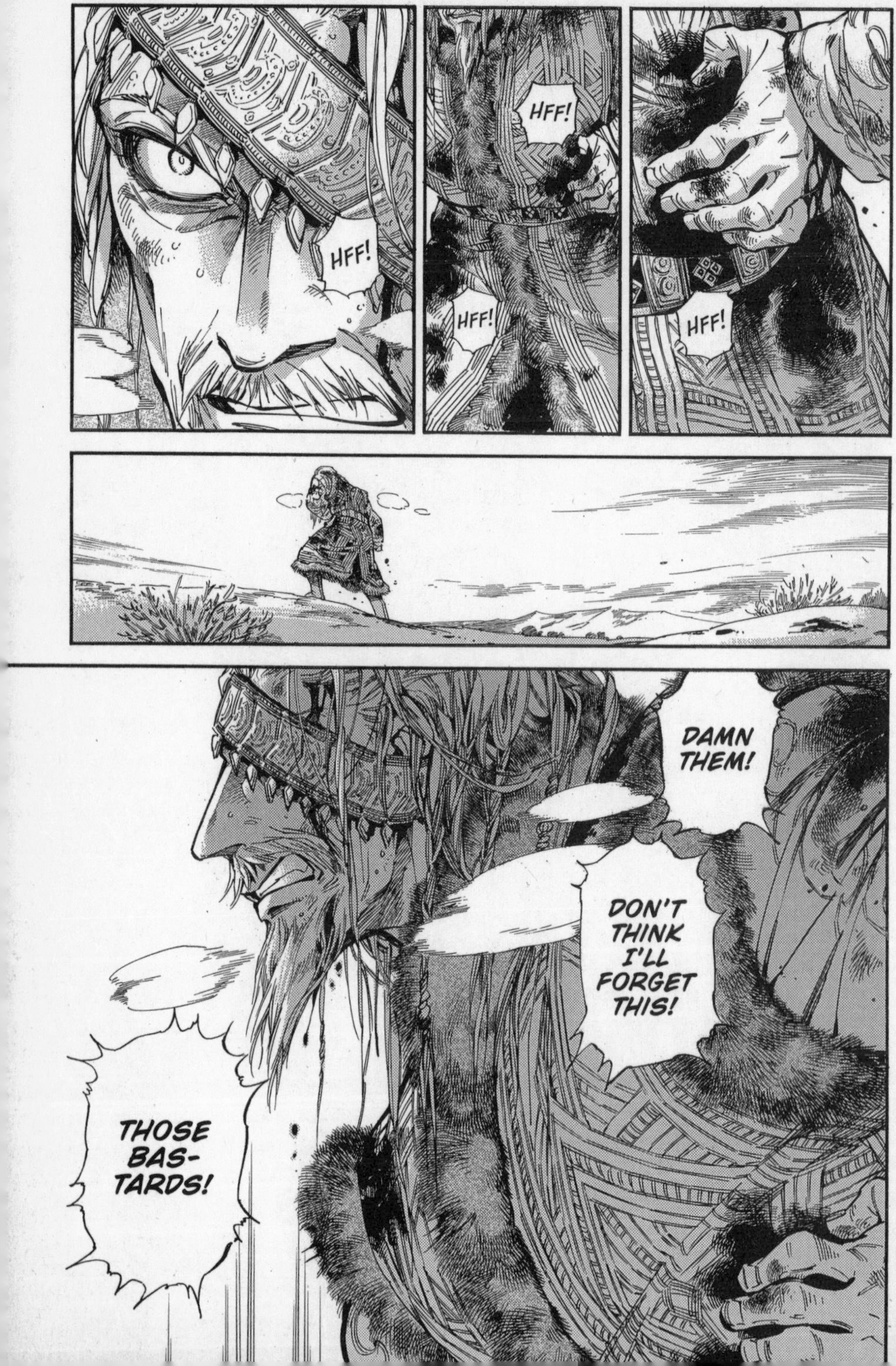
HFF!
HFF!
HFF!
HFF!
DAMN THEM!
DON'T THINK I'LL FORGET THIS!
THOSE BAS-TARDS!

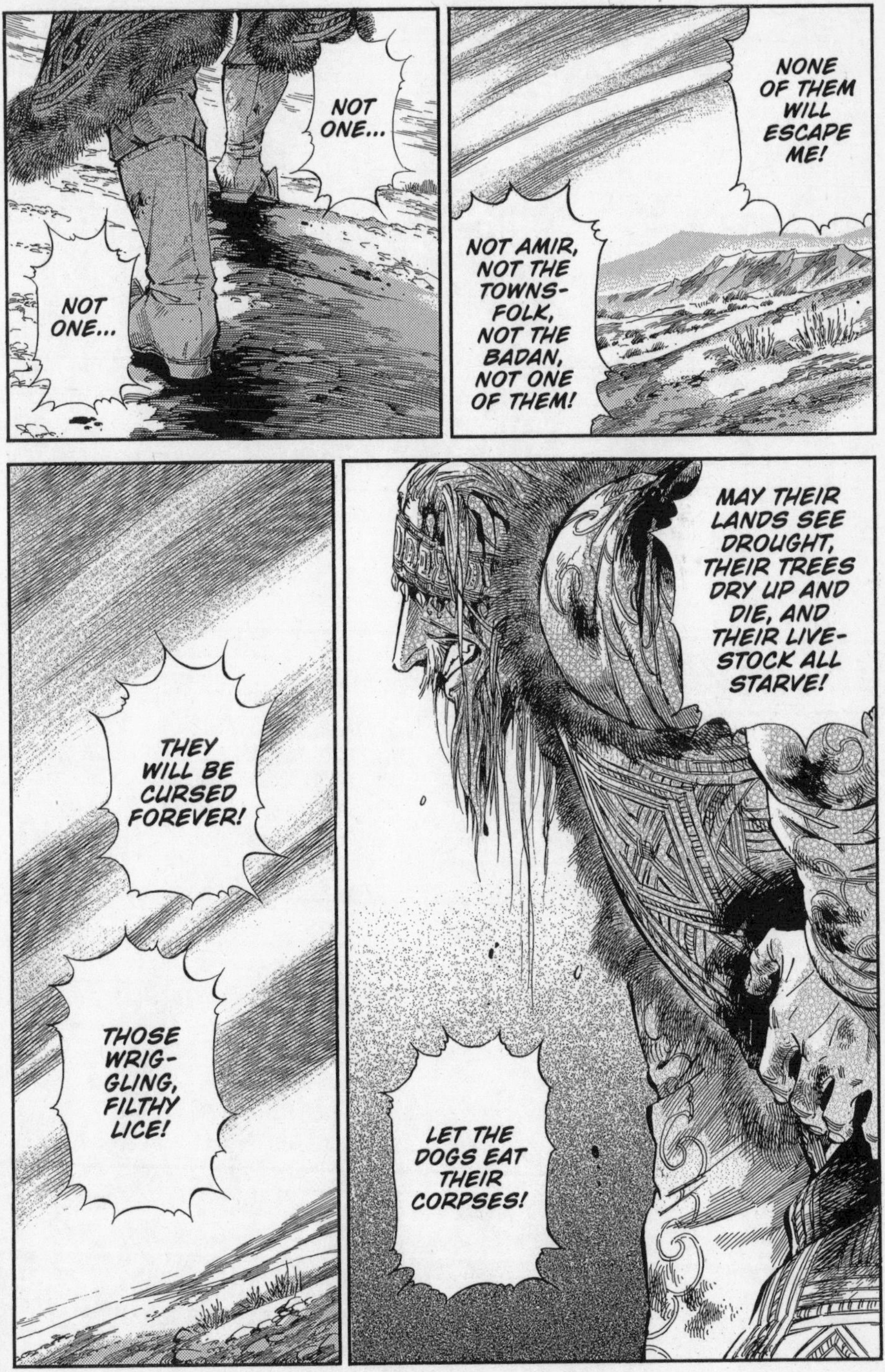
NONE OF THEM WILL ESCAPE ME!
NOT AMIR, NOT THE TOWNSFOLK, NOT THE BADAN, NOT ONE OF THEM!
NOT ONE...
NOT ONE...
MAY THEIR LANDS SEE DROUGHT, THEIR TREES DRY UP AND DIE, AND THEIR LIVESTOCK ALL STARVE!
LET THE DOGS EAT THEIR CORPSES!
THEY WILL BE CURSED FOREVER!
THOSE WRIGGLING, FILTHY LICE!

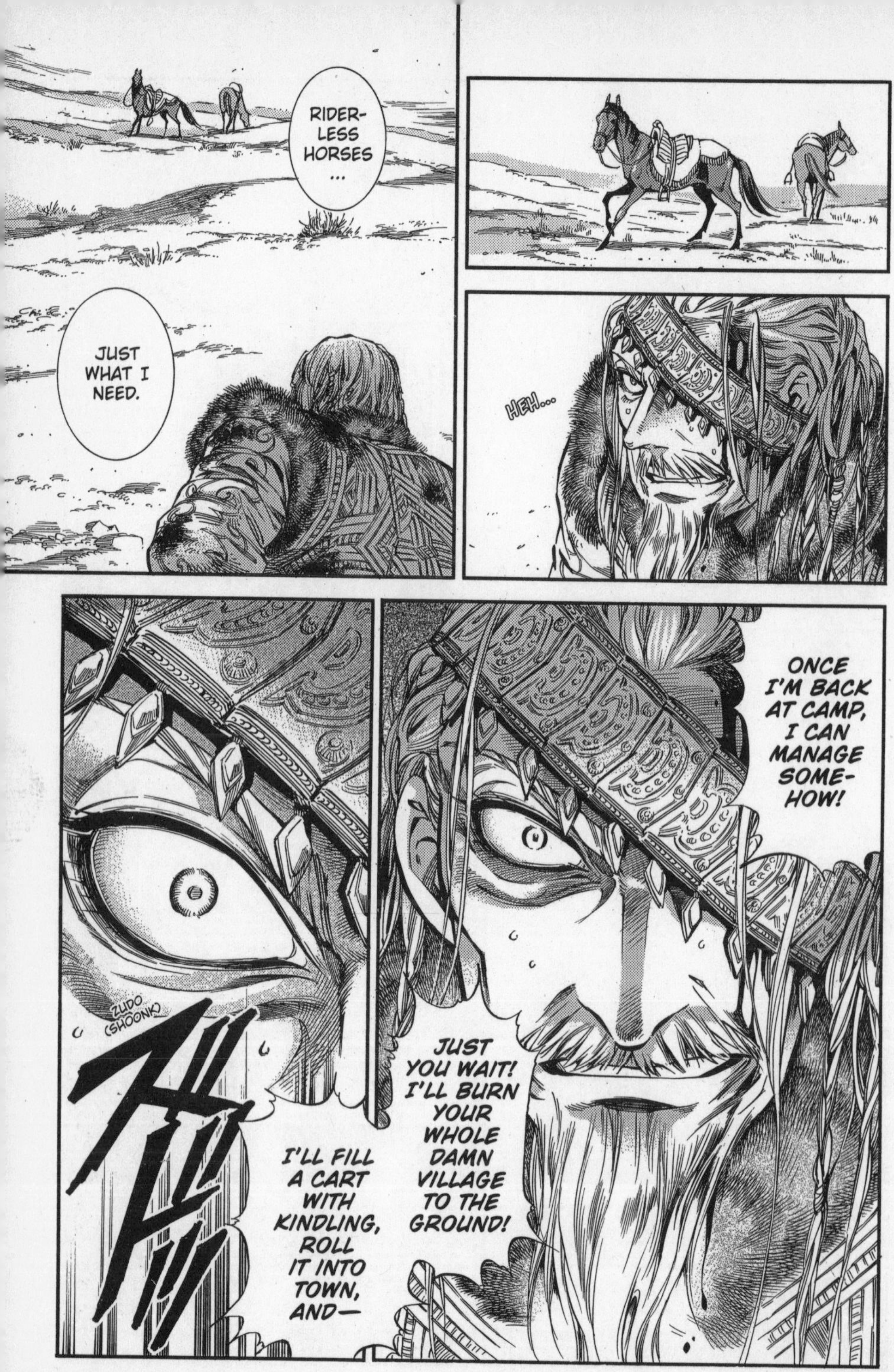
HEH...
RIDER-LESS HORSES ...
JUST WHAT I NEED.
ONCE I'M BACK AT CAMP, I CAN MANAGE SOME-HOW!
JUST YOU WAIT! I'LL BURN YOUR WHOLE DAMN VILLAGE TO THE GROUND!
I'LL FILL A CART WITH KINDLING, ROLL IT INTO TOWN, AND—
ZUDO (SHOONK)

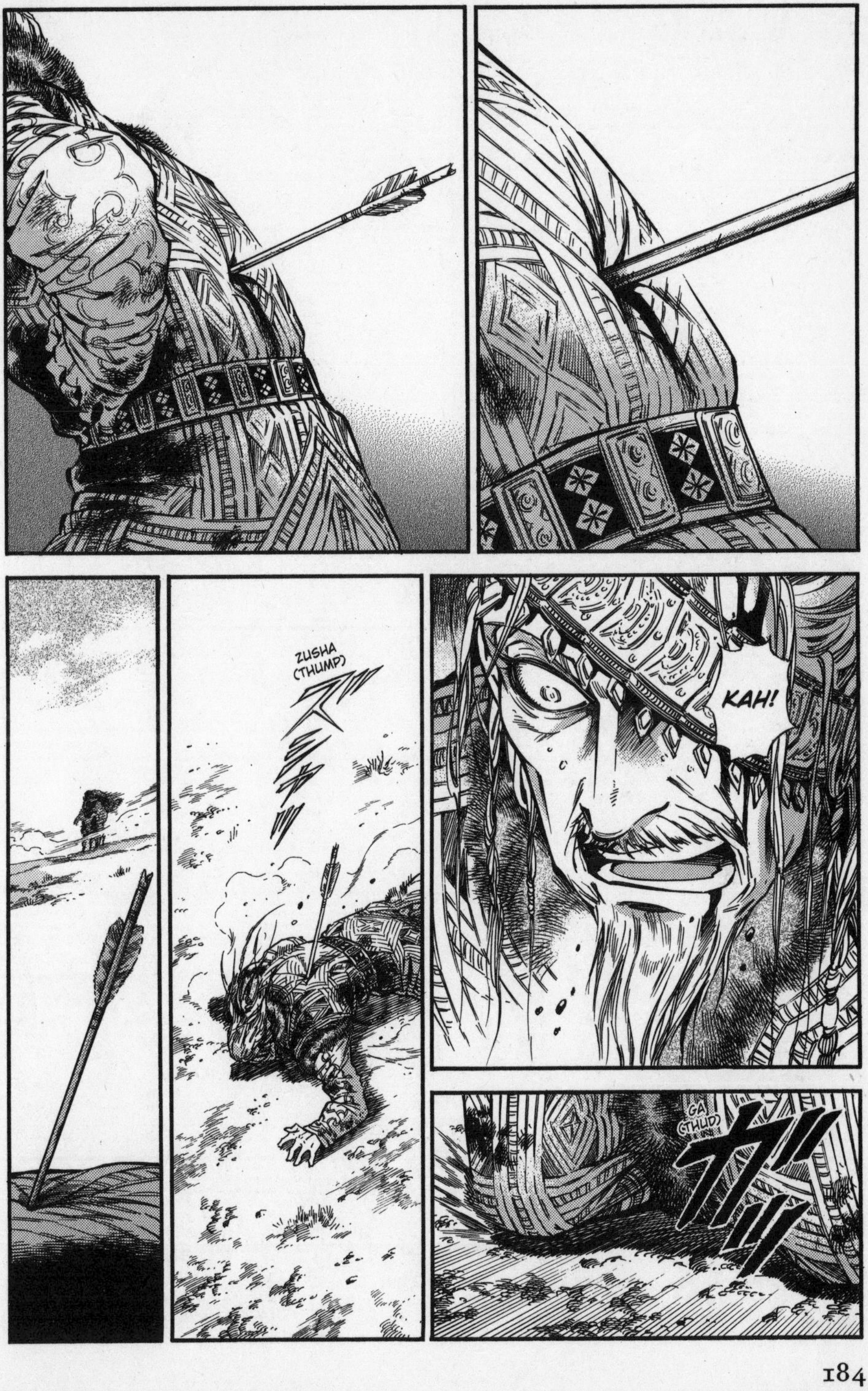
KAH!
ZUSHA (THUMP)
GA (THUD)

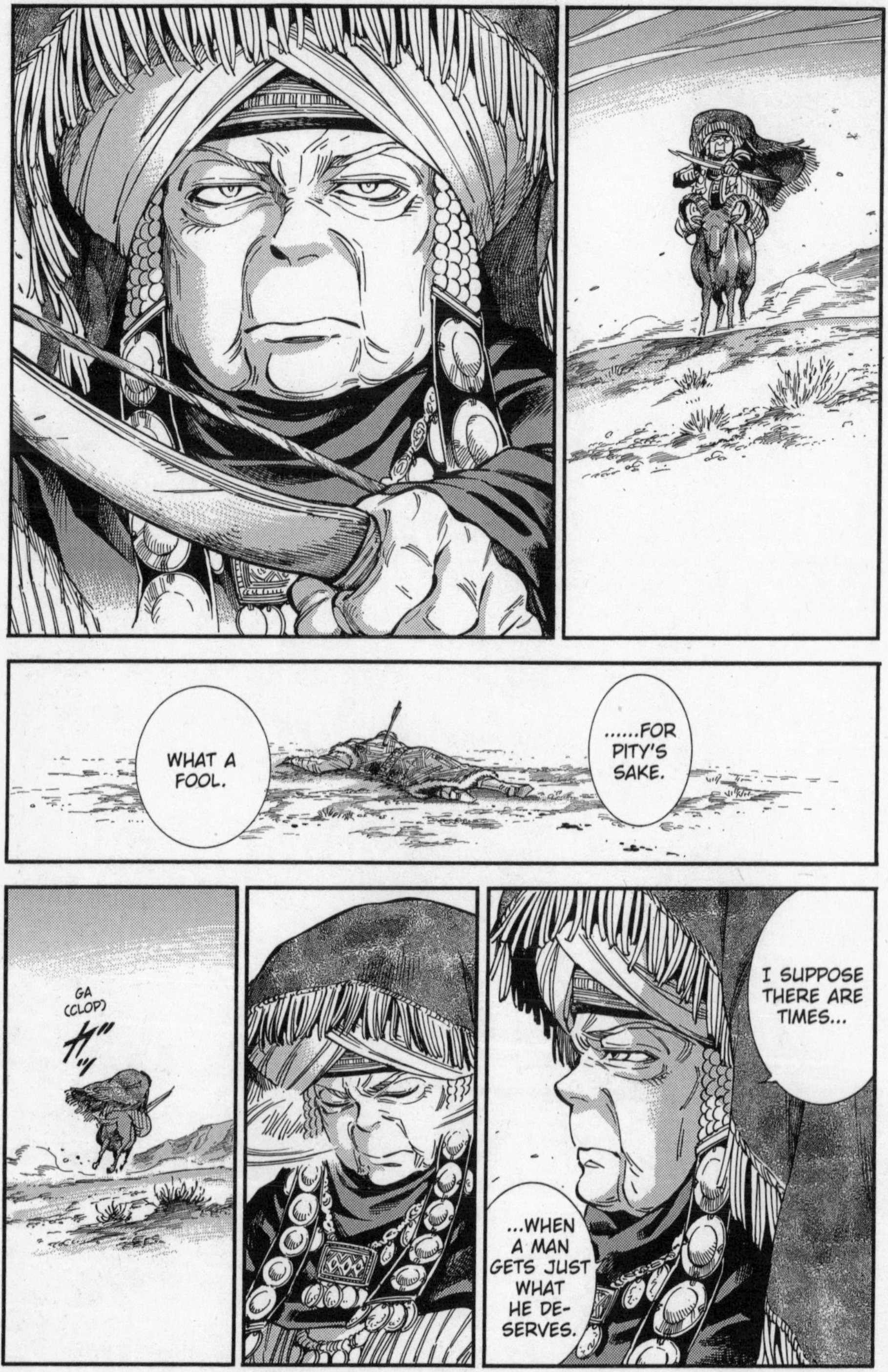
......FOR PITY'S SAKE.
WHAT A FOOL.
I SUPPOSE THERE ARE TIMES...
...WHEN A MAN GETS JUST WHAT HE DE- SERVES.
GA (CLOP)

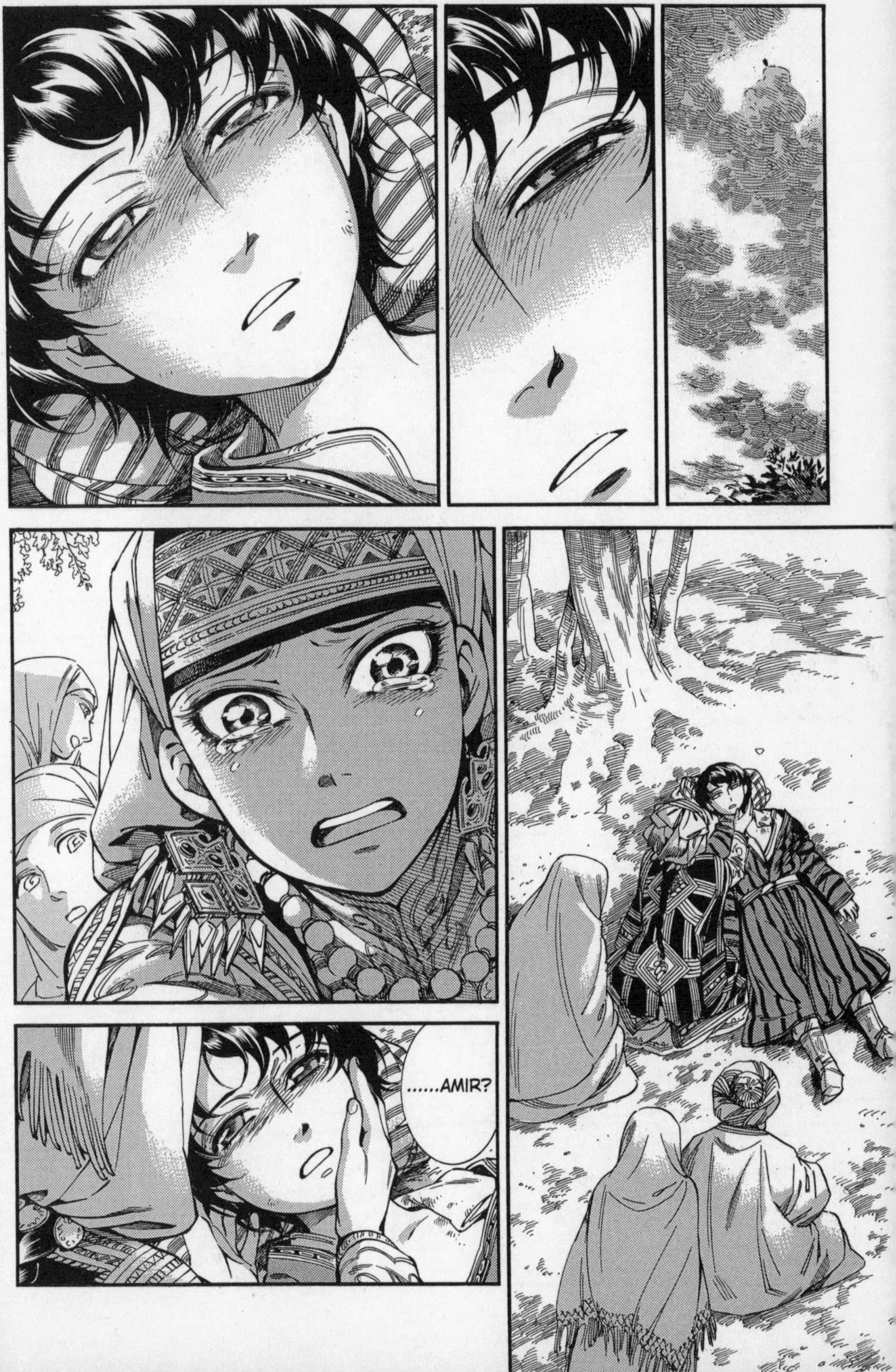
......AMIR?

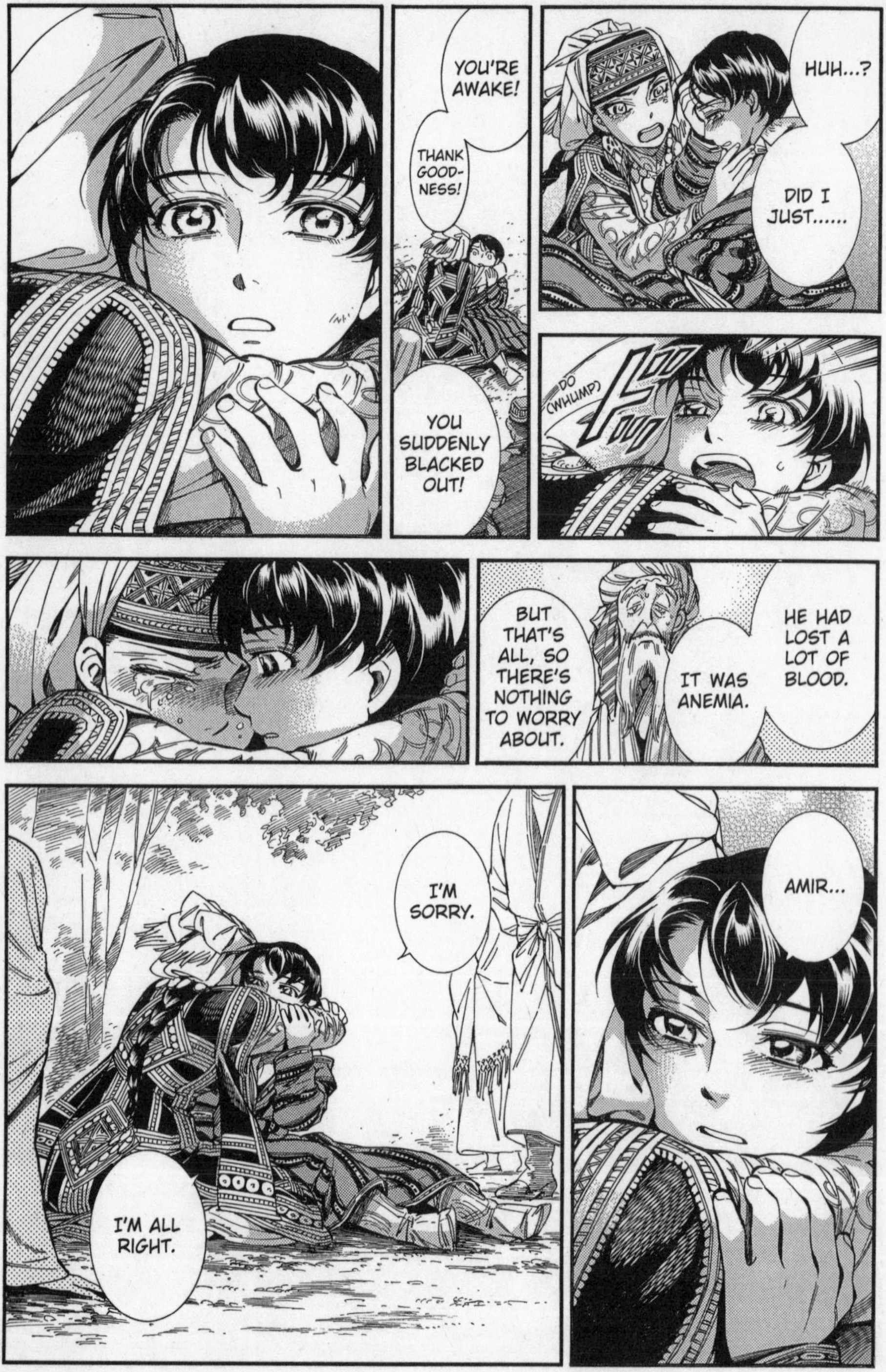
HUH...?
DID I JUST......
DO (WHUMP)
YOU'RE AWAKE!
THANK GOOD-NESS!
YOU SUDDENLY BLACKED OUT!
HE HAD LOST A LOT OF BLOOD.
IT WAS ANEMIA.
BUT THAT'S ALL, SO THERE'S NOTHING TO WORRY ABOUT.
AMIR...
I'M SORRY.
I'M ALL RIGHT.

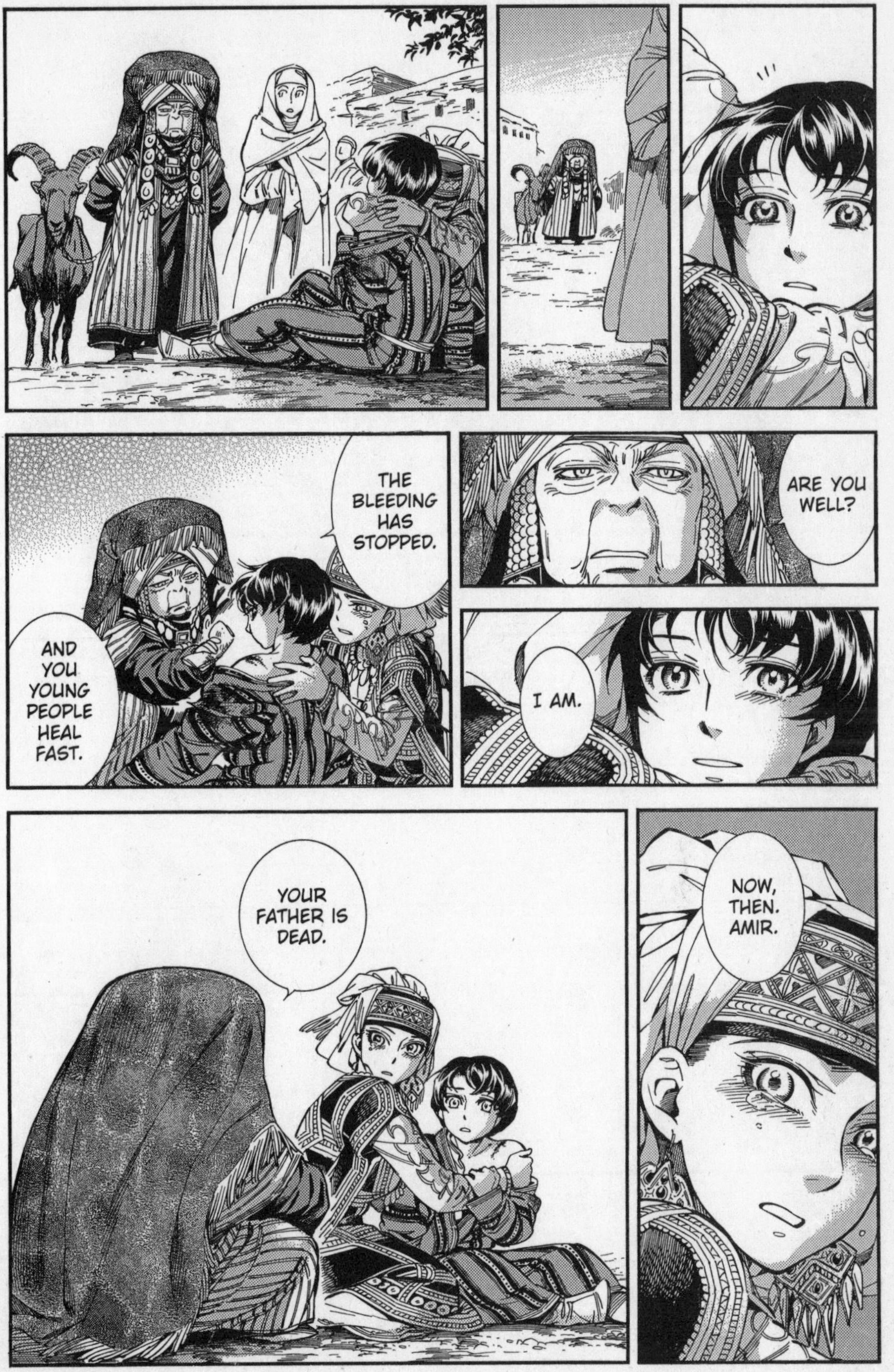
ARE YOU WELL?
I AM.
THE BLEEDING HAS STOPPED.
AND YOU YOUNG PEOPLE HEAL FAST.
NOW, THEN. AMIR.
YOUR FATHER IS DEAD.

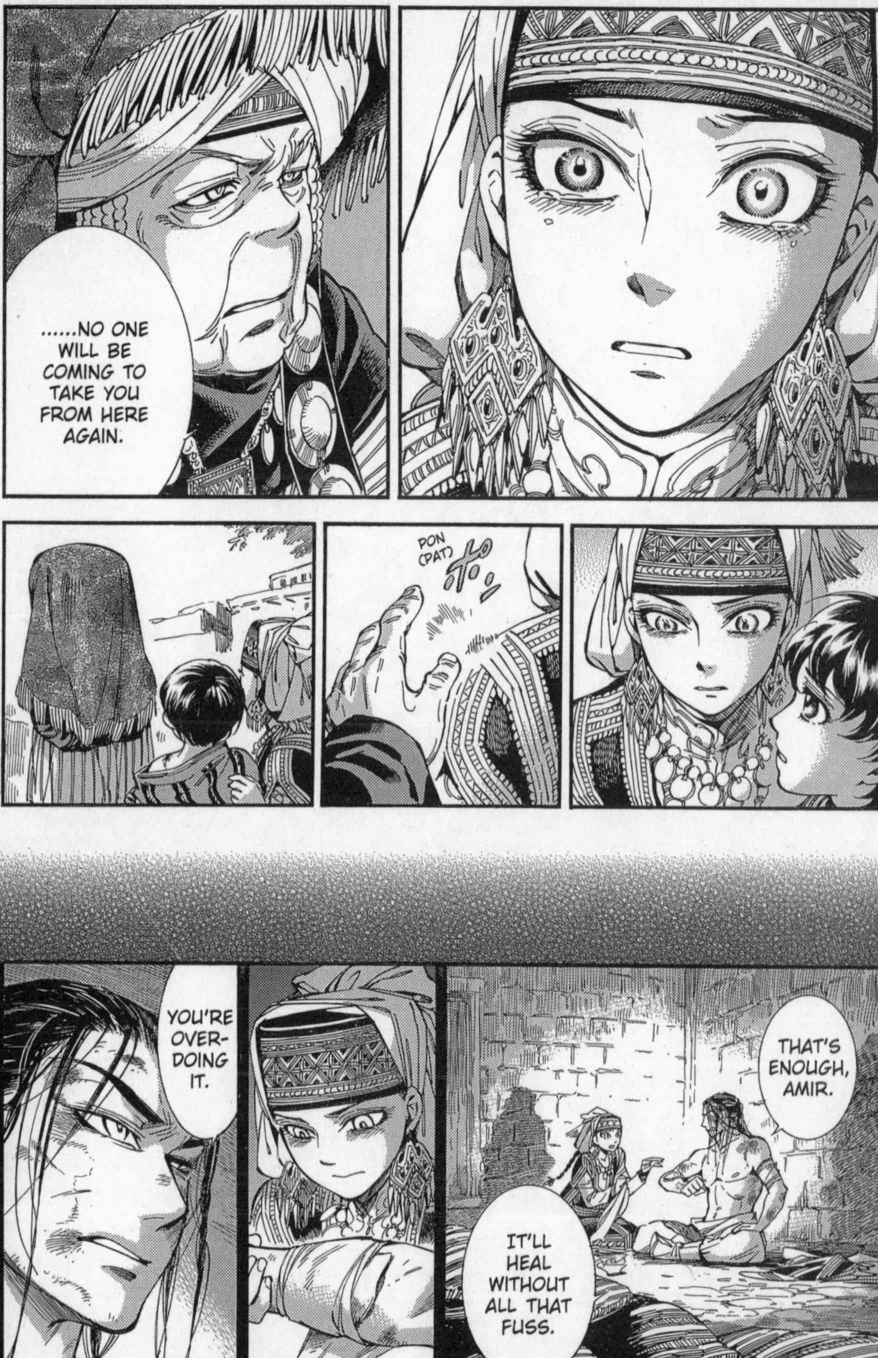
......NO ONE WILL BE COMING TO TAKE YOU FROM HERE AGAIN.
PON (PAT)
THAT'S ENOUGH, AMIR.
IT'LL HEAL WITHOUT ALL THAT FUSS.
YOU'RE OVER-DOING IT.

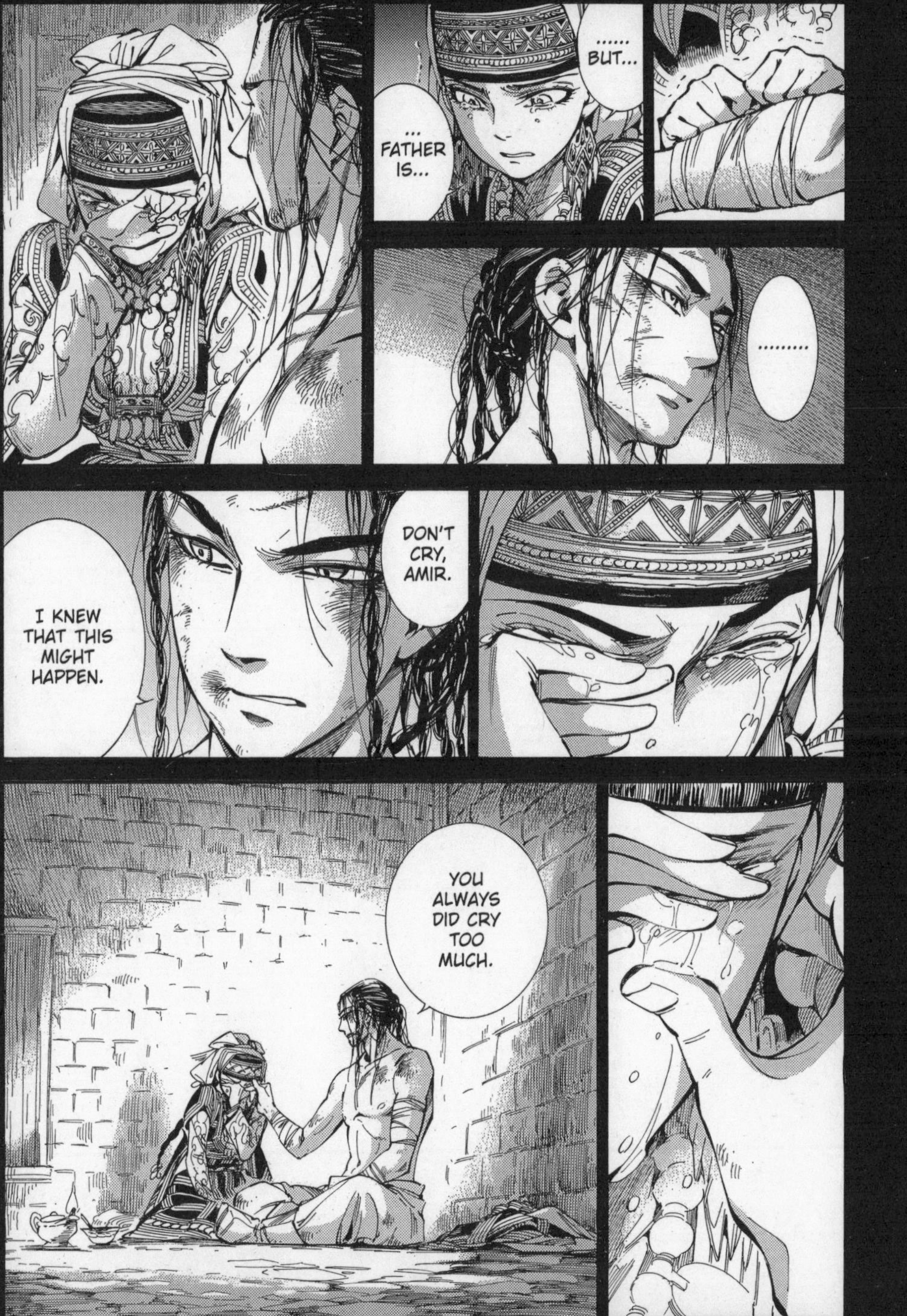
......BUT...
...FATHER IS...
....
DON'T CRY, AMIR.
I KNEW THAT THIS MIGHT HAPPEN.
YOU ALWAYS DID CRY TOO MUCH.

✦ CHAPTER 35: END ✦

AFTERWORD

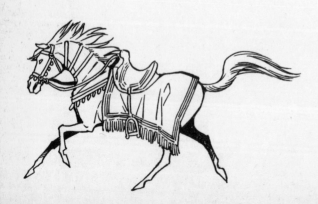

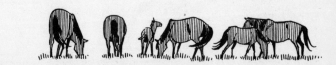

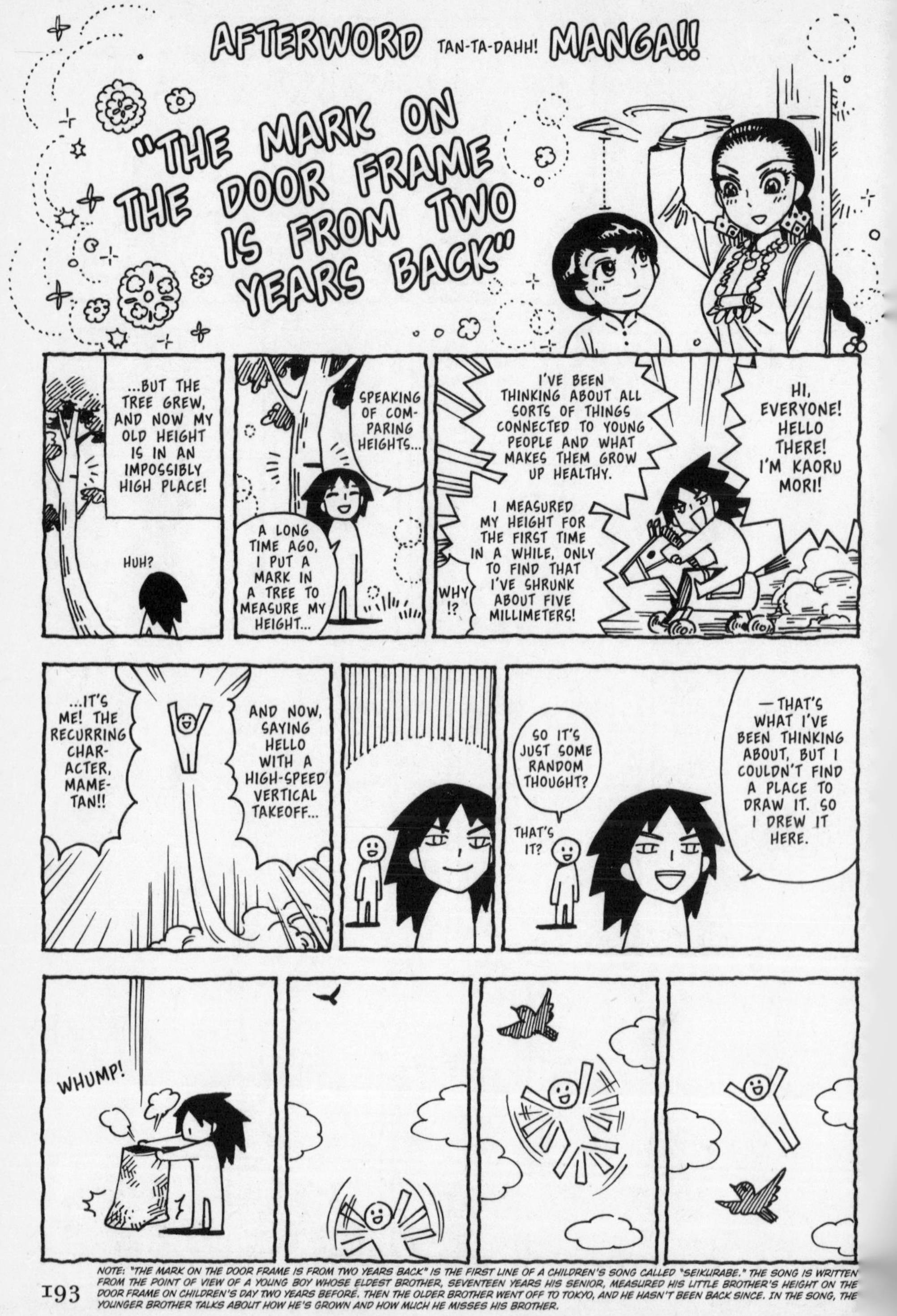
AFTERWORD TAN-TA-DAHH! MANGA!!
"THE MARK ON THE DOOR FRAME IS FROM TWO YEARS BACK"
HI, EVERYONE! HELLO THERE! I'M KAORU MORI!
I'VE BEEN THINKING ABOUT ALL SORTS OF THINGS CONNECTED TO YOUNG PEOPLE AND WHAT MAKES THEM GROW UP HEALTHY.
I MEASURED MY HEIGHT FOR THE FIRST TIME IN A WHILE, ONLY TO FIND THAT I'VE SHRUNK ABOUT FIVE MILLIMETERS!
WHY!?
SPEAKING OF COMPARING HEIGHTS...
A LONG TIME AGO, I PUT A MARK IN A TREE TO MEASURE MY HEIGHT...
...BUT THE TREE GREW, AND NOW MY OLD HEIGHT IS IN AN IMPOSSIBLY HIGH PLACE!
HUH?
—THAT'S WHAT I'VE BEEN THINKING ABOUT, BUT I COULDN'T FIND A PLACE TO DRAW IT. SO I DREW IT HERE.
SO IT'S JUST SOME RANDOM THOUGHT?
THAT'S IT?
AND NOW, SAYING HELLO WITH A HIGH-SPEED VERTICAL TAKEOFF...
...IT'S ME! THE RECURRING CHARACTER, MAME-TAN!!
WHUMP!

NOTE: "THE MARK ON THE DOOR FRAME IS FROM TWO YEARS BACK" IS THE FIRST LINE OF A CHILDREN'S SONG CALLED "SEIKURABE." THE SONG IS WRITTEN FROM THE POINT OF VIEW OF A YOUNG BOY WHOSE ELDEST BROTHER, SEVENTEEN YEARS HIS SENIOR, MEASURED HIS LITTLE BROTHER'S HEIGHT ON THE DOOR FRAME ON CHILDREN'S DAY TWO YEARS BEFORE. THEN THE OLDER BROTHER WENT OFF TO TOKYO, AND HE HASN'T BEEN BACK SINCE. IN THE SONG, THE YOUNGER BROTHER TALKS ABOUT HOW HE'S GROWN AND HOW MUCH HE MISSES HIS BROTHER.

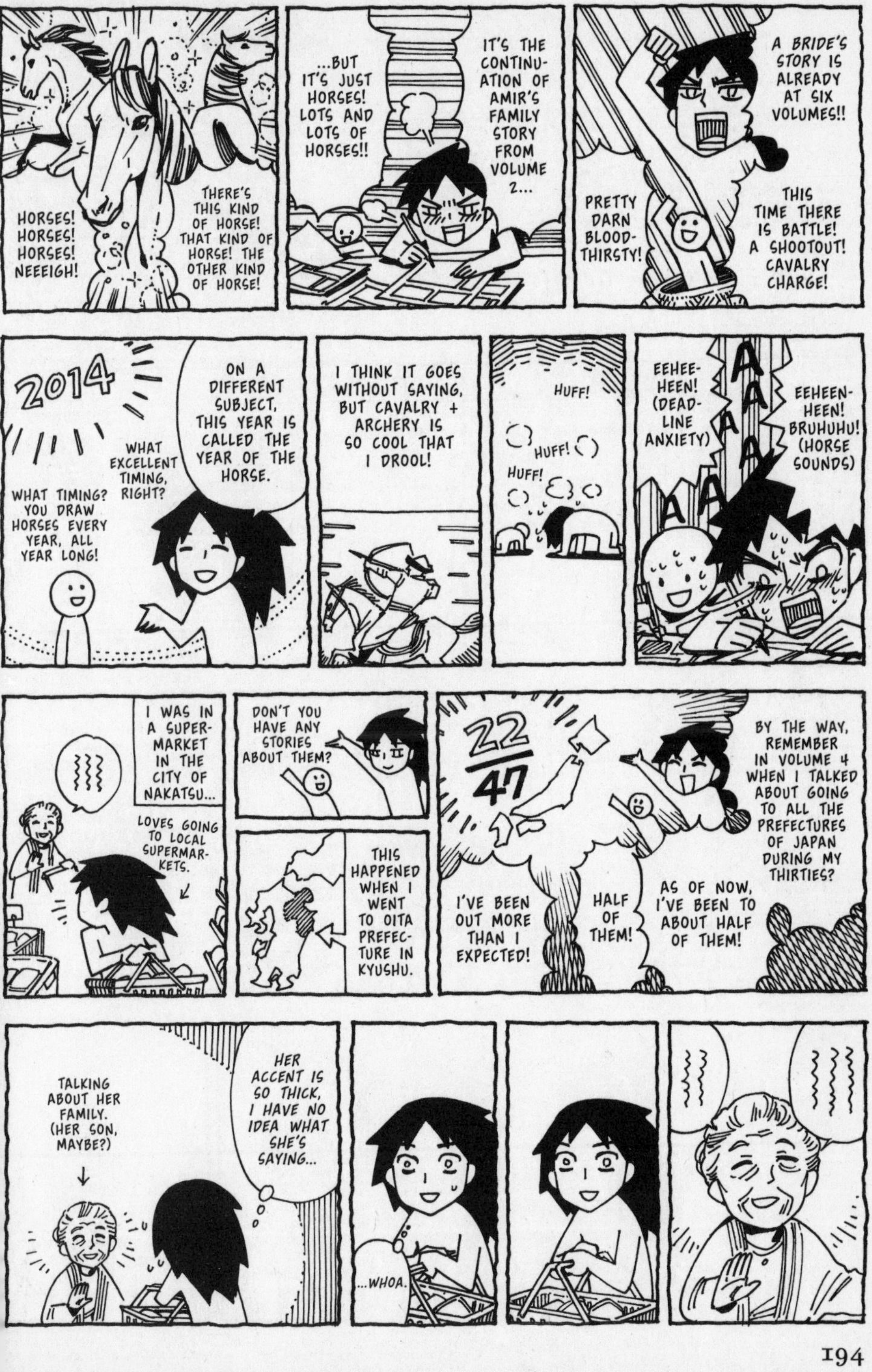
A BRIDE'S STORY IS ALREADY AT SIX VOLUMES!!
THIS TIME THERE IS BATTLE! A SHOOTOUT! CAVALRY CHARGE!
PRETTY DARN BLOODTHIRSTY!
IT'S THE CONTINUATION OF AMIR'S FAMILY STORY FROM VOLUME 2...
...BUT IT'S JUST HORSES! LOTS AND LOTS OF HORSES!!
THERE'S THIS KIND OF HORSE! THAT KIND OF HORSE! THE OTHER KIND OF HORSE!
HORSES! HORSES! HORSES! NEEEIGH!
EEHEEN-HEEN! BRUHUHU! (HORSE SOUNDS)
EEHEE-HEEN! (DEAD-LINE ANXIETY)
AAAAAAA
HUFF!
HUFF!
HUFF!
I THINK IT GOES WITHOUT SAYING, BUT CAVALRY + ARCHERY IS SO COOL THAT I DROOL!
ON A DIFFERENT SUBJECT, THIS YEAR IS CALLED THE YEAR OF THE HORSE.
2014
WHAT EXCELLENT TIMING, RIGHT?
WHAT TIMING? YOU DRAW HORSES EVERY YEAR, ALL YEAR LONG!
BY THE WAY, REMEMBER IN VOLUME 4 WHEN I TALKED ABOUT GOING TO ALL THE PREFECTURES OF JAPAN DURING MY THIRTIES?
22/47
AS OF NOW, I'VE BEEN TO ABOUT HALF OF THEM!
HALF OF THEM!
I'VE BEEN OUT MORE THAN I EXPECTED!
DON'T YOU HAVE ANY STORIES ABOUT THEM?
THIS HAPPENED WHEN I WENT TO OITA PREFECTURE IN KYUSHU.
I WAS IN A SUPERMARKET IN THE CITY OF NAKATSU...
LOVES GOING TO LOCAL SUPERMARKETS.
...WHOA.
HER ACCENT IS SO THICK, I HAVE NO IDEA WHAT SHE'S SAYING...
TALKING ABOUT HER FAMILY. (HER SON, MAYBE?)

A BRIDE'S STORY ⑥

Kaoru Mori

Translation: William Flanagan

Lettering: Abigail Blackman

A BRIDE'S STORY Volume 6
© 2014 Kaoru Mori
All rights reserved.
First published in Japan in 2014 by
KADOKAWA CORPORATION ENTERBRAIN
English translation rights arranged with
KADOKAWA CORPORATION ENTERBRAIN
through Tuttle-Mori Agency, Inc., Tokyo.

Translation © 2014 by Hachette Book Group

Yen Press
Hachette Book Group
1290 Avenue of the Americas
New York, NY 10104

www.HachetteBookGroup.com
www.YenPress.com

Yen Press is an imprint of Hachette Book Group, Inc.
The Yen Press name and logo are trademarks of
Hachette Book Group, Inc.

First Yen Press Edition: October 2014

ISBN: 978-0-316-33610-9

10 9 8 7 6 5 4 3 2 1

BVG

Printed in the United States of America

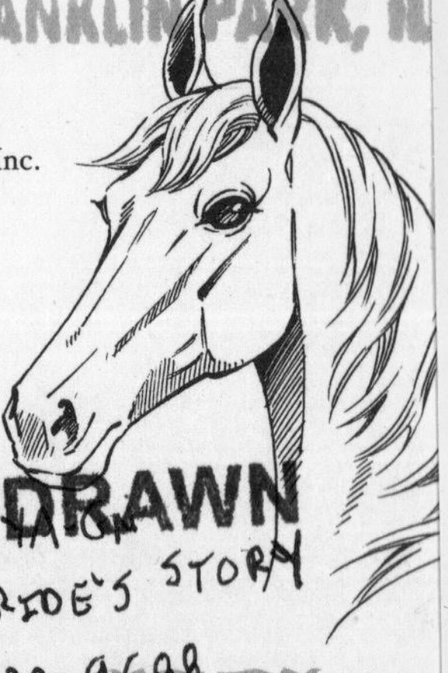

SURE, EVEN WI A THIC ACCENT IT'S STIL JAPANES
I THINK THIS OLD LADY'S ACCENT WAS PARTICULARLY THICK.
SURE, THERE ARE DIFFERENT WORDS AND TURNS OF PHRASE, BUT I'M SURE I WOULD UNDERSTAND...IS WHAT I THOUGHT...
...BUT REALITY WASN'T WHAT I EXPECTED, AND IT WAS A BIG SHOCK.
THE FAMOUS TRANSLATOR, DONALD KEENE, MENTIONED THAT WHEN HE SITS NEXT TO SOMEONE TALKATIVE ON A PLANE, HIS GO-TO TOPIC IS DIALECTS (IN THEIR MOTHER TONGUE).
I HAD THOUGHT THAT DIALECTS WERE SLOWLY VANISHING, BUT THEY'RE STILL PRETTY STRONG, HUH?
IZZAT SO?
BY THE WAY, MOST OF CENTRA ASIA SPEAK TURKIC LANGUAGES BUT THERE ARE MANY DIFFERENT DIALECTS.
(TURKEY)
TURKIC LANGUAGE GROUP
DURING THE SOVIET TIMES, THE LINGUA FRANCA WAS MAINLY RUSSIAN.
UZBEK
KARAKALPAK
KAZAK
KYRGYZ
TURKMEN
UYGHUR
(IRAN)
PERSIAN LANGUAGE GROU
TAJIK
THEY CAN COMMUNICATE, BUT IT A DIFFERENT LANGUAGE GROU
IMAGINING USING ALL DIFFERENT KINDS OF DIALECTS IN A BRIDE'S STORY...
...SEEMED LIKE IT'D BE PRETTY FUN!
LOOK HERE, EH?
NO KRAFT DINNER TONIGHT, EH?
CARE FOR A SPOT OF TEA?
THAT'S WICKED HAHD!
THAT'S GONNA BUILD YOUAH CHARAC-TAH!
TALKIN ABOUT DIALECT DRAWS YOU IN
IT'S A GO-TO TOPIC!
OKAY, FOR NEXT TIME WE'RE GOING TO SWITCH GEARS.
I THINK WE'LL CATCH UP WITH SMITH AND ALI AND SEE HOW THEY'RE DOING.
ARE THEY STILL ALIVE OR NOT? (IS THAT A JINX?)
ALSO, SINCE PARIYA DIDN'T SHOW UP MUCH IN THIS VOLUME, I'M GOING TO DRAW HER HERE.
YOU REALLY... DON'T HAVE TO.
WHAT AM I EVEN HERE FOR!?
HEY!
SO LET'S MEET AGAIN IN THE NEXT VOLUME!
WE'LL SAY GOOD-BYE IN DELTA FORMA-TION!
END.

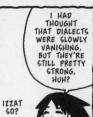

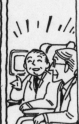

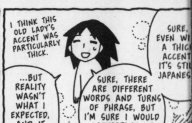

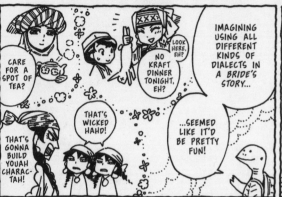

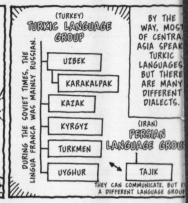

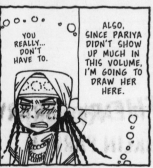

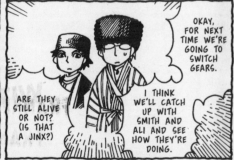

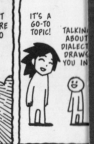

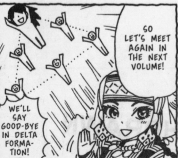

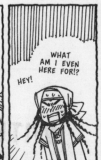

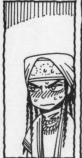

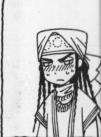